What readers are saying

online about

Epiphany
THE
SILVERING

(Book 3 in the *Epiphany* series)

'Once again, Ms. Terry does an amazing job of working the plots of
both the faery world and present day as the characters come to realize
they are connected through the Dream Sphere where the past,
present and future exist simultaneously...Brilliantly
entertaining...Captivating, wondrous and uplifting!'
Stephen Fisher – Readers' Favorite Reviewer
USA

'...Every bit the knockout!'
Rosey
UK

'A monumental achievement...I am in awe of
Sonya Deanna Terry's ability to guide the reader from Australia to
England and from the spiritual realm to the world of finance.'
Ray Simmons – Readers' Favorite Reviewer
USA

'...High octane imagination...a book that delivers
a powerful punch.'
Marta Tandori—Mystery/Suspense Author
Canada

'A riveting adventure from start to finish...a perfect blend of
flashbacks, time traveling, philosophy, romance, conflict and
sharp, witty dialogue...'
Veritas Vincit "Bill"
USA

'Everything I hoped it would be and more...The layered plot is clever
and unfolds nicely as each revelation comes to light.'
LA Howell
USA

'The *Epiphany* books are beautifully written—I could
not put them down.'
Kevina Bradley
Australia

'An awesome sequel...the characters are extremely realistic and make
you want to keep reading.'
Karsun
USA

'I could never have guessed at or expected the reversals and
outcomes. They fell into place in a most incredible way, completing
plots and tying up loose ends. While *THE GOLDING* glows,
THE SILVERING sparkles...from myriad points.'
Elf Dreaming
Australia

Accolades

GOLD MEDAL
Global Ebook Awards 2016
SILVER MEDAL
Readers' Favorite Awards Contest 2017
GOLD AWARD
Literary Titan Book Awards 2017
(The complete *Epiphany* series)
B.R.A.G MEDALLION
Book Readers' Appreciation Group 2018
(The complete *Epiphany* series)

Epiphany
THE
SILVERING

Sonya Deanna Terry

SEAHORSE

S T

TALES

Published by Seahorse Tales
an imprint owned by Sonya D Terry

Structural edit by Deonie Fiford
Front cover image by Laura Moyer of The Book Cover Machine
Front cover design by Jesh Snow of Jesh Designs
Back cover & spine design by Lorie DeWorken of Mind the Margins
Additional elements by Vecteezy

Earth provides enough to satisfy every man's need,
but not every man's greed.

MAHATMA GANDHI

Only when the last tree has died and the last river been poisoned and
the last fish been caught will we realise we cannot eat money

CREE INDIAN PROVERB

October: This is one of the particularly dangerous months to invest in stocks. Other dangerous months are July, January, September April, November, May, March, June, December, August and February.
MARK TWAIN

Remember that not getting what you want in life
can be a wonderful stroke of luck.
DALAI LAMA

Your vision will become clear only when you look into your heart.
Who looks outside, dreams.
Who looks inside, awakens.
CARL JUNG

And Jesus went into the temple of God, and cast out all them that
sold and bought in the temple, and overthrew the tables of the
moneychangers, and the seats of them that sold doves
MATTHEW 21:12

Do not be dismayed at good-byes.
A farewell is necessary before meeting again. And meeting again,
after moments or lifetimes, is certain for those who are friends.
RICHARD BACH

Money is not the most important thing in the world. Love is.
Fortunately, I love money.
JACKIE MASON

Prologue

An excerpt of a letter from
Edward Lillibridge
to his eighteen-year-old son

— Written in the autumn of 1767 —

My Dear Son Ned,

   It is midnight, and you are sleeping.
I am here at the table with a candle at my elbow, penning
the most difficult letter I have ever had to write.
  They are coming for me. Samuel Withers saw them in the
village—has warned of their approach. I am bereft, and yet my
mood is softened by an odd state of serenity, a knowing I suppose,
that I shall soon be with God.
  My son, I implore you to forgive me for my actions. I have
foolishly endangered myself. I must pay the price. My dogged
pursuit of The Truth has rendered me conspicuous to 'the powers
that be'. My eagerness to convey our true ancient history was
considered to have brought shame upon the Church, and I am seen
to be a criminal, a charlatan, unworthy of my parish, and now, it
appears, unworthy of my life. They are sending their men this
night. And so I write with a shaking hand my final farewell to
you...

Chapter One

<u>Character List</u>
at the back of this book

The community hall quivered with gabble.

Rosetta Melki sat back and watched Darren, farther down the row, absorbed in reading the poem she'd volunteered to recite. She turned to Royston at her left to ask who would read first. He was busy talking to another poet in the row ahead of them, a frail and sombre-eyed woman named Valerie, his arms waving about with frenetic verve. Darren, on the other side of Royston, signalled to her. He reached past forward-leaning Royston to return the poem and gave a thumbs-up.

Eadie, seated at Rosetta's right, related an incident concerning her runaway shopping trolley and an unfortunate carton of eggs. Halfway through, she lapsed into silence. Something, or someone, had caught Eadie's attention.

Rosetta nudged her elbow. She hadn't yet asked Eadie about her date three days earlier. 'So, what's your verdict on him?'

Eadie turned back to her. 'Very nice. Oh, you mean *him*?'

Rosetta chuckled. 'Who did you think I meant?'

Eadie gazed around the room and shrugged. 'He was there a minute ago.'

'The guy you went on a date with?'

'Course not! Why do you think that?'

'Think what?'

'That he'd be *here* at a poetry night?' This is the last place Carl would want to go. Carl's not in the slightest bit sentimental.' Eadie lifted a coy shoulder and stared blissfully into the distance, a tell-tale sign she was falling for someone. 'And I think it's kind of nice that he's not poetic.'

'Tell me more!'

Eadie cheerfully confessed that she and her date had very little to talk about. Despite this, there'd been an all-consuming attraction between them, so much so, it had overridden the need for words. 'I mean, talking isn't everything, is it?' Eadie rationalised.

'No, I guess it's not,' Rosetta said, trying in vain to adopt Eadie's point of view.

'I mean, it's how they make us feel. That's the most important thing, isn't it?'

'Well, yeah. Absolutely.'

'And he isn't down-putting with me.'

'Eadie, darl, that can't be considered a plus. It should be a given. Please promise me you'll stop undervaluing yourself.'

'No, what I really mean to say is...' Eadie contemplated the speckled ceiling in her search for the right words.'...He's the opposite of down-putting. He's sweet and encouraging and gentlemanly and protective.'

Striving to hear over the babble in the room, Rosetta listened intently to an account of a date Eadie described as 'heavenly'. Carl had made Eadie feel utterly feminine. 'Something to do with how he looked at me and listened to me,' she said.

Rosetta smiled, nodded and tried to push away a chink of sadness that had settled into the centre of her heart. Eadie's last comment could easily have been a description of Matthew Weissler. The night of Adam's tragic passing had been perversely enchanting. Vivid lanterns, fragrant flowers in a vase, the haunting notes of a well-meaning musician who Matthew had joked was following her. There'd been a sublime mix of laughter and heart-to-heart confidences. She'd even revealed her extreme aversion to spiders! Throughout the dinner, Matthew, seated opposite, seemed to have exuded an aura of sunshine. Recalling Matthew as golden was an exaggeration, probably an idealised image of his face illuminated by the candle's glow.

Eadie paused to wave off the cellophane lolly packet Royston offered and continued with, 'And at one stage, Carl held my shoulder really gently to direct me to his car. If there'd been no-one around I would have thrown my arms around him and kissed him passionately.'

Rosetta thought back to that night again when Matthew, guiding her to the restaurant's exit, had momentarily placed a hand on the small of her back.

Claude, the Poets' Garret host, began to ahem. The gabble died down. Members engrossed in the trestle-table display of local authors' poetry books took their seats. Greetings and meeting notes rattled on inanely, and then Claude asked an attendee named Julian to read the opening quote for the Wise Words segment, generally something well-known and ancient. The quote Julian chose to share was one of Rosetta's favourites, an observation by Taoist philosopher Chuang Tzu. In a voice that resonated with warmth, he read Chuang Tzu's story of having dreamt he was a butterfly one night, fluttering hither and thither, believing, to all intents and purposes that he was a butterfly and a butterfly only.

' *"And now"*,' quoted Julian, ' *"I do not know whether I was then a man dreaming I was a butterfly, or I am now a butterfly dreaming I am a man."* '

A spattering of rhythmic applause and then quiet anticipation of the first poet. Distracted by a rustling sound, Rosetta turned to see a hand waving an open packet of Jersey caramels in front of her. 'Royston, how wicked of you,' she whispered, diving for one.

'Don't tell me. I already know. You're going on that diet tomorrow.'

Rosetta winked, nodded and whispered, 'Jersey caramels! A flabster's nightmare.' Taking one more, she added in an overdone Greek accent, 'Ah well, I no complain.'

The host, about to introduce the first poet, grumbled about the inconvenience of small print, then hurried off to locate a pair of reading glasses.

Eadie turned to Rosetta and said dreamily, 'As well as everything else, Carl's lovely looking.'

'Bonus,' said Rosetta, trying to get her mouth around the second Jersey caramel. 'Whatseerookrike?'

'Nice. Really nice. Not geeky, or podgy, or too short or too tall, or too skinny. But not too good-looking either. Not as attractive, say, as the guy standing near the lectern. He was watching you earlier.'

'Watching me? Who—'

'In a yearning kind of way. The guy is *hot!* What's a hot straight guy doing at a poetry night?'

Never one to let a man of superior looks escape her eye, Rosetta spun round to face the front but only saw Claude, the host, brandishing a pair of thin-rimmed spectacles and saying, 'Vera Crompton has very kindly lent me hers.'

Lowering her voice, Rosetta said, 'So where *is* this man? It's been a while,' and was annoyed to find her throat hoarse from the last Jersey caramel, turning her words into a blare that smacked of husky desperation.

Sombre-eyed Valerie in the row ahead swivelled round to face her with an aggressive swish of her black-dyed bob, lowered her pencilled brows and scoldingly told her to *Shush!*

Eadie fell into silent giggles.

The host scooted across to the lectern, head bowed apologetically.

Rosetta had only managed to glimpse the new poet's athletic physique, jeans and purple paisley shirt before Royston's lolly packet annoyingly spoiled her view.

She mouthed 'No thanks' to Royston. The waggling packet retreated. She turned her attention to the poet again and took in a sharp breath. Wait. Surely that wasn't...?

But it was.

The poet at the lectern was Matthew.

Matthew Weissler was in the room. Right now!

Wishing she could hit the pause button on her runaway pulse, Rosetta tried to make sense of it all. He'd told her at Amaretti's that he'd gone to Poet's Garret only once—to practice his public speaking—and would never go there again. He was more of a lyricist than a poet anyway, he'd said.

She went to whisper to Eadie, 'That's *Matthew,*' but no words were accessible.

'Our first-up poet tonight is a second-time visitor to Poets' Garret. I'm terribly sorry, Matthew. It appears Vera Crompton's spectacles are useless on my vision. Would you mind telling us the name of your poem?'

Matthew's eyes were wide. Much wider than usual. He ran a hand through his ash-brown hair, cleared his throat and said, 'I wrote it the other week and meant it to be a song, so it'd actually sound better if accompanied by guitar.'

'Does this mean you're volunteering to sing it, Matthew? Acapella?'

Matthew grinned, then sobered. 'Sure, Claude, if you will first.'

Trying to slow her breathing, Rosetta gazed at him in awe, realising she hadn't remembered the extent of his charisma very accurately at all. The Matthew she saw now was even better looking than the Matthew she remembered, and *that* was saying something. The shirt that clung smoothly to the angles of his shoulders was a conglomeration of swirling patterns: pink and aqua and yellow against a background of hideous purple. On anyone else it would have looked ridiculous. On Matthew it looked amazing.

'Shame about the shirt,' Eadie whispered. 'Do you think he might be a little bit crazy?'

Unable to tear her eyes away from the Poet's Garret guest before them, intent on hearing what Matthew would say next, Rosetta shook her head from side to side, in a distracted effort to say he wasn't.

Claude gave the audience a rundown of the difference between a sonnet and a poem, and Matthew said he wasn't sure whether his literary attempt was either.

'And what did you say the title was, Matthew?'

Matthew unfolded a piece of paper—solemnly—as though about to reveal some really bad news. 'It's called "Mystery Woman".'

'Please put a big hand together for Matthew Weissler with "Mick's Three Women".'

Rosetta could understand the host's error. Matthew had gulped between the first two syllables.

Valerie in the row in front was murmuring to her neighbour, 'I suppose he goes by his middle name. Introduced himself to me once.

7

Greek name I'm sure. Sounded like "Tinnitus" but I don't always listen correctly.'

Matthew's eyes were still possum-wide. His voice tumbled out in a rasp. 'Um...it's actually *mystery*,' he said, and in a low mumble added, '*Mystery* woman.'

'I'm sorry,' said Claude. 'Mystery Women.'

'Woman. Just the one. Any more and I'd be in a constant state of confusion.'

'Oh, woman is it? Singular? Gosh, it's not just my vision tonight. It's my hearing as well. Anyone could be excused for thinking I was losing my senses. A big hand for Matthew Weissler with "Mystery Woman".'

Everyone clapped. Everyone except an open-mouthed Rosetta.

ROSETTA HELD HER breath and waited for Matthew to commence. Matthew frowned down at the page in his hands. Claude tiptoed away.

Someone in the audience raised their hand. Claude turned and acknowledged them. From where she was sitting, Rosetta couldn't make out what the person was saying. A mop of dark hair was the most she could see. The head wasn't much higher than the back of the seat. A child perhaps? An arm flew sideways. A finger pointed to one side of the hall. Rosetta watched as Claude and then Matthew turned in unison to their left. Leaning against the wall was a shiny electric guitar.

Claude nodded in approval and said to the anonymous gesturer, 'Of course,' and Matthew, dashing towards the wall, was saying, 'Thanks! That's really good of you.'

Matthew concentrated on plugging in and setting up the guitar. The audience members murmured amongst themselves.

Claude took up the microphone again and said, 'Ladies and gentlemen, what Matthew is doing, I want you to understand, is not in any way against the rules. You may have noticed my recent request on the Poet's Garret newsletter for musical contributions. We're making every third Tuesday "Lyricist Night". Has anyone else brought along an instrument?' Claude scanned the crowd hopefully.

No response.

'Not to worry,' said Claude. 'There's always a next time. And as for you, Matthew, being a bit different to everyone else tonight will make you all the more memorable! Are we ready?'

Matthew, now looking less cerebral and a lot more rockstar, acknowledged he was right to go.

At Claude's request, Rosetta and the rest of the audience welcomed Matthew a second time with applause. Claude, head bowed humbly, scuttled off in the direction of the trestle tables. Matthew, eyes growing wider again, launched into his performance.

In the first few seconds, Matthew strummed some chords.

The discomforting stretch of silence that followed made Rosetta cringe. Without taking her eyes off the reluctant entertainer, she leaned forward. Matthew was gazing at the floor, looking lost. He was clearly suffering from nerves.

A man in the row behind her fell into a coughing fit. Poets' Garret members in a row further down were shifting restlessly in their seats. And then, instead of singing, Matthew spoke.

'I'm not much in the habit'

Strum!

'Of guessing who's a rabbit
And soon I learned I'd got it doggone wrong'

Rosetta leaned back in her seat, feeling faint and uneasy.

'But lady you could be
Almost anything to me
And still I'd want to sing this tribute song'

A pause. Rosetta waited. Matthew's voice rose into a melody.

'Mystery woman
Hurtling down the street
Mystery woman
With the bouncy feet
You keep me guessing
But guessing games are kind of neat'

'Great voice,' whispered Eadie when he sang the next stanza.

Encouraged by the comment, Rosetta admitted, 'I was thinking that too.' Prior to that she'd doubted her own objectivity.

'I'm still guessing.'

He was onto another stanza.

'Guessing, guessing...
I'm still guessing.'

He repeated the line twice more. And then he repeated it again.

'Guess-guess-*guess*-ing.'

Rosetta tried not to feel concerned about the monotone mantra he'd lapsed into.

'Still guessing.
I'm...hoo-hoo-hoo-hoo...guessing'

Eadie, unable to stifle her giggles, said to Rosetta in a hushed voice, 'I'm *guessing* the poor guy's forgotten the rest of his lyrics.'

'You keep me...ee...guessing.'

Torn between respect for Matthew's attempt at a song and amusement at Eadie's remark, Rosetta relented to laughter. She folded forward, guiltily trying to silence her snorts. Eadie, giggling contagiously beside her, had demolished any hope of regaining a polite state of seriousness.

Eadie's flippant little throwaway line wasn't the entire reason for Rosetta's mirth. Joy was bubbling over her in bucketfuls. Matthew was here. In the same room. Singing a song about *her!* And it couldn't have been seen as sarcastic. Matthew's send-up of their first encounter wasn't cold or cruel. There was nothing Rosetta could have taken offence at, except perhaps, and only if she resorted to being picky, his poor use of the words 'sad', 'bad' and 'mad'.

Finally able to compose herself, she lifted her head and went back to watching him.

Matthew's eyes, gorgeous and green, found hers. She caught her breath. Matthew's calm expression clouded. His gaze fell away from her. A furrow crept onto his forehead.

Oh God, she thought. He saw me laughing.

For an awful moment, Matthew faltered. And then he sank into another uncomfortable pause. When he resumed, the lyrics crashed into each other. Was he singing in English? Or...

Matthew, visibly stunned at his blunders, gave up on playing and observed the other poets seated before him. His eyes, Rosetta noticed, closed briefly. He looked once more around him, face breaking into a fleeting smile, and started up the guitar. The music he strummed this time—chords leaping into a succession of lively rhythms—was thankfully free of confusion.

    'I'm guessing
    I'm confessing
    That I'd like to be your friend
    And hope Charades can still be played
    But this time till the end'

ROSETTA FLUNG OPEN the door of the community hall. The murmur of a poet reciting a piece about unrequited love filtered from Room 5. Matthew had taken a seat in the end row when he'd finished his song. She'd been acutely aware of that. Throughout the other poets' recitals, she had glanced over her shoulder in the hope of exchanging a smile and a wave. Matthew, seeming not to have noticed, had stared ahead, dolefully almost. And then he had vanished.

Frosty air nipped at her fingertips when she stepped onto the car park's asphalt. Wrapping her shawl more firmly about her, she hurried across to the rows of vehicles by the far wall of the building. No sound of anyone reversing. He might not yet have left.

Where had her self-control been? Matthew had gone out of his way to sing an apology, not that he'd needed to, and she'd humiliated him by giggling. If he meant what he said in his song, he'd chosen to overlook their last farewell when she'd stormed indignantly off. Not her finest moment. What would he think of her now?

'Please, Guardian Angels,' Rosetta whispered, 'if Matthew hasn't left yet, please guide me to where he is.'

She rounded the corner of the building and drew to a stop to scan each car that formed a row adjacent to the community centre. Green Holden, beige Ford, red Toyota...beige Toyota...decrepit blue something-or-other...red Merc, red...was that a Jaguar? A cherry-red Jaguar? It was! Matthew was still here! She threw herself into a sprint.

She rollicked across the asphalt. Her calf-length skirt's many panels tangled between her knees. She clutched both sides of her skirt and held the fabric taut, wishing she'd worn the boots with the lower heels. The stilettos on these were slowing her down. She was more of a chunky-heeled runner than a dainty, dancey one. Any minute now, the Jaguar's engine might start up. If she didn't get there soon, she might never have the chance to clear things up with him.

Rosetta urged herself onwards, alert to anything that might sound like a motor, but all she could hear was the tap-tapping of her boots and the jingle-jangle of bracelets, earrings and necklace, the result of her recent penchant for wearing an eclectic combination of new accessories all at once. She loved them all. Could never decide which to exclude. They were punishing her now: jolting from her ears, bouncing against her wrists, hammering at her collarbone.

Would he be angry? Too angry even to speak to her? Matthew didn't seem the peevish type, but he wasn't someone she knew well. Mama's ferocious reprimands screeched through her memory. *Men hate women laughing at them.* At the age of fifteen, Rosetta was shelling peas at the kitchen table. Her snipey seventeen-year-old foster brother had strutted in sporting a 'chicken-boy' haircut. Her laughter had been prompted more by surprise than anything else. She'd felt a searing *thwack!* against the side of her face, Mama throwing a boiled potato at her. 'Leave Stavros alone,' she'd ordered. 'And never laugh at a man. Men hate women laughing at them.'

She could only try. At the driver's side of Matthew's car, Rosetta tapped on the frost-whitened window. In an effort to see inside, she slid the side of her palm across the window's wetly cold centre, calling, 'Matthew! You in there?' She stooped to peer in. The driver's seat was empty.

She rose from the car window and swivelled round. No-one in the car park. So if he hadn't left, where was he? Might have gone to the centre's poky little tea room where poets congregated for supper. She dashed back towards the lit-up porch where ferns, wild and abundant, gleamed dark and light green against a backdrop of overlapping ivy leaves.

The view through the swinging glass doors was disheartening. She could see no-one in the darkened tea room, and the chairs outside it were vacant. Backs of poets' heads were visible through the doorway off the corridor. Matthew had not returned to his seat.

Puzzled by this, Rosetta sat down on a small brick wall beside the steps. She couldn't return to the room now. It might disturb whoever was reciting. She checked the time on her phone, comfortingly iridescent in the darkened gloom, and decided to wait it out. The meeting would be finishing up with tea and biscuits soon.

She'd go back once the poets drifted out. In the meantime she would have a look at the little memorial garden neighbouring the community centre. She'd stumbled across it the night Adam made his first call to her and had loved the lattice trellis and red-leafed rose bushes. The rows of glossy-leafed camellias were probably in bloom now that winter was here.

ROSETTA ROSE FROM THE community-centre steps, tippity-tapped down them and moved towards the memorial garden's silver birch silhouettes and lattice archways with their backdrop of camellias.

A flurry of movement caused her to stop. The crest of a head with slightly wavy hair bobbed above the hedge. A fist reached up in a mock cricket-bowling gesture. Great. Her hope of some peaceful contemplation ruined. Teenage boys, there to drink or get stoned. She listened out for the typical gravelly murmurs and shouts. Nothing. Was there such a thing as a quiet group of youths? Maybe there was only one.

Footsteps clomped beyond the hedge's archway. Between the gap of camellia hedge appeared not a boy but a man, tall and attractive, shrouded in shadows, the owner, probably, of that bobbing head and impulsive sportsman tendency. He turned, and the moonlight caught his profile. Matthew!

She hastened her step.

He turned again and strode along the garden's twisting path. She increased her step to a run.

Matthew was looking first at the sky and then at the ground. He planted a hand on the back of his neck and shook his head.

Rosetta's heels were now clippity-clopping frantically, having altered from a trot to a canter to a gallop. The tug of her clunky earrings was jolting her ears once more, and her belt, an Egyptian hipster chain made up of coins, clinked and tinkled like a poker machine spewing out winnings.

Alerted to the noisy giveaway, Matthew turned.

Rosetta halted. Her chain belt clanged in protest, then sank into silence. She launched into a leisurely stroll. If she acknowledged him too soon he might repeat that hurtful avoidance of eye contact that he'd carried out so blatantly in the row behind her.

She had to calm her runner's puffs before reaching him. It wasn't the best time to recognise unfitness when lathered in perspiration from tearing around the car park like a border collie rounding up sheep. She would activate that gym membership at North Sydney starting on Monday. Tuesday at a pinch. Wednesday was probably better...Wednesday of the following week.

MATTHEW COULDN'T HELP but stare. There she was! So relaxed and unhurried. The memory of how she moved, talked and smiled had driven him crazy over the past few weeks. That slow, sensuous way she had about her, interspersed with bursts of energy when enthusiastic or passionate about something; her wide glossy mouth; her low, loud laugh and *that* walk: confident in a queenly sort of way with an unconscious swing of the hips. All those and more had taunted him when he'd thought back to that night at Amaretti's.

Why was it that whenever he was around her, he was doomed to turn into a klutz? First, the near-accident when he'd transported her from Harrow's to her home, then a butter-fingers attempt at holding an unopened bottle of wine, and now a pathetic shot at winning her respect with a carefully mulled-over song, the words to which he'd lost track of once he'd spotted her in the crowd. At least he hadn't forgotten the bit about wanting to be a friend. Surely that had to be seen as a peace offering.

He glanced eagerly across at her. She hadn't progressed much from the spot she was in when he'd forced himself to look away. Her chin was tilted upwards, and her head was turned to the right. He wasn't at all sure whether she knew he was there. If she did, she'd deliberately taken her time getting to him. Understandable of course. Why rush to speak to someone who'd singled you out and mocked you publicly with a badly delivered ditty? No wonder she'd laughed at him! She'd *laughed*. The memory tore at him like a claw in his chest.

He could never live it down. Not ever.

And to add to that, he'd gone and worn the loud shirt he'd got in Naples. Bernadette hated that shirt. Yelled whenever he wore it. Said it looked like jellybean vomit. Lately he'd been wearing it in rebellion.

He gazed down at the pale pink flower he'd plucked up absent-mindedly after retreating into the rose garden to take a call from Charlie. It was the same species of flower the musician had insisted he hand to Rosetta. Funny that, how the guy was at the poetry meeting tonight. Funny how there were some people you continually ran into whether you liked it or not.

'Matthew...'

In response to Rosetta's sultry voice, Matthew turned to face her, temporarily tongue-tied by the dark, commanding eyes that met his gaze.

She smiled. Gorgeously.

'Aw...hi,' he said.

Remembering he'd been getting nostalgic over a flower, a pink one of all things, he promptly let it drift to the ground, hoping she hadn't seen him cradling it in his palm.

ROSETTA WAS LOST FOR A SECOND OR TWO. Matthew was looking at her expectantly. He was smiling a little. She now had a chance to talk with him. Things couldn't be better!

Standing before him, before tall, beautiful Matthew, felt surreal. Why did he always do that? Bring the same floaty feelings to her each time they met? She shouldn't be feeling divinely alive or delightfully airy with someone who mightn't be single still. It wasn't right.

She had to say something. Anything. She contemplated the camellia Matthew had thrown to the ground. Beside it lay a dozen or so more, stomped into smoothness on the wet concrete path. 'I always feel,' she said finally, 'a teensy bit sad when I see plants and flowers mistreated.'

'Right,' Matthew said. In one swift move he rescued the abandoned camellia. She didn't have the heart to tell him she'd been referring to all the others. He hesitated, then held it out to her, adding, 'Although this time it's without any prompting.'

'From the accordionist at Amaretti's? True!' She collected the poor fragile bloom from Matthew's large hand. His other hand remained by his side. Was he wearing his wedding ring? If he was, she knew he'd patched things up with Dette. And if he wasn't...well, it didn't really indicate much. Lena Morris could vouch for that. Before Andrew arrived in her life, she was tricked into dating a 'ringless' man until his supposedly non-existent wife made a traumatised visit to her health foods shop. Eadie too at one stage, but ever-astute Lena had spotted Eadie's new boyfriend at the markets, wearing a papoose and *Hubby with Bubby* T-shirt.

'Did you see him?' Matthew said.

Rosetta blinked. 'See who?'

'The accordionist. He was in there tonight.'

'You're joking!'

'He was in the third row. Directed me to a guitar that had been there all week.'

'Really?'

Matthew was grinning. 'Yes,' he said gently. 'Really. It was a Gibson Slash, too, the Rolls Royce of vintage guitars.'

The man with the dark mop of hair! If these synchronicities kept up, she'd know that hair anywhere. She wanted to tell Matthew about the same guy turning up on a singles cruise, playing the violin, but there was something more urgent to say, something she wanted to ask him. She steeled herself for the answer. Now or never. It was killing her not knowing where he was relationship-wise.

'How's Dette?'

'Bernadette?'

'Yes. How is she?' Rosetta's nails dug into her palms. Were they getting back together?

'I don't know, to be honest.' He kicked at a stone on the path and shrugged. 'Haven't seen Bernadette, or the girls, since they left. She wouldn't tell me where she was going.'

'Oh G—' About to say: *Oh God,* Rosetta stopped. The last time she'd gone to say that to Matthew was when he'd told her he'd left Dette, and she'd stupidly said: *Oh good,* in a slip-of-the-tongue response. Instead she said, 'That's a bit of a worry for you, Matthew, not knowing where they are.'

Matthew regarded her with a perplexed side glance. He placed a hand on the nearby trellis. Was that his left hand or his right? Her senses were scrambled. She was torn between watching and listening: wanting to hear his next words yet battling to calculate mirror-reverse amid the distracting thumps of a bumpity heart.

'I'm not worried,' he said. 'Not worried at all. I know they're okay.' Cynical half-laugh. 'She has the decency at least to answer my texts. I last heard from her a couple of days ago.'

Left hand. It was his left. And definitely no wedding ring. And yet he'd just said he'd contacted his wife to find out where she was. Did that mean he was missing Dette?

'These things have a habit of working out,' Rosetta said cautiously.

Matthew appeared surprised by the comment. He unclasped the frame of the trellis and lowered his arm. 'Nothing to work out there though,' he said. 'The marriage is over. We've both realised we're not good together.'

Not good together. He was admitting to being really and truly available. Oh good! Oh God! Matthew's rhyming offer of friendship had just got a thousand times sexier.

Rosetta drew in a breath. 'The song was excellent, Matthew. Really great!'

Matthew's sidelong look was sceptical. 'You serious?'

'Absolutely! I know a good voice when I hear one. I'm a singer myself. From one singer to another, it sounded unreal.'

'You sing too?'

'Sure do.'

'Thanks. I...hope I didn't embarrass you with it.'

Beaming, Rosetta shook her head. 'Good rhythm. Nice and pacey. And your lyrics were excellent. I laughed a lot.' She wasn't going to add: *for the sheer joy of seeing you there.*

'So it was the lyrics!' Matthew placed his hands in his pockets. Smiled broadly. 'I owe it to the accordionist for pointing out that guitar. A stanza without music has never made sense to me. What were the chances of running into him again?'

'In a city like Sydney? Practically zilch.' She told him about the singles-cruise encounter, when the same man they'd seen in Amaretti's and the bar with the autumn-toned lampshades—who went by the name of Chippy—had traipsed after her around the boat, frustratingly playing the violin in a conversation-killing screech. 'Pretty much ruined my hope of meeting anyone nice,' she said, laughing. 'One day I'll get back at him for that.'

Matthew raised an eyebrow. 'What'd I tell you? You've gained a fan.'

'I've been meaning to tell you,' Rosetta began. How could she put this elegantly? 'Um...well, meaning to apologise actually. I...*Eeeeeeeeeeek!*'

A prickly sort of terror seized hold of her.

Something was crawling across her wrist.

She flung the camellia to the concrete and brushed down both arms.

'All okay?' Matthew asked.

'No!' Her voice had turned squawky and alien.

She drew in a horrified breath. Clawed at her wrist again. Breathing was difficult. Her mouth slackened and struggled to form words.

She breathed out a groan and flicked again at her arms. '*Spider,*' she sputtered. 'Sp...sp...*spider!*'

○

NOW WAS NOT A GOOD TIME for arachnaphobia, at the start of a humble-pie session with Matthew Weissler, but Rosetta had no say in the matter. Each action was at the mercy of the wrist-tickling spider.

She ran on the spot. Jumped up and down, shaking her arm.

In the midst of it all, Matthew dashed to her side, took a step forward and another step back while her maniacal dance spun out of control.

Light from the lamp post she'd neared illuminated the back of her wrist for a second. She could see it now. Something tiny and scurrying. Not a spider. Not even a baby spider. It was an ant. A placid, harmless little ant that had ventured from the camellia. 'Oh!'

'Gone now?' said Matthew.

She brushed the culprit to the ground. 'Just an ant,' she mumbled. She'd needed to think quicker. A moment longer and she might have realised she could keep up the spider thing to save face.

'Ha!' Matthew's voice brimmed with amusement. 'Is that all it was?'

Rosetta gulped and stared at the ground.

'Although,' Matthew's tone was thoughtful. 'I guess they're easily mistaken when you're going only by feel.' His voice was deliciously warm and very close, and he had emphasised the word feel.

Going by *feel.* She liked that. If she were really going by feel at that moment, she wouldn't just have been listening to Matthew. She'd have been gliding her hands over Matthew's shoulders, sliding them over his arms to where the rolled-up sleeves of his interestingly multi-colour shirt ended and his forearms began, and enjoying the novel sensation of Matthew's skin.

Matthew's hand settled on her back. He smoothed it across the ends of her hair.

Zing-Zingity-Zing!

She drew in a breath and looked up at him.

He was smiling down at her. 'You all right now?'

His hand was moving over her back in firm, small strokes. Whirls of sparkling warmth ran over her spine and curled around her toes and fingertips.

She tried to nod. His touch had spun her into a state of unspeakable happiness.

And then...chaos.

A sharp twinge gnawed at her scalp. The twinge became nastier, sharper. No. It couldn't have been. Not a real spider this time! Not in her hair! She squealed.

'In my hair, in my hair,' she said helplessly. 'Something's in my hair!' She flung herself forward and swiped at the roots. Matthew ran a brisk hand over the top of her head to flick whatever it was away from her. Something was biting. Savagely.

'Ow!' she said in a screech. 'Ow! Ow!'

'Rosetta, Rosetta,' Matthew was saying. 'Stop moving. Stop now.'

She froze.

'It wasn't a spider.'

'An ant again then?' Rosetta was mortified.

'No, it wasn't an ant. It was me.'

Still doubled over, she swung her head round and gaped at Matthew.

'I'm really sorry about this. My watch. It's caught in your hair. Must have been pulling.'

His back-pat had caused a tangle.

Upon Matthew's advice, Rosetta levered herself from her cringe while Matthew choreographed his trapped arm to move with her. 'I can't undo the clasp,' he said. 'Your hair's too caught up in it. Got any scissors?'

'I have!'

'That was a joke.'

'No, seriously.' Rosetta's purse, which she'd strung from shoulder to hip when looking for Matthew, was on the ground, a side-effect of that unfounded ant-panic. 'Do you think you can reach that? I have nail scissors inside a manicure set.'

'I couldn't do that to you.'

'I'm fine with you going through it.'

'Not necessary. Almost sorted.' Appearing to know what he was doing, Matthew twisted her hair into ineffective spirals. 'This might take some time.'

Three voices from the car park called her name. Rosetta whirled round, taking Matthew's watch and arm with her. She winced from the needling pain it triggered.

Royston was standing beside the new luxury car Rosetta had bought him the week before. He waved to her. Eadie and Darren glanced across at her with raised eyebrows. The awkwardly close proximity she and Matthew were locked in probably looked like something special had been interrupted, like she was too lost in Matthew's presence to join her friends and leave. Some of that, she supposed, wasn't too far from the truth.

Eadie and Darren were gawping now and whispering to each other like gossipy sixth graders.

In a voice that only Rosetta could hear, Matthew adopted a reasonably good sit-com drawl and pretended to call to them, 'It's not what it looks like.'

In the moments that followed, she and Matthew gave in to peals of uproarious laughter while conscious of remaining static to avoid further damage. 'So this is what it's like to be a hysterical statue,' Rosetta remarked.

'And not a historical one?'

They managed, in the end, to exercise what the good folk on Sesame Street called 'co-operation'. Matthew edged crab-like to Rosetta's purse, and Rosetta edged crab-like alongside Matthew. He leaned sideways to retrieve it from the ground. Rosetta leaned along with him. She didn't have much choice. It was either that or risk baldness from a yanked-out strand.

Matthew located the mini manicure set, looked dubiously down at the scissors and passed them to her. 'Can't do it,' he said. 'Can't hack into your hair.'

'You wouldn't be hacking into it. You'd only be freeing up the ends.'

'Still couldn't.'

'Help me out here, Matthew! I'm not good at this siamese-twin thing. Couldn't you just—'

'Well, it's gorgeous hair, for a start. I'd feel like a vandal. I'd feel like I'd gone and shot Bambi.'

Rosetta pushed a thumb through one of the looped scissors handles. 'You've got to remember, Matthew, that the only thing you'd be guilty of vandalising is other people's Amaretti's gelato.' She walked her fingers along the strands connecting with Matthew's Rolex and efficiently snipped them free.

'Well done,' Matthew said, stepping away from her.

He placed both his hands on her elbows then, making her feel effervescently light, as though she were wading through rivers of champagne. His effect on her was immense. Powerful. It took all her willpower *not* to melt into Matthew's formal semi-embrace, despite a wild hope of every formality deserting them.

'I'll let you get back to your friends,' Matthew whispered.

'Ah yes. My friends.' Finally able to tear her gaze away from his earnest face, she looked across at Royston, Eadie and Darren. They were now in Royston's car, looking discreetly in the other direction.

'Rosetta...' Matthew's voice had become deep and suggesting.

'Mmm?'

His hands fell away from her. 'I'd like to keep in contact if it's okay with you.'

Determined not to bypass another opportunity, Rosetta took a freshly printed business card from her purse.

Matthew examined the card. 'Very nice,' he said. 'I like the holographic design.'

Rosetta shrugged this off. Silver holographic lettering was easy when you could afford the best printers in Sydney. And how she presented herself in a card didn't matter anymore. Even if she'd had only her former 'cards' to hand over: one of the flimsy gold-texta-squiggled squares she'd improvised with during her struggling single mother days, as long as the contact details were legible to Matthew, she wouldn't have cared.

'Er...I'm sorry. I thought...' Matthew was puzzled. 'But your name's Rosetta!'

She'd forgotten that her business cards had her new professional name on them, the name she now used at uni. Avoiding the question-prompting revelation of having been adopted, she told him how Odetta had been her mother's choice. 'But my friends have always called me Rosetta.'

'I like Rosetta,' said Matthew.

The awareness of him looking at her for quite some time caused her eyes to lower and her words to gain speed like a school-girl's. 'My baba's choice. He named me after the Rosetta Stone.'

'You're Egyptian? You have to be from somewhere exotic like that.'

'I'm a New Zealander. Half Maori. But I was raised by Greeks.'

'An exotic blend then.'

Ushering the subject back to Matthew, she said, 'And you've spent your younger years in England.' He'd mentioned it at Amaretti's, but the initial giveaway was the charming accent and quaint way with words.

'Yeah. I'm catching a flight there tomorrow morning, believe it or not. I've got to go to London about a possible career change.'

'Tomorrow!'

'Uh-huh. It should be good actually.'

England. Rosetta froze. Working in London and not Sydney. She was about to lose him again.

'It's just to check out a few things. I'm sort of in a quandary as to what to do. My brother wants to introduce me to a few people.' Matthew hesitated. 'Just business people. And, whatever the case, whichever I decide, it'll be good to catch up with the family.'

He hadn't decided yet!

Matthew nodded towards Royston's car. 'I came here on his advice. Returned *Our True Ancient History* to him, and he threw into the conversation that you'd be here on Tuesday night.'

'Ooh, did he really, now?'

'He did. I enjoyed the book actually and...Rosetta, are you seeing someone at the moment?'

'No!' She'd said it in almost a shout. If she hadn't wanted to seem desperate before, she sure sounded that way now. 'How long are you going for?' she asked, trying not to appear too hopeful. 'Or is it a one-way ticket?'

'I'll be there for a month,' he said. 'If I do decide to move, I'll need to come back and sell everything up.'

Realising she'd been holding her breath, Rosetta relaxed her shoulders and exhaled softly. Not a one-way ticket. A month. She could live with that. As for Matthew leaving Australia for good...well *that* didn't bear thinking of. It would mean having to forget about him forever.

Tonight Matthew had become a friend.

The friendship, though, was fragile. It might have to end.

An unpublished chapter of

Our True Ancient History

from Reverend Edward Lillibridge's
original *handwritten* manuscript

Frowning over Alcor's question as to who she had been in a previous life, Maleika gave her reply. 'No brother,' she said. 'I do not know who I was in my incarnation before this one. The divisions of recall are still firmly locked. Please enlighten me.'

Leaving her earthly life behind in permanent slumber had been a serene and lovely journey for Malieka. Her soul-self had travelled to the Dream Sphere through the silver cord that linked her to the physical world, and Alcor, her Dream Master, was now asking if she remembered who she had been in a prior earthly existence.

Alcor waved a hand across Maleika's forehead. As soon as he did so, a memory returned. Inside this memory she was hurrying across an expanse of grass towards a man of great beauty. The man's wings were angelic yet his aura, while silvery, lacked the pearl-white element belonging to those of the celestial realm.

The man was changing form, melding rapidly with the brown feathers of his wings and rising majestically into the air. He had mutated into an eagle.

The eagle circled the sky before soaring down to a tapered pillar. And then his feathers lit up, as though seared by the workings of thunder goblins. Maleika could hear her voice, sharp and agonised, felt her feet crushing into the cold grass as she ran. 'Storlem,' she cried. 'My love!'

The remembrance of pain overcame her.

'Oh Storlem,' Maleika whispered, surprised to find a tear escaping from her eye.

Alcor spoke. 'Who were you Maleika, in your life before this one?'

'I was Orahney,' Maleika said.

'Autumn faerie, bewitcher, soothsayer,' said Alcor. 'Renamed Zemelda by the Grudellans.'

Maleika pondered Alcor's sapphire eyes. Again she said, 'I was Orahney!' although this time she said it incredulously. 'Brother, how can this be? Orahney visited me.'

'In dream-self form,' Alcor told her.

'With respect, brother,' said Maleika, 'this all sounds rather ridiculous. Are you saying that I was visiting myself?'

'Precisely. We often encourage Dream Sphere visitors to assist their later selves.'

'And so I had lived in the Pre-destruction Century.'

'Would you like to hear of your next incarnation?'

'Indeed I would.'

'You have spoken to me recently about the possibility of becoming a water sprite.'

'Yes,' said Maleika decidedly. 'Carlonn and Zhippe lead such free lives. They play with the otters in the river and seals in the sea, and their descriptions of ocean gardens are quite breathtaking.'

'I am very pleased then,' Alcor said, 'to advise you, Maleika, that your next existence will be lived as a mermaid.'

'How wonderful!'

'And you will spend many of your days within a glorious sanctuary of corals. Neptune's haven of wonders.'

'And who shall I live my life alongside?'

'Interestingly, Maleika, your undine clan members will remain in earthly existence for many millenniums.'

'Undines are known for their longevity,' Maleika remarked.

'Indeed they are. And so, once you return to the earth you will see Zhippe and Carlonn again in their present form. They will have much to tell you of their travels to a faraway island, and of weapons beyond anything we can imagine obliterating the earth's surface. Zhippe and Carlonn will go underground when the warring comes about. They are survivors.'

'Thank goodness for that! They have helped me enormously in this most recent elfin life.' Remembering their journeys forward in time, Maleika shook her head smilingly. 'Zhippe helped me in my work with the woman of the future, as did Carlonn and Karee.'

'Is that so?'

'Do you not remember, Alcor, a life I was to guide? You handed me a personality at one stage, along with an appearance and elementary knowledge of the ways of those in the future.'

'Of course,' said Alcor. 'You were not, as I remember, so good at manoeuvring those boxes on wheels that they all get about in.'

Maleika placed her hands on her hips. 'Considering I had such little time in which to learn, I believe I did well.'

'I suppose you did,' said Alcor laughing. 'Let's say you did then, shall we? And speak of it nay more? Now come with me,' he urged, 'and let us gaze into the distant future.'

Chapter Two

To:.........Rosetta Melki
From:.....Matthew P Weissler
Sent:.......15 June 2008
Subject:...*Fight or Flight*

Hi Rosetta,

Great to catch up with you at the poetry night. How have you been?

I arrived at Heathrow 4 a.m. this morning. Caught a black cab to Cartwright Gardens in Bloomsbury, then lay down on the sofa of my suite to catch the early morning British news. That's the last thing I remember. It is now 6 p.m.

Woke an hour ago after a nasty dream that I'd missed my plane due to The Isle of Wight declaring war on every nation in the Southern Hemisphere. An alarming example of 'fight or flight'.

My hotel is situated on a crescent that's lined with concave Regency apartments and the odd shade tree. It's pretty misty out there now—dusk and haze intermingled. No wind about, and the clouds are silver-grey. Reminds me of my high-school days in Wimbledon when I'd return home after a two-hour bus trip. Dad would inevitably be in his armchair reading the evening papers, and Mum would be sitting by the window beneath the clackety clock, doing crosswords in the fading light and sipping tea.

I hope your friends didn't mind the hold-up on Tuesday night. If they'd known it was a case of either me being dragged into the car with you or the two of us working out an alternative to our entanglement, they would have said, 'Take all the time you need.' Sports coupes don't take kindly to extra passengers.

Gotta split. As it turns out, it's actually closer to 9 p.m. than 6. Picked up my watch on the bedside table but read it upside down by mistake. The joys of jet lag...

I've just broken off to answer a call from my brother—was due to meet him at The Ivy an hour ago.

Wanted to discuss Lillibridge's book with you but am now virtually halfway out the door. Would love to hear your thoughts on the story. Email back when you can. It'll be great to hear from you.

Cheers,

Matthew

To:..........Matthew P Weissler
From:.......Rosetta Melki
Sent:........17 June 2008
Subject:....Re—*Fight or Flight*

Hi Matthew,

Thanks for your email – and nice to hear from you!

How was the meal at The Ivy with your brother?

That dream of yours sounds intriguing. Scary though! I'd love to hear more about it.

My day today was mostly taken up with rehearsing for the Bondi Diggers Comp. We made it through to the finals—Yay. Craig is on guitar, and I'm on 'vocals'. We're singing a Danna Nolan song, and while we ourselves naturally like the tune, we have no idea how it'll be received tomorrow night. Whatever the case (and you, as a singer / songwriter, would probably agree) there are few things more fun than creating music. Craig and I loved every second of our trials (and errors).

I was pleased to hear you say the other night that you enjoyed *Our True Ancient History*. As you know, my friends and I formed a study group earlier in the year with the intention of uncovering the secret Lillibridge is rumoured to have woven through his story. Some say the work is based on truth rather than a work of fiction, so perhaps the secret is a past we could never have imagined.

Others believe it's more of a prophecy than a hidden history. The original manuscript of Lillibridge's is rumoured to have contained allusions to a time in the future known as The Silvering. The edition you borrowed from Royston is the only one I'm familiar with. There's a rare mention of The Silvering in that version in a small verse at the front. I think I might have pointed it out to you when we were chatting on my verandah. That was before Royston turned up unexpectedly—and spirited the book away from us!

Love the sound of your street view. It all sounds so serene at that time of evening, a mixture of Georgian-era grace and muted light. Did you wake up the next morning to sunshine or rain? Or something in between?

I'm looking forward to hearing your views on the book. Please keep me up-to-date, too, on the places you visit. I've never been to the United Kingdom but cherish the idea of going there. My ex-husband Angus was a Scotsman (and probably still is!!) We'd planned a trip to his homeland early on in our marriage. That was around seventeen years ago, but the plans changed abruptly when our baby daughter arrived. Izzie and I hope to go there some time next year. The two of us can't wait to start planning the trip because Izzie will finally get to meet her dad's parents.

I agree that Royston's new car would have been a bit of a problem if we'd remained entangled. I might have ended up in your lap!

Best wishes,

Rosetta

To:..........Rosetta Melki
From:.......Matthew P Weissler
Sent:........18 June 2008
Subject:....*Ban scissors!*

Hi Rosetta,

In my lap? You in my lap? I'm now wondering whether locating those scissors and detaching your hair from my Rolex was such a good idea.

The Ivy with my brother was really good—thanks for asking. A great catch-up. He introduced me to a mate of his, a top London business consultant whose name is Kirk Rummery. The guy's an ace, apparently, at setting up law and accounting firms and making them work. He's Scottish like your ex. Let's not hold that against him though!! He wants to go into partnership with someone here. Can't say I'm not tempted considering his track record—he's started some of the biggest names from scratch through innovative promotion and design.

So, you want to hear more on my 'fight or flight' dream. I think you'll regret having requested this. It was more stupid than scary, and I hate having to admit to dreaming it, but since you asked so attractively for the details, I'm compelled to elaborate.

In the dream, I decided it'd be a smart idea to disguise myself as a soldier and sneak into the UK via one of the battalions. I was lining up for roll call, and everything was going along surprisingly well. The major even had my name on his list to call out. (I've no idea how I managed that) and then an inspector marched up to me. I did the usual thing of regimented saluting etc. and the inspector said: 'Sorry, sir. You'll never get in with these.' He was pointing to my shoulders, and I argued that I did a lot of swimming and that my shoulders, therefore, were up to the task, but he walked away, muttering, 'Won't fit in the plane.'

Then I saw in my peripheral vision that I had wings. Huge, clumsy wings. So I picked up one of my army boots (it had a Maxwell Smart phone built into its sole) and dialled Midas Touch Jewellers for advice. Their chief jeweller assured me that my wings were highly appropriate for defending our territory and that to be rejected on account of these was discrimination. The military, they advised, would have to either fit their jets with a bigger doorway or allow me to fly independently alongside them, via my wings.

Fortunately I was woken by hunger pangs. And now I'm suffering from Fear of Ridicule. Relating a dream about Midas Touch morphing into a legal counsel is kind of embarrassing, so I ask that you save my pride by avoiding laughter at all costs.

I was intrigued to hear about your singing. You're obviously very good if you got into the finals of the comp. Any chance of me getting to hear that song of yours and Craig's? I've included a link here for SongSend. Have you heard of this? It's a sharp bit of technology. You just upload one of your songs and send it through the portal. You've got no excuse now for depriving me of your voice. Best of luck tonight at Bondi Diggers, not that I believe you'll need it.

Great to hear all those speculations concerning *Our True Ancient History*. Can't exactly tell you why I loved the book. I just did. Reading it felt like rediscovering dusty treasures from my childhood—I was really there, with each of the characters, and that's saying something considering I'm not a real fan of fiction.

Does your book group have an opinion on who 'The People of the Sea' might be? Could Lillibridge have been inferring on his first page that he based his story on the ramblings of whimsical fishermen?

Hidden history? Hard to say. Sounds dismally far-fetched to me. The only history I find interesting is the concrete stuff, the life of the author for example. I've been doing a bit of research on Reverend Edward Lillibridge. Apparently he was a controversial preacher. The king's men dragged him off to the gallows for his non-orthodox parish ramblings. Do you already know all that? I think you do. In fact I know you do since I got this info from your website. You're a dark horse, Rosetta Melki. Unless there's someone else in Burwood who shares your slightly unusual (and very lovely) name, I'm guessing the creator of the Friday Fortnight website is you.

Your suggestion that the book might contain a prophecy really interests me. What is The Silvering exactly? What do you make of it? Has The Silvering happened, do you think, or is it yet to happen? Perhaps it's all a load of fantasy.

What I found especially interesting on your website was a guest blog-post by one of the Irish Fortnighters who discusses Lillibridge's bizarre references to 21st century technologies. I'm baffled by the mention in Croydee's narrative (Chapter XXVIII) of cinema projections when he likens them to the holographic reflection of the body king residence:

Never one to give in to challenges, Croydee pondered his dilemma. 'I am perfectly safe,' he reasoned, for his observation of this hologram was simply like an individual from a future timeframe walking into a picture palace and wading through image beams.

The blog entry's mention of 'boxes on wheels' and 'view-cubes' spewing meaningless noise and imagery to a sadly deficient receiveship' in Pieter's narrative (Chapter V) also got me thinking. The blogger states that many readers believe the descriptions to be of cars, in the first instance, and then TV. How someone in 1771 could have envisaged so accurately inventions that were, at the very least, a century ahead in the future is more than a little mysterious. Do any of us know for certain that the book wasn't written later than claimed?

I'm impressed with how your Friday Fortnight idea has skyrocketed internationally: England, Ireland, Sweden, France...How does it feel to be responsible for all that? Did you know there's a group in Cornwall that's recently started up? My brother and I have a holiday home in Newquay. He naturally gets more use out of the place than I do, so I'm well overdue for my turn. Will stay there Friday night. That way I can go as a guest to the Rosetta-Melki-inspired Cornish book-study group. I'll check up on the group members for you. Will make sure they're complying with your rules. I can be your secret agent. I can be anything you want me to be...

London's pretty dreary at present. Nothing romantic or glamorous to report. Will include a detailed travelogue for you, in my next email, after I've been to the seaside. Far more picturesque and enticing.

Keep smiling and bye for now,
Matthew

To:.........Matthew P Weissler
From:......Rosetta Melki
Sent:........19 June 2008
Subject:...Re–*Ban scissors!*

Hi Matthew,

Good to hear you enjoyed The Ivy and got to meet a potential business associate. He sounds like a whiz!

That dream of yours was very entertaining. I tried to imagine you gliding alongside the jet and peering in every so often on the startled passengers the way Superman does in movies. Do you mind if I ask what kind of wings you had? Were they light and gossamer like a dragonfly's or feathery and birdlike?

The comp at Bondi Diggers went well. I've included the recording of our song for you on the Song-Send icon attached. I agree it's a great technology. I'll definitely make use of Song-Send in the future.

The comp had oodles of amazing contenders. One of the acts deserving of an award was a girl of fifteen (a few months older than Dette's Sara and one year younger than my Izzie), a harpist and singer. I heard her during rehearsals. Her song was simple but extraordinarily beautiful, and the harp along with it just added to the tune's celestial aura. Craig and I were utterly in awe.

I was upset with some of the other under–eighteens because they referred to this girl as 'Fish-Face'. She took it good naturedly, saying it was because her name (Serena) sounds the same as a brand-name for canned tuna.

Last night, at the finals, I helped Serena prepare backstage. I told-off anyone who didn't address her by her proper name, and I did her make-up and hair. (She wanted a French braid—a style that's really 'in' at the moment). Her hair is red, similar to my daughter's, although finer and silkier, and I commented on this. She asked questions about Izzie and was interested to know about Izzie's netball club, and her friends and her art. Didn't talk about herself at all, except for a dream she'd had the night before, of swimming beneath the sea. In the dream, she'd looked back at her feet and discovered she had a dolphin tail. Weirdly enough, *I* had the *same* dream a few weeks earlier—coral and seals included! So don't go thinking it's silly to dream you have wings, Matthew. Dreaming you're an aquatic mammal is just a *leetle* bit sillier, don't you think?

Speaking of wings, Craig and I happened to be waiting in them when Serena was called up to perform. She looked like a little mermaid sitting there in her aquamarine gown with the loose-ends of her plaited hair curling over one shoulder. The song she sang was sublime, and so standing backstage listening to the judges' verdicts was more than a little unsettling. My fingers were crossed so tightly they were beginning to hurt! I wanted so much for Serena to get a high score, but one of the judges declared she was 'a tad too nice.' Told her she had to be less innocent, more 'sexy,' and suggested she instead sing R & B songs. Craig and I, as you can imagine, were appalled. We'd expected at least 18 out of 20, but the poor kid was given (quite unfairly, I believe) an incredibly low score. Craig and I were called up to perform our song. Everyone seemed to like it, including the judges, who rated us highly and gave us second prize—a trip to Vancouver!

Neither of us could envisage travelling together to Canada within the six months of the prize's validity (I've gone full-time to complete a uni degree I'm doing, and Craig's completely taken up with his new mining company) so we checked with the organisers that it would be okay to give our prize away.

Doing that felt more comfortable for us. We didn't feel altogether deserving of the prize, especially because of the twenty odd years' experience we had over the teens, and Serena, who has never been overseas due to modest finances, had a voice we considered to be outstanding. Craig and I both agreed that seeing her joyful smile at receiving our gift was worth a hundred Second Prizes. She's going to friend Izzie on Facebook since I told her Izzie hopes to enrol at a Canadian uni and wants to get firsthand accounts of the place and its people.

And that's all my news on the singing comp! Quite an involved story, I know, but the point of it, Matthew, isn't about rewarding someone for good work. It's about reaffirming to a youngster that her crystal-bell singing is beautiful just the way it is and that she must never allow those who ignore its purity to corrupt it.

So you've located my Friday Fortnight website! Okay, Matthew, I give in. You've found me out. I don't tell anyone about it directly. Anyone who is not really, *really* interested in the book would probably find the site a bit obsessive, so I kind of have this notion that it will be stumbled across by those intrigued enough about *Our True Ancient History* to google it. Welcome aboard. (I see you've joined as a member—Congratulations!)

I am so excited about you visiting the Cornwall Fortnighters. Please tell them 'hi' from me and that I'd love to meet them all one day. Tell me everything you can. I'm dying to find out about their discussions. If you're still volunteering to be anything I want you to be, then be a movie camera...please?? Convey to me absolutely everything that was said and done there. I'm so happy you're going. You'll be kind of like an ambassador for our Aussie group.

I really want you.. to be there as a representative.

About Lillibridge's mention of 'The People of the Sea.' This is a bit of a mystery to Friday Fortnighters, but I'm determined to uncover who the original storytellers were. It's likely they were illiterate, and fishermen as you suggest, or shanty dwellers. Being the educated (and poetic) man he was, Lillibridge no doubt felt compelled to create a written version in honour of them. In doing so, he perpetuated a tale that might otherwise have vanished before reaching the era we live in, along with all other folklore that we'll never get to read.

Regarding The Silvering. My feeling is that it's to occur within our lifetime. Conan Dalesford has sent me across his latest guest-blog concerning this. It's quite insightful. He believes a re-emergence of the Currency of Kindness is our only hope. It's either that or we end up with a planet made un-liveable through decisions that centre on profit equalling destruction. I'm due to upload it in time for July's study-group meetings but have sent it to you in an attachment—a preview. Hope you feel honoured!

You asked how it feels to be responsible for Friday Fortnight going international. It feels amazing, although I can't take all the credit. If it weren't for Royston and Eadie and Lena and Craig, the idea for the book study meetings would never have got off the ground.

I just happened to be the one to envision a website and keep up a supply of pretzels every other Friday.

Am looking forward to your next email. Descriptions of English country landscapes that are enticing and/or picturesque will be enthusiastically received.

Enjoy every moment!

Warm wishes,

Rosetta

To:.........Rosetta Melki
From:......Matthew P Weissler
Sent:.......21 June 2008
Subject:... *Wings, fins and other things*

Hi Rosetta,

Congratulations on your win! I've listened to your song a few times now and think you're way too modest about coming second. I would have guessed first prize. Your voice has a smoky quality—full-bodied like a good wine and very, very alluring...

I think what you and Craig did for Serena was brilliant. Vancouver is at its best in autumn. I recommend early October as one of the nicest times to visit.

Still at Cornwall. Attended my first Friday Fortnight meeting. You asked if I could be a movie camera for you. Sorry. Didn't work. I clicked my fingers twice, too, and said the magic words. To make up for these diminished powers, I bought a movie camera and asked the group permission to film the meeting for you, hence the VideoSend attachment.

Prior to the beginning of it, when they're calling out 'Hi Rosetta,' we sat around and chatted. They wanted to know a bit about you, and I had to admit I haven't known you all that long. Glynis, the lady who got their group started, said that you appeared to be 'very striking' on the website's Sydney homepage (where you and your friends are sitting by a fireside holding up your books.) Someone else, one of the guys, asked if you always looked that beguiling or whether it was just a good photo. I told them the photo, good and all as it was, did not do you justice.

It was a really great evening. You'll see my mug crop up in the first few seconds of the video and then it will stay there, as part of the group, within the entirety of filming. Don't be alarmed. I'm not in possession of Go-Go-Gadget arms. Glynis's eleven-year-old grandson was staying over, and he volunteered to capture the meeting so that I could participate. He filmed us quite well from the shoulders up, and then there's a lovely bit of footage of the ceiling, which goes on for quite some time. Bear with it if you can...you'll still hear what we're saying.

You will then see a close-up of the design on Glynis's carpet, and then there'll be a blurred zoom-in of Glynis's husband Dudley and a further zoomed-in version of the abovementioned's nose. This will go on for approximately seven minutes, and then everything's back to normal.

It's funny you should mention mermaids in your last email. When I got to Cornwall on Friday afternoon, I drove down to Zennor to look at the church there, Saint Senara, home of the famous Mermaid Chair (photo attached). It's fascinated me from childhood, ever since my parents took my brother and me to see it one gusty Sunday, as does the legend behind it, mostly, I suppose, because the hero of the tale happens to be called Matthew. When I hear people relate the story, I'm convinced they're talking about me. Not that I'm egotistical or anything. Considering that the world does revolve around me, I'm remarkably unassuming.

So anyway, I get back from Zennor, drive out to the Friday Fortnight people in Tintagel, and Harriet (the blonde girl sitting to the left of me in the 'documentary,' not the tallish short-haired one, the one sitting opposite Dudley) tells me that Lillibridge wrote the odd short story in his time. Someone Harriet knows has managed to collect together a few of Lillibridge's possessions from descendants. She said this person has two letters Lillibridge wrote and a newspaper clipping of a short story. And get this. The title of the story is 'The Legend of the Mermaid of Zennor: Retold by Reverend Edward Lillibridge.' Uncanny eh? The legend's been circulating since the fifteenth century. Lillibridge, like me, was charmed by the legend, so much so, that he decided to write his own version. Harriet says the mermaid's name according to the legend is Morveren. Lillibridge maintains that this is her name, yet apparently has her saying at one stage to Matthew, 'My true name is Morveren, but my sisters call me Marani.' And so he thereafter refers to her as that name only.

You can find The Mermaid of Zennor on Wikipedia. Alternatively, you can read my very bland summary. If you already know the story, please disregard this next paragraph, and the ones to follow:

Back in the 1400s lived a great looking bloke named Matthew, whose singing voice was earth-shatteringly good. [Remind you of anyone?] He sang like a blackbird, this Matthew. It's little wonder then that he was invited to sing at his local church.

A mermaid named Marani heard Matthew's songs and was so very entranced by his spellbinding warbles, she climbed out of the sea, donned a flowing gown and hobbled upright on her fishtail into the church. Marani was quite a stunner. She attracted many an admiring glance when she took a seat in the middle row. Matthew saw her there when he was singing, got completely tongue-tied and botched his words. [Actually, that didn't happen in the story, but I'm familiar with the stupefying effect of locking eyes with an audience member you happen to find desirable.]

This visit from Marani kept up on a continuous basis, probably for around eleven or twelve weeks. When the parish saw her shuffle in each Sunday, they admired her devotion, having concluded that this bewitching maiden with the dark eyes and flowing reddish hair was built of tough stuff, since no spouse nor family member assisted her in journeying to the service. They wondered at the damage to the feet they presumed her to have.

The mermaid's actual reason for attending had nothing to do with psalms and sermons. The truth was, Marani had fallen head-over-fins for that old smoothy Matthew. [And who could blame her?] Eventually, however, pain from the bruises on her tail made attendance impossible.

Matthew could never forget the stoic siren. He's down by the sea one day, rehearsing his evensong hymns and, shock-of-all-shocks, the woman he only knows by sight who he's by now madly in love with, swims languidly up to him! She sings then (in a smoky sort of voice) and he serenades her with the snappiest songs he knows. She and her fellow mer-people tell him stories from long ago.

In the end, Matthew cannot do without her. She beckons him into the sea. He follows...and is neither seen nor heard of again.

Whether or not Matthew survived is debatable. The stories are always left up in the air. My hope is that he turned into a mer-man and lived happily ever after with Marani. Like most people, I don't warm to unhappy endings.

I haven't yet answered your question (about my wings.) Feathered? Yes. And definitely birdlike. Good guess. The same subject came up on Friday evening. They were talking about dreams they'd had—after our cameraman got bored and ambled off to bed—so I told them about mine, and half-expected them to think: 'Uh-oh! Sandwich short of a picnic,' but they were surprisingly tolerant. And then Harriet brought up the eagle-winged guards introduced in Chapter VI, saying Lillibridge's description of these 'genetically-tampered troopers' (winged guards who temporarily changed into eagles at dusk) would have inspired the dream. She couldn't have been more right. My dream wings had been a deep, dark brown, like those of eagles.

The Currency of Kindness that Dalesford talks about in the preview you sent me sounds very nice but rather delusional don't you reckon? I'm all for ethical consumption and am passionate about wiping out slavery, but capitalism works in its own funny way. Communism never has. I challenged him on that over dinner, the night of his Sydney book launch.

But I liked Dalesford's previous guest-blog, 'Remembering Lemuria'. It was interesting reading his 'past-incarnation reminiscences' of technically advanced ancients whizzing around The Land of Mu in crystal-powered boat-shaped baskets. Far more practical than a pair of cumbersome wings!

What's it like weather-wise in old Sydney-town? Probably no different to here. At times the English summer will mimic an Australian winter.

The other attached photo features my brother and the business-whiz Scotsman (Kirk Rummery) on a great night out at The Monkey and Barrel, a Tudor-style pub.

Looking forward to hearing from you again.

Love,

Matthew

To:.........Rosetta Melki
From:......Matthew P Weissler
Sent:.......21 June 2008
Subject:...*Lillibridge Documents*

Hi again Rosetta,

Too early for another email you're saying?

Just a note to update you on what's happening.

I'm off to Charles Gloucester's place tomorrow. He's the bloke with the short story and two letters. Lives in a farmhouse manor apparently. Harriet insists on giving me a lift there. Personally I'd rather drive, but she's cagey about giving out Charles' address, so I might as well go along for the ride. She's a really lovely girl, really humorous, so the company should be good. Will ask Charles if he'd mind if I take a copy of that clipping so you can include it on your site. Harriet has said she's been thinking for a while of doing the same, so we might as well get that done when I go there.

Shall keep you posted.

Matthew

To:.........Matthew P Weissler
From:......Rosetta Melki
Sent:.......22 June 2008
Subject:....Re—*Wings, fins and other things*

Hi Matthew,

Thank you so, so much for going out and getting a movie camera and filming your meeting at Cornwall. It was amazing getting to see the participants. I felt like I was there in the room with them...up until Glynis' grandson progressed to the architraves, the biscuit crumbs on Glynis's floor and the pores of Dudley's nose (very cute!) It adds some quirkiness to an otherwise 'serious' documentary!!

I'm so happy you're going out to visit Charles Gloucester. I've been looking all over for further material evidence of Lillibridge's existence, as has another Fortnighter Lena (the friend whose place you drove to after Amaretti's).

And now you've gone out and found that evidence—with the help of this Harriet. She's very beautiful, isn't she. Now that I mention Harriet, I remember how familiar she looked, on your Cornwall Fortnighter video. I hate to say this (because I have no reason whatsoever to doubt her) but she happens to be identical to someone I saw in a magazine – a *crime* magazine would you believe. *(Britain's Most Wanted)*. I was reading an article in it at the hair salon, and the story gave me the creeps. The woman in question is a serial boyfriend-killer, and because of that they've dubbed her 'The Black Widow'.

I was fascinated to read about Lillibridge's retelling of The Mermaid of Zennor. I'd never heard the tale. Thanks for providing that—a sad, beautiful story, and also for the amazing photo of that carving on the church chair. I have since googled it and am ravenous for any piece of information I can get on the topic. I've always felt all legends have more than a smidgen of truth in them.

About the Currency of Kindness blog post by Conan Dalesford. I can vouch for him in saying he does *not* see his suggestions for a fairer financial system to be any sort of political ideology. I think what he means to do in that post is hypothesise on what the effect might be if some of those at the top of the food chain were to allow more flow, rather than a miserly stagnation that puts pressure on those at the bottom of the food chain.

He argues that everyone should be allowed to earn as much as they like and is adamant that the majority of Earth's inhabitants do not wish to be excessively rich.

None of us knows, though, what the ancient Currency of Kindness truly was. How can we categorise a concept we have no frame of reference for? The only known examples in our present world have been capitalism and communism. What I know of both of these systems is that inside this current game of monopolisation, they're very much alike. Both are content to churn out losers, the unfortunate many who, despite their fair playing, miss out. And losers are in the majority. Regardless of whether we're rich or poor, all of us are controlled by our desire for money. What is so tragic about all of this is that nine-hundred-and-twenty-five million people in the world don't have enough food each day to sustain a healthy life.

925 000 000! That's one in six of us. What I'd like to know is:

Who is it that blocks off access to food, shelter, physical comforts and worthwhile employment on a planet belonging to everyone? Where did granting or denying an individual's birthright originate? And why does it continue?

Must rush, Matthew. I'm leaving in an hour's time to catch a flight to Alice Springs. Am going to Craig's new town for two weeks. It'll be so lovely to see where he lives, and I want to look into the crystals venture he's starting up. I had no idea this company he's formed has been three whole years in the making. It's not like Craig to be so secretive.

I loved that pub photo you sent through. Those Tudor buildings are a work of art. Who's the mysterious man with the smouldering eyes? He looks like the kind of guy I'd like to get to know.

Looking forward to hearing about your visit to Charles Gloucester's farmhouse—Can't wait to hear about the Lillibridge documents!

Regards,

Rosetta

ROSETTA WAITED WHILE ROYSTON opened the door of Craig's four-wheel drive. She climbed into the back and yelled out a 'Hi again,' to Jim Murray in the front seat. 'Conan! Great to see you!'

Such an impressively stately older man. Twinkling deep-blue eyes regarded her warmly. 'I'm very grateful to you, Rosetta, for having me as a guest-blogger on your Friday Fortnight site,' he said as they sped along the Stuart Highway.

'But I'm very grateful to you, Conan,' Rosetta said. 'All of us are! Your insights into Lillibridge's book are amazing.'

The trip out to the crystals mine that belonged to Craig, Jim, Conan Dalesford and two others, took much longer than Rosetta had expected. Conan nodded off to sleep. The languid murmurs of Jim and Craig's conversation filtered sporadically through to the back.

Royston nudged her with his elbow. 'Ooh, so these are the silk-weave pants you were telling me about. Very chic. And you can't go past white in this sort of climate. They go well with that red cotton blouse.'

'I got them because they're so cool and summery. I love this sort of heat, Royston. Makes me think I could happily move to the Northern Territory.'

'That's your Chilean genes talking,' Royston said. 'Heat does nothing for me.'

'True. You're more of a winter boy.'

'You can say that again. Even Sydney's too warm for me in the summer. One day I'll move to the mountains.'

'You love snowy alpine regions, don't you?'

'I owe that to having lived in eighteenth-century Norway in my last incarnation. I was a woman in that life. A well-to-do, educated woman, and I translated English texts. That's according to the fella asleep in the corner here.'

Rosetta looked again at the dozing prophet and smiled. 'Well, there you go. That explains it. But how do we know whether our influences are genetic or from a past life?'

'That's just it. How *do* we know and how can we? No-one can know it for sure. We're all a crazy-beautiful mix of physical matter and spirit, so my feeling is that each one of us is subjected to the promptings of both.' He lightly tapped her knee. 'So, how's Matthew-Baby?'

Rosetta laughed heartily. 'He's not quite that.'

'Oh no? Then make sure he becomes so.'

'It's not even like we've been on a date.'

'Then suggest a date to him on his return.'

With a flick of her head, Rosetta said, 'There's no way I would do that. It's up to Matthew to do the asking.'

'I don't get that. It's obvious from what you've told me that he's interested. Why should it matter who asks who out?'

'Royston, please! Allow me a bit of Greek mystique will ya?' She pressed the side of her head against Royston's, and they chuckled together quietly. 'I'm not going to throw myself at him.'

'So you're going to "keep" him "guessing" as per his lyrics?'

'Just a little. I don't want him to think I'm so easily caught and therefore just as easily dropped. Actually, I was loving corresponding with Matthew. Right up until the last email he sent, and then...'

'And then?'

'And then I started to question the person he was.'

'Why's that?'

'His outlook turned out to be kind of...well, I'd hoped we'd see eye-to-eye more. To be honest, I was shocked at his cynicism. He made a comment about the Currency of Kindness being "like communism". Do you remember me telling you that?' She glanced at Conan to check he was still sleeping and lowered her voice. 'Matthew totally misunderstood what Conan had said so beautifully.' She gazed at her toenails, crimson-bright against the car's charcoal floor. 'And now a week's gone by, and I haven't heard back. When we first started emailing he got back to me within a day or two.'

The heaviness descending on her heart was not unlike the discomfort ignited by that final image of Angus: a formerly devoted husband laden with suitcases and dashing out the door while their one-year-old daughter screamed in her shock-weakened arms. She wouldn't dare admit to anyone that the fear from that time, when the man she adored deserted her for someone more showy, still haunted her fifteen years on: a squirmish, seeping terror of remaining alone. Undesirable. Unmemorable. Second best.

'But Royston, I don't want to befriend people who I have to tiptoe around with my opinions.'

'I hear what you're saying.'

'Better still, I'd like to share my beliefs without risking *any* opposition! That's why I love you guys.'

Royston placed a hand on hers. 'You've got to realise, love, that the man you fall for isn't tailor-made to complement your own world view. Disagreeing can be healthy.'

'You're right. It'd be unreasonable to expect the opposite. I'm probably too hung up on getting the ideal response.'

'Sounds like Matthew is someone whose opinion you really value.'

'Um...no it's not like that. It's—'

'In your heart of hearts, he's the ideal guy. And on the odd occasion he doesn't agree with you, the secret hope you're harbouring is shaken a little. It's like...*Oh no! His answers aren't perfect!*' And then your potential Mr Right morphs into the dreaded Mr Wrong.'

'He's *not* my Mr Right. I never called him that!'

'Oh, hush. My eyes don't lie. The two of you were getting along pretty well in the memorial garden. Just dandy. The irony is, Rosetta, you already know Matthew's not perfect.' Royston pointed at her teasingly. 'He wears gaudy shirts, for a start.' Adopting a cartoon voice, Royston mimicked the one-liner Darren had uttered when they'd driven back from the poetry evening: '*Nice shirt. Where's the volume control?*' He shook his head and grinned to himself. 'And you've got to look on the bright side. Matthew goes along with a lot of what you believe in. Either that or he's just pretending to go along with it so he can chat you up. No, don't bother protesting. I'm joking. There's no doubt he's genuine about liking Lillibridge.'

'But there's one other thing.'

'There's something more is there, hm? Tell Uncle Royston then. He's all ears.'

'My other concern is Harriet. Remember the girl in the video with the very heavy eyeliner?'

'And long blonde hair?'

'Hm.'

'I know the one. Looked like a young Brigitte Bardot. Very pretty.'

'Matthew mentioned her quite glowingly in his last email.'

'Did he now?'

'And it's four whole days since he went to Charles Gloucester's with her. What if...actually I can't even say it. Don't want to think about that possibility.'

'Then don't. Instead do something positive. Send him another email.'

'That'd seem clingy, like I'm checking up on him.'

'A photo then. Send a photo.' He held up his phone. 'A casual "Greetings from Alice Springs". I'll take a snap of you once we're at the mine.'

Rosetta nodded slowly. It bothered her that Matthew had gone from signing off 'love,' in his second-last email to a detached and formal '—Matthew' in the email mentioning his impending day trip with 'lovely' and 'humorous' Harriet.

Shame she hadn't packed her tarots. A reading from Royston might shine some light on the subject. She'd considered throwing them into her tote but later reasoned conducting readings for herself based on her *mild* obsession with Matthew would be way too much of a temptation.

Royston tilted his cap down over his face. 'We should be there in another hour or so. Hasta la Vista. I'm off to the Dream Sphere.' Within minutes Royston's snores rumbled in chorus with the whirr of wheels and the murmur of Craig's and Jim's voices.

A photo might prompt Matthew to remember he owed her an email. She'd send a photo. Biting her lip, she thought of the comment she'd made about the photo Matthew had sent of himself, his brother and his brother's friend Kirk, at a pub. Matthew had been snapped with his eyes half-shut. Although probably considered a bad shot, she'd flippantly emailed him a question about the guy with the 'smouldering eyes.' Saying he looked like the kind of guy she'd like to know was probably coming on too strong. Had Matthew been put off by that? Determined to forget her worries and heed the call of sleep, she settled back into the car seat, closed her lids and blanked out the world.

She was shaken from her doze by the vehicle lurching into a series of jolts. They had turned off the highway. From the driver's seat, Craig called, 'Rise and shine, sweetheart, we're nearly there.' He was negotiating a barely discernible track that undulated through saltbush.

She blinked herself awake. Conan Dalesford, having woken before her, was engrossed in a phone conversation with his wife Jannali. Across the clear turquoise sky was an effect that made her catch her breath. A rainbow had formed ahead, not in the usual way, not as an arc. Ribbons of soft colour streamed vertically and diagonally and radiated outwards. 'Incredible,' she said in a drowsy croak. 'Craig, have you ever seen this before?'

'Seen what before?' The top of Craig's springy hair, visible above the headrest in front, swivelled to the side.

Mesmerised by the sky's outlandish display, Rosetta shook her head. 'I've never seen a rainbow like that.'

'Rainbow?' Royston was craning his neck to look out the window.

'Not over there,' Rosetta said. 'Up ahead. Near that clump of red rocks.'

'Couldn't be,' Jim Murray said. 'There's no rain around, no storms. Those multi-coloured sunnies of yours could be giving the wrong impression.'

Royston regarded her with a withering look. 'I thought you told me you were updating those,' he hissed.

'I am, but I thought I'd wait till I went on this holiday. I'll get some tomorrow.'

'Okay, I'm in on that. I'll help you select some before I leave for the airport.'

'Excellent, Royston. Thank you! No, they're still there, Jim, all the colours, and I've removed my beetle-backed shades. Can't any of you guys see that?'

Conan Dalesford was pocketing his phone and watching her with an enigmatic smile. 'I think, dear lady, that you're seeing energies.'

'Oh my goodness, am I really? I've always wanted to see energies. Occasionally I'll get a glimpse of someone's aura—or a hint, at least, of what I imagine an aura to be—but only of an evening when the lamps are on. And it's only ever a soft-ish pulsing glow. Nothing like this.'

'You're seeing the energies surrounding the crystals-mine. I see that too, but not with my physical sight.' Conan pointed to a spot between his eyebrows.

'The third eye,' said Royston in a respectful tone. 'It's the soul-seeing vision.'

The walk to the mine from Craig's vehicle was otherworldly. While Craig and Jim and Royston wandered ahead and talked, Rosetta trailed behind wordlessly alongside Conan Dalesford, rapt by the ethereal splendour emanating from the site. She was no longer aware of her physical self; could no longer feel the ground beneath her feet. Whenever the sublime craziness threatened to neaten into logic, she descended into small fits of uncertain laughter. Conan said nothing, just laughed along with her, an amiable echo.

They reached a crater of red dirt and the harsh, square lines of off-duty machinery, reduced by distance, unmoving, no different to a scattering of toy tractors. The mine was set in a huge hollow. A tall security fence enclosed other equipment and a shed. Gouged out of the surface was a shallow excavation, similar in size to the Olympic Pool that Rosetta swam at, in the harbourside precinct of Milsons Point. She'd been delighted to learn the pool was a mere five-minute walk from her new home-suburb of Lavender Bay.

The bands of colour descended here. Not upon a pot of gold but upon a silver vapour hovering above pale pink gems that graced a mound of earth beside the hollow and were cordoned off with mesh fences.

A sound rose up, the clear, whimsical strains of a chorus.

'Do you hear that, Rosetta?' said Conan Dalesford, his voice mellow. 'Are you listening with your etheric ears?'

The chorus rang sweetly of celebration, but also of longing. Elation and melancholy intertwined. 'I hear it, Conan,' she answered, only mildly aware of the warm tears sliding over her cheeks. 'It sounds like the voices of angels.'

'Or the voices of sprites perhaps?' said Conan. 'Their hearts are singing.'

'What's the song saying, do you think? Are their hearts telling us something?'

Conan Dalesford drew to a stop on the path, nodded, then shrugged. 'Perhaps that we all need to be kinder.' And yet the words Rosetta heard, which swam around her in crescendos, were: *We sing your joy.*

Craig was now loping towards them, calling, 'Come down, Rosetta. Come and check out the crystals.' Within the blur of light and colour and sound, Rosetta became aware of Craig hanging onto her hand, of Craig guiding her down a slope to the mesh-encaged sparkles. He draped an arm around her. Kissed her forehead.

We sing your joy.

A whirr filtered through the soft angelic trills, a whirr and a click. Royston hurried forward with his phone. Showed off the photo of two figures: Rosetta and her buddy in front of the glimmering crystals.

'Nice picture,' Craig said. 'I like how it's a close-up. Can you send me a copy?'

Royston's voice, guarded and reluctant, overtook the whispery melodies. 'Rosetta has first rights cos she's claimed it for Matthew.'

The sight, the sounds and the bittersweet bliss melted away, and Rosetta attuned to the real world, to that...*flicker in time we call reality*, as Lillibridge had put it. 'There is something so, *so* special about this discovery Craig,' she said when they drifted back to the vehicle.

'And you believe in me now?' Craig's tone was triumphant.

'I've never not believed in you, I just didn't realise.'

'I did keep it from you for quite some time.'

'That's so unlike you, Craig.'

'Well I know how easily I go overboard about new ventures, so I wanted to be sure this time. I was scared it was all too fantastic to be real. But this is going to work. It's already working. We're at a really exciting stage now that we're seeking investors.'

Rosetta turned and surveyed the mine one last time. Silence once more. A sky devoid of that radiating spectrum. No more magnificence. Just a soothing, floaty feeling that whispered of a future potent with promise.

On the drive back, Royston commented on her untypical verbal restraint.

'Just lost in thought,' Rosetta said.

'Well you *have* had a profound experience.'

'Maybe even spiritual.' Stars like ragged ice-cubes pierced the dusk, and the moon was silvering its way subtly over the horizon. 'It was kind of like...' Rosetta contemplated the feeling of completeness the crystals had inspired. 'What can I say? It was like...an awakening.'

They drove on in silence. Before long, Conan was wrapped in sleep again, head tilted forward, the whiskers of his beard pressing rhythmically against his chest with the car's motion. Royston's eyes were closed as well.

Rosetta stared out of the car window at the darkening sky. The awful secret she'd been harbouring for the past few days was gnawing at her. It was as though her encounter with the crystals had altered her conscience from a mumble to a scream. She had to tell someone. Royston would understand, or at least she hoped he would. She placed a hand on his shoulder. 'Roystie,' she said softly. 'You asleep?'

'Hmmm. Yes.' Royston opened his eyes and winked at her.

'I've done something really awful.'

'Awful? When?'

'Last week, when I emailed Matthew.'

Curiosity sparked, Royston blinked three times and stretched out of his slump. 'Okay, spill the beans.'

'I did something nasty. It was jealousy. I just couldn't bear to think of Matthew liking that woman.'

'Which woman? Oh you mean little Brigitte?'

'Harriet.'

'So what did you do? Dial a hit-man? Send her a cake laced with poison?'

'I made something up. I told Matthew she looked like The Black Widow in *Britain's Most Wanted.*'

'Wait a minnie, who's The Black Widow?'

Rosetta pulled a printed page from her handbag. 'Read this,' she told him. 'It's what I last emailed him.'

Royston read her email. She watched him uncomfortably. When he looked up from the page, mouth twisting in confusion, Rosetta sighed, conceding that she'd read an article in the hair salon about a criminal at large, a serial boyfriend-killer dubbed The Black Widow and that the only likeness to Harriet was the shade of hair. The woman in the photograph would have been at least sixty-five, and she'd sported a chin-length Prince Valiant haircut.

Remorse was never a nice feeling. How could she have reacted so viciously to Matthew's mention of Harriet? At last she said, 'It feels like a Three of Swords.'

'The love triangle card? Red heart, grey background?'

Rosetta gulped and nodded. 'And I'm pathetically afraid that I'm the expendable sword. Do you think that's the reason Matthew's not replying to me? Do you think he knows I've tried to deter him from her?'

Royston leaned back in the seat. Hooted with laughter. 'Don't ever make a habit of those lies,' he said finally. 'Your own face could end up in *Australia's Most Wanted.*' He laughed some more.

Rosetta did not laugh along. Instead she stared at the back of Jim Murray's head, hot with shame. She would never have thought she was capable of doing something this sly, of making cruel insinuations that someone's appearance made them sinister.

Royston went on. 'You had *me* fooled when I looked over it just then, and I know you a darned sight better than Matthew does. There, love. I've texted the photo to you. Email it now to him, and for God's sake, lose that melancholy!'

Chapter Three

Note from the Publisher of *Epiphany*
This chapter includes a letter from Edward Lillibridge. If you feel as though you've already read part of it, that's because you have. (An excerpt appears in Chapter Three of Book 1, *Epiphany – THE GOLDING*.)
Read on to see the letter in its entirety...

MATTHEW SMILED DOWN at the blonde huddled beside him. 'Another pint, Harriet?'

'Yes, please!' Harriet looped her arm through Matthew's, surveyed the bar and grimaced. 'Looks like you'll be waiting a while, Matt.'

Adopting an old-timer voice, Matthew said, 'Now don't you go troubling your pretty little head about that. Find something to amuse you while I'm queuing.'

Playing along, Harriet gave an exaggeratedly juvenile nod, skipped on the spot and drifted off to find a table.

Charles Gloucester, a reclusive man in his nineties, had been fond of the phrase 'Don't you go troubling your pretty little head.' He'd addressed Harriet this way a number of times. Harriet had ultimately asserted, 'I'm not *troubled* Mr Gloucester, just eager to learn of these documents you've so kindly offered to talk to us about.'

Their visit to the rambling red-brick manor flanked by beech trees had been rewarding, but an element of defensiveness marred their initial rapport. Before Charles produced Lillibridge's papers, Matthew told him about the Friday Fortnight website, explaining that Friday Fortnight groups were non-profit and dedicated to providing fans of Edward Lillibridge with information about his life. Harriet then asked how Charles would feel about sharing the documents with Friday Fortnighters.

Charles had marched, red-faced, to the door of his sitting-room as though threatening to make a thunderous exit. 'Do you know how precious those letters are?' he'd yelled. 'Sending them to someone who is going to stick it up on that net thing noticeboard will only turn them to dust! They're over two-hundred years old!'

They'd told Charles the net was not a noticeboard but an electronic network, accessible only by computer and, if happy to contribute to the Friday Fortnight website, would he agree to visiting a local printer with them and get copies made of his documents? Charles' temper cooled when he'd heard this. 'So it's on computer, you say, eh? So that's what all this internet fuss is about! I never understood where you young people went to read all those things.' He'd then said that the 'Lillibridge Computer Club' sounded like a splendid idea.

When Matthew had seen Lillibridge's papers, yellow and delicate, pinned into scrapbooks and crumbling at the corners, he'd told Charles and Harriet he wasn't at all sure they should handle the documents. 'I couldn't live with myself if I tore one of them.'

'That's what I'm afraid of also,' Charles had said, tut-tutting.

'We wouldn't do that to you, Mr Gloucestor,' Matthew had assured. 'It'd be grossly irresponsible.'

With Charles' permission, Matthew and Harriet had instead photographed the documents on the spot, with their phones. Charles was enthused by this technology. 'Well I never!' he'd said. 'Who would have thought a telephone could do all that?'

Once Matthew bought his round of pints, he sat at the table Harriet had found and looked out for Kirk Rummery. 'Chatting someone up, most likely,' said Harriet, pouting. 'Find him will you, Matthew? I don't want him straying too far.'

He found Kirk in the beer-garden. No women standing admiringly around him, unusual for the dynamic Scotsman. 'Hey Matthew,' he said, accepting the tankard held out to him. 'Meet my new friends, Steve, Ray and Geoff. These gentlemen are going into business in a couple of months, and I'm giving them a few hints.'

Matthew introduced himself, exchanged perfunctory pleasantries, then returned to the table and Harriet's concerned expression. He threw her a wink. 'Now don't you worry your—'

'Ooh, shut up!'

'He's talking business.'

'With who?' Harriet demanded.

'Steve, Ray and Geoff.'

At the mention of non-female names, Harriet's face relaxed. The two of them drank and chatted quietly, and admired the view from the velvet-curtained windows of twilit gardens surrounding lattice-windowed cottages. Matthew got them each another pint. Kirk was in no hurry to return, and Harriet, now more than tipsy and displaying a slow-motion jitteriness at Kirk's delay, was saying, 'I really like him, Matthew. I mean really.'

'And I'm sure he feels the same about you. He'd be an idiot not to.'

'But the problem...' Harriet was gazing out of the window, swaying ever so slightly. 'The problem is...he's like a butterfly isn't he? Hard to catch. Never stays put.'

Matthew shrugged.

'I think it's because he's an Aquarian.' Harriet stared at Matthew then, dark-lashed brown eyes reminding him of those belonging to a certain alpaca. She pointed at his chin accusingly. 'I liked *you*, Matthew,' she said, 'at first. You find me attractive don't you?'

'Um...'

She was still pointing at him. Her mouth was open a little, and her finger was starting to zigzag. Becoming conscious of this, she frowned at her hand and lowered it to the table. 'You do,' she drawled. 'I know you do. But there's a barrier.' She took a reckless swig of her beer, then set it down with a loud clunk.

Matthew drew Harriet's attention to the vintage jukebox on the other side of the room and moved her ale to his side of the table. 'Why don't we go and look for Kirk,' he suggested.

Harriet insisted they stay put. 'Why so coy? I knew, Matthew, that physically, you liked me a lot.'

Matthew grinned, sheepish. They'd told him at the Cornwall gathering about her powerful intuition. And in addition to a knack for predicting the future, Harriet apparently had an ability to glimpse past lives.

'Yeah,' Harriet said, nodding to herself. 'A barrier. Something in your aura.'

'In my aura?'

'Mm. Something that signified new love about to happen. And I knew for certain that it wouldn't be with me.' She flicked at the corner of a drink coaster with her pink-painted fingernails. 'Shame really. I got a glimpse of us in another life. We had a son. I was your wife.'

'Yeah?'

'Yeah.'

He was reminded of a documentary he'd watched as a teenager, about people retrieving memories of other incarnations with the assistance of a past-life-regressionist who specialised in hypnotherapy. They'd been able to recall places they'd supposedly lived two or three hundred years earlier, when their soul supposedly embodied another physicality. And then researchers in this documentary had dug up historical documents, exceptional details like floor plans that matched the regressed clients' descriptions. For a while Matthew was convinced about past lives. Youthful naivety, he supposed.

Harriet pouted. 'But you don't want *me*, darlin'. You want the Queen of Pentacles.' She picked up her handbag, rummaged through it and produced a sizeable pack of cards, explaining, 'The Queen of Pentacles is a dark-haired, dark-eyed woman. A *wealthy* dark-haired, dark-eyed woman.' With clumsy care, she sifted through each of them until she found a vivid display of crimsons and golds. 'Here,' she said, handing the card to him. 'Remind you of anyone you like?'

'You read tarot cards!'

'Certainly do.'

'So you're a real live tarot reader!'

'Certainly am.'

Matthew was impressed. 'I've never met a tarot reader before.'

Harriet reached for her confiscated beer. Unable to find it, she shrugged and went back to peeling apart the coaster.

Matthew scrutinised the card in his hands. Its picture was of a long-haired woman—with light olive skin—swathed in a gown of deep claret. Her throne was engraved with curling oak leaves. In her hands was a huge golden medallion with a star engraved on it, which probably signified money. Above her was a trellis of twining roses and at her feet, a rabbit with a grey splodge on its back. Matthew immediately thought back to the night he encountered a Rosetta he was yet to officially meet, halting him in the middle of Burwood only to leap about the road, and his resultant poetry-night presentation about the bouncy-footed woman who insisted she wasn't a bunny, obviously a drunken party dare that she'd been too ashamed to disclose.

In a single abrupt move, he turned the card face-down and handed it back to Harriet.

He was due to send her an email. He'd been hesitating. It wasn't as though Rosetta going to see her ex in Alice Springs had made him insecure. He had no claim on her. She had every right to remain interested in Craig. And no-one was forcing him to reply.

'So, Harriet, what did you say that card was meant to represent?'

'Someone who's either an earth sign...' Harriet examined the card thoughtfully. '...Or an earth-sign rising.'

'Which is?'

'Capricorn, Virgo or Taurus.'

Neither of these sounded like anything Rosetta had mentioned about her horoscope.

A photo had arrived in his inbox the day before of Rosetta, radiant in red, arm-in-arm with Craig, the former boyfriend. Matthew had immediately deleted the picture, deciding that pursuing her would inevitably result in disappointment. Did he really want a future that involved extricating himself from yet another delusion? His attraction to fickle women needed to end with the marriage.

And the marriage was soon to end, thanks to the prompt action of former workmate Marc Garrison. The Marital Status section on his passport now read: *Separated,* and Bernadette had given her official agreement to a divorce the day after Matthew left for England.

'The Queen of Pentacles is someone who's sensual, earthy...generous with money. As far as appearance goes, she's dark, as I said, and physically sturdy, and her overall demeanour is fairly composed. No one would regard this woman as thin and nervy.'

Matthew nodded in recogntion. At that moment, he spotted Kirk swaggering jovially in from the beer-garden.

Harriet's face changed from crumpled to luminous. Her lips curved into a smile as she watched Kirk walk towards her. 'Really like him,' she mumbled, mostly to herself. 'Really do.'

Matthew thought of Rosetta's emailed comment about the 'mysterious' man in the photo he'd sent her, with 'smouldering eyes' or whatever, who she said she'd like to get to know. Even minus the smooth-talk, bloody Kirk still hauled them in.

The truth, Matthew concluded, was staring him in the face. Rosetta was using the 'Kirk' comment as a deterrent. It was her way of saying to him: 'Sorry, Matt. You're not my type.'

Later that evening, when the three of them joined the taxi rank throng, Matthew stood apart from Harriet and Kirk, who were rapidly becoming an item, and kept watch for cabs. He could hear Harriet telling Kirk about a guest blog on Rosetta's website—the one Conan Dalesford had written on reincarnation that suggested the characters in the book were reborn into 2008 and had brought their names with them. Dalesford had made the way-out assertion that a handful of *Our True Ancient History* fans could safely assume they'd existed in Elysium Glades. The only evidence needed? A Lillibridge character's name hidden within their own. Kirk was pretending to be intrigued.

'I'm convinced I'm Orahney, the faerie in this history of Lillibridge's,' she was saying drowsily.

Holding Harriet by both shoulders in order to prop her up, Kirk said, 'Do you really, now?'

'Mm-hm. I'm just missing one letter in my full-name and that's a "y". Now if I were to marry you, Kirk Rummery...heh heh heh.'

'Heh heh! That's a good one. Okay, let's get married tonight, gorgeous, and then you can grow yourself some faerie wings. Fly me to work tomorrow, if you don't mind. That'd be really good. Better than taking the bus.'

'I can't be sure though.' Harriet swivelled her eyes drunkenly to the sky. 'It's not as though I've *seen* my life as Orahney.'

Kirk threw Matthew a gritted-teeth expression.

Matthew indicated the line of black cabs crawling their way up the street towards them.

'But when I met Matthew, I knew in a flash who I'd been in my life with him.'

'Oh you've had a life with Matthew, have you?' said Kirk. 'And not with me? I'll get jealous.'

'No! Don't be! Matthew and I have an unspoken agreement. We're attracted to each other, but we're not going to pursue anything.'

'That's very good of him,' said Kirk. 'To not pursue you.' He gave Matthew a thumbs-up. Matthew turned the other way, snorting with laughter.

'Y'see, I was Iona.'

'You were, Iona? Ah, I see.'

'No, you don't see. Not yet. And you're humouring me, Kirk, which is bloody annoying. I've been shown it all in a vision. I have memories of other lives and they're very logical. Like recollections from childhood. Clear and crisp but compar...*hic!* compartmentalised. I don't get to see what precedes or follows the memory.' Harriet took a precarious step forward. Kirk tightened his grip to steady her. She stepped back again. 'I was Iona Lillibridge, and Matthew was Edward.'

Matthew responded with a nod. 'Spot-on,' he said, then waited for the 'tricked you' grin.

Harriet was not smiling. Not even slightly. She was staring at him in disapproval. 'It's not a joke, Matthew, it's for real. You were Edward Lillibridge in your last life. *Our True Ancient History* was written by you.'

Hi Fellow Fortnighters!

Hope your Friday groups are continuing to flourish and that you're enjoying your discussions on Lillibridge's version of history as much as we are.

Fantastic news! A former antique dealer by the name of Charles (surname withheld as requested) has kindly allowed us to post, on this site, copies of two precious documents he has in his possession: letters written by Reverend Edward Lillibridge! The authenticity of these documents has been verified by Anna Callan—a descendant by marriage—who sold these to Charles in 1996.

The first has already been uploaded. We hope you enjoy viewing this window into Lillibridge's 18th-century existence! The second one will be uploaded by the end of September. We in Sydney plan to discuss each of these documents separately, over two successive meetings. You might like to do this too!

Keep up those fabulous emails. We absolutely love hearing your personal views, not only on *Our True Ancient History* but also on the author, a fascinating individual who would no doubt have been overjoyed if told he'd be the source of such lively speculation almost two-and-a-half centuries on.

Our deepest thanks to the generous Charles, and to Friday-Fortnighters Matthew Weissler and Harriet Neilson for their dedication to making these precious handwritten texts available to us.

Here's to the Currency of Kindness!

Warmest wishes,

Rosetta Melki and friends

NB: The date of this letter from Edward Lillibridge is unknown. You'll notice a printed version below the original document (easier on the eyes!) Many thanks to Harriet Neilson for going to the trouble of transcribing this.—RM

My Dear Sister Meredith,

Summer has slipped by and the wood gathering has begun in earnest now that autumn is here in her flame-hued finery.

I wish not to disturb you, Meredith, nor to pry on your good husband's efforts at the markets. I would be most grateful, however, if you informed me as to whether this regular allowance of four shillings is enough now that you have another babe to care for. If it is not, I can insist Ned work harder to sell another bundle. He is not quite so lame as before. It therefore shan't be the trouble for him that it's been in days gone by. Please, sister, do not hesitate to speak plainly of your circumstances.

Ned is becoming sturdier with each passing season; a fine grown fellow he soon shall be. I have every faith in him becoming

a decent provider. As you know, I have educated him, and he now writes considerably well. A landowner in neighbouring Perranporth is at present talking of a parish for him within the next five years. Only yesterday, at the end of my sermon, the gentleman approached me on the subject. I was, as you can imagine, brimming with delight.

The boy has led me of late into an extraordinary situation.

Several days ago he traipsed to the wood on the morn, telling me he would return to the cottage in time for dinner. Midday passed, as did the afternoon. Ned was nowhere to be seen.

When orange and violet streaked the heavens, and smoke whirled and curled from chimneys in the dale, I stood on my doorstep, paced for a spell and watched the shadows beyond the oak grove, anxious for Ned's return. Ned did not arrive home, and so I donned my cloak and ventured into the darkly mossy sanctum of the towering pines and elms.

At the edge of a clearing, I encountered a clue. Ned's wood-cutting axe lay discarded upon a nest of pine needles. My heart became chaotic then. All through my chest and head was the thud of fear. I could not for the life of me see any sign of my dear son, and I thought of my Mrs Lillibridge, peaceful now in her grave, and my thoughts dwelt horribly on the morbid. In my fettered imagination I saw two gravestones side by side and felt the familiar ache of woe that Iona's demise has so thoroughly instilled in me.

It is with great relief I report to you, Meredith, that this awful image I had conjured, of my son buried beside his mother at the mere age of one-and-ten years, was not to be a forbidding omen.

Presently, I heard the promising sound of rustling leaves.

I dashed towards the leaves that alerted me and found my son by a thicket, prone upon the ground with eyes closed. I cried out his name in despair.

The thicket's leaves parted then, and there before me stood a woman of considerable beauty, her dark hair not gathered modestly upwards as one would expect of the fairer sex.

In an accented voice, she said: 'He fell from the tree.' She gestured to the boughs of an oak above. 'He attempted to chop one of the higher branches.'

Ignoring her, I knelt by my son. Trembling and frantic, I listened for a heartbeat. Meredith, I speak the truth when I tell you I am certain his heart had stilled.

'Please…' The woman—a Gypsy—persisted with bothering me. Me in my ill-feared mourning! 'Allow me to return this boy to health,' she said. 'Allow me, sir, I beg of you!'

One who is immersed in the horror of a loved one's passing is loath to succumb to doubt when a ray of hope offers forth its glorious beams.

After consenting to her plea, I looked on dismally as the stranger waved her hands about in the air. She warbled a song—strung together with nonsense—and clutched at a pendant adorning her neck, presumably stolen, for it was an elegant gem of palest rose, one that would more than likely fetch a pretty penny at a London jeweller. She removed the pendant and placed the stone upon my Ned's left ankle.

Resigned to exclaiming, 'Cease mocking me, woman,' I was taken aback when I heard the word 'Father?' And there, in the clearing of the woods, was my awakened son: recovered, sitting upright, a startled stare marking his ashen expression, blinking at the Gypsy, who bowed her head and retreated whence she had come.

Once I had established my lad was all right, I hastened after the mysterious Samaritan, intent on conveying my gratitude. Upon reaching her, I was overflowing with questions. 'Where are you from?' I asked. 'How do you know of such… magic?'

The woman explained, in her awkward way, that she had refused to marry the man to whom she was promised. Because of this show of spirited resistance, she was abandoned by her Gypsy tribe and forced to fend for herself in the woods.

Her magic, she said, was the result of spells passed down from druids of the Middle Ages: spells that were secrets of the faeries and elves and undines and fire-sprites. Such a fanciful tale, Meredith! Nevertheless, as an awed observer of the miracle that came about, who was I to doubt it? She told me the jewel is blessed with curative powers, a sacred treasure passed down from the world's ancient past when magic existed and reigned supreme.

Feeling indebted to this charitable spell-binder, I immediately offered her a situation at our cottage, as housekeeper. Since Martha's leaving us to wed and move to Chestershire when Spring brightened the meadows with splashes of flora, Ned and I have been managing poorly.

And so you find me now with a son who is as alive as ever he could be, and a gracious housekeeper by the name of Lucetta. I refer to her, however, as Lucy, for it is far less foreign-sounding than the former.

She has been known to address me as 'Matthew' by mistake, which I find perplexing as it sounds nothing like 'Mr Lillibridge'. Goodness knows who Matthew is! Given that an unwedded woman does not refer to any gentleman by his Christian name, I suspect Matthew is a child from the past, a nephew perhaps.

She is quite a stately creature. Her eyes are golden glinted and watchful, like those of a tigress, and she is quick and clever and an admirable cook. I insist that she wears her hair in the proper mode of ladies, to which she complies, although I believe this only occurs when she knows I am about. Thrice I have returned from the parsonage to find her sweeping the doorstep or peeling potatoes, her raven tresses flowing about her like wild vine.

I do hope this finds you well, dear sister, and that you, and Mr Rathbone, and your growing little family are all bright-eyed, rosy-cheeked and comfortably fat.

I look forward to your reflections on life at Hazelton.

Fondest wishes,

Edward

Another unpublished chapter
from Reverend Edward Lillibridge's
original *handwritten* manuscript

'**D**id you manage to fulfil your assignment for the woman of the future?' Alcor asked.

'I don't believe I did,' said Maleika. 'We certainly tried. I provided Zhippe with a task, a role similar to that of the romance god Eros. Sadly, as I understand it, our work has been in vain. Karee, my dear rabbit friend, dashed across a road to halt one of the lovers in his red...What do they call their boxes on wheels?'

'Motorised chariots,' Alcor told her.

'Yes. His motorised chariot. It was only the man who spoke. The woman scurried away in shame.

'And then Zhippe entertained them when first they spoke—with somersaults and the like—to symbolise the saying they have in that future time about falling in love being "head over heels," but we weren't at all sure they understood its meaning because they did not make plans to meet again.'

'A task indeed,' said Alcor.

'And so Zhippe played them pretty tunes when first they dined together. This did not work either. The woman sprite fled from the man once more. She stomped solemnly away from his motorised chariot. He continued to sit in the chariot, alone, and I've never forgotten the dejectedness in those charming green eyes.'

'The fellow's name is Matthew,' Alcor advised.

'Yes. It is too.'

'An additional Brumlynd has worked on this assignment. Pieter has been responsible for repairing Matthew's soul connection.'

'Alcor, this news is most pleasing. Perhaps Pieter achieved more than me...and the undines...and Karee. What I do know is that the rose sprite and Matthew wrote letters to each other when he journeyed to another land. I do not know what became of the two. I abandoned all assistance. I knew I was near to death, and that I had my own life to concentrate on.'

'Perhaps, Maleika,' said Alcor, his eyes glimmering with mischief, 'perhaps you were concentrating on your own life all along.'

'Brother, I don't understand.'

'You do not need to at this point.'

At Alcor's invitation to gaze into the distant future, Maleika stood opposite one of the Dream Sphere's doorways and watched as a scene played out before her.

A construction with a crystal dome became evident. Seeing it made her shiver, for its interior was not dissimilar to the one in which gold-skins had cruelly drained faeries of their heart-powers. She remembered back to that day in her lifetime below, when she and the two undines had stepped into that hologram: a memory, an echo of what had already passed. The palace of the present had been relinquished, conjured into another timeframe, the Oracle had said.

Alcor, now by her side, instructed, 'Pay close attention, Maleika.'

A newcomer was introduced to a seated crowd by a man who appeared suspiciously golden-skinned.

'And now,' said the messenger, 'We introduce King Nikolaus.'

Maleika shook her head in disapproval. 'A king of all things!'

'Continue to listen, Maleika,' said Alcor in a hushed tone.

The messenger, who was holding one arm outwards, added, 'Please put your hands together in welcoming King Nikolaus.'

As Maleika waited for the gold-skin to take his place in front of the applauders, Alcor whispered, 'Your horrified reaction is not unlike that of your younger son.'

'You have shown this same scene to Pieter?'

'He has observed it in the Dream Sphere, yes.'

'Of course,' said Maleika. ''Twas an announcement concerning a woman by the name of Det-ah-Wise-la who would help in restoring this world to its former beauty. When Pieter told me of it, we discovered a hooded one from the Grudellan Palace eavesdropping on our conversation.'

She cast her mind back to that fateful night.

'And who should this creature be?'

'The name is...er...it is difficult to recall.'

'Take another sip of Remembrance Essence, Pieter.'

'Oh!' Pieter had said. 'Det.'

'Det,' she had repeated.

'Ah...'

'Take another sip, Pieter.'

'Wise...'

Maleika had nodded encouragingly. *'Wise.'*

'La!'

Surfacing from the memory Maleika said to Alcor, 'Thank goodness Pieter is safe and well, and living in the Land of Mu.'

'His life is to continue for many more years. Lemurian crystals will keep him and his princess wife ageless.'

'How wonderful! And as you have told me before in my previous Dream Sphere visits, he and his beloved are the originators of a new type of individual! What is the name of this addition to the earth plane?'

'Humanity,' said Alcor with a smile. 'Which is what you see before you now, Maleika.'

'So they are not gold-skins! And now this Nikolaus fellow has begun to speak.'

Alcor gave another wave of his hand and the scene before him froze. 'You will view this again from the beginning, but firstly remember, Maleika, that each person present in that scene is a descendant of Adahmos and Eid, aeons later.'

'Intriguing! Oh, Alcor, Adahmos will only ever be Pieter to me. My son Pieter. The son my Orahney-self told me of. I now understand why my Orahney-self advised me that his earthly purpose would be important.'

The king, who according to Alcor was not of gold but a member of humanity, told the crowd that seven-and-ten season-cycles prior, a certain part of their history had been revealed.

He then mentioned a numeral which sounded a little like 'two cows and a knight'. Alcor advised this was the name of a season-cycle—which was referred to as 'Two-thousand-and-eight.' In this particular year, the king told them, crystal receptors containing the heart radiance of an ancient people had been discovered. This furthered humanity's advancement greatly due to the gems' surprising source of energy.

The king made reference to knowledge of their origins. Clues to a pre-history, he explained, had been buried for aeons, just as the crystals had. 'We are now no longer in the dark.' The eyes of King Nikolaus, dark yet bright and very much like Pieter's, gazed upon his audience kindly. 'Prior to the work of archaeological teams led by the notable Professor Schwartz, the devic/Gold's Kin theory was deemed nonsense and dismissed as the mere imaginings of "space cadets".'

'Whatever is a space cadet?' said Maleika to Alcor.

Willing the scene to pause, Alcor said, 'Do not trouble yourself with this, Maleika. It is a term used in the future to describe those who are foolishly fanciful.'

The scene continued on from where Maleika had interrupted it. 'Dreamers,' said Nikolaus.

'Well we are all dreamers,' said Maleika, indignant now. 'Sprites spend half of their lives in the Dream Sphere. Is this king inferring that dreamers are foolishly fanciful?'

'Certainly not, Maleika. Now if you refuse to pay attention again, I will close the scene down altogether! I am getting rather tired of having to pause this for you.'

'My apologies, Alcor. Do proceed.'

The scene recommenced from the king's last words.

'"Space cadets." "Dreamers." Those whose feet weren't firmly planted in reality. Gradually the theory gained in popularity, firstly as a sort of urban myth. A legend. A fairy tale many of us wanted to believe.

'And then evidence emerged.

'Humanity is now only too happy to embrace the notion that we are more than we ever thought we were.

'We all now recognise our devic heritage.

'We all now recognise, in view of our true ancient history, how the enforcement of a currency originating in the exchange of gold— and the limited distribution of such—was designed to increase our capacity for dissatisfaction.

'As a member of the Wealth for All Committee, I am honoured to witness a way in which we can work together in developing a harmonious prosperity.

'The falling away of warring has meant deprivation of basic life needs exists no longer.

'Today, as we all unite with the same wish for each member of the world family: that each member of this vast family of ours experiences ongoing harmony, comfort to the level of luxury and further creation of beauty in Twenty-twenty-six and beyond, I would like to share with you at this tenth Sonic Unity Gathering the results of our international mandate concerning the Currency of Kindness...'

Maleika, unsure as to why Alcor was showing her an event so far ahead in the future, listened politely. Certainly this sounded all very pleasant, but she had never doubted the Currency of Kindness would return to Earth.

MATTHEW STARED ACROSS THE table, thoroughly bewitched by the woman opposite.

'More champagne?' he asked.

She nodded and turned away, her attention caught by a clatter of drums, the heralding of a show about to begin at the other side of the restaurant.

On the flight back to Sydney he'd been weighing up whether he should return to England for good. He'd cooled on the idea of rushing back to pursue Rosetta. He'd stuck to his word of course. Emailed the phone-photos of Lillibridge's papers plus Harriet's copy-typed version and then focused on not focusing anymore on someone he was beginning to fall for.

At Heathrow his plane had been delayed. When he'd spotted her reply in his inbox, he'd gulped. Ignoring the anticipation that anything she wrote to him prompted, he'd logged out of his emails and tried to concentrate on the DVD Harriet had given him to watch on his device. It was an old movie she no longer wanted: *You've Got Mail* and, annoyingly for him, surrounded a romantic relationship formed on the basis of electronic communication. Only half interested in the story playing out, he wondered what sort of response Rosetta had given. A quarter of the way through the movie, unable to bear the suspense any longer, he'd shut it down and logged into his inbox.

The reply had brimmed with her trademark enthusiasm, grati-tude running thick and fast. She'd said she was looking forward to catching up with him on his return. Said also that a photo she'd thought looked like Harriet was not like Harriet at all when she'd rechecked the crime magazine it was in.

Getting that last email had played on his mind for much of his waking hours on the trip back. That and Harriet's conviction. On the night Harriet insisted he was Edward Lillibridge in a previous life, Matthew stayed awake, re-reading Lillibridge's letters, flicking through the copy of *Our True Ancient History* he'd purchased at the Portobello Markets and marvelling at the familiarity of it all. He'd told himself there was little wonder since he was reading it all twice. Why the book and letters had seemed like old friends the first time, he couldn't explain so easily.

And then he'd re-read Rosetta's past emails and grinned over the fact that there'd been a little accidental return planted in the one dated June Nineteenth, between the words '*I really want you...*' and '*...to be there as a representative.*' Rosetta emailing to him in one clear line: 'I really want you.' A very nice thought. He'd obsessed thereafter, over what it would be like if he could get her to want him in reality.

By the time his plane had touched-down on Australian soil, he'd persuaded himself that asking Rosetta out was hardly a threat to his future. He would remain in control. A date, after all, was an opportunity for both parties to get to observe each other. A little like a job interview, only the screening was mutual.

He ordered from the airport florist the most elaborate array of roses they had available—to be sent to the address on Rosetta's business-card—and asked in the accompanying note whether she'd like to go out Saturday. If she made an excuse, he'd assume she was seeing someone.

She told him in a phone-text she was free. Thought dinner was a 'really great' idea.

On the night of their date, he brushed aside fears of turning into a butter-fingers nerd, splashed on his aftershave, then wondering whether he'd overdone it, towelled most of it off. Before he was due to leave, he paced up and down the hallway. Once he was in the car, imagining what it would be like to see her again, he realised with a shock that he was speeding.

He found her new address quite easily, a penthouse overlooking the glistening stretch of Lavender Bay. He buzzed the intercom; smiled as he heard her low, laughing voice; stepped into the lift and straightened his collar and jacket.

At Apartment Fourteen, he knocked. The door swung open to reveal a vibrantly exotic temptress. She was wearing a dress of claret velvet that subtly emphasised every alluring curve. Eyes far deeper and darker than he'd recalled, wide glossy mouth locked in a spellbinding smile. She'd taken his breath away.

And now he was sitting opposite her, not caring if she were fickle or a flirt. Regardless of how flighty she might be, he was determined to win her over.

The drum roll dimmed. A spotlight danced across the restaurant's stage curtains. Rosetta turned to him, beaming in anticipation. He smiled back.

He looked around the restaurant in approval. Her choice. And he admired her taste. He knew Chavelle's from the odd work gathering. He and his staff had gone there two or three years back to celebrate Harrow's thirtieth. The restaurant had since been done up to resemble a palatial eighteenth-century drawing room. Its oriel windows, framed by heavy damask drapes, revealed the luminescent beauty of Sydney Harbour's ferries, bobbing across the midnight-blue smoothness like mobilised lanterns.

The menu had quite an array of vegetarian dishes. He was proud of the way he'd stuck to his new diet; was especially glad he'd given up meat now that he was on a date with Rosetta. On the drive out to Charles Gloucester's country house, he'd gazed out of the window of Harriet's car, at the gentle-eyed cows resting their heads on the wooden fences, and felt a pang of guilt at all the beef he'd consumed throughout his life. They were no different in temperament to Edward and Lucetta: Conan Dalesford's alpacas. Just like alpacas, these animals didn't kill, nor did they eat anything living, and they had the ability to feel affection and pain. He'd only that morning re-read Lillibridge's grotesque description of Rahwor gulping down a screeching poktador, and vowed that day he would never return to consuming animals.

The lights on the stage grew low. 'And now,' roared the announcer, 'please welcome our talented harpsichordist Carla-Ann and her twin brother, the astounding magician Jippie!'

A face peered around the curtains, a face that was instantly recognisable.

It might have been the champagne or the dizzy delight of seeing Rosetta again, but the laughter Matthew lapsed into was almost unstoppable. He turned to his date. She was laughing as well.

Oblivious to the tricks the accordionist/violinist/poetry-night attendant/magician was performing, they continued to laugh, glancing into each other's eyes, and then down at the table, and then back into each other's eyes.

'Who would have thought?' Matthew said.

Chapter Four

ROSETTA LOOKED ONCE MORE at the magician bounding energetically towards the centre of the restaurant stage.

She'd spiralled into a fit of surprised laughter when Jippie—or was it Chippy?—had emerged from behind a spot-lit curtain.

The man opposite, the man who had sent her an extravagantly lovely arrangement of pale pink roses, had been equally amused.

Was it really the magician's arrival, though, that made sharing an in-joke with Matthew this much fun?

She lifted her glass of champagne and set it down again. A giggly mood coupled with the elation of being in the presence of someone she adored: quite likely cause for regret if combined with the effects of alcohol.

Matthew gestured to her drink. 'Everything okay with that?'

Swallowing back further chuckles, she nodded.

'I can get you another if that's too dry.'

'It's perfect,' she told him. 'Absolutely perfect.' Did perfect and absolutely work? Or was perfect no good with an adverb? Why was she so self-conscious?

When she'd opened the door to Matthew—tall, dynamically masculine, smelling faintly of an aftershave she would love forever—a blaze of rapture had zipped through her body, and her heart had flipped into overdrive. Heart, body, soul. He enthralled her totally.

Matthew had brushed his hand across her elbow when they'd entered the gilded archway of Chavelle's, causing her a brief moment of confusion. Instead of saying: *So gorgeous here* when they'd been led to their table, she'd said, 'So, gorgeous...' Involuntary pause. '...Here?' and then cringed at the way it had sounded, like a too familiar term of endearment. The worry was Matthew getting freaked by how much she felt for him. She'd scared Angus away hadn't she? He'd leapt from her life like a toad springing away from an unstable lilypad, and the degrading memory of his toadish disdain was a stern *tut-tut* that loudened with each new crush.

The magician concluded his unremarkable tricks to the tune of a tinkly-bright harpsichord, care-of his sister Carla-Ann.

A call came through to Matthew. He checked the name of the caller. 'Sara,' he said. 'I'll phone her after the meal.'

'No, Matthew, go ahead,' Rosetta told him. 'I'm dying to take another look at those funny little guppies, so I'll see you shortly.'

Matthew admitted it might be important and answered his step-daughter's call. Rosetta moved from her seat and made a point of studying the fish in the restaurant's aquarium. She had already admired it before with Matthew when they first arrived. The tank spanned half of the room.

Dinner out with Matthew! After the florist's van-man buzzed on the intercom the week before and said 'A delivery for Ms Melki', the smile had rarely left her face. She'd almost given up on her favourite correspondent asking her out, especially after those unsettling mentions of Harriet, but whatever had happened over in England was really beyond her control and admittedly none of her business. All that she needed to know was that Matthew was back in Australia for good, and here with her tonight.

She turned from where she was standing to steal a glance at him. His head was bowed, and he was speaking into his phone in lowered tones. Although her 'gorgeous' reference was accidental, few would regard it as inappropriate. Matthew looked just that tonight. His choice of open-collar white linen shirt and dark blue suit was more formal than anything she'd seen him in, and standard, it seemed, for Chavelle's patrons. She was glad she'd risked overdressing with the velvet dress and her calf-elongating platforms, or 'glammed-up manacles' as they were less-than-fondly known. Towering heels hindered her speed and made her feel like a tottery dolly, but she wasn't planning on chasing after Matthew like she had the night of their wrist-watch and hair entanglement. Or stomping away from him either.

Imagining the feel of linen beneath her fingertips, and the enticing warmth of its wearer's skin, Rosetta tried to concentrate on the sleepy terrapins. Their shells contrasted greyly against the flamboyance of flickering corals.

'See anything in there you'd like to dine on tonight?' A waiter was at the right of the tank, folding napkins.

'No way.' Appalled at the idea of chefs murdering innocent turtles, Rosetta turned to stare at the waiter. 'Vince!' She moved towards him. 'I knew I recognised your voice. You've changed jobs!'

'Chavelle's is my second job,' he said. 'I'll still be attending to you and your friends on your Thursday fortnight evenings at Sydney Tower. I've done Saturday nights here for the past three years.' He snickered and shook his head. 'You didn't really think we'd serve you up guppies and terrapins did you, Rosetta? I mean, I know the French have a different kind of approach, but...'

'Trust you to put me through that. I should be alert to your practical joking by now.'

'So where are the girls tonight?' Vince wanted to know. 'Where's the "dolphin fountain" one? I've got my eye on her.'

Eadie's unfortunate attempt at gulping down a mouthful of Perrier had become a running joke with Vince. But Vince had insisted to Eadie he thought she was 'cute'.

'She's out with her new boyfriend.'

'Damn! And let me guess. You're out with your new boyfriend too.'

Rosetta pretended to look coy and pushed at his shoulder. 'I'm on a date. A first date!'

'Boyfriend-to-be then. You wouldn't have described the date as *first* if you weren't sure about the guy. Does he know you have to order in French here?'

'You're kidding.'

'*Non mademoiselle.*' Vince folded his arms. 'My nationality's the reason I have this job.'

'What happened to your accent?'

'I emigrated when I was young.'

Matthew finished his call. Rosetta returned to the table when he was placing his phone back in his pocket and told him, 'We're expected to order in French.'

'You're kidding.'

Settling into her seat, she watched as Matthew fidgeted with a napkin. His uneasiness surprised her. 'I'm trying to remember who ordered when we came here from work,' he said, shifting uncomfortably. 'I think it might have been a banquet. Pre-ordered. So where did you hear that?'

'*Bon soir Monsieur.*' Vince was at Matthew's side, greeting him in an odd flurry of haughtiness. '*Votre sélection veuillez.*'

Matthew drummed his fingers on the table and looked the other way. Rosetta attempted to reassure him. 'If you don't know French, then I—'

'No problem.' Disarming smile.

Vince had never stipulated any rules at the other restaurant. Perhaps his Maitre'd at Chavelle's was a *My-way-or-the-highway* sort of boss. Ah well. Four years of language classes at Star of the Sea Ladies College meant she could jump in if needed.

Matthew frowned at the menu.

Vince addressed Matthew briskly. '*De hate, Monsieur, sil vous plait.*'

'Er...' Matthew hesitated. '*Je* Matthew...*Elle* Rosetta. *Nous affame.* Er...*Janvier...Fevrier...*'

January? February? Rosetta studied Matthew's face. He was rapidly scanning the menu pages, forehead crinkly with concentration.

'*Mars, Avril...*'

Why was Matthew reciting the calendar?

Matthew's eyes flicked up from the menu. 'So you're not a French speaker, Rosetta!'

She rushed to correct him. 'I ... er ... know—'

'No?'

The misinterpretations weren't just restricted to French tonight. Why did *know* have to sound like *no?*

'No, I...er—' Aware the laughter she was trying to quell could easily escape in an inelegant roar, Rosetta forced herself to look away from Matthew's anxious face.

'Not a worry. All sorted.' Matthew returned to re-naming the menu items.

And then Vince's French cling-clanged with deviations. '*Certainement comme vous ce qui.*' The waiter's accent had gone from soft-syllabled Parisian to Bengali-attempting Berliner, and he'd responded to Matthew's Franco months with a series of Gallic numerals. French born? A total fabrication!

Rosetta leaned back in her seat. Who was fooling who?

Matthew's face broke into an apologetic grin. 'I'll order the rest in English.'

Once Matthew had ordered a generous array of exquisite-sounding dishes, including the one that made her squeak 'Yum!' under her breath when he read out the menu's translation, their multi-faceted friend, the one with the mop of dark hair and debatable name, waltzed onto the stage again and produced a rabbit from his top hat, a rabbit with snowflake-pale fur and eyes like damp sultanas.

To a couple at the table opposite, Jippy said, 'Give Karee a pat,' and Rosetta couldn't help noticing, when the diners ruffled the rabbit's ears, that the animal's back was splodged with grey.

A third unpublished chapter
from Reverend Edward Lillibridge's
original *handwritten* manuscript

Nikolaus, a messenger at a future event—and one of Maleika's distant descendants—was reciting advice the Oracle had once given.

'And now
Those few
Will choose Anew
To delve the caves
Of darkness through

A gilded vortex
Fringed with blood
Those linked in memory
Maimed by mud
The shadowed prowl
To herewith prey
On star-spun souls
Their heart-warmed *fey*'

'Well I never!' Maleika, watching from the Dream Sphere, had recognised the words.

'This,' Nikolaus told his audience, 'is what the Oracle advised the elf-woman named Maleika, as stated in Lillibridge's book.'

'Alcor! Is it true the young man is speaking of me?'

'It is true, Maleika.'

'Nikolaus is telling fibs. My visit to the Oracle has not been recorded in any book!'

'Not yet, Maleika,' whispered Alcor. 'But your undine children will speak of you, and of the other Brumlynds too.'

Nikolaus continued. 'The first part of the Oracle's message concerns itself with indicating to Maleika that all of Earth's peoples will be drawn into the Cycle of Suffering, which our planetary population has only recently managed to evade. Everyone on Earth, throughout each of their incarnations, has had to endure the ills inflicted upon them by the body kings' insatiable desire for power.

'Their fondness for warring and for inducing starvation, and their masking our thinking with ignorance regarding the nature of our spirit-selves, has plagued us ever since they arrived in our earthly dimension. They succeeded in cancelling out sprites' natural sense of harmony. They put an end to sprites' balanced exchanges that relied *not* on ownership of gold. They hampered sprites' abilities to create beauty through magic and closed off access to the fuller senses.

'The next lines of the Oracle's message deal with the type of suffering that was to ensue; that although linked through the memory of an ideal world, much of this remembering will be muddied. To quote Lillibridge in his prologue, many of the ancients, the water sprites in particular: *...lost their inspiration to cry for gladness, so it was then and there that they disintegrated into the tide of obscurity, aeons later remembered only in the dreams of wise men and in children's utterances, which younger souls housed in older bodies dismissed as something known as 'non-sense': another term body kings used when denying reality's presence.* 'The next six lines indicate that those of devic origin, which body kings referred to derogatively as their "heart-warmed *fey*" would eventually become an extinct race.

'And now I shall recite the second half of the Oracle's words:

'But trace all progress
Through this maze
Of solar stealth
And toxic haze
To one point where
Those lives are freed
Thus vanquishing the glut of need.

'The verse I have just recited,' announced Nikolaus, 'indicates The Silvering. All of us here are well aware of The Silvering and are truly honoured to be alive during the commencement of this magnificently rewarding era. Thanks to the discovery of Elysium crystals, our own hearts are liberated of disharmony.

'Then crumbled is the horned ones' Wall
Where grizzly beasts are prone to fall
And once a winged man acts with grace
By gifting magic framed in lace
The Silvering will fast descend
To mark the greed-lack ailment's end

'For now Maleika put to rest
Your search
It is a fruitless quest

'This verse was a gentle urging from the Oracle for Maleika to release her concern over her son's absence. Pieter's fate, which was to involve repeatedly incarnating back into a Gold's Kin ruled world, would ultimately lead to the crumbling of the horned ones' Wall.

'The horned ones' Wall.' The king's tone had become thoughtful.

'Yes, *the horned ones' wall*,' said Maleika softly as she observed the scenario. 'Please, Nikolaus, explain what it means. I never did understand this reference.'

Nikolaus resumed his speech. ' "Is it a place?" you might ask.' Nikolaus hesitated. 'To this I would answer that yes, the horned ones' Wall is definitely a place. "Where is it then," you might ask. "Why have we not yet discovered it?"

'To this I would reply: you know it well. The Oracle's reference has been aptly hidden, and yet what I am about to inform you on this historic occasion is that the crumbling, another glorious effect of The Silvering, has finally occurred.

'It came about this morning. Two hours ago we were liberated from the final strands of Gold's Kin enforcements! The horned ones' Wall no longer stands. And the name that the horned ones' Wall is more commonly known as...I believe most of you have already correctly concluded the answer. The name of this now non-existent place is...'

Awe-struck by the momentous event, Maleika drew in a breath and awaited the king's explanation.

THE PLATTER DISPLAYING FRUITS, both orchard and tropical alongside an assortment of provincial cheeses, had now been replaced with bronze cups and saucers.

Rosetta was cherishing every moment at Chavelle's. The divine food, opulent surroundings, view of the moonlit harbour and quirky entertainment wove a special kind of magic around her, and that was before adding Matthew to the mix. But Matthew had his own brand of magic, a powerful blend of depth and attentive compassion, and his ability to see certain situations through the wry lens of humour never failed to make her laugh.

She'd told him about the exciting progression of EGS, something she didn't share with everyone because it was so very close to her heart, and he'd listened in fascination. And he wanted to know all about her, which she had to admit was refreshing after her last date, an interesting but one-sided conversation in an empty restaurant with another green-eyed guy.

She shouldn't have made comparisons—Adam had suffered so much as an addict—but she couldn't help recalling the quote read out at last week's Poet's Garret meeting that seemed to pertain to both him and Matthew. The poet up front had related the famous tale of Winston Churchill's mother, Jennie Jerome, who had dined out with two premier politicians: British Prime Minister Benjamin Disraeli and his rival William Gladstone. Miss Jerome was asked about her impressions of each man, to which she replied, 'When I left the dining room after sitting next to Gladstone, I thought he was the cleverest man in England. But when I sat next to Disraeli, I left feeling that I was the cleverest woman.'

Disraeli-esque charm had not been Adam's forte.

The coffee pot's warmly bitter aroma enticed Rosetta to sample the roasted beans. She filled Matthew's cup and went about adding almond milk and sugar to her own. 'The meal was heavenly.'

'I won't take the credit for it, having booked rather than cooked.'

'*Magnifique* sauces and salads, yummy soufflé, *fromages et fruits* and now perfectly made liqueur *café!*'

'That's pretty good pronunciation for someone who doesn't know French. Now where's that waiter?' Matthew signalled to Vince and asked for the bill.

'No worries Mun-shurrrr.' Vince snickered huskily, then hurried away.

Matthew, Rosetta noted, was watching Vince in disapproval. He leaned forward and whispered, 'Was he saying *Monsieur?*'

'I think so, yes.'

'Vince is *not* a Frenchman.'

'Why do you say that? Because of his lack of an accent?'

'Because of his terrible French. He's a definite Aussie.' Matthew appeared to be smiling to himself.

Terrible French? *Pot. Kettle. Black.* Rosetta toyed with the pearly linen corners of her napkin. Unable to resist a ribbing she said, 'And you would know, being so fluent. Your French sounded brilliant.' She watched him carefully for his response.

He drew his wallet out of his pocket and looked away from her with a mildly guilty grin. 'I think it's important to have a handle on other languages.'

'Me too.'

'You grew up in a Greek household, didn't you?'

'Certainly did.'

'Do you speak...ah here's our man now with the bill.' With a flourish, Vince placed a small tray on the table. Matthew threw his credit card onto it.

Rosetta answered Matthew's half-finished question, although she answered it in Greek and added, also in Greek, 'By the way, I find you irresistible.'

'Ha!' Matthew leaned back in his seat. 'I actually know the answer to that. *Kala!*

He'd answered: *Yes, I'm good.*

I find you irresistible : Yes I'm good.

'I wasn't asking whether you were well,' Rosetta said evasively.

In a hurried afterthought, Vince placed beside the tray a small dish of handcrafted chocolates moulded into berets and snail shells.

'Then what were you saying?' Matthew asked. 'That I'm overly suspicious of people who claim they know French?' He directed his comment coolly at Vince.

Rosetta berated Matthew in a whisper for being unfair, but Vince was unperturbed. He saluted to Matthew and sauntered off to greet a group of diners.

Unable to contain herself, Rosetta fell into giggles. 'I would never say you were too suspicious. It's good to have a healthy amount of scepticism.'

'So you were complimenting me, in Greek, on my powers of discernment then?'

'Something like that.' Powers of attraction more like it.

She plucked up Matthew's credit card from the tray to examine the silver hologram with its snatches of rainbows. She ran a finger over the raised edges of Matthew's name. Matthew P Weissler: a man she was aching to kiss. 'What does the "P" stand for?'

Matthew looked down, grinning.

'Ooh, you don't have to tell me if it's a name you're not comfortable with. I'm just stickybeaking.'

'No, that's fine.' Matthew's voice lowered. 'Er...it's Porter.'

'Porter? As in a bell-boy?'

'Um...yeah.'

'Do you have one of those square-topped caps they wear in 1940s movies?'

'I have several. Stupid name, I know.'

'Porter's a perfectly reasonable name, Matthew! I'm just teasing, and you have my utmost permission to tease me all you like about my name. Do you know what the meaning of Porter is?'

'Its meaning is "guard or gatekeeper". My mother chose that in preference to my father's suggestion of Perth.'

'Perth? Call me ignorant, but I thought Perth was a place-name only.'

'It's Scottish and it means "from the thorn thicket".'

'Wow. It all sounds so Grudellan: "guard or gatekeeper", "from the thorn thicket". So you're alluding to being a body-king trooper in a previous life?'

'Aargh. My cover's blown! Speaking of names, though, I remember you telling me your real name was Odetta.'

'Ah yes.' Now it was Rosetta's turn to be guarded. This was mostly kept discreet, her official name for work and uni only.

'Do you dance on tiptoe?'

'On tiptoe? Are you serious?' Rosetta peered over the rim of her cup at Matthew's laughing eyes. 'I'm about as graceful as a chicken with chilblains, but what's that got to do with the topic of birth names? I'm afraid I've failed the test.'

'You? You couldn't fail any test.'

'Wait. Is this to do with ballet?'

Matthew conceded that it was.

'A ballet heroine?'

'Yep. The heroine in Swan Lake.'

'Ooh, I'm doing okay here with guesses. I'll try guessing something else. You're a ballet fan?'

'Incorrect. You failed that particular test.'

'But you said I couldn't fail any test!'

'At that stage I was only taking into account tests that assess looks, personality, humour and spoken Greek.'

'So you know a bit about ballet, without being a fan.'

'Your assumptions are getting better, Rosetta. I'd grade that one a seven. I had to sit through Swan Lake with dance-mad Sara a couple of years back. In the car on the way home I heard all about the black swan Odile, and the white swan Odette. Odetta would have to be the Italian version of that.'

'It is. It is the Italian version, you're right.'

'I still like Rosetta.'

Whether he'd meant the name or the person the name belonged to, wasn't exactly clear. Rosetta stirred her espresso until the spoon's clatters echoed back at her in joyful repetition.

He was looking at her intensely. 'Really *like* Rosetta.'

She placed her spoon on the saucer and watched the flame of the candle that leapt about like an exultant fire sprite. She lifted her eyes. Surrendered to Matthew's gaze. The delicious sensation of *falling* enveloped her.

Falling. Such a careless thing to do.

To fall was to dance with danger.

She'd fallen for him a while ago. Had wished for a moment like this ever since he'd carried her luggage onto the verandah and told her his marriage was history.

Falling was frightening. And exhilarating. And overflowing with glimmers of possibility.

Matthew spoke again. 'I was thinking we could drive across to Balmoral...have a walk along the bay there?'

'Good suggestion, Monsieur Gatekeeper. I love the beach at night.' Balmoral. An esplanade illuminated with Edwardian street lamps.

Matthew collected the credit card Vince had returned, smiled at her briefly while placing it back in his wallet, then ventured off to compliment the staff.

Rosetta watched him as he moved smoothly away from the table. She stared into her wineglass. Champagne. Soothing and enlivening, just like Matthew.

Everything about him: the way he moved, the subtle lines that formed around his eyes when he listened with a half-smile to her sometimes disjointed stories, the kindness in his voice and kissable quality of his lips...All of this, all of Matthew, was crazily intoxicating.

I'm drunk with love, she thought. And the person responsible is Matthew Porter Weissler.

ROSETTA ROSE WHEN MATTHEW returned to the table. He was saying goodbye to their devious waiter. 'See ya round, Vince,' he said. 'Keep up the water skiing.'

'I certainly will, Matt.'

At the top of the stairs, Matthew gestured for her to go first. 'Definitely an Aussie.'

Rosetta murmured agreement. She should really tell Matthew about Vince's love of stretching jokes beyond their limits.

She trailed her fingers over the polished mahogany bannister and stepped onto the downward winding staircase. 'Matthew, I'll let you in on a secret.'

'Hm, what's that?'

'I actually do know French. Quite well.'

'Are you sure about that?'

'Aw, Matthew! Why would I say that if I didn't?'

'A good question, Ms Melki. But just to ensure you're genuine, I'll set you another test.'

'And put me through even more exam-induced jitters?'

'Life isn't always fair.' He caught her eye and flicked his eyebrows. 'Translate what I ordered.'

Turning to Matthew, she said, 'So you want me to repeat in English what you said to Vince?'

'I do indeed.'

'Okay.' Rosetta stifled a smile. Don't laugh, she told herself, remembering Matthew's awkward attempts at ordering and Mama screeching that men hated women laughing at them. Once again, she saw her foster brother turned chicken-boy and felt the side of her face smart at the scorching smack of a hurled potato. 'What you said was: "I Matthew. She Rosetta. We hungry. January February March April..." '

Matthew laughed quietly. 'Well, I'd like to let *you* in on a secret.'

'And what's that?'

'Like you, I happen to know French quite well.'

Rosetta found this hard to believe.

'I'm serious. I was being deliberately daft. The truth is, I know Vince quite well, or remember him at least. He was in charge of a lot of the celebratory dinners Celia organised for my team. Dead-keen water-sportsman. Born and bred in Adelaide. Self-confessed prankster.'

'*Aaaaagh!* I was just about to tell you he wasn't for real!'

'You mean you kept it secret? If that had been one of my tests, you'd be expelled by now.'

'*Phew!* Glad I escaped that!'

'I have to hand it to you,' Matthew said. 'You have a pretty good capacity for inspiring loyalty. It took a great deal of work to get him to reveal your plans. The two of you conspiring by the aquarium didn't entirely escape my notice.'

'But that's not true! I played no part in...' Rosetta's descent into laughter quelled any hope of arguing her innocence.

'He went along with the plan cos he fancied you.'

'No! He didn't—'

'Did.'

'What I was going to say was he didn't go along with any plan. Not my idea at all.'

'But he did fancy you.'

'For sure!' Rosetta pretended to preen her hair vainly.

'The magician did too, I reckon. That Jippie bloke's been following you around for weeks. Two admirers and it's not even midnight.' For a moment Matthew hesitated on the staircase. 'Actually, I think my calculations are out.'

'Ah, no! Don't tell me you meant to say zero!' Rosetta turned back to Matthew.

He was standing on the step above, smiling down at her. 'I meant to say three.' His voice had grown warmly seductive. 'There's one other who admires you. More than you can imagine.' He stepped down to the stair she was on and nudged her elbow.

Momentarily, she closed her eyes to savour the feelings this evoked. She nudged him back.

'I'll total that at three for the moment,' he said. 'Three definites, although I suspect there's probably a helluva lot more. Then I'll work on cancelling out the competition.'

He slid his hand onto hers. Sparks like lively champagne bubbles washed over her. She turned and looked up at his eyes, his mouth. He was watching her very seriously. She leaned into his shoulder and sighed, gloriously, ecstatically happy.

He wrapped his fingers around her hand. He held her hand as they made their way down the stairs. In silence they walked to the restaurant's underground car park, and he continued to hold her hand.

The Jaguar's lights blinkered on in response to Matthew's key. He opened Rosetta's door for her. 'This is a tricky door,' he said. 'Doesn't always open from inside. I'm getting it fixed on Tuesday.'

She slid into the passenger seat, looking forward to their trip to Balmoral. A glittering display met her eyes when Matthew drove out of the parking station, a dizzy array of starry city lights that edged the road to the Harbour Bridge, their reflections in the water below a showcase of liquid gems.

They were crossing the Bridge now. The moon, golden and full, seemed to be watching them from afar. During the drive to the North Shore, they talked freely. Matthew's fascination with Edward Lillibridge and his writings was possibly even greater than hers. He was keen to research the author's life and even revealed a quiet hope of collecting everything Lillibridge had written.

They had now reached the bay. Muted beams from the Bathers' Pavilion filtered through an eerie mist. They cruised down a winding street towards the beach.

'And it turns out Lucetta and Edward became quite friendly,' Matthew commented.

'Yes. They fell in love.'

'I now know why Conan Dalesford referred to his alpacas as soulmates.'

Rosetta had cuddled one of those alpacas on her Alice Springs trip. 'If I'd had a magic wand, I would have battled with the temptation to shrink the two and sneak them home in my pocket.'

'I enjoyed that first guest-blog of his. The one with the mention of lexigrams in names.'

'Royston believes the "Alcor" part of Conan Dalesford's name indicates one of his past selves.'

'Huh? Surely not! Surely he doesn't think Dalesford was the Dream Master in the book.'

'Do you believe in past lives, Matthew?'

Matthew veered into a parking space that overlooked the white sand of Balmoral Beach and slowed the car to a stop. He pulled the key from the ignition, rested his hands on the steering wheel, turned to her and said, 'I did, then I didn't, and now I do. I really do believe we've all been here before.'

'What changed your mind? The last time I mean.'

Matthew jangled his keys then slipped them into his pocket. 'Nothing in particular,' he said, although his tone suggested he was making light of something he'd been thinking about in depth. She tried to decode Matthew's expression. His profile, slightly lowered, was a mask of moving shadows from the breeze-tickled tea-trees outside.

He flicked on the ceiling light, reached into the back seat and handed her a book, which he revealed to be his own edition of *Our True Ancient History*. 'I got that in London at the Portobello Markets,' he said. 'I could have got a newer one, but I liked the emblem on this.'

Rosetta ran her hand over the cover. Under the title was an engraving: a golden eagle on a pedestal with wings outstretched.

She took in an uneasy breath. The sight of the emblem blanketed her in darkness. A sensation of heaviness descended upon her, a feeling of foreboding. Of warning. Was someone in the Dream Sphere attempting to tell her something? Would romance with Matthew fail to blossom?

'Let's walk, shall we?' Matthew opened his car door.

Pessimism is poison, she chided herself. Things between us have moved along beautifully so far. Nothing's going to go wrong.

She lifted the handle of the car door. It refused to give way. Wondering whether she'd spoken too soon about everything running smoothly, she smiled to herself.

Matthew, already crossing the front of the car, signalled to her with a double thumbs-up before rushing to her door and opening it. 'I do that a lot,' he said. 'I lock all my women in.' He held out his hand to her. Laughing, Rosetta took up Matthew's hand while he pulled her to her feet. 'It's so I can rescue them.' He released her hand and led her to a lamp-lit footpath that wound around the deep, dark blue of the bay. 'Kind of a tradition.' He was now walking alongside her. 'And it's also a preventative measure. The malfunctioning door handle keeps women from bolting when I reflect on their rabbit impersonations.'

Playfully, she bumped against him. He bumped against her in return. He slipped his arm around her. Unable to stop beaming, unable to continue moving, Rosetta leaned into Matthew's body. A cascade of joy was thundering through her. She turned around to face him. Got lost in the depth of his eyes.

The night was soundless, save for the silken swish of wavelets and the hoot of a faraway owl. They were standing opposite each other on a secluded path. The only thought she had was *I want him to kiss me*.

He leaned towards her and pushed aside a strand of hair that had fallen across the side of her face, the feel of his fingertips igniting her skin.

He leaned in closer. Closer. His lips brushed against her own, almost in question. He drew back.

She searched his face.

He was gazing at her, lids half lowered.

Again she melted into his eyes. Again his mouth found hers. He tasted of champagne. The sensation of his kiss was like diving into a bubbling ocean: a warm sea of champagne that whirled over and through and around her. Sparkles. Euphoria. Dazed, wild, *crazy* love.

Matthew whispered in her ear, 'You certainly passed that test.'

Smiling, she ran a hand over the back of his shoulder.

Still whispering, he said, 'I'd give that kiss one-thousand-and-one per cent.'

He straightened from his forward lean. Then he pulled her close to him and kissed her again. She pressed against the firmness of his body. The pressure of Matthew's lips increased. His hands were on her waist. She reached up to his shoulders and wrapped her arms around his neck, kissing him back with abandon. This was who she wanted. She had never felt so alive. There were times when she'd thought she'd lost him, but now he was here, kissing her, and although she'd imagined this countless times, she'd had no idea how powerful it would ultimately be.

He was holding her now and smiling. She breathed a happy sigh. 'I missed you,' he said. 'Loved getting your emails.'

'I loved getting your emails too,' she admitted.

His voice was low and growly. 'There was a gap in one of the ones you sent to me.'

'Hm?'

'A gap,' Matthew said, his voice still low. 'Between you saying, "I really want you" and "to be there as a representative".'

'Really?'

'Yes. Really. And although I knew you hadn't meant to do that, it drove me crazy.'

Rosetta, absorbed in the safeness of Matthew's arms, remained silent. She had meant every word of it in the email. Hadn't fully expected him to pick up on the subtlety of that strategically placed return.

Contact with Matthew Weissler had set up a yearning that strengthened with every encounter. She wanted him. Wanted only to be with Matthew.

One-thousand-and-one per cent.

Chapter Five

Hi again Friday Fortnighters!

Spring is around the corner for us here in the Southern Hemisphere. Frilly blossoms are sprouting on prunus branches in Kirribilli's avenues (Kirribilli is a suburb neighbouring my own—and home of the north-pylons of the Sydney Harbour Bridge). To all of you in the Northern Hemisphere: by now you are probably enjoying the cosiness of cooler days and nights as autumn approaches. No doubt clans of seasons sprites similar to those Orahney watched over are hard at work painting the leaves all sorts of fiery colours!

I can't wait for you to read this second letter of Edward Lillibridge's that Charles has so kindly allowed us to display on this site.

Thanks again to Harriet Neilson, of Cornwall in the UK, for transcribing Lillibridge's letters so diligently, and to the incredible Matthew Weissler who has become a dedicated and highly valued member of Sydney's book-study 'gang'. Matthew's inspiration over the past few weeks has, for me personally, been as dazzling as the summer sun.

Enjoy!

Warmly,

Rosetta Melki

My Dear Sister Meredith,

I enclose two extra shillings with pleasure. Ned has thankfully managed to sell six-and-ten bundles at the village on market day. As a result the three of us dined very well throughout the week just passed. I therefore cannot allow any more time to elapse without sharing our good fortune with my faithful sibling.

I am most pleased, Meredith, to learn that your youngest is flourishing. She sounds as though she is quite exhausting. That boundless vigour you describe does indeed make these kinds of children testing to raise. You must view her nature as a blessing. Your child is displaying a robust form of good health, which will serve her well once she enters womanhood. With age will come calmness. I indeed witnessed this occurrence in none other than you, Meredith. The energy you scattered about as a youngster has been channelled into the admirable abilities of a keen worker. There is fire aplenty in your spirit! I have no doubt your Mr Rathbone is well pleased with his choice of wife, both for the practical help you provide him in the growing and sale of his cabbages, and in the unfailingly dutiful care you bestow upon his offspring.

Meredith, I wish to convey some very important news of mine. I implore you to not be startled by what I am about to disclose. Although my association with the individual I am yet to mention has not been perceived by all in the parish as an appropriate one, I am hopeful that you and Mr Rathbone will find it in your hearts to complete my happiness with your blessing.

I am engaged to be married to Lucy, my housekeeper. My opinion of her manner, conduct and thoroughness was always of the highest. With time, this opinion became quite overwhelming. While I struggled with my regard for her, many of the tenderer feelings I harboured grew difficult to ignore. And so I decided that the only right and proper action to take was to either propose marriage or secure employment for her elsewhere.

I am apprehensive of your response to this news. At this stage of reading my letter, you might well be exclaiming: 'Well I never! Edward has been taken in by a common Romani!' In the expectation of this presumption, let me first indicate that I consider myself to be an excellent judge of character. Throughout my work at the parsonage I have learnt to distinguish between kind-heartedness and deception. Secondly, and I beg your pardon if you have thought nothing of that which I suggest, Lucy is in no way common. She is a very proper woman: modest, loyal, and eager to learn British traditions. Ned has taught her to read and write, and through being in our company she has quite nearly eliminated all of her accent.

She has become a wonderful companion to Ned and me. Of a night we sit by the fireside, and she tells us stories of magical peoples in faraway lands while stitching a tapestry.

Meredith, please do not pass on the following paragraphs to your husband. You must always take heed of the fact that our belief in the magical, in the good of the druids, could one day be to our detriment. It is only thirty years since the burnings ended. My arrival in this world two-and-thirty years ago saw the introduction of a fairer Witchcraft Act, however, we must not entertain complacency. Another uprising against those who <u>believe</u> might come about.

I am sure you would be fascinated by Lucy's tales. Like druids, she has the gift of faerie sight!

She tells me she has not always been in possession of this ability. It emerged when she first received that mysterious pendant, a gem set in an exquisite filigree of metal which is sometimes referred to as 'lunar-gilt', being of both gold and silver, and happens to be the same piece of jewellery that assisted in restoring Ned to consciousness. When travelling from village to village in her family's train of colourfully painted waggons, she was expected to earn her keep through telling fortunes, either by surveying an individual's palm or examining the tea leaves from an emptied cup. One of the people whose fortunes she told was a ship's captain who fell instantly in love with her. Lucy's family was quite eager for her to marry this fellow, for he was amassing great riches through merchant work. She maintained that marrying the captain would be unjust. She did not love him. To marry someone she did not love, she told her father, would be a wicked thing to do, yet still, her father continued correspondence with the poor unwitting voyager and accepted gifts on her behalf, including the rose-hued pendant.

In a letter accompanying this gift, the captain explained that the pendant had been given to him by a shipmate dying of fever. The expiring wretch had told Lucy's suitor that he had purchased this piece of treasure from a Dutch sailor while exploring New Holland, that newly discovered southern land of the Pacific Ocean. The pendant was pilfered from one of the native tribesmen.

Upon wearing this, Lucy became aware of all creatures invisible. She has friends, Meredith, down at the seaside, and their origins are neither human nor animal. They are sprites. Water sprites! 'People of the Sea' she calls them. Once she has finished her work for the day, and prior to her commencement of our dinner, she wraps a shawl about her shoulders, seizes her basket and hurries off to the shore. After our supper, once we're seated by the fire, she tells the two of us a story her ethereal companions have conveyed to her. It is a continuing story; quite intriguing; a devic account of humanity's unrecorded past.

Each evening before I retire, I note down all that I have heard, with the intention of expanding on this at a later date into a proper documentation of Lucy's narration. Ned and I look forward greatly to Lucy's retelling of the water sprites' tales. Whenever we are settled by the hearth at the day's end, each with a tankard of Honey Mead, Ned will be heard to say, 'Tell us, Lucy, what did Zhippe and Carlonn offer this afternoon?' And then we are treated to another instalment of their fabulous version of history.

Lucy claims that we do not have only one life. Since wearing the gem, she has gained an awareness of having visited

Heaven. This very unassuming woman, a Gypsy housekeeper who I have grown to respect greatly, visits Heaven often! So fanciful seeming, Meredith, and yet I cannot help but believe her! I have always known that our existence is far more expansive than we imagine; have always believed, like you have, in secrets that are yet to be learnt, secrets that are kept from us by the same fearful power mongers who ensured those with the presence of intuition were branded witches, then tortured or murdered. There were once thousands with these gifts of insight, I am told. My heart weeps at the cruelty. Innocent lives were destroyed en masse. What a different world it would be now if those lives were permitted to continue peacefully!

According to Lucy, all of us visit this place of paradise in soul form when we retreat to our slumber, although she refers to it not as Heaven but as 'The Dream Sphere'. She also believes our soul returns to the earth to live again. Once she'd begun wearing the gemstone, Lucy found herself able to recall who she had been in a life prior. 'I was a mermaid,' she told me, and I laughed uproariously. ''Tis true, Mister Lillibridge,' she said. 'You and I were lovers.'

Well! I sat up and took notice then because I was by that stage clearly smitten with this young and alluring creature, and hoped that if she were correct in assuming we had lived other lives, she and I being once linked in matrimony could indeed be true.

Do you remember, Meredith, how I mentioned in one of my letters to you that Lucy had a habit of temporarily forgetting my name? That she mistakenly called me Matthew? It so happens that she recognised me from a life that has passed.

At my urging, she confided in me about that life of hers as a mermaid in which she's certain I was involved. The story was none other than the Legend of the Mermaid of Zennor, the *folktale we heard many times as children. I again laughed heartily, much to Lucy's dismay. 'You have told me a fable,' I said to her.*

She scowled at me then, and I felt rather dreadful for having been so harsh. 'What makes you think this story hasn't stemmed from a truth?' she demanded to know, and I had to agree that I have, in the past, suspected fragments of truth in every tale that circulates.

And so I have written Lucy's version of 'The Legend of the Mermaid of Zennor.' Lucy maintains that Matthew did not address her as Morveren. In this particular tale, the mermaid tells Matthew Trelawney, 'My true name is Morveren, but my sisters call me Marani.'

Last Sunday, when I read this to the Parish after my sermon on the oppression of the poor, Mr Darlington of the local newspaper lavished me with praise, telling me it was a splendid tale and asking: would I permit him to publish it?

My documentation of Lucy's siren story is to appear in The Tintagel Times in twelve days' time. I shall post you a cutting as soon as it is in print.

Fondest wishes,

Edward

ROSETTA CLIMBED OUT OF THE POOL, flung on a robe and caught the elevator up to the fourteenth floor. She entered her suite and strolled down the cupboard-lined hallway, an array of white louvre doors that led to the kitchen and living area where the parquetry flooring took on an amber sheen in the morning sun. A song from the early 1980s, 'Woman in Love', which her mother Daniela had sung two years after Barbra Streisand made it a stellar hit, was stuck in her brain. As a kid she'd often laughed at that song, at the self-centred intensity of it, and at the way it inferred passion was a deadly serious thing. Much to her mortification, she'd found herself humming it in the car on her way to uni.

Izzie was at the dining table, breakfasting on the spinach-ricotta lasagne served the night before at the dinner party Rosetta held, in Matthew's honour.

'Mum, the pasta's out-of-this world.'

'Thanks, hon! Glad you like it.'

'One of your cooking class recipes?'

'Yep! Love those courses at the Kirribilli Neighbourhood Centre. Well, most of them.' Trying to ignore the results of her sculpture class on the coffee table, a depiction of Eros that could have been authentic if it weren't for the floppy bow-and-arrow emulating a bunch of wilted celery, she flicked on the TV, moved to the kitchen and started up the coffee machine. 'What'll it be today? Cappuccino, latte, flat white, Vienna?'

'Hmm. Maybe a Vienna this time.'

'Hazelnut syrup?'

'No thanks.'

'Aw, go on. Indulge. It's Friday!'

'Nope. Two lots of hazelnut Viennas in one week is way too indulgent.'

'I wish I had your willpower, Iz.'

On the news, a New York stock exchange official was talking in urgent bullet-points about the market having dipped to its lowest since 2001. 'Doesn't sound good,' Rosetta said vaguely, opening the fridge. She'd have to ask Matthew what it all meant. 'Ah no! We're out of...'

'Out of what?' Izzie said.

'Just testing. Did I get you scared?'

'Beyond scared. I was psyching myself up for a dash to the Lavender Bay shops.'

'In your dressing-gown and all? *Cor!* Lucky you caught on!'

'Matthew seems nice, Mum.'

'You like him? Oh, good!'

'Of course I do. Not that I ever thought I wouldn't. Sara always said her stepfather was cool.'

'Did she really?'

'Yeah. Said he was great because he never got cranky with her or Laura like Grant does. And he always took them really cool places, like Disneyland and stuff.'

'That's Matthew.' Rosetta frowned at the bag of ground coffee beans so as not to appear too starry-eyed. 'He takes *me* really cool places too.' Already he'd treated her to three weekends away, and they'd only been dating forty-five days. A chalet in the Blue Mountains, complete with open fire—they'd driven there on the first day of spring—yachting on the Hawkesbury the following week. Still floating about her in wisps of delight was their most recent trip to the seaside resort of Terrigal, an hour's drive from Sydney, where their balcony suite overlooked the Mediterranean style plaza and turquoise calm of the sea. In the evening the sea had become a rippling expanse of silver, a kaleidoscope of fragmented moonlight that wove itself fluidly through silhouettes of jagged pines.

Since they'd started spending nights together, Rosetta had joked to Matthew about struggling to recall where she was each morning. Matthew had admitted he suffered from the same sort of amnesia. Little wonder. Up until the lease ended on his Milsons Point penthouse, he had no fixed address. The Neoclassical he'd shared with Dette and the girls, a sought-after showpiece listing luxury features like the *Sound-of-Music* staircase and awe-inspiring Viennese chandelier, was already sold by the time he returned from England. 'I just wanted to get my fifty per cent across to her and out of the way,' he'd said, 'So I sold the Cabarita Heights property.' Matthew did have the option of moving to his penthouse. Property laws allowed him to issue his tenants with an eviction notice, but he hated the idea of giving anyone a *Move-out-in 30-days* demand. Instead he'd notified them of his intention to sell, halved their rent for good measure, then stayed at the Intercontinental until they'd given their departure date.

Rosetta felt sad the evening she'd first visited his apartment. Matthew's Milsons Point harbour view was far more spectacular than hers, and she'd especially loved his gilded Egyptian bathroom and sumptuous conifer terrace. 'Do you have to sell it, Matthew?' she'd said. 'It's so magnificent.'

'Half of it belongs to Bernadette unfortunately,' Matthew had said. 'She hasn't agreed to the post-nup, but I'll get something just as nice. And I'll keep a look-out for you in the meantime. It'd be great to see you snapping up something permanent.'

'Excellent! While I love being high up, I miss having a garden. There's something about being close to the earth you just can't beat. It's probably my earth-sign ascendant that makes me like that.'

'What's an earth sign? Besides Capricorn?'

'That's very astute, Matthew. Who told you Capricorn's an earth sign?'

'Someone I once nicknamed Lucetta.'

'That wouldn't happen to have been me, would it?'

'Correct! When we first met, you chatted with me at my send-off about astrology. And while I stood there, hating Adam Harrow for the time he got to spend with you, you told me Capricorn was an earth sign.'

'That's right, I did! You have such a good memory!'

'Only when it concerns you.'

She'd then told him she had a Taurus ascendant, or 'Rising Sign' as most people would say.

Matthew had said something quite out of the ordinary then. 'Like the Queen of Pentacles,' he'd suggested, 'who appears in the tarot?'

She'd been overjoyed to hear he'd not been averse to tarot cards. He hadn't thought them 'weird' as so many people did. She'd agreed that The Queen of Pentacles represented an earth sign or earth-sign rising, and that, funnily enough, she'd always used The Queen of Pentacles as a significator for herself.

'So what's a significator?' Matthew had asked.

'It's the card that's placed face-up on the table. It represents the looks and temperament of the tarot reading's recipient.' Matthew's would undoubtedly be the King of Cups: light hair and eyes, mid-thirties or over, a water Rising Sign.

She'd told him then that she'd done quite a bit of tarot reading over the years.

He'd been impressed but had thought she'd only done this for fun. Disappointingly, Matthew found the idea of a fortune-telling livelihood rather hilarious. 'I can't exactly imagine you reading cards for money,' he'd said. And then he'd described a comical image of

Rosetta in a shawl at a table outside a caravan, purring to passers-by, *'Cross my palms with silver.'*

Rosetta's 'New-Age drifter' fear had got the better of her. She'd thereafter resolved to never tell Matthew that reading tarots had helped her garner the scary amount for the electricity bill, coupled with the late penalty when her scrimping fell short.

Descending back into the TV-blaring present, Rosetta stared at the cups on the bench. 'Er...hazelnut, Iz?'

'Ha! You must have forgotten we've been through that. No thanks, Mum.'

'I'm not senile, Izzie.'

'Don't worry. I believe you.' Izzie went back to reading the newspaper, and Rosetta went back to the memory of first visiting Matthew's apartment.

He was getting her a glass of red in the open kitchen. She wandered across to his mantelpiece, the one by the bay windows, and pushed her fingertips over an array of books it shelved. 'Did you know you have eight versions here of *Our True Ancient History?*' she said.

'And I thought I had only the one!' Matthew gave a nod. 'Yeah I've started collecting them. They're chronologically arranged. The edition on your left was published in 1880, and then it goes on. 1890, 1920, 1947, 1962...'

'Wow. Impressive!'

'I'm looking for an unabridged version. One that reflects the original manuscript more.'

'Wouldn't that be amazing: to own a copy with info we've never read before. It'd be like getting a DVD with bonus deleted scenes, only *one-thousand-and-one-percent* more interesting!'

'Even better would be the original.'

'Ah, the original manuscript! We can dream I guess. By now it would have incarnated into a pile of dust. Someone would have disposed of it long ago.'

Matthew lifted their wine goblets from the bench and threw her a mysterious look.

She adopted an over-the-top confused face as he neared her. 'Why the raised eyebrow, gorgeous?'

Matthew grinned, handed over her wine and kissed her tenderly on the cheek. She sank against him and kissed him back. Heavenly. Each demonstration of affection was heavenly.

'I'd planned to wait awhile before I told you. Wanted it to be a surprise.'

'What were you going to tell me? I love surprises, Matthew! But only once I know what they are.'

Matthew smiled to himself, turned, and took a seat on the sofa. He took a swig of his wine, settled it on the coffee table and turned back to her. 'I got a letter yesterday. From Cornwall. Charles Gloucester wrote to me.'

'Really?'

'Yes. Really. And according to Charles, the manuscript is a long way from being reduced to a pile of dust.'

'Matthew! You're kidding me!'

Matthew rose and sauntered to his kitchen bench. Atop the speckled granite was a covered stationery tray. From it he retrieved a page of lined notepaper. '*Dear Mr Weissler,*' he read. '*It was very pleasant to meet you and your lady-friend on your visit to my house on Sunday 22nd of June, 2008.*'

Rosetta tensed.

Matthew looked uncomfortable. 'Uh, he's made a mistake. Obviously thought Harriet and I were together.'

Rosetta shook off her fears and urged Matthew to continue. He read on:

'*As you know, the two letters in my possession addressed to Reverend Edward Lillibridge's sister, Meredith Rathbone, estimated to have been written somewhere between 1755 and 1770, were purchased from Mrs Anna Callan of Tintagel.*

'*Anna has since spoken to me on the telephone. She has informed me that she discovered another letter amongst her mother-in-law's belongings when cleaning out her attic, along with what appeared to be Lillibridge's handwritten manuscript. After having it valued three weeks ago, she discovered it to be genuine and worth a substantial amount. I am certainly not interested in getting it: the cost is too great for me. However, I thought it possible that you or the Australian lady with that electric noticeboard...*'

Matthew stopped. 'I think what he means is, "*electronic* notice-board," website being a more user-friendly term.'

He read on. '...*might be interested in purchasing the manuscript.*

'*Mrs Callan has permitted me to pass her details on to you, although it seems she is in two minds about selling. My feeling is that she would rather not. Still, it is worth a try, isn't it? She can only say no. Yours sincerely,* etcetera.'

'Lillibridge's original *handwritten* manuscript,' Rosetta said. 'A dream come true!' If Matthew didn't make an offer, then Rosetta certainly would. She pictured a pile of string-knotted pages with curling corners taking pride of place on Matthew's mantelpiece. 'If you don't make an offer, Matthew—'

'I'm sorry to tell you this, beautiful. I already have.'

'And?'

'And Anna's decided not to sell. I've kept her number though. I've set up a reminder in my BlackBerry to phone her every six months. With that sort of pestering she's bound to give in.'

'That's if she doesn't hang up first. Half-yearly calls!' Rosetta tsk-tsked. 'Such a monotonous nuisance! Seriously though, Matthew, that's utterly frustrating, although I don't blame her one little bit. There's no way I'd give up something as precious as that. Even if I knew nothing about Lillibridge or *Our True Ancient History*, I'd still want to keep it.'

'You and your love of old things.' Matthew's voice had grown gentle. 'I'm still on the lookout for a vintage home you can buy. One with a garden that conveys the sensuous earthiness of a woman with Taurus Rising.'

'Thank you, Mr—'House-in-the-Air'—air sign.' She waved towards the vivid evening sky outside Matthew's airy seventeenth-storey window, peach flamed clouds lined with burnished copper.

'Libra's air, is it?'

'Sure is.'

'So you haven't had any luck with the house hunting today?'

'None. Not that I'm complaining. I love having Matthew Porter Weissler as my new round-the-corner neighbour.' Rosetta trailed her hand across the glossy surface of a shelf beside the mantelpiece. At the end of the shelf was an eagle sculpture. She ran her fingers over its undulating feathers. 'This is beautiful,' she said. 'Where's it from?'

'Oslo I think. My team's retirement gift. You're very tactile, aren't you? It's something I notice a lot.'

Immediately, Rosetta dropped her hand to her side. 'I know. I'm too touchy-feely for my own good.' And then, all about her went black.

The sensation of rushing backwards.

A memory so dark and so vivid, it engulfed her in a smothering shudder. Cold grass beneath her feet...An ache in her heart...An eagle...The agony of loss.

Matthew's voice filtered through to her warmly. 'It's not a criticism, Rosetta. I actually love how you do that.'

Shaking the inexplicable image away, she said, 'Do what?'

Surprised, Matthew laughed. 'What I was just saying. I love how you run your hands over everything.' Matthew moved from the bench towards her, his green eyes shining with admiration. Her very own Gorgeous-GEG. Who would have thought she'd meet another, after green-eyed Adam let her down? Or that Adam would lead her to a man she'd fall madly and completely in love with? 'You take in surroundings mostly through your sense of touch.'

'I do?'

'It's a theory of Dalesford's. Your voice is low in tone, and you often look down when you're expressing feelings, a sign you're predominantly tactile. So run your hands over the books again and...' His voice became enticingly low. '...Feel free to touch...' His arms were around her now. '...Anything here.'

'Anything? Can I touch these beautifully strong forearms?'

His lips were now pressing against her own. A heavenly kiss. 'Anything at all.'

The aroma of coffee lured her back from the daydream. Izzie was beside her, having taken over making their Viennas. 'You were miles away,' she said with a smirk.

'I...er...was just wondering what I should cook us for dinner tonight.'

'Yeah right! Admit it. You were thinking about Matthew.'

Far from unusual. In the weeks following Amaretti's, and aside from the emails, most conversations with Matthew once he'd left for England had taken place in her head. Rosetta would have died if he'd known how frequently she'd imagined talking with him...the questions, the answers, his unique style of flirty banter. And when she hadn't been thinking about Matthew, she'd been congratulating herself on managing to *not* think about him, which kind of defeated the purpose.

The TV's blare was hard to ignore. Someone from the White House was addressing an urgent press conference.

We don't yet know how it will affect the market. We could be heading for the biggest financial crisis since the Wall Street crash of 1929.

This was starting to sound serious. She'd ask Matthew when he phoned tonight. Matthew's finance knowledge was incredibly sound.

Rosetta lifted the bottle of syrup. 'Hazelnut, Isobel?'

'For the third time, *thank you*, but *no*. And by the way, that's not hazelnut coffee syrup. It's not even syrup. It's Worcestershire sauce.'

King Nikolaus of that future time was about to reveal the meaning of the horned ones' wall. Maleika watched the Dream Sphere's holographic projection in awe.

As she watched, a cloud formed across the image. And then the scene that conveyed the Sonic Unity Gathering vanished altogether.

Maleika turned to Alcor. 'Whatever happened to the Sonic Unity Gathering that we were viewing?'

'I've halted the scenario for a moment or two,' said Alcor, smiling to himself.

'Alcor, why? I was just about to learn the full meaning of the Oracle's message to me.'

'And you will,' said Alcor. 'Firstly though, I would like to present to you an account of what became of Adahmos and Eidred.' He waved his hand, and a stilled picture appeared, of the elf by the Grudellan Palace's eagle statue.

'Do you know how this statue came about, Maleika?'

'No, not at all. It was there when I attended Eidred's crystalling in my disguise as a bewitcher; it was there when I visited Eidred in her chamber; but when I visited the palace's hologram when accompanied by Zhippe and Carlonn, it was absent.'

She thought back to the time she had infiltrated the palace in her search for Pieter. She'd mistaken Eidred for Orahney due to the Oracle's vague advice. She recited the message to Alcor:

'A flight of stairs
The lost one's room
Is sanctioned off in lofty gloom

Revisit where the eagle's flown
Its earthly shell
Is set in stone

'Quite useless advice,' she said.

'Indeed not,' said Alcor, shaking his head. 'Your daughter-in-law was sheltering Pieter. Fripso had led your son to his destiny.

'And although you will not remember this, you, in your life as Orahney, went to great lengths to create a cavern beneath your pyramid dwelling with your crystal wand. The cavern sheltered a dragon you had rescued, and formed a tunnel that ultimately led under the thorn thicket and into the forest. This was what you knew as "the dragon cave". Had you continued your journey through this cave with Croydee, the two of you might well have found stairs leading up to the home that you—and Croydee's "lost one"—inhabited a century earlier.

'My feeling,' continued Alcor, 'is that the Oracle did not wish you to locate Pieter in his "room," nor to perceive the eagle on the post to be a landmark directing you to the Grand Hall. I suspect the Oracle wished you to revisit the eagle because it symbolised someone you once loved, a guard who took on eagle form at dusk, as all troopers did.

'If you hadn't been in so much of a hurry, and if you'd understood that you were to pause at the eagle, your magic would have enabled you a glimpse into history. You would have witnessed the freeing that Adahmos carried out. Your heart would have healed a great deal if you'd gleaned the knowledge of Storlem liberated from his earthly stone shell. When he first arrived in the Dream Sphere while still under the influence of Rawhor's constricting curse, he was locked in the physical form of an eagle and chose to dwell on an alpine peak in a microscopic realm.

'Of course, your conscious memory, Maleika, would not have allowed you to understand either who Storlem was or the association you'd had with him in your former life, but your heart, your higher mind, would have understood. The Oracle, I believe, wanted to clear your reluctance to fall in love.'

In a tone that was playfully scolding, Maleika said, 'I was never afraid of falling in love! I was simply preoccupied with my duties as Clan Watcher. And I had already experienced one soulmate connection, with Wallikin. We were happy, and then he passed on to the Dream Sphere. I decided then that one marriage was enough.'

'You and Wallikin parented two children. You welcomed your youngest son into your world, and soon after, Wallikin left the earthly plane.'

'I was lucky,' said Maleika, suddenly sad. 'Lucky to share a small part of my life with him, but it's true our time together was fleeting.'

'Maleika, the loss of Storlem is still impacting on your heart.'

'Nonsense,' said Maleika. 'My heart is resilient.'

'It has created in you a pattern of abandonment.'

'I do not agree,' Maleika said stubbornly.

ROSETTA SNATCHED UP THE PHONE. With a defeated sigh, she lowered it into its cradle. She couldn't. Wouldn't. Thankfully her self-respect had barred any action she'd later regret.

Back into the study to check her emails. Two from Lena, one from Royston, none from Matthew. Two weeks. Two whole weeks and no reply, unless she took into account his cryptic answer to her first four messages. 'Rosetta. Really sorry I haven't been in touch. Just need time to...sort myself out. I'm in the process of moving.' Long pause. 'I'll be in contact when I've found a place.' Extra-long pause. Deep breath in. 'Don't know when that'll be.'

She'd immediately phoned back but was greeted with Matthew's voicemail. 'What do you need to sort out, Matthew? Please understand you can talk to me if something's bugging you.'

Three days later she'd tried to contact him again. 'Matthew, do you need any help with your move? Please let me know if you do.'

He'd ignored both messages. Her voice had been taut with anxiety in her third call. 'Matthew, all I can think is you're wanting to break up with me. If that's the case, so be it, but please, *please* allow me the courtesy of a clearer statement than needing to sort yourself out.'

She'd gone over the memory of each rendezvous, not with the rosy lenses of 'a woman in love' as she'd been in the habit of doing, but with the steely fine-tooth comb of a detective, to identify signs of rejection. Even in her most dispassionate analysis of it all, she could find no reason for his sudden coldness.

Every meeting had been charged with affection. He'd continually showered her with compliments. Perhaps the bombardment of honeyed words was just a veneer. The last quote presented at the poetry meeting's Wise Words section had been one of Cyril Connolly's:

'All charming people have something to conceal, usually their total dependence on the appreciation of others.'

Remembering this made her wonder whether Matthew was simply a silver tongued flatterer, someone who acted as though he were unequivocally devoted until a shinier prospect emerged.

She combed through the time she'd asked him in a phone call what he'd watched the night before. 'Did you see the Oscars telecast last night?'

'I started to,' he'd said mournfully, 'but I turned it off because you weren't on it. When can I see you again?'

She'd had no reason to doubt Matthew's sincerity. After all, she was just as effusive in her praise of him. And anyway, people said crazy couple-ish things when they first got together, although some people—in particular, the late Adam Harrow—were intentionally deceptive. Perhaps Matthew fitted that category.

He'd called her one afternoon to tell her he was watching day-time television. 'You learn something every day when you leave a full-time career,' he'd told her.

'So what are you watching?'

'Dunno. One of those shows where they turn their back on the person they're conversing with.'

'*Days of our Lives*?'

'Bingo!'

When he'd phoned her the day after, he'd been watching *Days of our Lives* again. 'I had to switch it off though, cos I got reminded of you.'

Unable to help feeling pleased that one of the glamorous soap stars had caused Matthew to draw comparisons, she'd said, 'How could *Days of our Lives* ever remind you of little old me?'

'The hourglass,' Matthew had said. 'There's an hourglass on the beginning credits.'

'How very sweet,' Rosetta had droned. 'How delighted I am to be compared with an inanimate object. Why an hourglass though? Do you see me as a good timekeeper?'

'I see you as very shapely. And I've become obsessed with your curves. When can I see you again?'

And now he didn't want to see her. Not at all. Perhaps never.

That afternoon, Lena called round with a boxful of DVDs Andrew no longer wanted. 'They're just comedies,' she said with apology. Rosetta assured her they'd be perfect for the Kirribilli Neighbourhood Fete.

Lena wandered down to the local outdoor café with her, to commiserate about Matthew's silence.

'I'm terrified he's gone back to Bernadette,' Rosetta said.

'Let's hope that's not the case,' Lena said. 'We shouldn't really jump to conclusions. So let's go through it again. You'd gone on a harbour cruise together on the Sunday, and Matthew left abruptly.'

'I wouldn't say abruptly.' Rosetta thought about it. 'Dutifully is more the word. He had to pick up Kirk Rummery from the airport.'

'Who's Kirk Rummery?'

'Matthew's new business consultant, a mate of Matthew's brother. Kirk's left the UK with a view to living in Australia. He's setting up Matthew's new firm in the city. Matthew told me he'd been on a scuba-diving trip to the Barrier Reef. There'd been a cab driver strike, so Matthew offered to pick him up.'

'Hmm.'

'Matthew didn't seem distant at all. He was cuddling me heaps, saying he wished he wasn't leaving so soon.'

'Leaving so soon,' Lena echoed with a sigh.

'Ominous words,' Rosetta agreed.

'So there's no reason to think he was in any way upset with you or the relationship when he left. There's got to be a logical explanation.'

Rosetta harked back to the Sunday she'd already replayed too many times. 'All I can think is he was quieter than usual.'

'In what way?'

'Well, it was really strange at the end of our lunch on the cruise. Matthew threw his credit card onto the tray, as he's always done—he never lets me pay! And the waiter came back and whispered something to him.'

'That the credit card was declined?'

'Something like that. So Matthew reached for his wallet, then realised he didn't have enough cash on him. He kind of blanched, but I told him it was no problem at all and that it was about time I contributed. So I moseyed on up and paid.'

'How did Matthew feel about that?'

'Mortified. He vowed he'd reimburse me as soon as he got to an automatic teller. I told him again I was more than happy to cover the bill. But he insisted on going to an ATM. He went to draw out the cash, but a notice flashed up on the screen: *Please see your bank*. It unnerved him. That was when he went quiet I think.'

'Probably feeling bad about not honouring his promise.'

'You're right. I think he did feel bad. Genuinely guilty. I tried to turn it into a joke and jolly him out of it, but he must have thought he'd let me down.'

'Poor Matthew. He obviously has no idea how much you're worth these days.'

'Ha! Yeah! Although even if he did know, he'd still insist on paying for everyone. It's a principle with Matthew. He sees himself as the traditional provider.'

'And what's this Kirk like?'

'I've spoken to him on the phone. I answered Matthew's mobile one morning, when Matthew was too sleepy to talk, and another time when he was paying for something at the shops. Kirk sounds lovely. Great sense of humour, gorgeous Scottish accent.'

'Single?'

'Seems to be.'

'Might be good for Eadie.'

'Don't know about that. I heard he'd been going out briefly with Harriet, one of the Cornwall Friday Fortnighters.'

'The woman who got the Lillibridge letters from Charles Gloucester?'

'That's her, yes. She and Matthew visited Charles when Matthew was in England. Anyway, about Kirk. Matthew read me out an email from Harriet, and the poor girl sounded really confused. And devastated. She wanted to know why Kirk had upped and left without so much as a goodbye and whether he'd given any clue to Matthew. And now it looks like Matthew's done the same to me. It's all so weird, Lena! What's going on with these guys?'

'First Matthew, then Kirk!' Lena resorted to flippancy. 'Maybe they've run off with each other.'

'Don't even joke about it.'

'Oops. Just remembered the guy from the theatre club you dated for a couple of weeks.'

'Ah, yes. Tony. My first real date after Angus disappeared.'

'Although Tony didn't *actually* leave you for a man.'

'No, he just tried to. So heartening.'

'I shouldn't mention something like that at a time like this.'

'You're so right,' Rosetta said, half amused. 'Stop that cackling please. My self-esteem's already at an all-time low.' For the fourth time that day, she found herself sighing, her outbreath creaking into a groan. 'I reckon I was dumb, Lena, to go for a guy on the rebound.'

'But Matthew adored you! I'm sure there were no second-thoughts about leaving Dette. None whatsoever.'

'I don't know. Marriage is a powerful tie. So many couples agree to end it, then realise they miss each other the minute they're apart.' She hesitated, not wanting to voice again her gloomiest fear. At last she said, 'He's gone back to her. I'm sure of it.'

'But she treated him so awfully,' Lena said. 'I really think Matthew was pleased to see the last of Dette. I know it all seems strange, but I feel sure you'll get an explanation. And if it turns out he's snuck back to a rotten marriage, then you're well rid of him. No-one wants a pushover who can't make up his mind.'

'Mm,' Rosetta said miserably. 'I thought he had strength of character, but maybe he hasn't.'

Once Lena had said goodbye, wished Rosetta luck in resolving the Matthew mystery and sailed off in her brand new dream car, Rosetta rushed back into her apartment to check her voice messages and emails.

She hadn't even got to talk to Matthew about the Global Financial Crisis. And she'd been so looking forward to hearing his expert opinion. He could have lost money, of course, but if that had happened she was sure he'd share news of that sort with her. He was a highly communicative man, probably one of the reasons he'd been so successful in his career. Assertive, very aware of the effect of his words, unswervingly diplomatic. She was repeatedly in awe of his consideration for others.

She hadn't admitted to Lena that something about Kirk had worried her. She thought back to the morning Matthew told her about a dream. He'd dreamt again about Lillibridge's Pieter. She'd sat huddled next to Matthew on his sofa—still in her winter PJ's and luxury robe—listening, enthralled, to his description of a dream that sounded sequential and real.

In the dream, he'd been wearing a suit and tie, his former bank exec uniform. Pieter had pointed to the tie and said, 'Why, sir, do you have a serpent biting at your throat?'

Matthew hadn't understood. Pieter had held up a mirror, and then Matthew saw his tie in an eerie new light. The triangular knot nearest his collar suggested a serpent's head, a serpent with its jaws clenched around his neck. The patterns on the tie resembled a serpent's scaly markings.

'Wow!' Rosetta had been spooked by the idea. 'I'll never be able to look at business-suited guys in the same way again, not if I hold onto that image of an asp attack. I'm thinking Pieter was giving you a symbol.'

'Me too. Something to do with disempowerment.'

'Disempowerment, yeah. And possibly even betrayal.'

Matthew had shaken his head. 'Can't quite work out what it might be.'

'Maybe he's trying to say the bank career was sapping your life-force.'

'Maybe. Anyway I asked him about my money situation. I said to him, "How can I earn back the money I'm giving away to Bernadette?".'

Rosetta smoothed her hand across Matthew's fingers. 'And what did Pieter say?'

Matthew's hand closed around hers. 'Pieter didn't say anything.' His thumb brushed soothingly across her wrist. 'Just wrote a word on the trunk of an autumn tree.'

'And what was the word?'

'This is the weird bit. While I was reading the letters in the dream, they started to fade. They faded like sky-writing does. All that was left of the word was "Fred M".'

'Fred M! How interesting! Maybe you're going to meet someone by that name who gives you an opportunity.'

'It's possible I guess.'

A week or so later, when they were driving to Terrigal, Matthew had said, 'By the way, I think I've worked out what "Fred M" means.'

Rosetta was intrigued. 'What does it mean?'

'Well...actually I don't want to say at this stage. I'll tell you if it all comes through.'

She wasn't to find out. His phone had rung. 'How much?' he'd said. 'Yeah, you're right. Ninety grand does sound reasonable. Put it through then.'

'Who was *that*, if you don't mind me asking?'

'Kirk,' said Matthew. 'He's in there setting up the office. Needed approval for some of the fitouts.'

Rosetta twisted round to look at Matthew. Behind his sunnies he was super-cool and devoid of any facial expression. 'Matthew, I hope you don't mind me saying this, but when I checked out the prices of fitouts for renovating Crystal Consciousness, nothing was in that sort of price range.'

'Kirk knows what he's doing.'

'I've got a really great deal with an office decorator. Perhaps you could get a second opinion.'

'Rosetta, sweetheart, I'm not low on cash.'

'Well neither am I and—'

'And much and all as I appreciate your concern, everything's under control. Now are you up for an ice-cream? Or a gelato? Cos I know a great place up ahead that I think you'll really love.'

Rosetta wilted at the memory. There wasn't a single part of her that didn't feel bruised. Coming home to an absence of messages felt like a strike to the stomach, a thump with the pointy end of a football.

She rose, lifted the crate of DVDs Lena had left her, and embarked on her walk to the Neighbourhood Centre, a steady march along a pavement splashed with sun and silk-tree shadows. Inside the volunteers' quarters, she lumped the crate down on the desk. 'For the fete,' she told Nerida. 'DVDs galore. *Whew!* Glad that's over. By the time I got to the gate I wished I'd taken the car.'

'You lugged that all the way from home, Rosetta?'

'Ah, it's no trouble. Good exercise actually—walking while weightlifting.'

'Oh, Rosetta. That's so sweet of you. I'm really sorry to tell you this, but old DVDs just don't sell.' Nerida was sifting through the crate. 'Especially not these kinds of movies. Not in Kirribilli. We'd just be left with something we'd have to throw out. Do you know anyone who'll watch movies geared at teenage boys? Nephews perhaps?'

'The only nephew I have is in New Zealand, and *he's* three.'

'Know anyone young at heart then?'

Rosetta clicked her fingers. 'As a matter of fact, I do!'

ROSETTA STEPPED OFF the treadmill, ran a towel over her forehead and flipped off her iPod earphones. 'Got to remain positive,' she told herself. 'The positive thing about Matthew turning his back on me is I've lost four kilos.' Running on the spot had been good for counteracting those ongoing bouts of anxiety. The treadmill, probably now in danger of breaking down from overuse, had at least ensured she didn't fall apart completely. On-the-spot sprinting, as well as putting on a brave face for Izzie—and telling herself it was better she found out how heartless Matthew was before she'd become any more entrenched—had kept her sane throughout each darkly agonising day.

The phone rang. She went to answer it. Stopped. She was past flying into an angry, hopeful frenzy when the trills chimed out from her study. 'Let it go through to voicemail,' she told herself. She was past working out something ingeniously vicious to say to Matthew. To both miss and despise someone: *how* was that physically possible? Why couldn't passionate distaste blot out all that useless sentimentality?

'Hello, erm...Rosetta,' An English accent. 'I'm erm...' A businesslike English accent. A woman. Someone related to Matthew? Matthew's mother? Sister-in-law? Someone to inform something awful had happened to Matthew? Oh God. He had to be all right. He *was* all right. She *knew* he was all right. She'd already checked all the hospitals; had checked them twice throughout the past three weeks. 'Erm...first I had better introduce myself. My name is Anna Callan. Now, a friend of yours by the name of Matthew Weissler...'

Rosetta rocketed across to the phone. 'Anna! Hi! How lovely to hear from you!'

What did Anna Callan have to say about Matthew?

Restrained laughter from Anna, followed by charming British apologies and a sheepish mention of having thought Rosetta to be an answering machine.

Wanting to explain to Anna that she had indeed gone through to voice-mail, Rosetta found herself incapable of uttering anything. Once the pleasantries subsided she said, 'You mentioned Matthew Weissler.'

'Ah yes. Now, I phoned him three or four days ago, and he told me I was best getting in contact with you, rather than with him.

I'm the one with the Lillibridge manuscript. It's handwritten in Regency-style cursive and is in pretty good shape considering its antiquity. I sold two of Edward Lillibridge's letters a couple of years ago, to a collector in Cornwall by the name of Charles Gloucester.'

'I see,' said Rosetta. 'No, I mean you're right, you did! I display both of those letters on my website.' Her breath caught in her throat. She swallowed. 'Er...so you phoned Matthew three or four days ago, you said?'

'Yes, three or four days ago. Perhaps it was more like four.'

'And he actually answered *you*.'

'Ye-es,' Anna's tone was puzzled. 'Yes he did.'

Wrong emphasis. Sounded unintentionally patronising. 'I mean, he *actually* answered you.' Patronising tone redirected to Matthew.

'Mm.'

Trying to calm her heartbeat, trying to stop the conclusions from disrupting her conversation with an international caller, Rosetta said, 'And he referred you to me!'

'He did.'

'And do you mind if I ask what exactly he said to you?'

'Ahem!'

Oh no, Rosetta thought. I'm sounding interrogative. And formal. And frosty!

To the caller she said, 'Sorry, Anna. There are a few distractions here...so I'll start again. I'm just so excited to have you phone. And really, *really* pleased that Matthew gave you my number. I'm just a bit mystified as to why Matthew referred you to me. I would have thought he was interested in the manuscript for himself.'

Anna agreed. 'He was,' she said, 'but I told him when he phoned that I wasn't parting with it.'

Rosetta already knew this. 'And what was his attitude like when you got in contact just recently?'

'Not too different. He was very nice of course. Not in any way busy or dismissive, if that's what you're concerned about. But he said that the best person to speak to was the woman who inspired him to learn about Lillibridge.'

'He said *that!*'

'Mm. He referred me to you. Passed on the details of your website and gave me your home number.'

Aha! So he hadn't fallen off the face of the earth.

Anna continued. 'First of all, I'd better mention that I've seen your Friday Fortnight website, Rosetta, and I must say I'm impressed with the details you've supplied on Edward Lillibridge's life.'

'Well, thank you, Anna!'

'And my husband and I just recently found a small locked box that once belonged to Edward Lillibridge, in my mother-in-law's attic, God rest her soul, which I'll be taking to get valued. It's pewter I think and probably not worth much at all, although when I rattle it I can hear something clinking inside, so I'll arrange for a locksmith to open it, but the reason for my phone call is to tell you there's another letter amongst my mother-in-law's possessions.'

'Another letter!'

'Yes. Now I'm quite happy to type up its contents and send it to your website...'

'That's brilliant of you!'

'...Because I think it's rather important. It concerns the authorship of *Our True Ancient History*.'

'The authorship? What does the letter say?'

'It says a lot, actually, and reveals something quite remarkable. What it indicates is this. The man who wrote the letters was *not* the man who wrote the book.'

Chapter Six

LIX

'Indeed I would, brother,' Maleika told Alcor.

'So you would like to see what happened to Adahmos once he freed Storlem's soul?' Alcor enquired.

'Of course! Although he will always be Pieter to me.'

Alcor waved his hand. 'You will laugh when you see what happens next,' he said, 'for the scene you are about to view concerns the crystalling you attended in your earthly life, in The Century of Ruin.'

The image of Pieter standing by the stony remains of Storlem sprang to life. Maleika observed the eagle frozen in time, its now soulless earthly shell reduced to the same material the pillar had been sculpted from, cold and grey. She felt a sudden stab of grief as she saw it. Bravely, she shook the feeling away.

Pieter was holding a wand, the same wand Maleika had wielded at the crystalling. He ran across the vast expanse of the palace grounds and past the dragon fountain that bubbled gold. As he neared the gates, he murmured an incantation. 'I hope I remembered this correctly, Orahney,' he whispered.

A dark cloak with a hood materialised within a beam of the wand. Pieter held the wand aloft, gazed heavenward and said to the sky, 'I call for the faerie Orahney who now resides in the Dream Sphere. Orahney, please send to Earth the sonic code that Maleika is to discover after a century is long passed.'

From the skies appeared a ray of orange. The wand's crystal lit up. The part the wicked one had chipped returned rapidly to its original form. Inside the crystal now was a crowding of symbols. Pieter wrapped the wand in the cloak. He marched forward. Haltingly, he declared, 'Wand of Orahney's, take yourself now to the dryad of the oak tree.' He then hurled the wand over the golden gates.

Maleika watched in fascination as the bundle flew over moon-tipped elms. At last it toppled from its airy travel and settled at the foot of a tree Maleika knew well, an ancient twisty oak.

The oak's dryad called out, 'Where in heaven's name did such a thing come from?'

Hearing this, Pieter called from the thorn thicket, 'A faerie by the name of Orahney has sent it to you. She wishes you to keep it. In your distant future, it is to be presented to an elf woman.'

'And who, might I ask, will this elf woman be?'

Pieter called out his reply. 'The receiver of this is to be Maleika, a Clan Watcher of the Brumlynds. She is not in existence at this time as she is yet to be born. The bundle will soon disappear. After two-and-eighty season-cycles have passed, it will reappear to you. When it does, I pray that you immediately ensure Maleika receives it, when she arrives there to meet Orahney, and that she dons the cloak and hastens to the Grudellan Palace with the wand. Words will appear to her in the crystal of the wand. When they do, she must repeat them.'

'We shall certainly honour this request,' the oak dryad cried. 'This wand and this cloak are safe with us. They will be passed on to my descendants, and my descendants will be told of that future time. The name Orahney sounds familiar to me. A faerie was stolen away by palace courtiers many moonths before. Perhaps...'

Just as Alcor had predicted, Maleika laughed. 'I was summoned, back before Pieter was born, to visit my Orahney-self at that oak tree,' she told the Dream Master. 'A dryad presented me with the cloak and wand. Although baffled as to why this was requested of me, I magically transported myself outside the doors of the palace temple. Once the bad faerie had cast her spell, I saw the words appear in the wand, and so I read them aloud. *The princess will not die*, the words said. *She will sleep. All of gold will sleep for one hundred years.'*

'Thus saving the fate of little Eidred, and helping to usher in the beginning of humanity,' Alcor said. 'The Gold's Kin gene is very strong. Even if Adahmos and Eid's daughter Lunara weds a deva in future years, the children she has will still possess the auric colours of mortals, which influence certain aspects of the mind and physicality.' He gestured to the scene they were watching.

Pieter was now kneeling over sleeping Eidred. 'Awaken now, Beauty,' he said.

Alcor spoke. 'The prince ventures from the thorn thicket and awakens the princess with a kiss.' He chuckled into his beard and shook his head. 'Here before us is a moment to be honoured throughout history. The story of the slumbering sun princess will survive aeons, Maleika, although it will take on many variations. It is to become a legend, known to future timeframes as *Sleeping Beauty.*'

Maleika was impressed. 'Well I never!'

Eidred had woken and was sitting up in a daze. Hastening to the basket beside her where little Lunara lay, she said to Pieter, 'A century has passed?'

Pieter was presenting Eidred with a bottle of Remembrance Essence.

Upon seeing this, Maleika clapped her hands. 'Well done, Eidred, my dear,' she said. 'Despite my son's discouraging advice, you found him the potion that demystifies Dream Sphere visits.'

Eidred, having taken a sip, blinked at him. 'Adahmos!' she said. 'I remember everything! We visited Orahney who is now living in the Dream Sphere. She told us we would not sleep for a century as this is only reserved for Gold's Kin.'

'How pleased I am, Beauty, to hear you recall.' Pieter gazed down at their daughter as Eidred gathered her up in her arms.

Eidred continued. 'You and I and Lunara are of silver. We are not restricted to this spell! Oh, and she said that she will be an elf in her next life.'

'And I am beginning to suspect who it is she will be,' said Pieter.

'Oh, beloved! Do you really believe it possible? Do you think Orahney is also Maleika?'

'I do. I believe my mother was being visited by herself when my birth was prophesied. We do that on occasion in the Dream Sphere. We journey to future lives.'

Maleika, watching this scenario in awe, now dabbed at a tear of joy. 'Yes, Pieter,' she whispered. 'It is true I was the autumn faerie in my former existence.'

'And she wishes us to flee Norwegia,' Pieter reminded.

'How wise of me,' Maleika said with satisfaction, 'although I cannot remember having ever advised it. I recall very little of my Orahney life.'

Pieter stood, helped Eidred to her feet, then clapped his hands three times. '*Sluken,*' he called. 'We summon you now, for we require your assistance!'

They both fixed their gaze upon Orahney's dwelling at the west of the royal grounds. From the doorway burst the dragon in all his sparkling grandeur.

'Croydee's lost friend,' said Maleika, dabbing at more tears.

The dragon lolloped across to them. After embracing the creature and patting him, Pieter announced, 'Orahney says you are prepared to transport us to the Land of Mu.'

'Indeed,' said the dragon, bowing his head. 'I have known of this for quite some time.'

A flash of light engulfed the dragon.

Eidred, clutching Lunara tightly, stepped back and squealed.

When the dazzling beams faded, Sluken stood before them as a giant dragon. His head was now as high as the loftiest of the Grudellan Palace's spires. 'Princess,' said Sluken in a tremendous voice that echoed throughout the grounds, 'it has been predicted by Orahney that you will carry a crystal with you on this day.'

Eidred reached under the pillow of Lunara's basket and held up a broken gem. Maleika recognised this to be a fragment of the godmother-wand that she'd hidden in Eidred's crib so long ago. 'Lunara was fretting earlier today, poor little creature. Restless she was, and tearful! Once I placed the crystal in her basket, all vexation disappeared.'

'This crystal will enable me to transport you,' Sluken told her. 'It will lend me the power to fly you to that other land.'

Pieter was incredulous. 'All the way to the Land of Mu?'

'Impossible otherwise,' said the dragon. 'Crystals enable flight when wished upon. I shall conjure you onto my back.'

Eidred spoke. 'We thought only that you'd transport us instantly, Sluken.' Cautiously she added, 'Are you certain we'd be secure?'

Upon the prince and princess's agreement, Sluken magically elevated them to a hollow in his spine. They sat upon a flat bony ridge, which did very well in forming a seat. Maleika thought the two looked exceptionally tiny. The dragon then conjured up velvet-soft ropes that wound around their torsos in loose loops, and over and around Lunara's basket. 'To keep you safe,' he told them. He then confided that he had no further Kindness Merits. 'Although I doubt we will need enchantments now that we have the crystal to propel our flight.'

The dragon flapped his great wings. Eidred laughed as they rose into the air. 'Adahmos,' she said, nestling against Pieter. 'This is so very exciting! We are going on a journey to that faraway southern land.'

'An extraordinary adventure,' agreed Pieter. 'Hark!' He pointed to a hill below. 'I see Fripso!'

Beneath them was Karee's small son, bounding through buttercups with a group of other rabbits. Eidred waved to him ecstatically as Sluken glided over the palace gates. Pieter merely smiled down at the buoyant animal, eyes ashine with teary pride. When Fripso stood on his hind legs to acknowledge them, his newfound long-eared friends mirrored the action.

Maleika smiled at the sight of the dragon flying high over the farewelling rabbits and forest. His tapering tail flowed gracefully behind him. They sailed over Elysium and across an enormous beach where sand of pale lilac shimmered beneath a pensive moon. Sluken crossed the shore. They were now soaring swiftly over the ocean.

Some moments into their journey, Eidred's voice rose up in a troubled shriek.

Pieter said, 'Ye gods, what is this I see? Have you dropped something, Beauty?'

Maleika observed a sparkling flint, a small pink stone somersaulting towards the dark-green depths.

The dragon lurched from side to side.

Eidred peered over the edge of the dragon's back. 'My crystal,' she cried. 'My crystal!'

Sluken's great paws flailed clumsily.

'Are you all right, Sluken?' Pieter called.

'Not entirely,' said Sluken. 'The power of flight seems to have left me. We cannot soar this high without the gem.'

And then the dragon plummeted.

Eidred screamed.

Maleika viewed the scene in horror as Sluken tumbled towards the sea.

MATTHEW SAT WITH HIS HEAD IN HIS HANDS on the thirty-year-old couch. A tatty piece of furniture. A relic that didn't belong in this expendable world. A comfy concoction of beige and black corduroy, faded and frayed at the edges. Unfitting for this time, this place, this reality. No different to Matthew, really. Matthew and his newly acquired couch. Has-beens.

Fighting off lethargy, he drew in a deep breath, rose to his feet and took two steps across the grey carpet to the phone. This was something he could do at least, to make himself useful: access calls he might have missed when dozing in front of *Days of our Lives*.

None of the messages were new. He listened again to the old ones. Hearing once more Rosetta's warmly rich voice, and her increasing concern with each call, made him cringe at his own cruelty. How could he have lacked the courage to phone? He'd failed to explain why he couldn't continue the relationship.

'...Market isn't sounding healthy, Matthew. Hope the Fred M in your dream hasn't anything to do with the Freddie Mac/Fanny Mae collapse. Call me when you get the chance, hey? I'm relying on your expertise here...'

'...Do you need any help with your move?...'

'...Matthew, all I can think is you're wanting to break up with me. If that's the case then so be it, but please...'

He flicked the messages off. Right now he couldn't even begin to explain to her what had happened. Doing that had been relegated to the too-hard basket. Once he made proper sense of it all, he would attempt to put into words the bizarre occurrences that had reduced him to lolling about like a boat without a rudder.

Boats had played a part in the beginning of the end. He and Rosetta had gone on a lunch cruise. It was just another typical day with Rosetta, a typically perfect day in an untypically perfect romance. Untypical for him, anyway. She was all woman. His woman. He had never been so recklessly happy.

He'd handed over his credit card. Concern had flickered in her seductive eyes when the waiter discreetly informed him of the problem with his credit card. Declined! She offered to pay. He'd winced at the idea of having treated his new girlfriend to a sumptuous lunch that he hadn't been free to cover. From that moment on he'd sweated over going ashore. He had to refund her as soon as possible.

Up until then he'd been on Cloud Nine, the usual thing. He'd been content to soak up the sight of both Sydney Harbour on that calm spring day and Rosetta, radiant in a dress of deep brown, the garnet pendant he'd given her gleaming redly against the creamy-olive sheen of her skin.

And then the notice on the ATM. It had hit him like a slap. Rosetta had said sweet things to him. Told him not to worry. Took it all good-naturedly, and yet he'd felt like an absolute idiot.

On the way to the airport, he'd phoned his bank. 'Your credit card has been frozen I'm sorry,' said the customer service operator.

'Frozen? What do you mean by frozen?'

'You've maxed your limit.'

'Come on! My limit's a hundred grand!'

'As I said, you've maxed your limit.'

By the time he was at the airport waiting for Kirk to arrive back from his Great Barrier Reef trip, he was thunderous. How could they have got it so wrong? He would have understood if it were the debit card Kirk used for the office set-up, but this was in no way related.

A glitch at the bank perhaps? Never! A bank getting a computer glitch? Never!

He'd resolved to ask Kirk once he arrived if he'd had the same sort of trouble with this particular bank. A national or international crash was possible he supposed. There *had* been rumblings in the market.

He stared across the tarmac, angry and frustrated. If it were Monday he would have told Kirk to get a cab on the account, then he would have dashed across to his bank. But it was Sunday, *bloody* Sunday, and all taxis were on strike, the reason he'd offered to zip Kirk back to the inner-city apartment the Scotsman had been living in since arriving in Australia six weeks earlier.

His phone had rung. Glaring at the sky that paled where it met the horizon, he'd answered it.

His brother.

'Matt, I've got something urgent I have to tell you.'

'Yeah? What's up? Everything okay with the market?'

'It's not about the market.'

'The banks then? I didn't catch the news this morning. Rosetta and I—'

'God! I reckon I'm too late if you're thinking there's something happening with the banks. Where are you right now?'

'At the airport. To pick up Kirk.'

'You mean to tell me that Kirk's no longer in Sydney?'

'He's...coming back from Queensland.'

'No he's not.'

'Huh?'

'I can guarantee he's not coming back, Matt. And he sure as hell hasn't gone to Queensland.'

'Whaddya mean? He said he was—'

'What Kirk says and what he does are two different things. Now answer me this. Have you left him in charge of any money?'

'This doesn't sound good. What are you saying?'

'I've just found out a couple of guys he worked for were ripped off severely.'

'You're saying he's a con.'

'Not exactly. All his credentials were verified. He's above board in that sense. I've sent you an internet article I located a few minutes ago. He's a gambler. A "reformed" gambler. He squanders company money on stocks and shares.'

'You're telling me this guy's a thief?'

'Just promise me you'll put a stop on any cards you've given him.'

The reality of it all had gripped at Matthew's throat; had shaken him into a stupor; had caused him to wait for that damn plane even though he knew it was more likely than not, futile. He scanned each exiting passenger, just to make sure he hadn't missed an opportunity to confront the man who'd found a way to access his credit card and bank accounts, the man who'd ratcheted up his expenditure to an impossible amount. The man who, right now, at this moment, as Matthew sat inside a dingy flat, was causing him to feel worthless while the fraud squad went ahead with their investigations.

How could he have been so stupid? He mulled over his slack response to the friendly phone calls that had come, presumably, from the new office in the city that Kirk was setting up. For all Matthew knew, the last of those calls could've been from Bermuda. Why hadn't he been there to supervise Kirk? Why had he relied on the recommendation of his brother and others?

Why? How?

He'd been stupid. Stupidly in love. Stupidly confident that life was filled with good people. He'd thrown his usual caution to the balmy spring breeze; had been a total yes-man to Kirk's spending suggestions, too content to while away his afternoons and evenings with the woman he idolised. Too eager to focus on the promotion side of things: drumming up clients, meeting with former colleagues, doing stuff that could have been put off until after he'd visited the city each day to make sure Kirk was actioning all they'd agreed upon. Instead, he'd chosen to limit his CBD visits to Tuesdays and Fridays. Rosetta had sensed his idiocy. He realised that now. She'd tactfully questioned his impulsiveness on their way to Terrigal.

Terrigal! The memory was heart-constrictingly painful. They'd walked along the beach when the moon was silvering the sand. He'd quietly contemplated the years ahead. The stars smiling down on them were solitaire diamonds.

He frowned at the corduroy couch. The future? The future was bleak.

If it'd been only the embezzlement he had to worry about, he would have been able to explain it to Rosetta. He'd have to sink into further levels of perceived foolishness, of course, by admitting to being cheated, and he'd have to wait until those investigations were carried out, but at least he'd be prosperous enough to buy an engagement ring worthy of her. Eventually.

But then there'd been the crash.

The Global Financial Crisis had put the lid on all lofty notions of committed bliss. Now that he'd been brought to his knees financially, there was no way he could entertain the idea of dating anyone, let alone proposing to them.

And he'd thought the elf in the dream was benevolent.

Fred M. The elf had spelt out a word, a name that had rapidly dissolved. A few days later, Kirk had emailed him info on a

United States share company. The name of the company had virtually leapt off the monitor, was as prominent as a neon dollar-sign.

Friedman.

Kirk insisted it was good.

Matthew instantly put more than he ever had on this mortgage lending corporation. The elf had wanted to help him with finances. Here was the answer! Friedman. Fred M. It was too much of a co-incidence not to be right.

The elf had been wrong.

Friedman and three other Wall Street stocks had mercilessly plummeted. And then the whole house of cards. Matthew, perusing ensuing reports with incredulous eyes, had gone numb with disbelief. Bulls and bears! A downward swiper had wiped out *el toro*.

In desperation he'd phoned Conan Dalesford for some insight. The Alice Springs author hadn't been much help. He'd drawn a tarot card for Matthew and said that the Five of Cups signified looking back on what was lost and shunning remaining treasures. Told Matthew to 'wake up' which seemed rather down-putting, although it wasn't the first time he'd heard that advice. Back when Pieter made his introduction within a dream in the neighbourhood park, the same two words had been uttered.

'You see, our fuller senses are sleeping, son,' Dalesford had told him. 'You need to awaken from this collective amnesia.'

'So what's meant by "the fuller senses"? Do you mean I have to access my sixth sense?'

'Sixth, seventh and the rest of 'em! The Silvering will see us remembering who we are.'

And that had been the sum total of it. Dalesford had said a hurried goodbye, and Matthew had put down the phone, feeling far from enlightened by the advice.

A knock on the door.

'Yeah?'

A familiar female voice. 'Matthew, it's me.'

How did she know he was here, in Grant's former flat?

He'd been in a filthy mood when he ran into Grant the week before, outside the mall. Grant had been trying to tell him something about Bernadette. 'She wants to see you, Matt.'

'Why? Half my fortune not enough for her?'

'No it's not that at all...it's...*Mate!* You look bloody terrible.'

'Listen, Grant, I've gotta get going. The real estate agency closes at five. I've been embezzled, I've lost out on the crash, and I've nowhere to sleep. So unless you can direct me somewhere cheap and nasty...'

Grant had held up a set of keys. 'My flat.'

'I couldn't do that to you.'

'I'm not in there anymore. I moved out before the lease was up. Bernie and I...' His eyes slid away from Matthew. 'Actually I'll tell you about that some other time. Look, Matt. Sounds like you've been through hell. Take the keys. It's fully furnished.'

'Nah. Look I don't need...' Matthew exhaled forcefully.

'Rent's all paid up. I've left two weeks prior to the lease finishing. Take the keys. It'll give you some breathing space till you decide on where you're gonna go.'

Matthew had accepted the keys with reluctance. In a barely audible groan, he'd said, 'Thanks.'

'We wouldn't want you sleeping in Hyde Park with the winos,' Grant had said in a jokey chirp, and he'd tootled off to the hardware store.

'No,' Matthew had said bitterly. 'We wouldn't want that, would we?'

And now he was enduring sleepless nights, thanks to a vocal blue heeler—that got into everyone's rubbish—and unthinking, raucous neighbours who piled up his bins, to overflow, with their beer bottles.

The knocking persisted. 'You in there Matthew?'

'Yeah. Just a minute.'

He yanked open the ill-fitting door.

Bernadette in a pink-suit, an envelope in one hand. She was smiling, her face aglow with something he'd never seen on her before. She looked different. She looked happy. She looked differently happy. 'Hello, stranger,' she said. '*Gawd!* Look at you! You've gone a week without shaving. And you've lost weight! Someone like you can't afford to lose weight!'

'Good to see you, too, Bernadette.'

Bernadette giggled. 'Sorry, Mattie. Me and my bluntness! So are you going to let me in?'

Not bothering to hide his displeasure, he drifted away from the door and gestured, half-heartedly, to the couch.

She marched into the lounge room, placed the envelope on one of the unpainted chests of drawers and said in an amused voice, 'What about me?'

'What do you mean, what about you?' Hadn't he already given her an ample slab of his inheritance?

She bowed her head and pointed to the skirt of her lolly-bright suit. Her hair, no longer golden-red but blonde, fell forward in damp, jagged strands. 'Well, what I mean is, it's the pot calling the kettle black isn't it? What about me? I'm a complete mess! Mud all over my outfit! A truck came by just as I was crossing the road and—'

'A puddle flew up at you?'

'Yeah! Can you believe it?' Bernadette was shaking her head now, laughing at her misfortune. Bernadette experiencing any sort of inconvenience had never resulted in laughter. Was this Bernadette Weissler standing before him or a clone with the self-pity gene removed?

'What's more, I'm drenched,' she said shrugging one shoulder.

'It's raining out there, is it?'

'You didn't know?'

'Windowless lounge rooms are useful like that.'

'Ah yes, you're right. Grant's place is horribly devoid of light and air. I've got something really important to tell you. Grant told me he'd given you this place because you were in a bit of trouble. I...actually, Matthew, before we talk, could I ask a favour of you?'

'You've never been shy of it in the past.'

Bernadette ignored the biting remark. 'I'm on my way to Rotary, then I'm going straight to Laura's parent-teacher interview. Haven't got time to go home. Would you mind very much if I used your bathroom to clean up a bit?'

Sighing, Matthew said, 'Sure. There's a bar heater on the left-hand side if you need it.'

'Thank you. Do you have something I can change into while I'm waiting for the skirt to dry?'

'Use my robe if you want. It's on the inside of the door.'

'Thanks so much, Mattie. Appreciate this.'

Appreciate? Since when did Bernadette appreciate anything?

At the door, she paused, turned, and said in a tone that could almost be described as guilty, 'Um...Matthew...'

'Hm?'

'I know this'll sound tacky to you, but...er...I'm living with Grant now.'

'Well, well,' said Matthew blandly. 'Why am I not surprised?' She disappeared behind the bathroom door. Unable to resist, Matthew called out, 'It's obviously done you good, this latest bout of fickleness. You seem pretty upbeat for someone who's lost out in the GFC.'

The door snapped open. Bernadette and her bedraggled hair appeared round it. 'Lost out? What do you mean?'

'Well, the money I gave you was invested wasn't it? In superannuation and the like?'

Bernadette tilted her head in confusion. 'What's superannuation got to do with anything? And what's the GFC?'

'So you haven't heard about the crash! I'd be phoning your financial adviser if I were you. The news ain't gonna be pretty.'

'But Matthew! Why would I do that? I haven't *got* a financial adviser!'

'Whoever's handling your money then.'

'You mean, me?'

'You?' Matthew scratched his head. 'Where did you invest your fifty per cent? Stocks and shares? Bonds? Property?'

Bernadette blinked. 'I didn't invest in anything. I put it in the bank.'

'You mean you put it in a long-term deposit with one of the American finance companies.'

'No. I just put it in the bank.'

'In the bank I worked at?'

'Nuh-uh. Not an investment bank. Just a normal bank. In my savings account.'

'But four per-cent interest is abysmal!' Then again, how abysmal was dealing in the share market at a time like that?

She ducked back into the bathroom.

'Jeezers,' Matthew said under his breath. 'Where's the justice in that?'

Bernadette, after having feigned devotion throughout their five years together, had got her lawyer to insist on no less than half of everything he owned. It was this that had driven Matthew to take a punt on Friedman. His hope of restoring his grandfather's legacy was wreathed in the remorse of having lost it in the first place. And now, due to sheer naivety, Bernadette had blithely kept her money safe. She'd been swanning around oblivious to the fact that since September the world economy would never be the same again.

And Matthew was standing on worn carpet, in an almost windowless flat, staring at a couch that wasn't even his own.

Where was the justice in that?

Note from the Publisher of *Epiphany*

This is where *Epiphany* begins. You are likely to remember it from the introductory scene in Book 1. Read on to discover where it leads...

ROSETTA flicked on the windscreen wipers, staring out at the procession of umbrellas and smudged reflections.

No green light for ages. Plenty of reds, though. She could have done with those before going out with him. Some sort of signal: *Slow down!...Stop!...Don't go any further!*

There were probably warnings everywhere, but she had blissfully waved off qualms. Saw every doubt to be a pebble on the Path of Perfection. The path had been strewn with spring flowers. It meandered past a river of champagne and disappeared into a forest smelling of campfires and hazelnuts...and a certain divine aftershave.

Wearily, she pictured that metaphoric trail, musing over where it might have led. She half-closed her eyes. Heard the rustle of feathers. Felt her heart drag to a stop. Imagined shouting the name of an eagle-winged royal guard. *'Storlem!'*

A bewitcher witnessing her lover turn to stone. She shook herself out of the reverie. 'Why would I do that? Why would I imagine I'm a character in the book?'

It wasn't just any book of course. It was Lillibridge's book, and she knew it wasn't fiction. Empathising with characters was fine at Friday Fortnight meetings, but a random flare of sounds, feelings and images while steering through a heavy September downpour wasn't altogether useful. Not that she had much say in it. The mystique of a hidden ancient history never failed to entice...and what made everything even more intriguing was Conan Dalesford's claim. He was adamant the souls of Lillibridge's 'characters' lived on in this current timeframe.

Rosetta knew she would never have been any of those sprites in a former life. Sure, her Odetta Ryland birth name contained all the letters in *Orahney*, but her 'o' and 'r' weren't side by side. That decided it. Anyone in the sea people's story, which Lucetta related to Edward two-hundred odd years ago, was said to have that sequence.

Matthew on the other hand...Rosetta exhaled sharply. What did it matter that Storlem's name was a lexigram of *Matthew Porter Weissler?* She'd never mentioned it to him; it all sounded so crazy! Her secret theory was Matthew having lived the life of an autumn faerie's suitor, the Gold's Kin courtier silvered by heart-crystals, a brown-winged angel guarding the gates by the thorn thicket.

The book fascinated him. He had an affinity with eagles. Almost laughable. Way too ridiculous, and yet...in one of his dreams he'd had feathered wings. In another he'd conversed with Pieter of the Brumlynds, and that was before knowing anything about *Our True Ancient History*.

The green blinked on dubiously, a squashy emerald ripple through the rain-smeared windscreen.

Four weeks now.

Four weeks of falling into a bottomless pit of despair. Four weeks of treadmilling like a mouse on a wheel and abandoning the apartment in a fevered rush once Izzie left for school. Solitude equalled torment. She couldn't bear being at home with only her grief for company.

She'd kept herself exhaustingly busy. Took a course in remedial massage at the Neighbourhood Centre and got scarily absorbed in her law degree, having even drummed up a Wednesday afternoon study group with eight fellow students. She'd kept strict tabs on everything the business consultant did towards glamorising the Crystal Consciousness store and made a point of visiting at least one of her friends daily.

Earlier that afternoon, when Izzie left to catch a Sunday matinee with a couple of schoolmates, she paced the living room, seized by a scorching need to escape. There was no-one she could realistically arrange to see. She'd already called in on book-club buddies Eadie, Royston and Lena twice during the week. If she cropped up any more they'd be boarding up their doors. A crate of DVDs had then caught her eye, an oversupply of bad comedies bound for the bin. In a rush of inspiration she'd whispered, 'Grant!'

And now she was on her way to Grant Belfield's, hoping he'd be home. It'd be good to see her former neighbour again.

She surged the car forward, peering through the spattering torrent. A sign sailed past.

Welcome to the suburb of Punchbowl

'My old stomping ground.' Remembering the barking blue heeler, overflowing garbage and encounter with a psycho intruder, she breathed a contented sigh. 'Glad I'm not still there.'

She leaned against the soft seat of her new car, the same model and colour as Craig Delorey's, and switched on the stereo. A plaintive voice rang out in impressive trills, lamenting the loss of trust. Feeling her heart start to weep, she changed the station. 'Gimme,' a familiar voice screamed. 'More. More. *Moooo-wah! Moomoomoomoo-moomomomoomoo.'* She gritted her teeth. The angry tones never ceased to remind her of a certain someone's obsession with Doctor Cyanide songs. 'Put a sock in it, Doc.'

She again changed the station. *'...Stock market crash is wreaking havoc on thousands of lives,'* a reporter blared. 'Hasn't wreaked havoc on mine,' she reasoned, then felt instantly ashamed of her complacency. She'd managed to retain all she had, but how many in the world hadn't? Poor old Craig was one such example. The punishing effects of a crisis experts were referring to as 'the GFC' had cost him a quarter of his superannuation. 'I'm not too worried,' he'd told her. 'These gems are gonna bring me good luck, and my salary will be taken care of. I'm stoked you're distributing them through Crystal Consciousness, Rosetta.'

She veered into her former street and slowed to a stop. The rain had eased. She reached for her maroon and silver umbrella, the one Eadie talked her into buying, the one Matthew always referred to, in his irresistible English way, as a *brolly*. 'Got your brolly, beautiful?' he'd say. She became aware of the leaden ache of sorrow. Why couldn't she stop remembering?

Retrieving the crate from the boot, she brushed a strand of dark hair away from her line of vision, a side-effect of keeping it long, and clunked down the concrete path. She passed the outdoor laundry, now brightened with roughly painted daisies. The exterior looked small. Friendly. Safe. For a while it had been a symbol of doom. The prowler, someone who would present himself to her further along in a far more appealing form, still lurked in dreams that descended into nightmares.

At Grant's door, she knocked while hugging the crate with one arm.

The door opened.

Matthew!

Her arms weakened. She tightened her hold on the crate.

Matthew was staring out at her.

His eyes, the eyes she loved, grew wide with shock. He was wearing an old T-shirt that contracted into wrinkles across his broad chest. Ragged shorts, bare feet. Unshaven. Gorgeous as ever, and yet something was missing. His dynamism? Slight hollows had formed beneath his cheekbones. He looked older somehow. Defeated.

Why here? Why was he here in Punchbowl?

The crate dragged heavily on her elbows. Not knowing what else to do, she shoved it clumsily across to him. 'For Grant,' she said.

Saying nothing, he accepted the crate. Stood holding it absently. His lips moved as though to utter something. He stared at her some more.

Her pulse was pounding. The skin at the nape of her neck prickled with perspiration. The sight of him was throwing her into a whirlpool of feelings. Disbelief. Elation. Fury. Outweighing all else was curiosity. Wanting to know why. Why had he gone? Why hadn't he loved her in return? What was he doing opening Grant's door?

He glanced back into the flat. 'Er...I'll...I'll join you there on the landing,' he said. He placed the crate on Grant's worn kitchen bench, and she noticed from the doorway that he was leaner than before.

She surveyed the living room in search of Grant. Everything about the flat was brown or grey. Plastic timber-look slats lined one of the walls. A corduroy couch made up of mediocre neutrals sat grumpily against the corner. The threadbare carpet was the dreary shade of an overcast sea.

Matthew, smiling now, stepped onto the landing. 'I'll get you a tea,' he said in words that tripped over themselves. 'Wou-would you like a tea, or...? Ah no. It's raining.' He swung round and looked back into the flat again as though concerned his caller would see something she shouldn't. 'Um...well, why don't you come in then? Come in and—'

'I just dropped by to give Grant some old comedy DVDs. If he's not there I'll...' Reluctantly she added, '...call round some other time.' A part of her wanted to stay right there with Matthew. A part of her hoped he would repeat the offer of stepping inside, that Grant would stay out long enough for Matthew to give a reason for having fled from her. She turned.

'Rosetta, don't go.' Matthew's voice had taken on a quiet urgency. He gestured for her to enter. 'Stay. Please. Just for a little while. Grant doesn't live here anymore. I'm... looking after things for him. Please come in.'

Thankful to remain with him a few moments more, she drifted into the grey and brown grimness. Still dazed at having encountered Matthew, she followed him to the couch and allowed herself to sink into it. She continued to sink.

'Sorry about the seat,' he said. 'It doesn't take kindly to being sat on.' She watched as he perched on the armrest. Turning to her, he smacked his hands together. 'Tea then? I don't think I have any of that cocoa you love.'

Cocoa? That she loved? So he still remembered things about her. Hadn't completely blanked out their time together. Resentment welled up like a simmering ocean. 'No thank you, Matthew.' Her voice was gravelly with tension.

He sank into the couch alongside her, so near that if she were to lean to the right, her elbow would connect with his. She gazed at Matthew, thoroughly amazed that she was in the same room after the certainty of never hearing from him again. Would he make an attempt to explain? Or were they just going to sit there on Grant's sinking couch? Two pebbles swallowed by quicksand.

Matthew drew in a laboured breath. 'You have every reason to hate me, Rosetta,' he said. 'I can't even begin to say how sorry I am.'

She turned to him. His head was bowed, and his eyes were locked on the floor. 'Try,' she said.

Matthew rubbed his forehead, pushed a hand through his hair and groaned. 'I've lost out on the GFC,' he said, 'and I've been embezzled. That new employee of mine turned out to be shifty.'

She straightened. Matthew's confession sounded promisingly like some sort of reason. 'Matthew, that's terrible,' she said. Unable to resist a sarcastic swipe, she added, 'Did anyone run away from you? Did anyone ignore all your calls?'

'I've been a bastard to you.'

She watched his fist thud down on the coffee table.

'There's no denying that. I can't explain what happened. The money disappeared, and I ran. Panic, I guess.'

'Are you saying that's why you turned your back on me, Matthew? Panic over money?'

His eyes, the eyes she would adore for eternity, met hers in recognition. He conceded with a nod. 'I didn't know how to face you.'

'Surely you didn't think I'd be upset! There's no way—'

'No, no. Not at all. I just...I'm just...not capable of dating anyone now that I've failed. I'm a financial liability, Rosetta.' He was covering his eyes now. 'There,' he said grimly. 'I've said it.'

'But how can that change anything?' She battled the urge to fling her arms around him. 'Money isn't important.'

Matthew gave her a sceptical side-glance.

'I'm serious, Matthew. It's awful you feel this way! I've never placed importance on who has what. You could be lying in the gutter. Drunk and destitute...with scraggly Doctor Cyanide hair, and I'd—'

'Never,' Matthew said. 'Never will you find me in that state. It's short back and sides or nothing.' His face broke into a slow grin.

She grinned along with him, remembering the silly jokes they'd shared. 'But whatever happens I'd still...' She replaced that risky word 'love' with something milder. 'I'd still *like* you.'

Matthew remained unconvinced.

'So if that's all it is, don't worry about a thing. I'll lend you whatever you need. I wouldn't care one iota, in fact, if you kept it. And if you need somewhere to live...' She eyed the peeling paint on the ceiling. '...You can stay in the investment property. It's over in Wollstonecraft.'

'Thanks for the offer.' His answer was abrupt. 'But I couldn't. These issues are mine alone to resolve.'

A sudden glimpse flew to her, of how Matthew saw himself: a benefactor devoted to lavishing those he valued with his own quiet brand of generosity. In the short time she'd known him, he'd pick up the tab in one subtle sweep before anyone at their table had time to protest. Money was his identity. The stately home with its elegant *Sound-of-Music* staircase. The harbourside penthouse and clump of acreages he'd mentioned in passing.

'Have you always been well-off?' she asked.

'Until now, yes,' he said. 'I mean, no. I had a pretty modest up-bringing. It was the inheritance at twenty-three that changed everything.'

'Matthew, you're still the person you were before you turned twenty-three and bought all those properties. You don't need any inheritance to—'

'Yeah, I know.' He brushed the words off as though he hadn't heard them. 'So, Rosetta, what have you been up to since we last spoke? How's the Crystal Consciousness venture going?'

'Good! Really good.'

'Keep a close eye on that business consultant of yours, won't you. If my experience is anything to go by, you're better off on your own.'

'He seems okay so far,' she told him. 'But I am keeping a close eye.'

He was turned three-quarters on, watching her. 'You look differ-ent,' he said at last.

Had he noticed the recent weight loss? She would never be slender of course. Waifish limbs and narrow ribcages were exclusive to the likes of Lena and Matthew's ex Dette and and the gymnast who ensnared Izzie's father. 'Different in a good way?'

'Don't know.'

Hopeful he'd realise the difference was her trimmer figure, she rose from the couch—fighting its determination to hold her captive—and spun herself into a twirl by the coffee table. 'Notice anything?'

'No.' Matthew's voice had lost much of its power. He was speaking in melancholy tones. 'Still beautiful.' He grinned at her, sheepish.

She found herself smiling back. 'Can you see that I'm not so bulky?'

'No,' he said.

Disappointed, she shrugged.

'You were no such thing. You were perfect.'

Heartened by the nostalgia in his tone, she turned and made the precarious weave between a chest of drawers and the coffee table, back towards Grant's couch. Matthew's next words were barely audible.

She asked him to repeat them.

'Your curves,' he said. 'Your curves are smaller.'

She sat down again. The couch encompassed her in a corduroy clinch.

'I've just realised what the difference is,' Matthew said. 'Your smile isn't big anymore. My actions have upset you. I'm so, so, sorry.'

He reached out then and caught up her hand. A feeling of breathlessness overcame her. The familiar warmth of the hand she loved enclosed her in a dizzy blend of desire and relief. She wanted to nestle into him, to kiss his beautiful lips, to throw her arms around his shoulders and never let him go. He was showing her affection! He was looking at her as though he still cared.

Perhaps this wasn't where the story ended. Perhaps she and Matthew did belong together after all. Perhaps Matthew was the king on the card that Molly Carr hid under a pillow. Molly's words echoed back: *It could be any day. Any day or night. You might be hurrying down the street...and there he'll be.*

Hurrying after a disappearing rabbit. Stopping Matthew in the street, the middle of Ashbury Avenue. For some inexplicable reason, they'd been fated to meet.

'Rosetta,' Matthew said softly.

'Yes?'

His thumb was sliding across her fingernails.

She closed her eyes, savouring the champagne happiness that washed over her in whirly tingles. King of Hearts. Her very own Green-Eyed Guy.

She would tell him everything. About how she'd been a struggling shop assistant and novice fortune teller, that she'd avoided giving him one of her flimsy home-made business cards for fear of being viewed as 'unsuccessful'. She would tell him she'd worked as a cleaner at his offices. Status was just illusory. What they believed to be their rights to this world had threatened to keep them apart.

A thump stirred the silence.

She opened her eyes—drowsily—emerging from another world.

Matthew released her hand and turned.

She followed his gaze to a door off the lounge room, a door that was creaking open.

She rose to her feet unbelievingly. Stared at Matthew aghast. Behind the door was her very worst fear.

'Rosetta...' Matthew said. 'I...was just about to say.'

SICKNESS rose in her stomach like a wave. Rosetta glanced back at the woman. Dette. Oh God. He was back with Bernadette.

In a blur she saw only the front door as she hurtled towards it, then the balcony ledge where raindrops dripped down it like tears, the wet concrete of stairs, the laundry's roughly painted daisies that mocked her with their cheery brashness...heard, against the drumming of her heart, her footsteps down the path...the clap of the car door as she closed it behind her.

Sobs tore through her lungs. She wept onto the steering wheel. Cried hysterically until she shook.

A phone rang faintly. Her phone. She could see it on the passenger seat, shuddering with each bleat. Lit up across the screen was the name of a friend.

Royston.

Royston! She needed to speak to Royston.

At the trembling of her voice, Royston's tone grew concerned. 'Are you okay?' he asked. 'You sound a bit weepy.'

She couldn't bring herself to talk about it. 'Just a bad day,' she said, her voice cracking with despair.

'Sorry to hear it. So! Are you right for the poetry night tonight?'

The last place she wanted to go: somewhere that would remind her of Matthew. 'Yes,' she said, willing herself to be strong. 'I'll see you there at seven.'

The sound of hastened footsteps caused her to jump. She checked the rear-vision mirror. Saw Matthew sprinting towards the car. He was calling out her name.

She could not let him see her like this. He must never know how much he'd hurt her.

'Thanks, Royston.' Her entire body felt numb. 'Glad you reminded me. Looking forward to it.' She closed off her phone and slid the key into the ignition.

Matthew was tapping against her window, leaning forward to peer in. She started up the motor, thankful the raindrops were masking her misery. They were scattered across the glass as though thrown without care. Discarded solitaire diamonds. An emblem of broken hope.

She stepped on the accelerator in warning to Matthew to step aside. Matthew's fist punched downwards as he moved away.

The rain pelted furiously. Lurching into the traffic, she glimpsed through her tears a small, dejected image in the rear-vision mirror. Matthew calling out to her, waving his arms in the air like a frantic Grand Prix flagman.

The image became smaller...and then smaller.

He was no more than a dot now. A grain of nothingness that she vowed to forget.

He was no-one. Going out with Matthew had never happened.

It had been nothing.

Nothing worth remembering.

She would no longer grieve for an illusion. She would get on with her life. And she would make an overdue pact with herself, a vow she should have made after Izzie's father had fled. To never love anyone that deeply again.

Chapter Seven

MATTHEW GLARED AT THE UPTURNED coffee table. 'It's all your fault,' he said to it.

Moments before, Rosetta had flitted away from him. Before he had time to say anything, she'd disappeared out of the door.

He'd gone to leap from the couch. It had clung to him, pulling him back to its cushioned depths. Fighting against the deceptively cosy force, he'd found his feet. Went to dash around the coffee table and collided with it instead. The coffee table had somersaulted forward and morphed into a frustrating obstacle to pursuing Rosetta, to clasping her in his arms and assuring her that he and Bernadette weren't together, that he could never leave her, let alone leave her for anyone else.

He'd been too late. She'd driven away before he'd caught up.

His heart felt like it had suffered a massive injury. What was she to think, anyway? He was painfully aware of his appalling neglect during the financial meltdown. Today he'd seen mistrust in her beautiful dark eyes, and he'd regretted every moment of his month-long standstill. Days had fallen into weeks, and he'd been too ashamed to phone. Shame. The shame of being ripped off, despite all his financial expertise, the shame of losing what he'd prided himself on. He felt out-of-control, emasculated even, deeply disempowered by his pitiful stupidity. Who was he if he wasn't wealthy?

A little voice murmured, 'I'll go now, Matthew.' He looked up. Bernadette back in her pink suit. He'd forgotten she was there. 'My skirt's dried now. Thanks for the loan of your heater and robe.' She crept past him, shoulders slouched meekly. 'Sorry about...' she stopped. Nodded towards the open door, the door Rosetta had escaped through. Astoundingly, the gesture did not appear to be a product of sarcasm. 'It'll work out, Mattie. I know it will.' She smiled. Her eyes softened with sympathy. 'I had something I wanted to tell you, but this isn't the time. I'll speak to you about it another day, okay? Bye-bye then.'

Now seated on the dipping lounge suite, engulfed awkwardly in its possessive hold, he watched her leave, realising—only after—that he hadn't said anything in return.

If Bernadette hadn't been there...No. It had been Matthew's responsibility to warn Rosetta. Several times in their short conversation he'd attempted to alert her to Dette's unexpected visit. Just as he'd begun on his awkward explanation, the bathroom door had bumped open.

And now, he was there again with his head in his hands, regrets floating down on him like ash from the aftermath of a particularly destructive bushfire. Seeing her again was an agony. Hope and elation weighed down with remorse.

He tried phoning again. Her mobile was switched off.

A knock on the door. Rosetta?

Matthew struggled to his feet. 'Yep.' Again he rushed towards the door. 'Won't be a sec.' Again he tripped over that bastard of a coffee table. Rosetta was back! She'd thought it over and was back to ask what he'd wanted to tell her.

He straightened his T-shirt and flung the door open.

It wasn't her.

His heart heaved. He frowned at the bloke before him, a nondescript individual. Medium build, neatly dressed, mouth stretched into a polite smile.

Spotting a black book in the visitor's hand, Matthew clutched the door-handle and said, 'I'm a Buddhist,' a trick Rosetta had passed on to him. Closing the door, he added, 'Thanks anyway.'

The door bounced back. Matthew looked down to see the shining leather of the caller's boot.

The owner of the boot responded with a laugh. 'That's news to me. You weren't a Buddhist when *I* knew you.'

Matthew's eyes snapped up. He took in the face of the religion peddler. Pale. Hair neither dark nor fair, a similar colour to his own. The eyes looked familiar though. The smile even more so. Matthew knew that smile. He did. Where did he know this guy from?

'I'd better reintroduce myself.' The guy extended his hand. 'Adam Harrow. I used to work with you.'

LX

Gazing anxiously at the scene before her, Maleika studied the wavelets of silver and gold. A dragon, two parents and an infant, stranded in the darkness on an enormous floating pillow! How would they escape such worrying circumstances?

'Your magic, Adahmos,' Eidred had told him as they fell. 'You have plenty of Kindness Merits left!'

Pieter, probably having forgotten his capabilities after living so long without resorting to them, had instantly created a solid cloud upon the water to cushion Sluken's fall.

Once they had landed onto the rapidly conjured softness, Eidred said in a wail, 'We shall never travel to the Land of Mu now. I stupidly forgot to tuck the crystal in Lunara's basket! It caught in the frill of my sleeve!'

Pieter looked dubiously at the sea. 'I will dive in,' he said, 'although it's doubtful I'll find it. I am yet to learn to swim well. If only I'd been born a water sprite.'

Maleika cupped her hand over her mouth. 'Pieter was never drawn to the water,' she told Alcor. 'I should have insisted Zhippe and Carlonn teach him to swim.'

Eidred placed a hand on her prince's arm. 'But what about your magic, Adahmos? Surely you can command the crystal out of the water.'

Pieter shook his head. 'I attempted this a moment ago, beloved. Sadly, creating the cloud summoned up all of my allocated magic for today. My Kindness Merits are now depleted.'

Maleika looked away from the scene. Shaking her head, she said, 'I know for certain, Alcor, that these two and their daughter go to the land of Mu. You have already told me this. How do they get there though? Looking for the crystal might well be futile.'

Bubbles broke the sea's surface. A head popped out from the water. Maleika took in a smiling face, hair like moss and eyes the colour of the water beneath. The creature raised its kelp-entwined webbed hand and waved to the landed dragon.

Maleika clasped her hands together. 'Ye gods, it's a merman!'

Another head popped up. A mane of blue-green hair framed the second sprite's face. 'And a mermaid as well,' Alcor observed.

Pieter promptly explained their plight. Within minutes, the mermaid had dipped back into the water to search for the fallen gem.

The mermaid emerged from the depths, announced with apology that she'd failed to locate the crystal and returned to her underwater haven.

The merman eyed them jovially.

Maleika could see that Pieter and Eidred were attempting to hide their misery over the crystal.

'So you are off to the Land of Mu, you say. I have always wanted to visit there. One day I will, I suppose.'

The mermaid emerged once more.

'"Twas silly of us,' Eidred said to the mermaid, 'expecting you to find such a tiny fleck. But thank you all the same for your efforts.'

The mermaid held her hand aloft. The precious pink stone was clasped in her fist.

Eidred gave a gleeful shriek and embraced a delighted Pieter.

'Well done,' Pieter said. 'Well done!'

The gem, at first glance, appeared to be lodged in a scrap of fishermen's net. On closer inspection of the scene, Maleika noted its attachment to a patch of flowery lace: a remnant of Eidred's torn sleeve. Moonlight danced over water droplets upon the crystal, lending its facets a twinkling lustre.

'You are most clever, madam,' said Sluken. Pieter and Eidred agreed wholeheartedly.

'I have never met any merfolk before,' Eidred said, 'although my devic husband has told me many stories of their compassion.'

The mermaid handed the gem to her companion. The merman threw the find to Pieter who immediately presented it to his wife.

Sluken spoke then. 'It is the gem from an autumn faerie's wand. If I had more Kindness Merits at my disposal, I would immediately turn that gem into an item of jewellery. The lady here could then travel without concern. 'Tis wrong to expect either of these young parents to keep the crystal from slipping. Caring for the child takes precedence.'

'Jewellery is something we can do,' said the mermaid. 'We would certainly have enough Kindness Merits between us to carry that out.'

The mermaid and merman clasped hands ceremoniously, closed their eyes and then sang. Their song caused Eidred to weep, so celestial were the tones.

'Beauty, look!' Pieter was visibly overjoyed. 'The crystal now suspends from your neck!'

Eidred glanced down. 'Why, so it does!' The pink shard of wand had been altered into a smooth, glossy oval. The curling filigree of Eidred's sleeve had solidified, its texture having changed from fine looped strands of cream-coloured silk to ornamental metal that encased and framed the crystal, and was neither gold nor silver entirely, yet displayed the qualities of both.

'A metal unknown in today's world,' the merman told them proudly. 'One day it will be known as "moon gold" or "sun silver". We have made it everlasting. It will survive many thousands of years.'

After many cries of gratitude from Pieter and Eidred, the dragon, now restored to flight with the crystalline power of Eidred's new pendant, rose swiftly into the deep, dark sky.

Maleika felt wistful when the scene before her faded. They would be safe in Mu with its native devic peoples and unrestricted connection to the Dream Sphere. Their new home, a land far from Norwegia, promised them the freedom to dream without fear.

The scene was soon to dissolve.

All Maleika could see now was a transparent Sluken ascending above the ocean.

Higher and higher the dragon rose, jewel-like scales glistening in the starlight. His elongated form, from which all colours of the spectrum shone, undulated with serpentine grace, a rippling ribbon of rainbows bound for that southern land.

AND HEREWITH CONCLUDES
THE SEA PEOPLE'S TALE OF
OUR TRUE ANCIENT HISTORY!

❧❈❧

Reverend Edward Lillibridge

MATTHEW, STANDING AT THE open door, shook his head. Laughed a little. To the stranger before him, he said, 'Are you for real? Adam Harrow's dead!' He gripped the door-handle once more. 'Next time you want to impersonate a bloke, try choosing one who's alive.'

'So you're saying you don't recognise me, Weissler.'

How could the stranger possibly know him by name? Matthew opened his mouth to ask this joker what he was up to and closed it again.

The smile. The shape of the features. The height. Couldn't be. Wasn't.

No. Harrow was dead. What was wrong with this guy? Why would anyone impersonate a jerk like Harrow?

'Look, Weissler, I understand your reaction, but I'm not impersonating anyone. Why would anyone impersonate a jerk like me?' The visitor smiled wryly. 'I'm not a fake. Not anymore.' He pointed to himself. 'Remember the blond hair, green eyes, tanned skin? All fake.'

'And your death,' Matthew said, angry now. 'You faked that too?' He narrowed his eyes to scrutinise the structure of the visitor's face. Observed once again the eyes. They were the colour of a sky before rain.

'The diagnosis was correct. My death was real. But something inexplicable happened.'

Something inexplicable drawing Harrow back from death? Impossible.

Matthew watched him cautiously. The way the guy expressed himself...it was undeniably earnest. Could this be true? Could it really be Harrow? The voice sure sounded the same. 'So what's your story?' he said, careful not to appear too agreeable.

'It's hard to explain. I revived in the ambulance.'

The paramedics must have kept working on him. A near-death experience. It was known to happen. Matthew eyed the black book. 'So now you're here to tell me you've found God.'

A gap of silence stretched between them. At last the visitor said, 'I guess you *could* say that, but no, that's not why I'm here. I've come to apologise.'

Harrow apologising? Never! Matthew folded his arms. 'Harrow wouldn't knock on my door.'

'What if I haven't just changed my appearance?'

'Whaddya mean?'

'What if I'm a different person now? I've had a near death experience, Matthew. I'll never be the same again.' His voice conveyed emotion. Nothing like Harrow. 'And there's something very important I have to tell you.'

'Yeah?' Matthew was wary. 'And what's that?'

'I was your son.'

'You were my *what?*'

'I was your son.'

Matthew snorted. Just his luck to open the door to a lunatic. 'Are you warped or what? You stand here telling me you've died and come to life, and now you're trying to tell me you're my *son? This isn't* Days of our Lives, *mate.*' He half-closed the door. 'You don't need to see me, you need to see a psychiatrist.'

'Was,' said the visitor. 'I *was* your son. Let me ask you something.' He held up the black book. 'Do you believe in reincarnation?'

The book's gold embossed title floated before Matthew's gaze. Not The Bible. A novel.

'Our True Ancient History,' said Harrow.

Matthew started. Felt the air rush out of his lungs. At last he found his voice. It was little more than a croaky whisper. 'Perhaps,' he said, 'you'd better come in.'

'OKAY HARROW,' Matthew said, taking a seat opposite at the kitchen table. 'What's your story? When did you read *Our True Ancient History?*'

'Only a couple of months ago. A guy named Conan Dalesford recommended it.'

'Dalesford!'

'You know of him?'

'Alice Springs alpaca farmer. Author of *Thoughts on Tomorrow's Tycoon War*. I would have thought Rosetta—'

'Nope, she never told me about the book. I contacted the guy after stumbling across Rosetta's website. A bit of a surprise to find someone I recently dated happened to dabble a bit in the subject.'

'An understatement,' Matthew said. 'She's done a really impressive amount of research, and she's been responsible for renewed interest in the book worldwide. I wouldn't call that dabbling.'

'No, not at all.' Harrow was apologetic. 'Wrong choice of words. Her website's intriguing. I'm full of admiration for what she's done. And the book itself...ah, the book!'

'So what's that got to do with you going on about being my...' Did he really have to say this? '...My son? Or was that just a ruse to get in the door?'

'It's complicated.' Harrow studied the laminex of the flat's dining table, appearing to plan his words. 'In a past life I was indeed your son. I've got to tell you my story. I have a special connection with Lillibridge's work.' Hands shaking slightly, he plucked the book up from the table, opened it, closed it, then put it down again. 'Er...this might sound pretty strange to you, especially if you don't believe in reincarnation, but...the truth is...I have reason to believe that I wrote *Our True Ancient History* in 1771.'

Unable to speak, Matthew gaped at him.

'It's hard to believe, I know. But I've been told that I'm the reincarnation of Reverend Edward Lillibridge.'

'That's ridiculous!' Fury welled up in Matthew's throat. His job, his wife, and now this. Harrow and his parasitic nature. The creep didn't believe in achieving anything on his own; was content to rely on sapping the painstaking work of others. *Our True Ancient History*: a sacred text cheapened by a sleazy cheat. 'You say you're not fake any-more,' Matthew said, voice gravelling with irritation, 'yet you're still trying to pose as something you're not. I hope you realise there's no accolade for having been "the reincarnation" of Lillibridge.' Sarcastically he added, 'You won't be paid royalties,' although knowing Harrow, the media was probably already lined up. 'This claim you're making. It's totally crazy.'

His own words echoed back at him. The level of anger Harrow's statement evoked was surprising. What was it that prompted this sudden territorialism? An elusive memory? Nostalgia? A deep affinity with Lillibridge's words? Could it be possible he'd taken Harriet's assertion seriously that night outside the English pub? *Totally crazy.*

'Look, I know it's hard to believe, Weissler, but I'm for real.'

Matthew rose to his feet. He'd had enough.

'Before you throw me out, I want you to hear my story.' Harrow gestured with his head for Matthew to sit down. 'Mate. Please. Listen to what I have to say. There's a lot to do with me that actually involves you.'

Swayed by the odd brand of sincerity in Harrow's voice, Matthew plonked back into his seat. The least he could do, he supposed, was allow the man to elaborate.

'I overdosed,' Harrow began.'Not that I meant to. Passing out happened a lot. I'd been on smack for fourteen years.'

'Explains some of the behaviour.'

'Explains but doesn't excuse. I hated myself for it. I was out of control, fevered and frenzied, like something was taking me over. When I'd go unconscious, whole hours would pass before I'd gain a sense of who I was. And then I'd kind of wake out of my daze to find myself all in black. Claws included.'

'Gruesome.' The clothing and claws sounded similar to the garb Harrow wore for his Doctor Cyanide tributes, at the bank's crazy charity nights.

'Gruesome's too kind. But I *became* that ghoul. When I overdosed that day, I found myself floating up near the ceiling of my house. I was thinking: Why can't I stay here and leave this pathetic world? And then I noticed Dette was beside me. I was there on my own as far as I knew, and I'd never expected to see her again.' Harrow was staring blankly ahead. 'I remember drifting back into consciousness, seeing her standing there with a gun, and then a gripping feeling took hold of my chest.' His words dwindled.

'Go on.'

'I rose up in the air again, looked down, and saw Dette getting distraught. She was screaming out to me. I told her I was fine. I called to her that I just needed to come down from the ceiling, but for all my reassurance, she kept yelling at me to answer, and then she ran around hysterically, sobbing and crying out my name.'

Feeling concern for Bernadette, Matthew pictured her as Harrow described, falling into a shivering heap on Adam Harrow's floor and shakily declaring she'd killed him.

'And I kept calling out: "But I'm not dead!"' Harrow related seeing Grant, 'a plain-clothes cop who had some authority with the other cops', and also Rosetta. 'I was hovering above them, mystified as to what they were doing in my house. I floated out to the terrace. That's when I saw you, Weissler. You of all people.' He directed a finger at Matthew. 'You were closing the door of your Jag, asking Rosetta what the cop car and ambulance were doing there, and I was thinking: *Finally I'll get my answer* and Rosetta said in this really sad voice that I'd died of a drug overdose.

'And then, I notice below, a covered corpse on a stretcher, and I realise that this must be me. I realise I'm a ghost.' He grinned, apparently conscious of how ridiculous it sounded. 'Even though I'd grown to loathe myself, even though I was intent on escaping my addictions and personality switches, I felt a sense of loss, like I'd failed to achieve anything significant.

'And so I'm there floating above my body as they're shovelling me into an ambulance, and I see a woman with long hair climb into the vehicle and press something small and shining against my ankle.'

'Rosetta?'

'Yup.'

Matthew doubted Rosetta would interfere with the paramedics' procedures. 'You sure about that?'

'Of course I'm sure. The woman in the ambulance was definitely Rosetta. Anyway, the next thing I know, there's this brilliant flash of light. The light is silver and quite blinding. Then I start to travel. I get this feeling of rushing through some kind of tunnel. I'm being propelled forward by...I don't know what.' He told Matthew that at the end of the tunnel was a light, more beautiful and far more dazzling than the silver one. 'And I always thought the life-after-death experience was a bit of a joke. A cliché, cos people's accounts of it tend to involve the same thing.'

'The tunnel and the light? I actually have heard of that.'

'But take it from me, Weissler. That's exactly what happens. I was clinically dead, but at the same time another part of me was very much alive.'

Harrow had sensed the light to be an angelic sort of being whose form was obscured by a luminous, far-reaching aura. The being made Harrow feel utterly secure. 'I'd never in my life felt so...' His voice mellowed. '...Well...*loved* I guess you could call it. The being's kindness was beyond description.'

He was shown the life he had lived and was advised not to judge himself when viewing it. 'It played out like a movie.'

'A movie with a thirty-three-year running-time?'

'It's beyond belief. Even though everything in my entire life was shown to me, the time it took to view must have been little more than a few minutes, but then, the place I'd gone to was free of time. Time just didn't seem to exist.'

The being then told Harrow he would see two former lives. The first life was difficult to observe because the person Harrow had been in this incarnation appeared to be twisted and dark. 'I was...and this will sound really weird to you, but, hey, what am I saying here that isn't weird? I was a kind of warlock; a sorcerer or something, and there was a king sitting above me, referring to me as "Rahwor". And behind this king was a mirror. I know this because I could see my reflection in front of the king's. And believe it or not, my appearance wasn't too far removed from Doctor Cyanide's.'

Matthew reviewed the impressions he'd had when he'd read about Rahwor. Oddly enough, the description of this character had always called up for him the unsavoury image of Harrow snarling 'Gimme' at the charity nights, but likening a dark sorcerer to a *badass* rocker like Doctor Cyanide probably wasn't uncommon amongst Lillibridge's readers.

'This king and I were discussing a woman I'd promised to pursue. The woman lived in the future and was threatening the plans of the empire in some way. I observed myself saying to him, "I shall confuse. Distract. Destroy".'

Eyeing Harrow sceptically, Matthew leaned back in his seat. Harrow planted a possessive hand across the cover of Lillibridge's book. Deluded. The heroin had scrambled his brain. 'And let me guess,' Matthew said. 'You trundled off and zapped a man-turned-eagle in mid-flight.'

'Yes!'

Matthew shook his head. He really believes this, he thought. He really believes he's a character in the book.

'In the last moments of that life,' Harrow was saying, 'I saw myself yelling at a guy who had turned into an eagle. The eagle was flying, and I was boiling over with rage. A weird, burning feeling escaped from my fingertips. I could see the heat. Streaks of electricity. Each of my fingers lit up like candles. Then the eagle became stock still. It morphed into a statue.'

Matthew had never liked that part of the book. 'I see,' he said, morbidly fascinated with just how confused his pathetic ex-colleague had become. 'What happened then?'

Harrow described transitioning into a dark and frightening death, finding himself trapped in a nightmarish world of monsters. 'And then something changed. A flash of silver shook me out of that world, the same blinding silver I witnessed when Rosetta approached me in the ambulance. My spirit was viewing the Grudellan Palace grounds then, and all I could see was a young guy—he was in gold regalia, looked royal to me—and he was standing over my lifeless body. He pressed a gemstone against my ankle.'

'Wait a minute.' Matthew leaned forward. 'Was that what Rosetta did? Was the shining thing she held against you a crystal?'

'I think so, yes, although what Rosetta held was small and flat, whereas the stone in this scenario was like a chunk of illuminated rose quartz at the end of a rod. All I knew, as Rahwor, was that Adahmos, Prince Consort—the guy in all the gold—was blessing me with Orahney's wand. So I actually think what Rosetta had was a gem of some sort. Not just any sort of gem. This was supercharged.'

That sounded more like Rosetta. Matthew knew she carried around a chip of crystal from Craig's new mine. She normally kept it in her cosmetics purse. When Matthew had suffered a flare-up with his knee, she'd handed it to him and the pain had vanished, just as it had with Dalesford's crystal. He'd said one day to

Rosetta, 'Someone should investigate the power in crystals. I reckon they're grossly underestimated.'

Rosetta had regarded him with a mysterious smile. 'Ah,' she'd said, 'this isn't just any crystal, Matthew. It's—' But he'd conveyed his love for that smile with a kiss that turned into a torrent of passion.

Another shard of sadness stabbed at his heart.

Harrow was continuing with the Rahwor delusion, claiming that after Pieter had 'silvered' him, he'd been drawn through a tunnel towards a bright light. The light introduced itself as "Alcor". 'Alcor said I'd received a promotion in evolution. I'd been delivered to the Dream Sphere because I was no longer of gold. He asked me if I'd like to stay there, and I said, "Of course! Never before have I known such beauty!" Alcor advised that in order to stay, I would need to undo all negative spells, and he told me how.

'And that's all I was shown of that weird ancient life. The angelic being, the one who greeted me when I died from that overdose, urged me to look at an additional life I'd lived. In this next scenario I was climbing an oak tree in some kind of forest. I tumbled, hit the ground and obviously lost consciousness because I floated above my body, like I did with the overdose. I could see myself lying below. I was a boy of about ten. I wore breeches and boots, and a puffy sort of shirt. A woman with long dark hair held a pink stone to my ankle. History repeated, I think, when Rosetta did the same.

'A man in a loose leather waistcoat, who I knew to be my father, was pacing by the oak and uttering prayers while the woman revived me.'

'That's...that's Lillibridge's story. He's talked in his letters about the Gypsy woman Lucetta healing Ned with a crystal.'

'But I've already told you this. I was Lillibridge. Not the man who wrote the letters. I was Ned, his son.'

Matthew groaned. 'Be logical here, Harrow. You claim you wrote the book, but Ned didn't write *Our True Ancient History*. Edward did.'

Harrow's voice rose with impatience. 'I'll get back to that in a minute. When I was hovering above the ambulance, I heard that police guy, the ex-husband of Dette's, refer to me as a cross-dresser. I was shouting at him, trying to tell him he was wrong. It wasn't my fault a change in personality controlled my actions whenever I was under the influence.'

'So what happened in the ambulance—after Rosetta stepped in with the crystal?'

'After I was shown those lives? Well, the being told me I hadn't finished my earthly existence. Told me I had more to do. Next thing I know, I'm wriggling my fingers and feeling heavy. The paramedic nearest me grabbed my wrist. She sort of squeaked and yelled, "He's got a pulse" and then everything sprang into action. Oxygen mask, injections, the feel of the vehicle speeding up, an emergency siren squalling in my ears.'

'It happens, I guess.' Matthew wasn't liking being drawn into Harrow's miracle mongering. Exasperated, he sighed. Why did he doubt Harrow when he himself had encountered the supernatural? What about his conversations with Pieter from Lillibridge's book? What about the dream Rosetta had told him of, about a visit from Molly Carr, a rabbit-owner whose combined first name and surname sounded the same as 'Maleika'?

They'd both had wide-awake dreams. And then there were the stars that invaded Rosetta's vision when she'd stopped him on the road. Around the same time, he'd been hearing Pieter's music. Low and haunting. The soft, sweet whistle of a pipe made from reed. 'Perhaps the sprites were leading us to each other,' Rosetta had said.

While neither he nor Rosetta had ever experienced *being* a character from the book, if reincarnation were real, then there was every chance that someone in today's world had lived the life of Rahwor. He hated to admit it, hated to acknowledge that Adam Harrow's rants might be genuine and not another of his manipulative deceits, but Matthew's latest motto since discovering *Our True Ancient History* was 'fact is stranger than fiction'.

The unlikely visitor's jittery, emotive account of out-of-body experiences, the effect of the crystals and a benignly welcoming afterlife was peculiar, of course, and not at all easy to believe, and yet the doubts over its authenticity were fading fast.

Matthew didn't want to succumb to it; didn't want to acknowledge such an outlandish notion, and yet despite its cringey absurdity, Harrow's claim echoing Harriet's, about an eighteenth-century incarnation, was sealing the lid on his scepticism. It had begun to feel true.

The story was beginning to make a certain type of sense.

Chapter Eight

MATTHEW CLUNKED A MUG ONTO the table for his unexpected guest. 'What did I tell you last?' Harrow said. 'Had I got to my Dream Master's explanation for reverting to Rahwor?'

'Nope,' Matthew said. 'You were telling me Rosetta revived you with the crystal.'

'Ah, yes.' Harrow took a gulp of the instant coffee Matthew had salvaged from the back of Grant's pantry. 'While I was in the afterlife, or "Dream Sphere", my super-luminous Dream Master explained that the trauma associated with drug-use crumbled the safety barriers that block distressing memories. This breaking down of my memory divisions had me inadvertently recalling not only the negative events from my childhood but parts of that low-vibe sorcerer life as well. Memory damage can sometimes cause a failure to discern between a current life and others. So when I was under the influence, I often *believed* I was still Rahwor. You could say I was trapped in a nightmare most of the time.

'The Dream Master told me I gravitated to drugs because of childhood trauma. I didn't think my upbringing was so bad, but once he mentioned it I realised I'd never been loved. I was born into wealth. Had everything money could buy, and now that I think of it I wasn't such a bad kid. Pretty malleable in fact. My major rebellion back then was studying literature when my entrepreneur father wanted me to follow in his footsteps with finance. I gave in to that, but initially I pursued my passion for words.'

Matthew knew Harrow had been a journalist, and everyone on the bank's trading floor knew of his father. American like Matthew's dad. Hailed as a Wall Street golden boy in the early 1970s.

'My father. Whoa! He had supreme intellectual powers, but he wasn't exactly your lovable type. Not like brilliant but benevolent Charlie Sanders. Did you hear about his retirement, by the way?'

'Celia said something about it.'

'Did you know Roddie got Charlie's director role?'

'Roddie eh? Well, whaddya know. Good old Roddie. And what's happening with you?'

'Writing. I've returned to journalism, a bit of freelancing for finance blogs and e-mags, and I'm pleased to say it's going well.'

'So it's bye-bye Wall Street?'

'Wall Street's a crumbled whim. I never made the grade as Golden Boy, and I've since lost my fascination with the NYSE.'

'Can't say I'm too pleased with Wall Street either. GFC losses.'

'You lost out? How much?'

Matthew declined to answer. He still had his pride.

'Winning on Wall Street never did my dad much good,' Harrow said. 'He was terrifying, and that's putting it mildly. And my mother...well, I'd have to say my mother was absent. She didn't have much in the way of emotion. There was cruelty directed at me. You could say my parents embraced Gold's Kin values. They were ultra-materialistic. Acquisition meant everything to them. So did appearance, all the surface stuff...and their hearts were the opposite of warm.

'Look, I make no excuses for myself. Going on drugs is the dumbest thing I ever did. I know that's where I went wrong, and maybe I got high to lose my vulnerability. Problem was, the smack ridded me of more than that. It hit the delete-button on my conscience.

'Anyway, when I got more into the hard stuff, I found I'd become obsessed with a name. For a long time, and I never knew why, I would hear a kind of an echo, sort of like *deja vu*, concerning someone by the name of Det-ah-Wise-la.' Harrow flicked the book open. 'Here it is. Chapter XX. Page 164. A body king spying on Pieter and hearing about the woman who would:

...one day restore the world to its former beauty.'

'That was Rahwor,' said Matthew. 'Rahwor promised the Solen he'd go forward in time and get rid of her.'

'Well I never did get to travel in time as Rahwor. I was poisoned by the rose thorns before I got the chance. Look at where it says "wise-lah". It's the surname of your wife, preceded by her first name.'

Matthew glanced at the page. 'It is not. I can't imagine Bernadette restoring the world to its former beauty!'

'I'm serious.'

'But it's nothing like her name. Unless you count the "Det" part of it, and that's pretty obscure.'

'I'm talking about how it sounds.'

Matthew mouthed the word. 'It's uncanny how the last part's the pronunciation of Weissler, but the name she goes by is "Dette", not "Det-ah".'

'What does her middle name start with?'

Matthew thought a second. 'R,' he said. 'Her middle name's Raelene.'

'Exactly.'

'All right. So it sounds like her name. But it's not spelt the same.' A chill trickled over Matthew's shoulder blades. 'You're not saying...No. This is just too weird.'

'Anyway, there I am, living my life as a trading manager, somewhere between lucid and crazed, and I'm fascinated with the name Det-ah-Wise-la.

'And then one day I'm at work, and I hear your assistant phoning some company, complaining for Dette about a purchase. The service officer must have asked her what name was on the warranty. She looked down at a bit of card, and said, "Dette R Weissler".'

'I vaguely remember giving Celia that to do. Dette had said they were unreasonable or something and asked me to phone on her behalf. So the name rang a bell with you?'

'Yeah! I just instantly recalled this puzzle haunting me, about having to pursue a woman by that name. I heard "Dette R Weissler" and something clicked into place. I was convinced your wife was the woman I had to track down. The idea was on continuous-play. I became obsessed.'

Matthew recalled the night that Bernadette threatened Harrow with a gun. Harrow's weird obsessiveness had driven her to it. 'You'd better promise me you never did anything to hurt her.'

'Unreservedly. Not counting the odd bit of bastardry of course, when I broke it off with her. Thank God I didn't carry through with that weird echoing command. Initially I followed Dette. Followed her here, once, to Punchbowl. I blanked out and found myself running away from the laundry in this block of flats you're now living in. Dette would bring her kids here on weekends.'

'This used to be their dad's flat.'

'I know. I stalked her wherever she went. That was until I realised I could use my charm. Not long after the Punchbowl incident, I found my golden opportunity. The cocktail party the bank held last year, the one that spouses were invited to...I hate to have to tell you this, mate, but Dette was going out of her way to attract my attention.' He shot Matthew a sheepish glance. 'Sorry about that. I was well aware of my ability to influence women. I had the right looks and status, not to mention an aptitude for brainless flirting.

'Dette didn't mean much to me. She was just another conquest, and I was addicted to sex. That other side of me, the hideous "Rahwor" side, wanted me to entrap her though.' Harrow cleared his throat, slouched forward and folded his arms. 'Er...I'm ashamed to say this, but there was a time when I came close to hurting Dette. You probably know by now that we went to Vanuatu together.'

Matthew gritted his teeth. 'All right. Get to the point.'

'On the second-last night we were there, I woke up out of a smack-induced daze. I was running after Dette. She was screaming and trying to get away from me.'

'What!'

'She was all right, mate. She fainted from fright.'

'You call that all right?'

'She recovered quickly...the doc at the island confirmed nil injuries. Her fall was cushioned by a clump of ferns. I discovered later that I was wearing the same thing I always wore when I woke from those dazes. A black wig I have—'

'Your Doctor Cyanide gear.'

'A total personality switch. I never had any recollection of having put the Doctor Cyanide gear on. All I ever remembered was waking from some sort of haze. How disturbing is that? Waking up in a costume you normally reserve for an annual charity concert?'

'Can't say I know what that's like.' Matthew tried to imagine chasing after people in Don McLean's '70s hair and sideburns. The idea was more than a little nauseating.

'I'd put it down to the heroin causing me to emulate an idol, like kids do when they dress up as Batman or whoever.'

'Once Dette fell to the ground, I regained my identity. For the first time, I'd been able to observe myself after a conscience lapse, and all I could feel was revulsion. It was hard to take. Discovering I'd terrorised someone was pretty frightening. I saw Dette lying there, and—'

'I can't believe you put her through that,' Matthew said. 'Can't believe it.'

'It scared me how close I came to...I knew I had to protect her from my bouts of insanity. That wasn't difficult. The fling was already over.'

'That's what you're here to apologise about? For scaring Bernadette half-to-death and encouraging her to cheat on me?'

Harrow's smile was conciliatory. 'No,' he said. 'I'm remorseful, about how I treated Dette. But as for luring her away from you...Well, be honest here for a sec.' Harrow eyeballed him seriously. 'Did you envisage staying married to Dette to the end of your days, once the two of you grew apart?'

'That's none of your business.'

'I think it is. Since my heart awoke in the Dream Sphere, I've become intuitive. I sense things about people. And I've gained amazing insight into the goings-on in this world. I'm seeing the bigger picture more.'

'And what's the big picture with seducing someone's wife?'

'I'm not saying it's right. I'm just telling you something bad can lead to something good. That marriage of yours spelt disempowerment for both parties. But you, Weissler, you'd be the sort of person to vacillate about splitting up.'

'That's not true.'

'All right then. Whatever you say. Answer me this though. Would you consider yourself to be long-suffering?'

Matthew thought about this. 'Well I'm not showing much evidence of that today, but I generally allow others a fair bit of slack.'

'See? That easygoing trait of yours was trapping you in a loveless relationship. Patience ain't always a virtue.'

Matthew was not going to admit to the second thoughts he'd had prior to Bernadette's return.

'In hindsight,' Harrow said, 'I realised I was doing you a favour. You weren't meant to be with Dette. I was the catalyst for your divorce. You and I aren't enemies, Matt. We have a connection from previous lives. I was Ned, your son, and…What I'm here to apologise about, is for turning you to stone.'

'Huh?'

Harrow picked up a pen and notepaper stacked at one side of the table and scribbled down the name Rahwor. 'Can you find my name in that?'

Matthew contemplated each of the letters. 'A lexigram,' he said. 'And an anagram. Contains every letter of your surname.'

'Bizarre, hey?'

'But that could apply to hundreds.'

'Now write down your own name. In full. No, not just the "P", the *whole* middle name. That's it. Porter, is it? See if you can find the name Storlem in that.'

Matthew crossed off each of the letters. 'Surely not!' He threw the pen down.

'I'd like to say it's just a coincidence, Weissler, but Edward Lillibridge, the guy whose letters appear on the Friday Fortnight website, the guy whose letters you chased up in Candlewell, according to Rosetta's blog—'

'I think you meant to say Cornwall.'

'Cornwall. Yes. He didn't write *Our True Ancient History.*'

'What makes you so sure? Those letters have been certified. They've—'

'You mustn't have seen the latest letter Rosetta uploaded. You're not in contact with her then?'

Another ache rose in Matthew's chest. 'No,' he said. 'I haven't seen her last post.' As soon as Harrow was gone he'd try Rosetta's landline.

'Hm, strange. I got the impression the two of you were pretty friendly based on the praise for you in her introduction to the previous letter.' He swigged the rest of his coffee and set his cup aside. 'My intuition's still in the trainer-wheels stage. I'm careful not to take every hunch too seriously.'

Thinking of Rosetta's hasty getaway earlier prompted another dose of guilt. His pathetic inertia had prevented him from doing anything that reminded him of the happiness he'd smashed apart. He'd planned to see Rosetta's website eventually, but the pain of reading her words was just as difficult to endure as hearing her voice on the message bank. Could it really have been four weeks? He'd tried to muster up the courage to visit and explain he was no longer worthy of her. He couldn't bear the thought of doing that. Each week had melded miserably into the next. The days had escaped him. Four whole weeks! Unforgivable.

Harrow drew from the back of his book a folded document. 'Here's a print-up of the latest Lillibridge letter from the Friday Fortnight site, with Rosetta's introduction to start. It's a letter dated 1767, and it's addressed to Ned. This is what you wrote to me in your past life.'

Matthew accepted the document. 'How did you find me?'

'Pretty *f***ing* hostile at first.' Harrow was grinning. 'Especially when I told you I'd written the book.'

'Not what I meant. This address. Who told you where to find me?'

'Private investigator.'

'You went to a lot of trouble then.'

'Yep. And for good reason.'

Matthew unfolded the page and began to read...

○

Hi Friday Fortnighters,

What a horrendous September it's been. Many lives have been thrown into turmoil because of the crash. I'm keeping my fingers crossed that all of you are faring well. If any of you have been unfortunate enough to be stung by the Global Financial Crisis, I hope with all my heart that you find good fortune again really soon.

And on this sombre note, I introduce a letter of Lillibridge's that has moved me to tears. I can understand the information in it might well come as something of a shock to you. Reverend Edward Lillibridge Senior was in fact the instigator, rather than the author of *Our True Ancient History*. In view of this recent revelation, I sincerely apologise for any information on this site that may have misled. The only research available to me in the past led us all to believe that the man who wrote the letters was the man who wrote the book. You could call it a 'learning curve' I guess. We're untangling mysteries about the book together, at the same pace, and at times we've been in the dark.

I am indebted to Anna Callan of Tintagel in the United Kingdom for her generous offer of the letter below. As with Lillibridge's other two letters, it's been dated by an expert and certified as an 18th-century document. Anna typed up the words in the letter and emailed both this and photos of the original pages for the benefit of Friday Fortnighters. Many thanks, Anna, for your wonderful contribution to our site.

I understand Anna is in the process of discussing the insights of this particular document with a historian. I believe an update will be necessary for encyclopaedic references.

As you will see, in this tragic farewell addressed to Edward Junior, (Ned for short), *Our True Ancient History* was the accumulation of three people's efforts.

Kindest regards,
Rosetta Melki

2nd Day of October
in the Year of Our Lord, 1767

My Dear Son Ned,

It is midnight, and you are sleeping.
I am here at the table with a candle at my elbow, penning
the most difficult letter I have ever had to write.

They are coming for me. Samuel Withers saw them in the village—has warned of their approach. I am bereft, and yet my mood is softened by an odd state of serenity, a knowing I suppose, that I shall soon be with God.

My son, I implore you to forgive me for my actions. I have foolishly endangered myself. I must pay the price. My dogged pursuit of The Truth has rendered me conspicuous to 'the powers that be'. My eagerness to convey our true ancient history was considered to have brought shame upon the Church, and I am seen to be a criminal, a charlatan, unworthy of my parish, and now, it appears, unworthy of my life. They are sending their men this night. And so I write with a shaking hand my final farewell to you.

Please look after Lucy. She has been a good stepmother to you. Our dear Lucetta. Such joy she has brought to our lives. How I loved those stories gathered from the People of the Sea! I look back on our evenings at the fireside when the three of us drank mead and sang songs to the tune of my lute, and I smile. The candle flame is flickering. I fancy it smiles as well. Nay, it laughs, a prancing fire sprite, celebrating my impending return to the Dream Sphere!

Look after her, my son. Ensure she is always cared for financially. When the sands of time pass and her bones become brittle with age, make certain that you, and the wife you choose, endeavour to cater to her every comfort. Treat her as you would your own mother. She does not deserve my abandonment.

Remorse, again, pricks at my heart. I should not have brought controversy upon myself. I should have exercised discretion concerning the story of Adahmos and Eid, and yet I could not abide by the biblical version. If, in my life, I have managed in my preachings to inspire no more than one individual then I shall die grateful, content in the knowledge that I have lived a life of purpose. Should this individual convey discreetly the correct account of humanity's beginnings, to his family, to his friends, ever cautious of those he is unable to trust, one day— whether it be decades or centuries I suppose is God's Will—one day, Lucetta's words of wisdom will be heeded, and with this will come the return of magic.

Our world has lost much of its beauty. Elysium Glades is a far cry from the 'body king' indoctrination of modern society. No longer do we dwell in a world of kindness. It is <u>gold</u>, of all things, <u>gold</u> that rules our motivations and drives many to commit unspeakable crimes. We no longer unite in the love of one family sharing a planet. We fear one another and inflict pain on our brothers. My son, if you strive throughout your life to assist in making our world a worthier place, you will have led a valuable existence.

You have done well. I am most pleased with your devotion to your work as a reverend. Your parish respects you greatly. You are still very young. At nine-and-ten you are scarcely more than a lad. Son, I request of you, on this night of my demise, to consider the following:

As you know, Ned, I am a devoted Man of God, but I have always harboured reservations about the veracity of The Old Testament's history of the world. Being a representative of the Church bestows public honour, despite the fact that we are preaching from a book that, while well intended, has become altered through time in its translation.

Although the livelihood of a parson is indeed a lucrative one, do not be afraid to change your occupation! Lord knows, you might need to with all the treachery that is about. I certainly do not ask that you behave as I have done. My zeal has been my undoing. When you waken and find that all that is left of me is this letter, I ask that you vow never to repeat the error of your father.

What I wish for you, however, is a life of safe adventure, the sort of life that enables you the freedom to explore other lands. My hope for you is that you hear the spiritual beliefs of peoples from all corners of the globe, thus broadening your own concept of the ways of this earth and the ennobling secrets of dimensions beyond our limited vision.

Humanity's senses have dimmed. We see only our world and nobody else's. When we slumber, we do not recall our visits to the Dream Sphere. While few people know of—or believe in—the ancient existence of body kings, their dastardly influence lives on and will probably continue to do so for many years to come. Body kings have done well in imprisoning our senses. They have kept us ignorant.

Tomorrow morning, once I am gone, I wish you to ready the horses for a journey to your aunt. Meredith has been a good sister to me. You must pass on the news of my death and promise to continue the support with which I have endowed her. She is to be sent four shillings every third Monday. Take Lucy with you on this journey to Hazelton. She must not be left in the cottage alone. These men might return. She must be protected at all times.

Before you leave, you must move the two of you from the cottage to the vicarage. Destroy all my preachings and anything else of mine that might incriminate.

Move everything there except the trunk in the corner of my bed chamber. This you must take with you to Hazelton. Locked within it are the papers on which I recorded Lucetta's stories. They are raggedly put together—a sentence here—a sentence there—and a small introduction, a 'prologue' of sorts, yet they capture the essence of that which she has told us. I had hoped to use these as a guide to the writing of a proper text. I had planned to infer its truth in the title. No doubt my insistence of its authenticity as a work of non-fiction would have landed me in further trouble.

One day, my son, you might wish to write the history yourself. I give you my utmost permission to work from the notes I have made. You must only ever call it 'a novel', however, and you must not approach any publisher in the Kingdom of Great Britain. Be mindful that your father's ill reputation precedes you.

Once you arrive at your aunt's cottage in Hazelton, you must leave with her the trunk from my room, and you must keep with you the key. Meredith is to destroy all letters I mailed her.

Be aware, my son, of those who have ensured my slaying. Do not underestimate their slyness. If you perceive animosity towards you, if there are threats as there have been with me, I ask that you plan an escape. In the event of such misfortune, you must firstly deliver Lucy to Meredith's and retrieve the trunk. She will be safe there in Hazelton with the Rathbones and will earn her keep through housework. You must then pack the contents of the trunk and your most treasured belongings, and once nightfall has descended, you must travel to Dover. There you will be free to board the next ship bound for the Continent. My son, you cannot be too careful.

The sale of our cottage should hold both you and Lucy in good stead.

I hear the men's horses. The sound of their hooves is echoing in the valley. It will not be much longer before they are here.

The ink on the line above has smeared. A teardrop has disturbed this letter's continuity. Forgive me, son, for now I weep. I am certain, however, that you will decipher it.

The candle has burnt low. As with my earthly existence, it is soon to perish. I shall snuff the flame before it decides to die. And when I watch the fire sprite vanish, when I see its lively form *dissolved, and as the smoke from my sole source of light rises mournfully to the ceiling, I shall say a prayer for you and your stepmother.*

The horses have risen from the valley. From the window I see my perpetrators, ghastly silhouettes obscured largely by the garden's well: the well that I built when you were but a tiny lad; the well that has consistently delighted us each summer with its embellishment of briar roses, planted many years before by your dear mother.

Live happily, my son. May you fully embrace the Currency of Kindness.

Until we meet again, farewell.

Your ever loving father,

Edward

MATTHEW FOLDED THE LETTER GENTLY. Stared at the kitchen wall without seeing it.

Outside a car roared through the street. What was it that had changed? Nothing. Nothing had changed. The tables and chairs had remained where they were. Harrow, a former rival, was still sitting opposite. The clock had continued to tick. The clock. All he could hear was its dutiful forward march. Had he noticed its loudness before? Its morose attachment to clunking rhythmically away from the past? The past. A place in which Edward Lillibridge lived and died, the place where childhood memories resided, now little more than brief grabs of colour, aromas and sound.

He reflected on the previous two letters. How could anyone have ever imagined, after reading Lillibridge's romantic accounts of eighteenth-century surroundings, that it would all end so sadly for him? For him. For Matthew. The grief of preparing a hastily written farewell had felt like it was happening to him.

Harrow spoke, his voice rippling quietly through the ponderous calm. 'I came here today to thank you.'

To thank him? To thank Matthew?

Solemnly, he added, 'I'm indebted to your kindness.'

'Kindness? You said you came here to apologise.'

The whirr of a lawn mower spiralled into existence.

Harrow didn't answer immediately. At last he said, 'That was my foot in the door.'

Transient glimpses of somewhere far away. The glint of a pale jewel encased in lunar-gilt, a woodcutter's axe, a valley alive with chimney smoke. The longing for a time dead and buried. Was that what had changed in Matthew? This feeling of deep understanding concerning his past?

Harrow spoke again. 'Before I revived in the ambulance, while I was in the Dream Sphere, I was shown my progression throughout three lives, three separate aspects of myself: Rahwor, young Ned Lillibridge, and who I am now. Of those lives, there was only one that I saw to be successful. One. In my life alongside you, Weissler, back in the 1700s, I experienced the kindness of a devoted parent. On the day I fell from the oak tree, my father's love was the magnet that drew me back into consciousness.'

'But the Gypsy. Hadn't she achieved this with the gem?'

'The gem revived my body, but what brought my soul back to complete the incarnation was the bond I had with my father. In this current life, I knew with all my heart that the crystal of Rosetta's had brought me back. I would have remained dead in the earthly dimension if Rosetta hadn't "silvered" me. Do you know where she got that crystal?'

'A friend of hers. He and his mates discovered a source just outside of Alice Springs.'

'I'd be finding out more about that if I were you. Imagine if everyone had access to them. Those crystals could change the world.'

'By bringing the dead back from the grave?'

'No, I don't mean that. In my case I hadn't finished my earthly existence. Once you're in the Dream Sphere, the temptation to stay is huge. It's indescribable just how beautiful that place is. I was reluctant to come back to this present life, but the being of bright light insisted.

The fact is, I have a mission to fulfil in my silvered state, and so dying at that stage wasn't my destiny.'

'So what was it?' Matthew began. 'What was it that made you think I was your father in that life?' Harriet and Harrow, two unconnected people living thousands of miles apart, had now claimed that he, Matthew, was the father of the younger Edward, Ned.

'Well it was weird,' Harrow said. 'There was something about that memory of my father, an atmosphere about him. It might have been in his mannerisms, or maybe it had been in his eyes. I don't know what it was but somehow, throughout the months of recalling having witnessed that life, I felt that this guy held a similarity to you.' He laughed slightly. 'That riled me. I mean, it's no secret that you and I weren't exactly best buddies. At first I said to myself, "My mind's playing tricks on me. There's no way *that* arrogant creep would have been Edward Lillibridge Senior." But the feeling persisted. I became intrigued with the Lillibridges.

'And so I googled some names I remembered from my "Ned" life, not expecting to find anything from that long ago, and came up with the book. Finding evidence shocked me a bit. It proved so much! I also found Rosetta's Friday Fortnight website. I was fascinated by some of the guest-blogs. Surprised too, at discovering that the guy who wrote them, Conan Dalesford, had my Dream Master's name inside his own. And I remembered I'd bought a book of his from the shop Rosetta worked at. Pretty odd for someone who hates visionary literature.'

'I was with you that day.' Matthew re-experienced the sticky drink cans against his knuckles when he'd reached into the bin and grasped the unopened package. 'You didn't waste much time chucking it.'

'I'd only bought it to impress Rosetta. Everything I did back then had an ulterior motive. Anyway, once I found these observations of Dalesford's on the website, I picked up the phone to dial Rosetta's number. There was so much I wanted to ask. Then I thought better of it because, well the truth of the matter is I'd been a jerk. We'd been out a couple of times. Nothing too heavy. Just...' his words halted. 'Instead I contacted Conan Dalesford. I asked in an email if I could visit him, then took a flight up to Alice Springs.

'He didn't say much when I stepped into the foyer of his house. Just greeted me with, "I've been waiting for you," and then he handed me this.' Harrow held up the black book on the table. 'Can you believe it? This is the first English language edition of *Our True Ancient History*.'

'Is that right? I collect various editions. If they weren't sealed up in a packing carton, I'd bring them out to show you. I had no idea the book was printed in any other language before that.'

'Neither did Conan Dalesford. Neither did I. But while I was there Dalesford sat me down and handed me a crystal that he'd run up in his workshop.'

'I know the one! I held that crystal in a city bistro and the room turned silver.'

'Yeah, it does that. Powerful gems for sure, but he refuses to make more of them. Says there's a stone out there now that's just as powerful, and apparently there's an abundance of it. Wonder if he knows about Rosetta's friend's venture. He wouldn't live far from that if they've set up in Alice Springs.'

'It's possible,' Matthew said. 'Come to think of it, Rosetta mentioned Craig was friends with Conan, the reason she found out about his books and ordered them into Crystal Consciousness.'

'That might explain it. Dalesford told me he could see from my aura that I was ready to connect my intuition. He led me into a creative visualisation meditation and told me to tell my heart that it no longer needed to bar me from my whole self. Dalesford's a fully-realised being. Did you know that?'

'Rosetta's friend Royston said something about it. I...didn't quite get what that was.'

'Fully-realised beings are people who have evolved to a point where they independently become aware of their other selves from all other lives. They're then able to recall former skills they've developed, like energising everyday crystals for instance. Dalesford learned how to do that previously, in a life he'd had in Lemuria. He also knew how to create underground escape tunnels from crystal power alone. They had to manifest a lot of them in Lemuria once Atlantis invaded. He has a tunnel under his house. One of his early experiments.'

'Yeah?'

'Yeah! We went through a trapdoor, and I checked it out. Its stone walls are quite similar to some of the tunnels at The Rocks on Sydney Harbour. So when I found out about all that previous-life knowledge this guy had, I wasn't surprised to learn he at one stage had a life as a Dream Master. Alcor, of course, was the guy I'd returned to in my life as Rahwor. Could have been your Dream Master too when you were Storlem. And Orahney's. Who knows?'

'Anyway,' Harrow continued, 'Dalesford often talks about "waking up". Apparently that's the very early stages of becoming realised. It can take years though, even lifetimes, to regain all past life memories, and it has a lot to do with clearing Gold's-Kin-inflicted pain. If we free ourselves of the past-life and current-life trauma that we store in our hearts, we're then able to access our personal history. We begin to get a sense of our own wholeness.'

'Whoa.' Matthew chuckled to himself. Hadn't Dalesford told him on the phone two weeks ago to 'wake up'?

'So I'm in this incredibly peaceful state during the meditation Conan Dalesford's guiding me through, and I'm able to feel the essence of the Dream Sphere again. It's like it's right inside my chest. And this feeling of rightness flows over me. The feeling expands and sends me into a floaty kind of timelessness. And I suddenly remember who I am. I suddenly remember that I'm not Adam Harrow of Vaucluse, recovering addict and former trading manager. I'm more than that! I'm a being of wisdom, and I'm deeply connected to the human race and beyond.

'And I feel instantly at one with everything and everyone. I realise that we're *all* beings of wisdom, each with something sacred and magical to share. We are joined together by beams of light that stream from our hearts.' Adam stopped. His voice had become hoarse. 'In my state of *seeing* fully, *feeling* fully, *hearing* fully, I felt empowered and humbled all at the same time. It was like how you feel when you've gone into a dark room and flicked the light switch. No, that's not it. It was like...It was a recognition of sorts.'

'An epiphany.'

'Yes!' Harrow's voice gained in volume. 'An *epiphany*. That's exactly what it was.'

FOR A WHILE, HARROW SAID NOTHING. He dragged a hand across his forehead, eyes downcast. 'In that meditative state, I saw what happened in my life as Ned Lillibridge after you wrote me that letter of farewell.

'You'd been on trial for heresy. Executed. I was torn between honouring and resenting you. I felt extremely cheated that you should have put yourself in danger. It felt like a major rejection, you having been so careless with your self-preservation. You'd left me, and I hated you for it. And yet, another side of me wanted to make you proud. I knew you were up there in the Dream Sphere, able to observe what happened in my life.

'I did my best to look after Lucy, but Lucy was inconsolable. Because she was so totally heartbroken, she became withdrawn. Occasionally she'd sort of mutter something about having lost her "faerie sight". I told her it was probably because her heart was clouded over with sadness. At one stage, after days of silence, she said to me, "Not even the gem, Ned. Not even the gem can help heal my heart." I worried about her. Tried to get her to eat, but she refused.

'She kept up her wanders to the sea, only she did this more often, every morning and at sunset as well. I would always follow her. I knew there was every chance either of us might be targeted by the bastards who took you away from us. She'd just stand on the cliffs for ages, staring out at the ocean. And then one evening, when I'd returned to the parish after having gone to collect water from the well, I found she'd slipped away somewhere. Her pink pendant was lying on the table, and there was this grey, knitted thing—it might have been a scarf or a shawl of some sort—and it was thrown down onto the floor.

'It was raining, and thunder had started up. I lit a lantern and ran to the beach, but I couldn't find her. I searched through the forest. I searched everywhere for Lucy. I went for an entire night without sleep, sodden to the skin from the downpour, trying to find my stepmother. The next afternoon a fisherman came to the door.' Harrow grew silent.

'And?' said Matthew.

Harrow shielded his eyes with his hands. 'Sorry. This memory makes me a bit emotional. I er...I.' He faltered. Sighed. 'I...was told by the fisherman that they'd seen Lucy on a rocky ledge in the early evening. Someone had shouted out to her that she was standing in the path of perilous waves, but she failed to heed their warnings. In an attempt to coax her away, the fisherman ran to the rocks.' He shook his head. 'That was when the wave took her.'

Matthew groaned.

'I realised then that the night I followed Lucetta I'd been too late. I became consumed with guilt, tortured by the notion of how different everything would have been if I'd reached her in time. I felt I'd let you down by not protecting your widow and had to remind myself that you and Lucy were happy in the Dream Sphere, and together.

'And so, even though I'd failed to save Lucy, I set about fulfilling every other request in that final letter of yours. I travelled across Europe with your documents. I'd taken them from the trunk at Aunt Meredith's in Hazelton. Sailed to Norway, the modern "Norwegia" where Lucy's stories were set. I instantly fell in love with the place, and I remained there till the end of my days.'

'So you lived a peaceful life from then on out?'

'Absolutely. I married a Norwegian-born girl who spoke English very well—the daughter of a British diplomat—and I worked tirelessly on your notes. Turned them into a documentation of all Lucy had told us, which was able to be passed off as fiction. My wife translated the story into Norwegian, and I described it as "a novel" to my publisher. It was published in Oslo in 1771 under the title of *Hvisker av Visdom*. Translated into English this means "Whispers of Wisdom".

'I lived to a ripe old age, and I enjoyed success with my publication. The book was quite popular. It was translated into all of the Scandinavian languages. I continually refused to sign over the rights to Great Britain. It wasn't until 1820 that I agreed to have it published there. I was elderly and on my deathbed with pneumonia. I had my will changed. I requested that the original manuscript I'd written in English be released to Dean & Son in London. I told them its title was "Our True Ancient History" a term you used in your letter the night you were taken away.'

Matthew was almost unable to speak. 'Amazing,' he said. 'And it explains why I've never found any edition published prior to 1820. I needed to google "Whispers of Wisdom" in Norwegian.'

Harrow agreed. 'Or Swedish. Or Danish. As I said, the books were translated throughout Scandinavia. Anyway, getting back to why I was so certain the older Edward Lillibridge was you. Once I was leaving Dalesford's place after his lovely wife Jannali persuaded me to stay for dinner, I said to him it bugged me that something about the father had reminded me of a former colleague.

'Dalesford laughed a bit and said, "It's a gathering of the clans it seems," and then he said, "Tell me, Adam. Do you harbour any animosity towards that colleague?" When I said I did, I thought I had the answer. I thought he'd tell me that if I didn't particularly like you then you could never have been Edward Lillibridge Senior. Instead he just said, "There's your answer. You've stumbled across the present incarnation of your father, and you haven't forgiven him. The battle you went through with drugs would have magnified that resentment. But you don't need me to tell you that. You can receive any truth by doing the heart meditation I taught you."

'So in my daily meditations, I came up with the answer. I worked out why I'd always despised you. Edward Senior's indiscriminate broadcasting of what he believed to be fact about the origins of money and humanity had brought about a tragedy for me during my life as Edward Junior. In that meditation I came to terms with the knowledge that you, as Edward Lillibridge, couldn't have acted in any other way. Although you'd counted the cost, you could do nothing less than press forward with your message.

'So, almost two-and-a-half centuries on, I'm there working at the bank, and I'm hating you for your honesty. You, I suspect, hated me for my dishonesty.'

'And for good reason I reckon.'

'Sure. But now all I want is to become a better person. Becoming a father has had a bit to do with that.'

'You didn't say!'

'I have a son, a beautiful boy of three-months. We named him Eddie, in honour of my Lillibridge dad...and in honour of *you*, ultimately, Matt. Of course I didn't know you were Edward when I named him. Weird, hey? Feel free to take credit for it.'

'I will. And I do. Always keen to take credit.'

'Lila and I got back together. She's the most incredible person I know. I'll never forgive myself for abandoning Lila during her pregnancy.'

'Lila Donevski from the bank!' Matthew stepped forward to shake hands. Harrow clasped his arm and clamped him in a hug. 'Lila's a gem, Adam. Congrats to you both.'

Adam Harrow checked his watch. 'Is that the time? I gotta get going.' Matthew followed him to the door. At the chest of drawers by the telephone, Harrow drew to a halt. He picked up the envelope Bernadette had left. 'What's this?'

'Dunno. I haven't read it yet. Why?'

'*Man!* Something in its energy field tells me you'd better read it! I've got a feeling it's to do with your future.' Harrow turned to take in the dingy lounge room. 'It might even get you out of this slum.'

A fifth unpublished chapter
from Reverend Edward Lillibridge's
original *handwritten* manuscript

Quietly observing the Sonic Unity Gathering, Maleika mulled over the words of King Nikolaus, that future member of humanity. 'It came about this morning. Two hours ago we were liberated from the final strands of Gold's Kin enforcements!

The horned ones' Wall no longer stands. And the name that the horned ones' Wall is more commonly known as...'

Much to Maleika's annoyance, Nikolaus interrupted himself. He said, 'In fact, I will speak of this further along in my presentation to you. First, I would like, if I might, to read aloud a speech I gave back in 2008.'

The window into Earth's future that Maleika and Alcor stood beside conveyed Nikolaus recounting the announcement he had made seventeen season-cycles prior.

' *"...Imagine a world that rejects the wheel of suffering; a world that refuses to perpetuate war.*

"Imagine a world free of corruption.

"Imagine a world whose every inhabitant is ensured a life of comfort, healthful nourishment, vitality, security, respect.

"... A place where wellbeing is paramount, where all experience contentment through work that is purposeful, energising and rewarding.

"Picture a world that has forgotten what it is to feel ailments such as fear, worry, grief.

"Picture a world whose many varied peoples have learnt, after having weathered the storms of deception, to trust one another once more.

"My dream is to help create a world whose people enjoy:

"... a clean environment free of toxic haze,

"... vibrant health,

"... a safe, peaceful space in which to reside,

"... a daily life that involves nurturing the local community,

"... interaction based solely on kindness.

"This, I believe, would have every possibility of coming about upon rejecting money in favour of a system I shall refer to as merit accumulation. The accumulation of merits, a measurement of kindness, would be designed to allow each and every one of us to prosper..."

'This was the introduction to a speech I made at secondary school as captain of a debating team. My team had won the choice of topic, and so we initiated an argument surrounding the statement: *The world is in need of an alternate exchange system.*

'The opposition team's arguments were fierce. When they won, we consoled ourselves with the notion that it is easier to argue for what is apparent than for what is considered to be a nebulous fancy.

'By the time the opposing captain had completed his speech, I was the object of much derision. My opponent had responded with statements such as, "There will always be the rich and the poor." And: "There will always be warring and ageing and sickness." He then said: "The battles over territories and resources will always be a fact of life because desire for what another has, my friends, is human nature. *Equality for all,* he says! And money? This guy believes there is to be *no money!* Just sweetness 'n' light amongst a bunch of aimless do-gooders!" He turned to me then and laughed in a way that ruffled my fifteen-year-old sensibilities. I could feel the indignation seeping hotly through my skin. "It seems," he said, "that it is more than my opponent's face that's turning Red."

'Was I attempting to sell a certain political stance under the innocent guise of idealism? In a word, no. Along with the current monetary system, I had criticised all forms of government and had, along with this, stressed the pointlessness of anarchy. My intention was to inspire thought on a system completely unlike anything we already knew.

'My opponent then closed his very convincing speech with, "Friends, I don't know about you, but I suspect our exchange-student buddy has faeries at the bottom of his garden."

'I wondered how best to respond. I could have waxed lyrical about an incarnation I once had as a Norwegian elf. Somehow, I don't think this would have gone down too well.'

A faint murmur of amusement emanated from the king's audience. Nikolaus continued. 'But this was much earlier in the millennium. Not many of us had woken at that stage from our collective amnesia.

'Back in 2008, many of us believed that the world was doing fine as it was, with its imbalanced distribution of wealth and its majority yearning to experience more than mere survival. Is it any wonder I lost that debate?

'When I was growing up I would often hear my father quote Norman Vincent Peale who once said:

"*Every problem has in it the seeds of its own solution.*"

This was a rule my father lived by. A few months after my debating team speech, the Global Financial Crisis introduced an economic downslide that was especially traumatic to developed nations.

'In that same year, although we didn't know it at the time, the seeds of a solution were discovered. Beneath the red dirt of the Northern Territory's Alice Springs in Central Australia, and within the open spaces of a nation that was once part of Lemuria, many seeds had been slumbering. These seeds were the solution to our lack-inducing financial systems.

'As you are aware, the solution within the ground I speak of is what we now know as the Elysium heart-crystals. Let's pause to remember how it all came about.'

Chapter Nine

Matthew shook the hand of the man opposite.

'Good on you, Matt. Welcome to the team. Looking forward to having you on board.' Craig Delorey's energetic enthusiasm and mercurial reflexes continually reminded Matthew of a gangly six-month-old retriever. From the minute he'd met this bloke at the Alice Springs airport, Matthew had liked him. 'Three to four weeks is fine with us,' Craig was saying. 'We still have some loose ends to tie up before you begin. The manager's house we have here for you won't be available for another month, so the timing's perfect.'

'Thanks for the advance.' He would need at least four weeks back in Sydney to get hold of a good barrister and set wheels in motion. He'd decided against representing himself in the Kirk Rummery case. The time would be better spent learning all he could about Craig's new company.

Craig threw a handful of ten-dollar notes on the bill tray to cover lunch and jumped to his feet. 'Anyway, better get on with things. I'm due to meet with a potential investor at two.' The palm fronds directly behind Craig—jagged strips against the brilliance of a Pro Hart sky—had formed a spiky sort of halo around his unruly hair. The image, clownish and all as it was, represented to Matthew something he imagined he'd recall in future years: the point at which everything changed for the better.

'What time's your flight tonight? I'll drop you off at the airport.'

'Six-thirty.'

'Too easy. I'll catchya at five.'

Matthew returned to his hotel, marvelling at how rapidly situations could change. At the start of the week, he'd been sitting with his head in his hands. It had only taken four days. Four? Or had it been one? On that greyed-out Sunday, he was certain he'd been condemned to a life of scarcity-induced stinting. And then there had been the knocks on the door and his ensuing roller coaster of reactions. Bernadette, Rosetta, Harrow. Each visitor had played a part in jolting him out of his catatonic state of self-pity. It was the last visitor, Adam Harrow, enemy from the past looking quite unlike his previous self, who had changed the way he'd looked at misfortune. By the time they'd walked across to Adam's car, no-one could have guessed at the contempt they'd once harboured for each other. Matthew had been surprisingly at ease in Adam's presence; had ceased protecting his own hotshot pride and confided in the newfound ally about his personal economic downfall.

Taking a seat at his hotel-room desk, he took a gin bottle from the minibar, poured himself a drink and recalled their parting conversation.

'Well Matt,' Adam said, 'you know what happens if you hang onto wet soap too tightly. It shoots out of your hand'.

'Yeah, right. Don't I know it. I've been up to my ears in suds for the past month if that's what you mean. Not used to being without a dishwasher.'

Adam laughed, not with his former jeering attitude but with genuine empathy. 'No mate. You, like the rest of us, are infected with the Gold's Kin malady. You were so afraid of losing your dough, you clung to it too intensely. Money tends to be slippery.' He reached into his pocket for his keys. 'And fear does affect judgement.'

Matthew protested he was losing his grandfather's hard-earned fortune to Bernadette, and Adam continued with: 'You wanted to protect your inheritance in deference to your granddad. But you know what? He doesn't care. He'd just want you to be happy. Your granddad's no longer imprisoned in the illusion. He'd want you, even while you're still on the earth-plane, to be free of the illusion as well.' Adam nodded towards his car at the other side of the street. He still drove that Porsche, a brownish, brassy yellow glinting gaudily in the afternoon light: *Morning Piss Gold* according to certain colleagues. 'Life's confusing, hey? Sometimes it's like driving a ten-tonne truck— at a hundred miles an hour—blindfolded. What do we know? Nought percent of nothing. We don't understand how greatly thoughts influence our reality, and clichéd as it might sound, they really do.'

Turning to Matthew, he said, 'You mightn't like me saying this, but I'm getting the impression you're too busy looking back at what you've lost. I reckon you need to now focus on what you still have.'

'Funny. Dalesford said that too. Something about still having cups standing.'

'He must have drawn a tarot card for you. Five of Cups, probably. When I was there he used the tarot cards on me as well, then he said, "You'll find your answer in those." The cards were completely relevant to my question. Anyway, mate, *you're* going to find solutions to most of your puzzles this week. I feel it in my bones.'

Solutions? This week? While the sentiment was comforting, Matthew knew his financial affairs couldn't be sorted out that speedily. By the time Adam had left, the sky was clearing. Brightened clouds nudged at promising patches of blue. The dingy lounge room didn't seem quite so oppressive when Matthew returned to it. Sunlight, alive with dancing dust particles, beamed through the kitchen window and onto the telephone. Still thinking of Rosetta, he picked up the envelope Bernadette left for him, the contents of which Adam Harrow had insisted would be lucky in some way.

His name was written neatly on the envelope in teenage-girl cursive. Inside it, the printout of a four-month old letter.

Hello Matthew,

You may not remember me, so I hope this note doesn't seem too presumptuous.

We've spoken a couple of times—at Grant Belfield's last week, and before that at your send-off drinks. I was invited by one of your colleagues (Adam Harrow). You kindly fetched me a drink and kept me company while Adam caught up with friends.

Just recently I remembered the conversation I had with you at the send-off, and your plan of starting up a law firm. I'm not sure whether this was definite. In case you are open to opportunities, I thought I would pass on some information about a new company that my friend, Craig Delorey, is starting up.

The company resulted from the discovery of a gemstone in the Northern Territory. It is extraordinary, and although it appears to be a crystal, it is unlike any crystal anyone has ever encountered. Geology experts have assessed this amazing stone. As yet there is nothing it resembles.

Craig, along with a group of mining experts and business associates, has been working on this project for approximately 18 months. They are ready now to launch the product and are in need of a manager with both legal and financial expertise. I remembered my conversation with you and wondered if you'd be interested in looking further into it. (Craig is a lawyer himself and says he wants someone who speaks his 'language'.) He's very approachable, so if you're interested in making enquiries, I'm sure he'd be happy to hear from you.

I've taken the liberty of mentioning you to him.

His number is (09 Alice Springs 5555 5155)

Yours sincerely,

Rosetta Melki

Rosetta's voice reaching out to him from the past. A pre-relationship communication. Cautiously formal in drawing his attention to an opportunity he was now, four months later, able to act upon. Quite different to the flirty notes he'd awaken to find under his pillow the mornings she left early for uni.

On that Sunday just passed, when he'd seen off Adam and read Rosetta's letter, he'd immediately remembered her mention of it. Something about an email attachment she'd sent to Izzie while in New Zealand, which Sara was supposed to pass on. She'd told him this at Amaretti's, that very first restaurant they'd dined at together. Dinner at Joe's.

Contemplating the pale yellow walls of his Alice Springs hotel room, Matthew took another swig of his gin. On Sunday he'd witnessed what could only be described as a miracle. A resurrected Adam Harrow, the transformation of a former rival. And the reason for Adam's revival was the crystal Rosetta had wielded, a crystal from Craig's mine.

On that Sunday, once he'd read Rosetta's letter, he'd rocketed across to the phone and dialled Craig's Alice Springs number, determined to find out more. If the crystals could bring a bloke back from the brink of death and transform him into someone with a conscience, what else were they able to achieve?

Today he swirled the dregs in his glass, mulling over a phone call he was about to make. She might even answer this time. He had a good feeling about it. He'd tell her everything. First he'd get the Bernadette explanation out of the way, then he'd let her know he could see a financial future. He grinned at the idea of telling her he was now employed by someone from her Friday Fortnight gang, that it was all because of that letter she wrote him when she'd been in New Zealand, all to do with the timing.

Craig had said, when Matthew first phoned, 'Yeah I heard about you a few months back. Heard *about* you but not *from* you. We no longer have the guy we initially put on, so you've rung at a good time.' He'd then asked how soon Matthew could get across to Alice Springs to discuss the position further. Matthew had hesitated. How soon could he get a loan from his brother? He'd been doing his best to avoid asking for help. And then Craig had said, 'Naturally I'll cover the cost of your fare and accommodation.'

Another month. Too long to spend away from her. It had already been agreed to, though, the month-to-six-weeks onsite that Craig had stipulated. Matthew needed at least this long to set up his management role. From there on out he'd be free to work from home in Sydney. Until then he could probably book flights back on weekends, to spend time with Rosetta. Once his salary started up he could do what he liked. Getting her to stay with him occasionally in the rented manager's house Craig was setting up wouldn't take much persuading. She loved hot climates. She loved Alice Springs.

He picked up his phone and dialled her number. He counted each of the rings. First...second...third, and steeled himself for disappointment. Easily seen intuition wasn't one of his strong points. He'd been wrong about the idea that Rosetta would answer him today. On the voicemail he asked her to phone him back. 'Hope my email cleared up the events of last Sunday, when you called in with those DVDs for Grant. I've got some really great news.' He slapped his phone back down on the hotel-room desk. It was almost a week since she'd refused to speak to him. Not that he could blame her. And fair was fair. When his money had gone down the gurgler, he'd been too gutless to pick up the phone when she'd called him. Rosetta not bothering to return his calls was karma.

His phone shuddered into a series of buzzes. He dived at it. Bernadette. She'd called a couple of times since Sunday. He'd been too tied-up to get back to her.

'Listen,' he said, after pleasantries had been exchanged. 'I want to thank you, Bernadette, for bringing round that letter you found amongst Sara's papers.'

'Not a problem, Matthew. It was the least I could do. Sara said it was from...She said it was from a friend of hers by the name of...ah! Can't think of the name right now! Sara's bought a little grey kitten from her.'

'Izzie,' said Matthew. Rosetta's sunny-natured daughter.

'That's the one!'

'And the kitten's one of Sidelta's.'

'One of whose? Can you wait a minnie, Matthew?' Bernadette was talking to someone. Was it Laura? It sounded like Laura in a bad mood. 'No, Laura,' she was saying. 'Dad and I have discussed it, and you're not to have your ears pierced until you're ten.' Back on the line again, she said, 'Sorry about that. What was I saying? Ah yes! The kitten's gorgeous. We all adore her.'

'Well, the mother cat's got a good coat on her. During pregnancy she looked like a sub in a mohair rug.'

'So you know Izzie's family?'

'I know her mother. Rosetta was the one visiting me the other day.' At the absence of a response, he added, 'You were drying your suit in the bathroom.'

'Aha. Yes, I've met Rosetta before.'

'You met her at my retirement night.'

'No. Before that. She went for that babysitting job I gave to Rhoda.'

'You're joking.'

'She cropped up at that bar a few days later, and I was thinking: "Uh-oh, this is going to be awkward: disgruntled candidate," but she turned out to be okay about the whole thing.'

Still unable to believe Rosetta Melki had gone to their house for a babysitting interview, Matthew shook his head. Why would a woman as well-off as Rosetta go for a job? Perhaps Sara had told Izzie about it, and she'd taken pity on the girls being left for two weeks.

Perhaps it had been more of a visit than an interview, to offer to have the girls at her place in Burwood. Trust Bernadette to twist the truth.

'Rosetta was there the day Adam died,' Bernadette was saying.

'Yup. Now about Adam Harrow—'

'She's into crystals isn't she?'

'How did you know that?'

'I was totally out of it with shock that day. Rosetta loaned me a crystal of some sort. It was pink. Really pretty.'

'Why did she do that?'

'She said the crystal would calm me down. And it did calm me down. I felt peaceful. I'll have to look in the shops for one of those.'

Another testimony to the crystals' bizarre soothing properties! He imagined how joyous Rosetta's response would be if she knew. If she were here right now, he'd get the chance to tell her about the brilliant healing she'd initiated by 'silvering' his ex-wife and Adam.

'They won't be available for sale in Sydney for another couple of months,' he told Bernadette. He began to add the news about his upcoming work with the guys who'd discovered them, and stopped. Talking about his new venture before Craig confirmed the role and offered him a contract wouldn't be wise at this early stage. He would make a note in his Blackberry to post Bernadette and the girls some of the sampler stones Craig had given him. He continued with, 'So! What were you wanting to contact me about?'

'Well, I'm phoning you now because I'd called around at a bad time on Sunday and didn't get to say what I'd wanted to say. I um...' Her voice rasped slightly. 'I wanted to apologise.'

'Apologise? Ha! Who have you been talking to? Adam Harrow?'

Silence.

'Mattie...' Bernadette's tone was concerned. 'Adam's dead.' She'd used the same tone when her great-uncle's diminished brain-cells had caused him to put his shoes on the wrong feet.

'Er...Adam is actually—'

'Is everything all right with you, Matthew? *Emotionally*, I mean.'

Bernadette using a word as in-depth as 'emotionally' was comical. Not so amusing was her allusion to him losing his grip on reality. Hardly surprising. Once Rosetta had fled the flat, he'd been too lost in grief to say anything much to her. Hadn't even said goodbye. 'All's fine with me, Bernadette,' he said. 'What do you want to apologise about?'

'Everything.' Bernadette groaned dramatically. 'You wouldn't believe how sad you made me when I saw you cooped up in that old place of Grant's. I went home, and I cried.' She sniffed then added, 'Cried and cried.'

'But I'm fine. I'm—'

'And I said to myself, "That's two of them!"'

'Two what?'

'Two men!'

'Well, you've proven it to yourself and the rest of us, Bernadette. You can't be content with one.'

'That is *not* what I meant,' she wailed. 'I meant that it's all my fault, what I've done to Grant, and what I've done to you. Grant would never have had to live in that...that revolting flat if I hadn't created the financial mess that forced us out of our home. Seeing you there too was so, *so* heartbreaking. I just kept shaking my head when I drove away, and I thought, "That's two of them! I've put two men into the same slum".'

Pride kicked in. 'That's no slum. It's—'

'Compared to what you're used to Matthew, it isn't exactly a royal palace.'

Matthew could hardly argue with that. 'Apology accepted,' he said. 'Thanks. Do you want to go now?'

Bernadette's simper turned into a roar. 'Absolutely not! For God's sake, hear me out, Matthew. Please.' Her voice went back to its usual softness. 'You know something? I look back on how I've been over the years, and I cringe. I must have been carrying around a lot of pain to have done what I did to myself and other people.'

So, what was she going to tell him? That she was getting professional help? Why the belated remorse?

'And I have to confess this to you. I know it will hurt, but here goes. I was planning on leaving you for Adam.'

'That doesn't hurt, Bernadette. It just highlights the extent of your gold-digging capacities.'

'Okay, so I admit it. Money's been a bit of a problem for me.'

'Not many people would call full financial support and a life of ongoing leisure a problem.'

'Point taken. Now, will you *shut* the *frack* up and listen to what I have to say? The solicitor I went to before the Vanuatu trip was a bit of a tough cookie. One of the girls at tennis recommended him. He'd worked beyond exhaustion in getting her fifty per cent of everything her husband had ever earned. Beyond exhaustion.'

'Poor bastard.'

'Oh no, he's not beyond exhaustion anymore.'

'I was talking about the husband.'

'The husband? Oh, right. Anyhow, I had no idea who to go to, so this guy sounded like a good idea. He was saying, "We'll sting him for half," and I was like, "Okay, sounds good to me," and then I went on my trip. But you know what? Something's changed in me since then. It was Adam's death that did it I think. Since that day, I started realising that we're all in this world together. It's not the *things* in our lives that are important, Matthew, it's the people!'

Matthew tried not to say something cynical. Ah well, glimpsed from the bright side, it had only taken her thirty-four years to wake up to that. He had to be thankful she'd thought it at all.

'And so, I went ahead and bought a home for the girls and me—it's an adorable little house, Matthew! And after I invited Grant to move in with us so we could be a family again, I couldn't help feeling bad about taking so much of your money. I told Grant I wanted to settle on a fairer agreement with you, and he was all for it.'

'Yeah?' Matthew went over Grant's words when he'd happened upon him at the mall, moments before accepting the offer of his flat. *She wants to see you.*

'That was my main reason for visiting. See, Matthew, the solicitor dismissed your post-nuptial agreement, and at the time I trusted that this was how everything worked, but it really bugged me when he told me how much I'd taken from you. So I asked him for a copy of your contract, and Grant found a solicitor on Yellow Pages Online, a local guy, and I told this guy how terrible I felt about taking fifty per cent. He was pretty understanding. We talked for two whole hours. First he asked me how much I paid the last solicitor, the expensive one—'

'Bernadette, he had no right to ask that, let alone keep you talking while charging you by the minute. I hope you didn't tell him.'

'But I did! I did tell him how much the expensive guy charged and it worked in my favour! He agreed to represent me for quite a bit less! So I'm phoning you now to tell you to expect a call from him.' Bernadette laughed. Her laughter quivered with nervousness. 'I'm agreeing to your pro-nup, Matthew. I'm keeping the house I got and my Audi, but I'm giving you back everything else.'

A sixth unpublished chapter
from Reverend Edward Lillibridge's
original *handwritten* manuscript

Maleika sighed impatiently. 'Alcor, as you may well have noticed, I am keen to learn what the Oracle meant by "the horned ones' wall".'

'Patience Maleika,' Alcor said. 'You will hear of it soon enough. Nikolaus is yet to announce this discovery.'

'I must say before we proceed with learning of the king's announcement that I cannot help worrying about the woman in the future. Despite Karee's assistance in leading her to her mission, there was only so much we could do. And as for Zhippe...well! He tried very hard to prevent the woman from falling in love with someone who wasn't Matthew, so with the help of a violin, the crafty undine deterred potential suitors when the woman sprite travelled on a small ship that went nowhere in particular.'

'Oh-ho-ho! Such ingenuity.'

186

'I thought it admirable of Zhippe, on his next visit to the future, to conjure a lute of sorts. The lute enabled Matthew to sing a love song. Most spoke poetically before a small audience, but Matthew chose music.'

'Did this win over the object of his affection?'

'I believe it did, somewhat. From what I could make of the scene, the two went into a garden of roses and camellias...to dance. And he holding her hair aloft as they did so. What strange customs they have in the future!'

Alcor waved a hand. Nikolaus's speech, hovering somewhere in Earth's faraway future, appeared once more.

Nikolaus was saying to the seated crowd: 'And during one very memorable spring season, a strange silver light swirled through the sky above Sydney Harbour. The light expanded to all parts of our world, inspiring wonder and joy in all who witnessed it. This freakish occurrence, now commonly referred to as the beginning of The Silvering, heralded a significant event in Earth's history.

'The Elysium Heart Crystals were already renowned for removing ailments. They affected many people in highly positive ways, but once the sky turned silver, these crystals rapidly increased in power. The crystals' healing abilities were no longer limited by geography. Research revealed that healings, both physical and emotional, were able to take place within up to 200 kilometres of any gem. Few escaped the magical results of this fascinating treasure.

'It has been suggested that the completion of major planetary cycles in 2012, as prophesied by the ancient Mayan race, enabled us to fully receive the crystals' remarkable "awakening" effects in the years that followed. And so, we now believe it was our evolution rather than any change instigated by the crystals, which allowed our transformation.

'The unifying sonic waves of the crystals began to "silver" us through reviving our inherent devic qualities. Once our emotions were cleared of hatred, despair, fear, jealousy and distrust, we began to understand each other on a whole new level. We began to enjoy a feeling of safeness and a desire for all to prosper.

'A return to nature came about: group by group, town by town, city by city. Self-supporting communities sprang up around the globe.

Many created co-operative market gardens for food supply. Many areas around the globe devised exchange systems, preferring their own form of cooperative currency, which previously would never have been possible.

'And here we all are in 2026.

'Ancient sprite wisdom is resurrecting everywhere.

'Our direct connection to the Dream Sphere has empowered us.

'With the return of our fuller senses, inspiration is flourishing.

'The enhanced clarity of our minds has led to the development of incredible crystal technology. We could never have envisaged this sort of technology in 2008, the year I made my secondary school speech on alternate exchange systems.

'Previous dire predictions about ridding the earth of pollution taking up to a thousand years were probably accurate at the time they were made. Innovative developments, however, have erased the relevance of these predictions. Crystal sonic-wave technology is purifying both the air and the water and is assisting in coaxing barren land to bloom. Our world was never meant to be devoid of vegetation. Deserts have been shrinking over the past few years and fertile land has increased significantly. We have seen an end to our dependence on fossil fuels. Free, crystal-powered energy has enabled us pollutant-free transportation and manufacturing. Of course, cleaning up the planet remains a work in progress. Each of us strives for a return to the world that was stolen from us, millenniums ago, by Gold's Kin.

'On this day in Perelda, Sweden, on this ninth day of August, 2026, I am overjoyed that I can now finally say that all I suggested as a fifteen-year-old captain of the Silver Tongues debating team at Burwood High in Sydney, Australia, all that I dreamed of and hoped for and remembered with sadness from ancient lives buried in the past, is gradually coming about. A world that could only once be imagined is now the place in which we live.

'And all this has happened because of you. You, the people on this planet at this auspicious time, were the ones who collectively embraced the Currency of Kindness.

'The Silvering allowed you to recognise your devic qualities. These qualities had never left you. They were only slumbering.

'We are all now familiar with our true ancient history: when the forbidden love of an autumn faerie and a Gold's Kin trooper played a vital part in the changes that are taking place in our lifetime. It is almost as though we are journeying back to that time, to re-experience it, the time before Gold's Kin embarked on their destruction of a world that knew no pain...'

Matthew strode through Sydney Airport, as happy as a kid at Christmas. He was back home with a revitalised sense of purpose. Just when he'd thought life couldn't get any better, Bernadette had phoned to relay her change of heart, a fresh new attitude that had cartwheeled into a wealth of goodwill. It was the crystal that had transformed her. Didn't Dalesford say the Alice Spring crystals restored harmony within the individual? That they opened the mind and healed the emotions?

He and Bernadette had talked some more after her astounding declaration. She'd been candid with him about how she'd felt in the marriage; had told him that marrying a workaholic was a recipe for sadness. 'You were never there. The loneliness just ate me up. I fell back into my spending addiction for comfort.' Matthew had argued that he'd always made a point of planning family days out every second weekend. Bernadette had replied, 'And you were wonderful with the girls, Matthew, really wonderful, but sometimes I thought you were better at being a dad to my kids than being a husband to me. I wasn't the only one who'd given up on our marriage.'

He'd only ever considered himself to be the honourable half of the partnership. Honourable and blameless...but why had he thought he was free of all blame? Because he hadn't severed the commitment once he fell out of love with Bernadette? How honourable had he been immersing himself in his work and golf and swimming as a means of avoidance? She was justified in saying that. He'd been selfish! After coming to grips with the revelation, he'd said, 'Bernadette, I think you're right.'

Heading towards the airport's lifts, Matthew dodged an unsteady toddler and a pigtailed girl skipping in buoyant circles. He steered around a woman wheeling a stroller and slid aside as the stroller swerved gracefully away from his feet. A slow motion waltz reflecting the rhythm of existence, of living harmoniously in this battle-weary world. Life on Earth: the daily dance of decisions; a place where all inhabitants were absorbed in a to-and-fro choreography. Everywhere in the airport was evidence of this. The head-jutting of a guy enjoying whatever was on his iPod. The click-clacking of harried passengers across a whitely reflective floor. He felt as though he were part of a Broadway stage show. Considering the euphoria he'd spun into since Bernadette's decision to return his grandfather's legacy, the idea of launching into a tap dance seemed strangely justifiable.

At the lifts, he took the small flake of stone from his pocket and savoured the familiar warmth it exuded. Who would have thought something so tiny could be capable of so much?

He collected the Jag from the airport's carpark and started out onto the main drag, bound for Lavender Bay. He wasn't taking chances. It was straight to Rosetta's. He had to speak to her as soon as he could; would knock down her door if he had to.

The petrol light flashed. 'Aargh! Almost on empty.' Not a service station in sight and only ten or so minutes' worth left in the tank. He refuelled the Jag at a Zetland BHP, gave its windscreen a once-over with the squeegee and drove across to the air pump, already in use. The guy inflating his tyres was kneeling on an arthritis cushion. He acknowledged Matthew with a grimace that said: *I'll probably be a while.*

Matthew leaned back in his seat. What would he tell Rosetta first? Would he tell her about the interview? Craig had greeted him at Alice Springs Airport effusively, shared a drink and a laugh with him at an outdoor bar, and listed some interesting examples of the crystals' uncanny healing abilities.

Once they'd got stuck into their dinner at a vibey organic cafe, Craig had said, 'Now, down to business.' The guy's change in demeanour was disconcerting at first. He'd gone from affable pal to cross-examining prosecutor to test Matthew's commitment. Matthew had answered each demand with unmasked enthusiasm. His running injury hadn't flared for months now, not since the night Rosetta taped her own crystal to his knee. He'd woken without pain, and the flexibility in his tendons had since improved. As for promptly restoring someone to health after a lethal overdose, Adam Harrow was living proof of the crystals' uncanny healing properties.

They'd then got onto the subject of *Our True Ancient History*. Craig told Matthew about the legend of the Land of Mu. 'We're standing in the middle of it,' he'd said. 'Australia was part of Lemuria. A goddess apparition appeared to a few of us in the bush one night. You would have read about Orahney in the book. We believe it was Orahney visiting us from the past. We're uncovering hidden beauty-creation, Matt. There's magic in those gems. Real magic.'

'Do you think...' Matthew had said, '...I know this is pretty way out, but do you think it could have been the same crystals Storlem and others exported? There's a chapter in the book where Maleika and a couple of other Brumlynds witness a magic-robbing ceremony. Chapter XXXVIII if I remember rightly.'

'I do indeed think that,' Craig had said. 'That's what I was referring to when I mentioned beauty-creation. I'm ninety per cent certain these crystals were the receptacles for sprites' heart-elixir. There's also, in one of the earlier chapters...Chapter V, I think it is, a part where Croydee talks to Maleika about a Dream Sphere prophecy regarding beauty-creation slumbering for aeons:

...unrecognised, deep beneath the soil of a faraway southern land.'

He'd shaken his head and chuckled. 'That's us! We are *the southern land*. The head honcho of the ancient Norwegian Gold's Kin made sure the gems were sent away. He was in fear of his people becoming silvered. The crystals were ridding hearts of hostility, and the Solen didn't like it.' Craig had leaned forward and lowered his voice. 'You gotta understand, Matt, I don't go around announcing this stuff to just anyone. I'd be laughed out of court! But if what we've discovered in Alice Springs has the power to *silver* people, right now, right here, in this current age, then the healing we can create in this world will be nothing short of incredible!'

They'd called in at Conan and Jannali Dalesford's alpaca farm.

Edward and Lucetta had galloped clumsily up to Craig's four-wheel-drive, and Lucetta, true to form, had nuzzled Matthew's neck. Seeing again the author and his wife had been one of the trip's many highlights.

Matthew told Dalesford about the elf writing 'Fred M' across a tree trunk. 'And other letters had faded, you say?' Dalesford had said. 'I'll ask about that in the Dream Sphere tonight.'

That had been on the Friday. On the Saturday, when they were travelling across to the crystals mine, Dalesford had enlightened him on the dream. 'From what I can gather, Pieter was in no way suggesting you put money on Friedman.'

Matthew had felt suddenly foolish. 'So he was warning me against it?'

'He hadn't written Friedman at all. That was your interpretation. He'd written one word in answer to your question, and one word only. The word had been *freedom*. Meaning, no doubt, that releasing half your fortune to your wife would liberate you from a loveless marriage. There was no need to try and recuperate it from elsewhere.' Dalesford clicked his tongue. 'Bulls and bears, eh? So you got a grizzly this time! I'd keep away from the stock market from now on if I were you.'

Demoralising advice for someone whose career had revolved around that.

A phenomenon had occurred when Matthew first saw the mine. Turning slightly away from the site, he'd become aware of a glowing band of silver that no-one but Dalesford could see. 'It's in my peripheral vision,' he'd told Dalesford.

'You're seeing the power the crystals emanate,' Dalesford had said. 'Rosetta saw rainbows.'

'Did she really?' Matthew practically lived for those all too fleeting mentions of Rosetta. Her name had been brought up again in the evening that followed when he and Craig were sinking chilled beers. 'Sorry to hear it didn't work out for you and Rosetta,' Craig had said.

Matthew had answered too quickly. 'You've spoken to her?'

'Yeah.'

What had she said? About them? About Matthew? It couldn't have been too bad. *Two-timing low life* would never have induced Craig to fly him across for an interview.

'Spoke to her yesterday, actually. She just said the two of you didn't work out.' Evidently she hadn't related her version of Sunday. 'I asked if she'd be okay with you working in the same company, but she just changed the subject, so I'm guessing that's an absent-minded "yes".'

Matthew had said nothing; had stared at the surface of his beer.

'So you're relegated to friend status.' Craig had patted his shoulder. 'Join the club!' He'd laughed and shaken his head. 'That's Rosetta. Great girl, but always on the lookout for some knight in shining armour. Not content with decent blokes like us.'

...Reflecting on the stab of grief Craig's well-meaning comment had caused, Matthew drummed his thumbs on the steering wheel. The cushion belonging to the poor arthritis sufferer was now alongside the second wheel. If there'd been an extra air pump nearby, Matthew would have jumped up and helped him with the other two tyres. He would give the man a sampler crystal. His own knee was cured.

He flicked on the radio. *Mr Sandman* trilled sedately from the speakers, the same song that had played when he'd driven Rosetta across to Lena's after their Amaretti's dinner. Back then the melodious lyrics surrounding dreams had felt soothing. Romantic even. This afternoon the lyrics felt lazy. Drowsy. Soporific. A hush fell across the hum of traffic over on the highway. He closed his eyes.

Sleep overtook.

A candlelit table...The interior of a lattice-windowed cottage. He was writing at the table with an ink-dipped white quill. Outside the window, and within a garden alive with the flamboyant rays of a sinking sun, was a small circular stone wall, abundant with climbing roses.

A woman with exotic eyes was watching him, cascading dark hair brightened by a pale pink rose, taken from the stone-built well. In her hands was a copper pot brimming with soup. She stood in an open doorway that led to a room with a fireplace; was telling him gently that supper was served.

He addressed the woman, his heart aglow with adoration. 'I will work tirelessly, my darling enchantress,' he said, 'to bring about The Silvering. It has every chance of occurring. Within one score-year, I would say.'

The woman lowered her eyes and shook her head sorrowfully. 'Not in our lifetime, dear-heart. One day though. One day, many years into the future, it will happen.'

○

''Scuse me!' *Rap! Rap!*

Matthew jumped. Opened his eyes.

'Excuse me!' *Rappity-Rap-Rap!*

A square velvet blob bounced against his windscreen. The tardy tyre-filler, cushion clenched in one fist, was gesturing for him to drive forward. 'I've clearly put you to sleep,' he joked once Matthew had wound down his window. 'All wrapped up now.' He gave a knobbly thumbs-up and hobbled back to his car.

Matthew filled the tyres distractedly. The dream felt as though it had played out before. 'Of course,' he whispered. 'I've read about the guy in the cottage. Chapter XLIX.' The chapter in which Pieter had observed eagle-winged Storlem's future lives.

A fine film of rain had formed across the windscreen when Matthew returned to his car. His drive through the suburbs and towards the Harbour Bridge was contemplative. Craig's comment about Rosetta's lofty and changeable standards continued to gnaw at him. He activated the windscreen wipers to clear a scattering of stubborn raindrops and shook away his doubts. The fickleness was Craig's opinion. Surely the relationship had been more than just a passing fancy for Rosetta.

Life was meant to be shared. Throughout history, he and Rosetta had spent lives together. He wasn't going to tell her that. The notion was too intense; could paint him as desperately eager to form the sort of commitment she might not be willing to consider. And yet, what had occurred in the distant past could not be denied. Rosetta's actions in reviving Adam with the crystal had reflected exactly Adam's past-life recollection of the Gypsy Lucetta bringing Ned back to life. Edward and Lucetta. Matthew and Rosetta. The past five weeks had been an agony. They weren't meant to be apart.

The rain had ceased by the time Matthew reached the Harbour Bridge. A deep, muted green speckled the harbour, along with crimson fragments of sunset. When he turned left at the end of the Bridge, the old anticipation returned. At Kirribilli, he glided under the arched railway underpass and through the roundabout into Lavender Bay. Rosetta's apartment block, normally the colour of unbleached calico, was pinkly orange in the evening's glow, a queen's castle overlooking the dancing jewels of a light-dabbed sea.

Upon nearing the apartment, he glimpsed a figure at the edge of the manicured lawns, a teenaged girl with golden hair. On exiting his car, he realised the girl hadn't been blonde at all. Redheaded Izzie, surrounded by the deceptively lightening rays of the setting sun, was standing outside the apartment complex with an overnight bag in one hand and a cat carrier in the other. She smiled and waved. 'Hi Matthew.'

'Hello, Izzie. Good to see you. Is your mum about?'

'Actually no! Mum's gone away. She left for the airport this afternoon.'

Swallowing back his disappointment, Matthew said, 'Right! I see! Where is she off to?'

'Alice Springs. She decided yesterday to stay there for a month. She needs to sort out crystals distribution with Craig.'

A whole month. He wasn't due back there any earlier than that. He contemplated the tufts of lawn that formed fringes around his shoes. When he looked up again, Izzie was regarding him with a sympathetic half-smile. 'Sorry about that!'

'Not a problem. I should really have...Do you know the exact date she'll be back?'

'Eleventh of November.'

Matthew nodded glumly. He was due to start with Craig on the tenth.

'She'll be back for a week, then we're off to New Zealand. I'll get to meet my uncle and aunt and cousins. Mum's starting a Crystal Consciousness store there.'

'New Zealand? Whoa. She doesn't waste time.'

'Sure doesn't.' Izzie nodded good-naturedly.

He gestured to her bag. 'And you...you're all right are you, on your own here?' Probably a stupid question. Rosetta would have ensured her daughter was okay to leave.

'Yeah, I'm fine.' Izzie nodded towards the concierge behind the glass doors. 'Security apartment and all. I could have stayed here on my own, but Lena offered to have me there, and Mum said she'd prefer that, so...' In a single shrug, she held up the cat carrier. '...Sidleta and I are waiting on a lift from Lena as we speak.'

'You and Sidelta deserting the place too! Your poor old apartment will get a complex.'

'That's true. But then again, it's part of a complex isn't it?'

'Now that's a point.'

'Anyway, it'll be good to have a change of scenery. Lena's son's got heaps of computer games, and I usually win the challenges, so I'm psyching myself up to claim victory again.'

'Enjoy yourself then. How long will you and your mother be in New Zealand?'

'A fortnight.'

'All right, I'll er...Would you mind telling Mum if you speak to her that I called round?'

'Not a problem.'

'Thanks, darl. Have a good time at Lena's. Make sure you win all those games.'

He crossed the lawn. Swerving towards the kerb was a new model Porsche with a fair-haired woman at the wheel. Lena. Noticing Matthew, she waved.

He waved back, returning the smile. He liked all of Rosetta's friends. Seeing Lena and Izzie again, and even Rosetta's apartment, was bittersweet in a way. Knowing they were connected to her made him sentimental. Knowing he mightn't get to see her for at least six weeks had immersed him in despair.

He strode towards Lena's car, then slowed his step. Would it be appropriate to talk to her? Lena would probably know as much about Sunday as Rosetta did.

Lena's hand hesitated in the air. She cut eye-contact abruptly and busied herself with rifling through her handbag. Fair enough. He sauntered to his car. The situation was awkward. Probably as far as Lena was concerned, Matthew was Rosetta's double-crossing ex.

How could he get hold of Rosetta now? He wouldn't risk upsetting her by taking an impulsive trip back to Alice Springs. Going there when he wasn't needed would only ring of obsession. Somehow he'd find a way.

His options were narrowing though, crashing down around him with stultifying certainty.

Rosetta had wrapped herself in a cloak of self-protection, and he had only himself to blame.

Chapter Ten

Spring, 2009

MATTHEW STOOD IN THE FOYER of Hotel Pallisandre and examined a plaque while he waited for Craig's phone call. The plaque was in memory of singer-songwriter-guitarist Jimi Hendrix who died of an overdose in 1970 while staying in London. Engraved on a brass surface was something the man was supposed to have once said:

'*When the power of love overcomes the love of power, the world will know peace.*'

The concierge had told Matthew that former British Prime Minister, William E Gladstone had made an almost identical statement in the 1800s.

Rosetta would have liked its sentiment. It was the sort of quote she might use in the Wise Words segment of Poet's Garret meetings if called upon to contribute. Whether she still attended those poetry nights, Matthew could only wonder.

Tomorrow it would be six months. Six months of not knowing how she was getting along, not knowing who she was spending time with, not knowing whether she was happy with the way life was treating her. Six months. The hope of speaking to Rosetta again was whittling away steadily.

He sank into a velveteen armchair beside the plaque and checked his phone once more.

What frustrated him was that in every other part of his life he had an element of control. Self-reliance was winning him points daily in his dynamic new career, his most recent coup the arrangement of heart-crystal distributorships in the UK and throughout mainland Europe. When it came to his shattered relationship, though, the stern whims of fate were all he could rely on. Those whims had let him down. Severely.

Psychics insisted the crystals cleared past emotional pain, but Matthew's heartache had proven itself incurable. Perhaps the pain was still too recent. Perhaps...but he didn't want to envisage carrying the heaviness of despair around for much longer; couldn't imagine life continuing as it was, with the absence of the person he loved most in this world. She'd been his very best friend. And now she refused to speak to him.

His phone rang. Craig. He pushed the phone to his ear. No response. Craig getting interrupted most likely. No doubt he'd call again within the next few minutes. Matthew settled the phone onto a side table next to an ostentatious array of feathery spring blooms and retrieved *The London Evening Standard* from his briefcase, the blaring headline about post-GFC protests reminding him of having crossed through Pall Mall yesterday.

'Monetary exchange doesn't work anymore,' a guy with a placard had said to him in a shout. 'It's the ninety-nine per cent versus the one per cent.'

'Yeah, I know all that. I worked in finance.'

The guy had caught up with him, demanding to know whether he thought it unfair. 'Wall Street has to close. We have to find a better way.'

'Hate to smash your hopes,' Matthew had said, 'but I don't think that'll happen.'

'Why so sure? Money can't be sustained. It's going to come to an end.'

'Not in our lifetime, pal.'

The guy had folded his arms. 'Not if it's up to the likes of you.' He'd shaken his head and looked pointedly at Matthew's top-of-the-range briefcase. 'Pal.'

Matthew had then produced a crystal from his pocket. 'Here. Try this.' He'd handed it to the placard-bearer and marched onwards. As he'd negotiated his way through London's peak-hour huddle, he'd heard a shout.

'Hey! Come back? Where'd you get this?'

The most Matthew could do while shouldering his way through the crowd was turn and acknowledge the activist with a thumbs-up. He'd been running late for a meeting. The guy had done what most people did when presented with one of the glowing stones. He'd clasped it against his chest. His face, mostly obscured by beard, had taken on an expression of blissful serenity. *Instinct,* Craig had said previously about the predictable chest clutch. *Something to do with the heart chakra.*

Seeing the date on the front page made Matthew shake his head. Twenty-fifth of April, 2009. Not long now till the close of the Millennium's first decade. A little over a year since he'd first encountered her. Who would have thought the madwoman leaping about on the road would become his prime obsession?

If she hadn't blocked his explanatory emails...If she'd let him speak to her when he'd visited on her return from New Zealand...Her response when he'd nervously buzzed the apartment complex intercom, was, 'Give me one good reason why I should see you.' He'd gone to tell her she'd been mistaken about Bernadette, but she'd dismissed him before he'd begun. 'Actually, Matthew, there's probably *no* good reason. The fact is, I don't trust you to come up with the truth, so we'd just be wasting each other's time.'

'But surely we could—'

'It's over Matthew.' The intercom had clicked off. He'd returned home in a cloud of gloom, knowing he should quit pursuing Rosetta, furious he had no way of proving his innocence. He had to respect Rosetta's wishes. His presence was upsetting her.

And now he was two months into a UK business trip and about to recruit a European Distributorship Manager while quietly cherishing the faint glimmer of a possibility. Glynis and Dudley, the Friday Fortnighters whose group he'd visited in Cornwall, had hinted at inviting him to dinner when Rosetta was due to visit them. If the two agreed to the purchase of a Crystal Consciousness store for Tintagel, there'd be plenty for Matthew to discuss with her. Now that he'd been promoted to international sales manager, he expected Rosetta would need to liaise with him about the newer Crystal Consciousness franchises on this side of the world.

Craig phoned once more.

'Hey Matt,' he said. 'Great news about that gambling crim. So Interpol finally caught up with him?'

'Yeah! Good to have my money back. Kirk Rummery returned most of it in the end.'

'Good stuff. So how's the head-hunting going?'

'I'm meeting my brother at The Ivy in half an hour, but I'd say his mind's pretty much made up.'

'So he's still strong on staying where he is?'

'Unfortunately, yes. Like I said before, he's entertained the idea, but he's also said he'd rather stay in his current line of work. So I've prepared you a duty statement.'

'Got that. Picked it up from the inbox a few minutes ago.'

'Just need your final okay, and then I'll start the selection process.'

'Sure. Although, Matt, I've been thinking...'

Matthew waited. Had Craig done a backflip on the Euro Distributorship Manager idea?

'When I put you on here I said your UK connections were what we needed. Remember that?'

'Of course. I don't reckon you could call my brother a connection though.'

'Ah, no, no. That's not what I'm talking about. This isn't a criticism. What you're doing there is fine. In fact it's better than fine. That's why I've settled on this proposal.'

'And what proposal's that?'

'Well, what I'm thinking, mate, is this. You're over there in England, in the place you grew up. You're footloose and free of a wife and kids, and a permanent address. You've got family over there, London's supposed to be one of the most exciting cities in the world...' Craig was listing benefits, painting the rosiest of pictures surrounding life in the UK. And why? He wanted Matthew to snap up the position himself.

'What I'm saying here, Matt, is this. You're great at the international sales. You know London like the back of your hand. Who better could we have as an EDM than you?'

No way. Never. He needed to remain in the same city as Rosetta. He might still have a chance.

'So what do you say, Matt?'

'No, look—'

'Wait on. Don't decide straight away. Think it over. I really reckon you could do the job justice. Hang on a minnie.' Craig was now speaking to someone in saccharine tones. The faint notes of a woman's voice echoed in the background. 'What's that, sweetheart? No, I'm not throwing *them* out. I've had them since high school. Aaaagh!'

Matthew was amused. 'Someone threatening to ditch your Papa Smurf underpants?'

'Not quite. It's my collection of *Mad* comics.'

'Can't throw out those.'

'Can't indeed.' His voice rose. 'Matt agrees with me, sweetheart. *Mad* comics are off limits.' He laughed a bit. 'Rosetta's insisting I put my boyhood behind me. Ha. Women! They'll never understand.'

'Rosetta's...She's...she's over there is she?'

'Sure is. You know how I said I'd be moving in April...'

'Of course. Forgot you were moving. That's good of Rosetta to help you out. She's...Now as I understand it she's scheduled to be here on third of May.'

'Not so sure about that, Matt. She was saying something about putting it off. Sweetheart, about your England trip...'

Matthew flinched. Craig calling Rosetta sweetheart. Fingernails down a blackboard.

'You sure about that, sweetheart?'

Matthew flinched again. *Stop saying sweetheart.*

'Strike while the iron's hot I reckon. Glynis and Dudley might purchase elsewhere, and Matt's over there. You could both go and speak to them...huh?...Right. Well, I guess...right. Okay then. You there, Matt?'

'Yep.' Realising he'd been holding his breath, Matthew slowly exhaled.

'It's not happening. Rosetta reckons September now. September or October. She's contacted Glynis apparently, and Glynis is fine with that. Said they're not looking to purchase till October anyway, so I guess it's a fair enough move.'

Matthew closed his eyes. Tried not to groan. He grappled for something to say. Something cheerful. Settled on, 'So, what did you decide on property-wise?'

'Funnily enough, it's turned out to be a joint decision.'

'In what way?'

'I don't think I've told you this. About Rosetta and me.'

Rosetta? Rosetta and Craig? What, *for crying out loud,* was going on?

'It's happened, mate. We're together again. After all these years. I asked her to be my wife and...'

No.

'...And she said yes. We're moving into a place just north of Alice. Looking forward to you seeing it. Spectacular views, gorgeous lap pool. Congratulate me, Matt. I'm engaged.'

Congratulate? Right now Matthew wanted to shout 'Theft!' Congratulate? Not a hope in hell. *You missed out there, mate,* Matthew wanted to say. *I'd rather mash you to a pulp.*

The reasons against Rosetta marrying Craig rained into his brain like machine-gun bullets. 'But Izzie,' he said. 'Izzie's in Sydney. And Rosetta's friends...' He didn't even care if he sounded disapproving. The guy he worked for had unexpectedly turned into a *fracking* traitor.

'Izzie had the choice of moving up here, but she's quite happy in Sydney.'

'Without her mother?'

'Well, the girl's turning seventeen in a few weeks. Rosetta's let her have the Lavender Bay security apartment, a rental she ultimately bought. Izzie's sharing the place with a couple of girls from school, and Rosetta remote-orders their groceries. They're stoked, all three of them. Rosetta said the "parties every night" remark was just ribbing, but I'm not so sure. When it comes to teenage girls—'

'Izzie's a sensible kid,' Matthew bit back. Craig obviously didn't know Izzie's dry sense of humour.

'Of course, of course. I'm stirring Rosetta, actually. She's glaring at me now with her hands on her hips. Ha. Just stirring, sweetheart. Izzie's not a party animal.'

Don't. Say. Sweetheart.

'So, think about the job, anyway.'

'I've already thought about it.'

'But before you say no—'

'I'm not saying no.'

'But you said no a moment ago. Matt, what's up? Everything okay with you? You sound a bit weird. Distracted or something.'

'I'm not saying no. I'm saying yes.'

'You're saying yes to the UK post?'

'Yes.'

'I haven't prepared the proposal though.'

'Doesn't matter.'

'The pay, of course, will be substantially better than the pay you're getting now.'

'I'll take it.'

'You'll take it? Matt! That's great news! Are you serious? You'll take it just like that?'

'Just like that.'

She'd been everything.

Everything to him.

And now all that mattered was getting as far away as possible from Craig, and Rosetta, and Australia, and every single one of those wrenching memories.

'Just like that.' Bleakly, he added. 'I'm moving to London for good.'

Autumn, 2024

Hi Friday Fortnighters!

Autumn is here in the Southern Hemisphere once again, a reminder of the faerie Orahney. Here at the Sydney and Alice Springs groups, we see Orahney as highly significant to our future.

It's nearly sixteen years now since I launched this website. We've all been acutely aware of the correlation between what the body kings began all those aeons ago and the limitations that are placed on us still. The study of Lillibridge's book has inspired plenty of online and in-group discussion on how we might restore the earth to its former beauty.

When thinking of the heart-crystals' initial discovery north of Alice Springs, I can't help but feel great reverence for the autumn faerie. Her astounding appearance to a group of campers may well have changed the course of history! We have no idea where all this will lead but feel sure that where we're heading is unimaginably good.

It's hard to believe Orahney's visitation was way back in 2008. The years are rushing by crazily! Since then, we've witnessed phenomenal occurrences—and on a daily basis!

Positive changes in people's health—both physical and emotional—are manifesting with miraculous regularity. You all know the stories. You, the Friday Fortnighters, are part of these stories. I am so hugely grateful that so many of you throughout the world have signed up as distributors. Because of your valued contributions, and thanks to the diligent work of Craig and Conan's team and my daughter Izzie in Canada (She does part-time public relations work for CEGS along with studying a second degree) we are enhancing this wondrous world of ours with soothing energies that increase our sense of responsibility towards each other.

Last week saw the emergence of yet another international Crystal Consciousness store. This time in New Delhi. As you probably already know, my fiancé Craig Delorey is a partner in my firm. (A too-lengthy engagement you say? It's probably the longest engagement in the entire history of the world, but who doesn't love being engaged? And we *will* get round to planning a wedding some day.) All profits from the sale of our Crystal Consciousness stores go towards financial aid for war-ravaged and disaster affected nations. Our mission, like the mission of many excellent organisations that have gone before us, is to assist in ending all aspects of slavery and eliminating all poverty. It's *not* so impossible. It *can* be done!

Craig and I are always on the lookout for volunteers in our Crystals Ending Global Suffering (CEGS) community enhancement projects. If you're interested in taking time out to see the world and are keen to work for ten days (or more) helping people in developing nations in their efforts to restore health / wellbeing / prosperity, we'd love to hear from you.

CEGS operates in seven different locations. You'd be working amongst super-fun people within a well-run organisation that offers locals the practical assistance they seek (whether it be the construction of schools, the restoration of clean water or the sowing of crops) and you will absolutely love working alongside them. An unforgettable experience. Click onto the application link below. If you're called upon, we'll fit the bill for your fares, accommodation and meals. Please direct any enquiries to our Melki-Delorey email.

To allay any potential confusion when you visit the site, I'll advise here that you're likely to see on the 'About Us' page a photo of a woman named 'Odetta Melki' who looks suspiciously like me. No, not my evil twin. Odetta is my other first name, which I've used in business for some time now, but friends and Fortnighters are fine to keep using the one below.

Hugs,
Rosetta Melki

Summer, 2024

Hi Friday Fortnighters!
Amazing news regarding *Our True Ancient History!*
Anna Callan contacted me last week to say she's putting the original unedited manuscript up for auction at Sotheby's London in April next year. I would love to get it and have arranged for a British

broker to attend the auction on my behalf. If the purchase comes about smoothly (and I can't see why it wouldn't) I will publish the 1771 handwritten manuscript on this site. So it's only four months away, our chance to discuss Lillibridge's *original* text, all things going well. Exciting times ahead!

And while on the subject of exciting times...We've booked our venue for the first ever Crystal Consciousness / Friday Fortnight Fancy-Dress Ball to be held in Australia's spring next year, on the 6th of October. The location we've chosen is...drum roll please...*Luna Park,* a Coney Island style amusement park situated on spectacular Sydney Harbour. I've heard there's to be a full moon that night, so we are pleased to have settled on a site whose name suggests that silvery luminary. The invitation is extended to Friday Fortnighters, Crystal Consciousness store owners/ employees and CEGS organisers / volunteers and, of course, all partners and friends. The dress-code is 18th century (costumes from the 1700s) or a character from *Our True Ancient History.* We have a limit of 500 tickets, and we're currently taking bookings, so if you're planning a trip to Sydney around then, we'd love to see you there.

And, hey, I've been thinking...Imagine if by 2030 we have all become 'silvered' like Eidred and Storlem were. What sort of innovations would come about? How much more peaceful would life be if war and slaughter and lying and territorialism ended, and we knew no threats? *In our lifetime!* We can only imagine...

To those of you in the Northern Hemisphere, enjoy your wintry Christmas, and all the best for a wonderful 2025!

Long live the Currency of Kindness.

Warmest regards,

Rosetta Melki

Winter, 2025

Hi Friday Fortnighters!

Which would you like first? The good news or the bad news?

We've received such an enthusiastic response for the Fancy Dress Ball.

Let's start with the good news.

Friday Fortnighter Arthur Dalwood of Crazy Daisy will be responsible for decorating Luna Park's Crystal Palace Ballroom. His plans are like, *wow*. I can't wait for you to see what he'll create! There are still tickets left, but they're dwindling fast, and the event is only two months away now. I'd hate any of you to miss out, so if you can manage to get your RSVPs across to us (as soon as humanly possible!) you'll be all set for an enormously fun evening.

And now for the not-so-good news.

My broker was unable to purchase Lillibridge's original manuscript back in our autumn. Despite his diligent efforts at Sotheby's, he was outbid by an undisclosed buyer. Unfortunately, my phone was out of order at the time, and the broker couldn't reach me. He was mindful of my purse-strings, saying, 'It had been pushed up to a ridiculous amount. I couldn't justify spending that much of your money,' which was very sweet of him, but between you and me, Fortnighters, I don't think he realised how much it would mean to me to share the document with you on my website. I would have happily paid any price, but then, it would hardly be fair to blame him for not being a mind reader! He did his best, and I'm grateful for that.

And, disappointed and all as I am, I can only wish the undisclosed buyer well. Sure hope he/she values that coveted handwritten treasure. What a treat to own it! *Grrr!* What a stroke of absolute luck, winning the bid like that. (But now I'm coming across all Green-Eyed Monster, so I'll close off the topic right here!!)

Below are photographs of our wonderful CEGS volunteers on location. It's so rewarding to witness everyone's achievements. A typical unpaid CEGS participant starts out keen to help someone they've never met and progresses to embracing the challenge of adventure. By the end of the volunteer's working holiday, a sense of satisfaction sets in at having made a tangible difference. Lifelong friendships are invariably formed in the process.

Keep up the fantastic work, volunteers! We adore what you do and are 'over the moon' that you adore it too. That's all for now!

Rosetta Melki

A seventh unpublished chapter
from Reverend Edward Lillibridge's
original *handwritten* manuscript

Oh dear, Maleika thought when observing the close of the future-man's announcement. I should really have pursued that rose-sprite assignment.

Her thoughts had turned again to the future-woman she'd attempted to help. Now she would never know the outcome. Was Rosetta in fact a sprite? Perhaps she was one of those people from humanity: part of the expansive descendancy of Maleika's son and daughter-by-marriage. Given her placement on the timeline, it could well be a possibility. Whatever the case, the poor creature might be grieving an inconclusive romance.

The elf woman bit her lip and sighed. It had been her own responsibility, after all, to ensure that Rosetta and Matthew remained together after having been magnetised. She supposed the stars she'd sent, to dance before Rosetta's eyes—whenever her decisions or actions led her in the direction of Matthew—had not been recognised for their significance.

She remembered back to her brief future-visit when she'd hinted to Rosetta, with the pictorial help of cards Rosetta referred to as 'tarots', how near she was to encountering this fellow. She'd told her they'd be beside each other in toil, already true in Rosetta's present, quite possibly to be repeated in her future, all things going well.

Rosetta—at the point in time Maleika had visited—was most certainly working alongside him, unknowingly of course. During the card reading, Maleika was given a glimpse of the work Rosetta did. She was a type of servant who dusted and polished her soulmate's place of work.

The man named Matthew was quite unaware of her. High within an unadorned tower, whose glassy exterior reflected the setting sun, he sat at a narrow table and played a piano of sorts that made particularly ugly music: *tap-tap tappity-tappity-tap* while staring into a rectangle similar to the Grudellan Palace's spy-lights. Numerals appeared in this rectangle, each wrapped in harsh geometrical lines, one on top of the other. Alcor had informed her that this man was a dealer in gold. 'Ah, so he is a servant also,' she had said.

'Not so much a servant as a slave,' Alcor had corrected. 'A slave to something known as "the dollar." A victim of currency.'

Brought back into the present, Maleika cast Alcor a furtive glance, hopeful the Dream Master would conjure again the holographic scene of Nikolaus in the future, and the meaning of that mysterious wall.

The scene reappeared.

She craned her neck forward and listened to the conclusion of the king's final announcement.

Chapter Eleven

Spring, 2025

THE WAIL OF A LONE VIOLIN rose up, dipping and weaving through strains of melancholy. Rosetta took a step forward. Laughed when a mint-scented mist whooshed about the hem of her flowing gown.

I'm really here, she thought. It's really happened. Elysium Glades resurrected.

She could never have imagined just how magical it would be. She stepped back onto a path that disappeared into a grove of pines and crimson-leafed maples. Beyond clouds of dry-ice mist, the violinist's chords soared and plunged, rich with dramatic verve. Where was the source of this music? She was yet to meet the entertainers Izzie had hired. Another twist in the path, and then she saw it: the Lillibridge cottage, a creation Arthur Dalwood and his team had assembled that afternoon.

She moved towards the central wishing-well displaying the same roses used in Arthur's Grudellan thorn thicket. Pale and pink, a reminder of the roses Matthew sent her, more than a decade ago, when he invited her on that first date. The camellias in the memorial garden near the Poet's Garret venue had also been that colour. She'd loved how Matthew, on hearing of her sympathy for discarded flowers, had immediately rescued one from the ground. A not-so-pleasant memory of that night was the ungainly false-alarm spider dance she'd been compelled to perform, when an ant had crept from that same camellia and scuttled across her hand.

Two years past a decade-and-a-half! Could it honestly have been that long? How could a few months of misguided adoration still feel like yesterday seventeen years on?

She shook herself out of her poetry-evening reminiscence and sat down on the well's stone wall. Why the stupid nostalgia? Tonight was party night! The man who had torn her heart to shreds wasn't supposed to exist in her memory. He was nothing to her. No-one important. Just one of Craig's distribution managers on the other side of the world.

The violin increased in volume. Rosetta leaned past the ferns and ran a thumb over the powder-puff hydrangea petals. No need for sadness. There it was again though, that sudden ache of loss. The music whirled into a Gypsy rhythm, a cascade of fiery lilts. She thought of the art prints she'd carted from home to home during her renting years, the ones that spoke of dancing feet and caravans.

She felt as though she were spinning now, lost in a dreamy procession of images and sounds. Sparks of flame from a lantern...the glint of a jewel...a boy, pale and angelic, golden hair contrasting sharply against the dullness of dead pine needles...the mellow tones of a man's singing voice...the ominous roar of ocean waves. All buried and forgotten. Tantalising glimpses of a place that felt like home. An attachment to somewhere she couldn't quite reach.

She rose from the wishing-well and turned to admire the garden one last time before stepping back onto the path. Impromptu flashes of places and people she'd never seen before had become a regular occurrence over the past few years. Craig continually insisted the crystals inspired that. 'They're waking your soul memory,' he'd say. 'You're gradually recalling past lives,' and she'd had to agree that numerous customer reports, of weird memories rising from nowhere, pretty much reflected her own experiences. Testimonials such as these had necessitated a new classification on the Crystal Consciousness database. Now, along with *Improved Health* and *Enhanced Wellbeing,* was a file with the title of *Fuller Senses* that overflowed with fascinating stories. She ran a hand over the crystal embedded in her bracelet. Who could have imagined these modest gems would change lives?

The music somersaulted into an Irish jig and seemed to be hovering nearby now, somewhere behind the mist. The violinist emerged onto the path, a diminutive man with large and shining child's eyes. He passed her, wielding his bow impishly, before vanishing into another layer of mist. Definitely a candidate for Best Costume. It was obvious who in the book he'd chosen to emulate.

Spiky autumn-toned hair, a scattering of fins. Everything about him described Zhippe the undine.

Zhippe. A member of the Brumlynd clan, half of the People-of-the-Sea pair, the sprite whose documented musings on the ancient past had, for a century-and-a-half, captured the imagination of millions.

Rosetta reflected on the lifespan of *Our True Ancient History* and the part Zhippe played in preserving it. How *incredible* it was, that this pure-hearted legend bearer had lived for *aeons*. From an idyllic beginning where the Currency of Kindness reigned, right through to the rise and fall of Norwegia and Ehypte; the dinosaur age that emerged after the Atlantean cataclysm; and, in more recent ages, the Roman invasions and Napoleonic wars.

It wasn't so long before Napolean that a Gypsy woman, Lucetta 'Lucy' Lillibridge, discovered the ancient water sprite twins frolicking among the waves of a Cornish sea, although she mightn't have discovered anything had she not worn the crystal pendant with its gift of faerie sight. From there, Zhippe and Carlonn's tale of money and humanity travelled from Lucy to Lucy's new husband Edward, related to him and his son after supper by the hearth and documented in notes he made which, upon his passing, were left to Edward Junior, or Ned as he was better known. And lastly from Ned to publishers, once Ned wrote the story based on his father's notes, a book sold first in Scandinavian countries and then in the Kingdom of Great Britain. Forgotten for a few decades until its revival in the early millennium, thanks to a tiny Aussie group who gathered round Rosetta's fireside one night, to chat about elves and body kings.

'Clear the way! Clear the way, please,' a familiar voice droned. 'Pregnant lady coming through.'

Rosetta responded with, 'Where are you, Roystie?'

'Stuck in a pea-souper with a mum-to-be, and not a single midwife in sight.'

A loud giggle from Eadie.

Rosetta stepped into the dry-ice clouds and flung her arms around the two friends. 'Well, look what we have here! A rabbit and a big-bellied mouse!'

'I *am not* a mouse,' said Eadie. 'I'm a rabbit like Royston is. Although I agree these ears are a bit on the short side.'

'Only teasing. You make a brilliant bunny. And I *love* those ears! How many are you expecting in your litter?'

'Eadie's meant to be Karee,' said Royston. 'And I'm her runaway son. So you've seen the Lillibridge garden, I note. Beautiful isn't it?'

'Absolutely! Took my breath away.'

'That designer Izzie engaged is a total magician.' Royston shook his head in awe. His bunny ears shivered in agreement. 'Jannali says he was a regular, once upon a time, at the Chelsea Flower Show.'

'Is it any wonder?' Eadie said. 'Isn't it amazing how he's woven autumn creepers over the trees? I could have sworn those pines were real.'

'They even smell authentic!' Rosetta breathed in the pine scented air. 'And what about that minty mist?'

Eadie looked at her blankly.

Royston patted her back. 'I actually think that's the after-effect of my mouthwash,' he said. 'Thank you for commenting.'

'You can't smell the mint? But it's divine. And there's that really spicy aroma wafting through the forest. It's a nutty, ashy sort of smell.'

Royston turned to Eadie. 'Have you been smoking pistachios again, missy?'

'So you can't smell that either?' Rosetta said.

Eadie continued to look mystified. 'All I can smell is Royston's cologne.'

'Simmering Pine it's called,' Royston said. 'My signature scent. I think that's where Rosetta's confusion lies.'

Rosetta shrugged. That didn't explain the aromatic presence of campfires and hazelnuts.

'You make a very good Orahney,' Eadie told her.

'Hear-hear!' Royston eyed Rosetta's costume approvingly. 'And *Orahney* does happen to be part of her birth name.'

Eadie snorted. 'Do you still believe in that? If it did happen to be true, I'd be fighting over the title of Eidred with Rosetta's daughter, although I'm sure if anyone were to be a teenaged bunny-adoring princess, it would have to be Izzie.'

'And Izzie might well have become royalty,' Rosetta deadpanned, 'if Glorion had stuck around. Lena's the same as you and me, Eadie. She doesn't believe she's anyone from Elysium Glades.'

Royston pointed out that Lena had never fancied the idea of having lived before.

Eadie agreed. 'And I don't know whether I fancy the idea either. Reincarnation's a bit spooky if you ask me.'

'But Rosetta,' Royston said, *'Orahney* is definitely in your birth-name. I discovered it just the other day. Got out a notepad and pen and scribbled down the name Daniela Ryland gave you.'

'Odetta Sophia?'

'Yes! Odetta Sophia Ryland. And then I said, *"Hallelujah! Just as I suspected".'*

'My "o" and "r" aren't in any way side by side. Sorry to shatter your illusions.'

'What's that got to do with the price of fish?'

'Didn't Conan Dalesford claim the twenty-first-century sprites had to have—'

'An "o" and "r" in their names,' Royston said. 'Yes. Or an "i" and "e," and he believes the ancient names are hidden inside current ones. Nothing to do with letters being side by side.'

'But I was sure...' Rosetta tried to recall. 'Well, I mean, there's Eidred and Pieter and Maleika. And Storlem and Croydee and Kloory.'

'Kloory: Also known as Royston Leckie,' Eadie said, clasping Royston's paw. 'Each letter of Kloory is in Royston's name.'

Rosetta pushed on with the side-by-side concept. 'Rahwor, too, if you want to count him. The letters aren't separate in any of the book's names.'

'I hear what you're saying, Rosetta,' Royston said. 'But did you ever consider the name Zhippe? Or the name Carlonn?'

'Ooh, I didn't. So the side-by-side rule was little more than an assumption!'

'Just your own little theory.'

'Ah well. What does it matter? It's all just hearsay.'

'Hmm.' Royston threw Eadie a wink. 'Non-existent name laws, phantom aromas, rabbits confused with mice...I think all this excitement's getting to her.'

'I'm not getting much right, tonight, am I?' Rosetta gave Royston a nudge. 'So, Fripso, my love, how do we find our way out of Elysium Glades? Craig's about to launch the baroque dance lesson.'

Royston led them back to the front of the ballroom where Craig was introducing the dance instructor. Eadie mumbled something about finding Carl and scampered off.

The instructor's voice trilled through the loud speakers. 'I'll now ask you all to form rows of twenty opposite your partners.'

From where she stood, Rosetta could see Eadie hopping across to her hubby. Carl was drinking punch beside the thorn thicket, a sure-fire candidate for the Whackiest Costume prize. He was done out as a mango eater. A small disagreement followed: Eadie marching on the spot in her giant bunny-feet slippers; Carl shaking his head, folding his arms and leaning against the wall with a defiant grin.

The ballroom echoed with an alarming *thump!*

Party guests swivelled their heads to the podium. A blast of thunderous squeaks was effectually swallowing the instructor's words. Craig rushed across to the faulty microphone. The instructor, red-faced, stepped aside as Craig examined an assortment of controls.

Back at the thorn-thicket display, Carl was giving up his hand to Eadie's outstretched paw. He followed her onto the dance floor, exaggerating his reluctance in a backwards lean.

Amid the microphone's clicks, squeals and boompity-boomps, Rosetta made her way to the open doors to greet another group of guests in various arrays of Gold's Kin and sprite costumes.

Someone whispered in her ear, 'Full moon tonight.' She spun round, saw no-one and continued towards the doors. And then the voice whispered again. 'Full moons are very, *very* romantic.' This time she saw who had spoken. The violinist—that artful Zhippe impersonator—was darting away from her with a wink. He looked familiar, although Rosetta was sure she'd never seen anyone with eyes as unusual as these. In this light they looked black and glinted with strange flecks of gold. 'Just reminding you about the importance of this evening,' he said, in an accent she couldn't determine, and then in a tone that no-one could have taken offence at, he added, 'Make sure you've got someone to snuggle up to.'

'I'll try.' Rosetta contemplated Craig on the stage, not unlike a porcupine in his bristling 'Croydee' chestnut-suit. 'Although for some reason, Zhippe, I don't like my chances.'

◯

MATTHEW CHECKED HIS WATCH and thumped his fist against the cab's door.

'Fair go, mate. I can't drive any faster. It's peak hour.' The taxi driver's drawl dragged him from his thoughts.

'It's not you I'm annoyed with,' Matthew said. 'It's the plane. Two-hour delay. Look, you'd better wait for me outside the Intercontinental and then we'll continue on over the Bridge.' No time to unpack, unwind and get another cab as planned. He'd have to check-in at the hotel, change his clothes, then duck straight out again.

'So you've just stepped off a plane from the UK!'

Matthew affirmed that yes, he had. The driver's pronunciation of the UK rang uncomfortably in his ears: *Yoooook-eye*. He'd forgotten how monotone Australian speech could be. Sixteen years away from it, and the stretched-out syllables sounded surprisingly foreign. Not the first time he'd experienced an awareness of his homeland's accent. As a virtual Englishman, hearing it at age seventeen had been a novelty. Aussies' calm partiality to lengthened vowels had seemed, back then, to echo the glamour of soap stars.

At the Intercontinental, he collected the key-card to his suite, showered quickly and got into his 'buccaneer' gear of loose unbleached poet shirt, fitted taupe pants and brown boots. He retrieved the surfboard cover, in which Harriet's mum had packed the rest of his costume, slapped on aftershave, pocketed the square, palm-sized velvet box he'd been guarding with his life, then rushed back out to the cab.

Crossing a city street not far from his old workplace brought back a flood of memories. His currency-slave discontent, thoughts awash with ways he could win more, earn more, climb higher than the rest. The bar with the fancy lampshades. The bad-song charity nights. Good old Charlie, trusty Davo, intolerable Adam Harrow, a greedier and needier version of himself.

Harrow's words at Grant's all those years ago echoed in his memory. *Wall Street is a crumbled whim.* His mind reached back to Lillibridge's book, a verse from the Oracle.

'Then crumbled is...'

No. Couldn't remember the rest. Too long ago since he'd read it. Why he'd related it back to a transformed Harrow and his altered Wall Street ambition was a puzzle. Ah! Crumbled. Of course. Adam's descriptor had reminded him of the verse.

Before getting in the cab, he signalled to his driver to open the boot and arranged his precious cargo diagonally while the driver, clearly pleased at getting an impromptu break without having to halt the meter, hummed discordantly along to an old Danna Nolan song.

They launched back into the traffic. Veering onto the Cahill Expressway, the driver nodded across at the glimmering green expanse to their right. 'On your right there, is Sydney Harbour,' he announced. 'Best harbour in the world they reckon.'

Matthew murmured agreement. He'd forgotten how extraordinarily vivid it was; had failed to remember the feeling of openness and freedom it inspired in him. Below, dinner-and-show boats were launching into their watery promenades, their outer lights shimmering silver-gold on the water's sunset-streaked surface. He'd been on one of those cruises with Rosetta. Their very last day together. If he'd known what was to come, he would have cherished those moments even more.

The cab was now gliding onto the Bridge, reminding him of his first date with her. They'd driven across it on their way to Balmoral Beach, and she'd said she suspected the moonlight was chasing them.

'Sydney Harbour Bridge,' the driver said. 'Beautiful structure.' Few would have been prouder if they'd built it themselves. 'Links the south to the north.'

'Certainly does.'

'And we're about to turn into a suburb known as *Milsons Point.*'

'That's the one.' Suburb of the penthouse he sold.

Undeterred by his provision of tour-guide hospitality, the driver said, 'Milsons Point is the first suburb you come to when you hit the north side.'

They swerved left at the roundabout. 'That's called *Lavender Bay* along there,' the driver explained.

Lavender Bay. The location of Rosetta's former apartment. Before Alice Springs. Before that decision of hers to marry Craig. Did Izzie still live there? Or had Rosetta ultimately decided to sell?

'I thought it might have lavender growing there when I first heard about it,' the driver was saying. 'But it's not named after the plant, it's named after a bloke.' A short silence. 'Funny name for a bloke.' More silence. 'How would you like to be called Lavender?' Wheezing laughter. 'And this street here is *Alfred*. Alfred Street it's called.' Matthew's old address.

Once they'd drawn to a stop at the Olympic Pool, Matthew paid and tipped. 'That's the Olympic Pool,' said the driver unnecessarily. The boot sprang open. 'Don't forget your surfboard.'

Matthew went to say, 'Eagle wings, not a surfboard,' but thought better of it.

The driver gestured towards the harbour. 'Not much in the way of waves here,' he said. He nodded towards the swimming pool. 'Or there.' Another bout of wheezing laughter. 'You ought to go to Bondi. Have you heard of Bondi Beach? Pommies love it.'

'I have actually heard of Bondi Beach,' Matthew said. 'Thanks for the tip.'

'No. Thank *you* for the tip. And for the little pink gem. My wife'll love it. Very generous of you.'

As the cab moved away, Matthew unzipped the surfboard cover and ran a hand over the brown feathered wings he and Harriet had found. They'd discovered them in a Sherwood Forest costume shop. 'Robin's Hood' it was called. Who would have thought? They'd scanned the Neoclassical aisle, and Harriet had talked him into trying on the buccaneer costume. Said he looked 'hot' in it.

He'd found the eagle wings in the Tribal aisle along with an assortment of Native American costumes.

'There you go,' Harriet had said. 'Along with the pirate outfit it's a perfect combination of Storlem and the seventeen-hundreds.'

There'd been a problem. The wings were only made to attach to a Hiawatha jumpsuit.

'Don't hire the wings then,' Harriet had advised. 'Offer to *buy* them instead, you wealthy old sod, and I'll get Mum to make modifications.' So Matthew had made the shop owner an offer he couldn't refuse.

He pulled the feathery mass from its encasement. They were his wings now. Bought for a princely sum. Sewn to a suede waistcoat, in keeping with the olde worlde theme.

He shrugged on the waistcoat and slipped into its inner pocket the small velvet box he'd grabbed from his suitcase. He'd be watching out tonight for when she was alone. The words he wanted to say when he presented it to her swam frantically through his brain.

His wings bounced against his shoulder blades on the short walk to Luna Park. Aha. There at last. Emerging from the Olympic pool wall was Luna Park's gateway, a giant, smiling face with sunbeams for hair, which instantly reminded him of the day he'd been offered the management role at an outdoor restaurant in Alice Springs: Craig and his halo of spiky palm fronds.

He strode through the face's clown-mouth archway and took in the other guests. Not many in costumes. Apart from a few cowboy hats, the dress code appeared to be casual. Doubtful now, he swung back to the entrance. A sign indicated he was at the right place: *Friday Fortnight Fancy-Dress Ball. Crystal Palace Ballroom and Function Centre, Luna Park East.* The map beside it depicted the venue as having a castle-themed exterior. It was situated at the other end of the carnival thru-way and involved quite a walk. Realising the crowd milling past him were there for the amusements and not for the company's ball, he rounded his shoulders in an effort to make his wings less obvious.

'What's he gonna do, Daddy?' a small voice said when he hastened past a fairy-floss stand. 'Is he gonna *fwy?*'

'Don't know.' The father's tone was indulgent. 'We'll just have to wait and see, won't we?'

Feeling as visible as a streaker on a football field, Matthew wove swiftly around the butter-scented popcorn carts.

A teenage boy yelled, 'Oi, Bird brine!'

Brine or brain? Brain in an Aussie accent.

A female voice hollered his name as he neared Crystal Palace.

Great. This was all he needed. A hunched-over dash through an amusement park while looking like a sideshow freak from the Mad Hatter Regatta...and then getting spotted by someone he knew.

THE OWNER OF THE VOICE, a girl who appeared to be in her mid-to-late-twenties, was also a costumed party attendee, her Viking helmet a testament to this. 'You're back for the ball,' she said to Matthew. 'I don't remember seeing your name on the guest list.' Rosetta's daughter: Izzie grown into a self-assured woman.

'Last minute change of heart,' he told her. 'My ticket-payment went through a couple of nights ago. I didn't recognise you, Izzie.'

'Probably because I've gone blonde.' Izzie pointed to the woollen plaits attached to her headdress. 'I was never very comfortable with the Anne of Green Gables look.'

'You looked lovely back then, and you look lovely now. Even with yellow wool for hair. So who are you here as?'

'I'm here as Princess Eidred.' To show off her gown, Izzie flung herself into an intentionally silly whirl. 'See the sleeves? Cool, hey?' Fabric sprouted from them and trailed in long triangles almost to the ground.

A tall, fair-haired guy in a lopsided crown stepped forward.

'Matthew, this is Ben,' Izzie said.

Matthew reached out and shook hands with Izzie's date. To Izzie he said, 'Is this the computer-game champ you were telling me about some years back?'

'Sure is. Good memory!'

'The name rang a bell.' Nothing to do with Rosetta could ever have been forgotten. 'Although I actually think you'd told me it was you who happened to be the champ.'

'Sounds like Izzie.' Ben was placing an arm around the girl and smiling down at her. 'She brags about her skiing skills too. And that's unfair, cos I haven't had the advantage of living in Toronto.'

Izzie chatted freely as they strolled towards the ballroom door. Told Matthew she'd graduated from a master's degree the year before.

As Matthew already knew, she'd been working part-time in the role of PR Consultant at Crystal Consciousness. What he hadn't known was that Izzie spent the other half of her working week co-ordinating CEGS volunteers' trips for Melki-Delorey Legal. Next year she was moving overseas for twelve months to start on a prestigious public relations role at the Australian Embassy in Stockholm.

Ben would return to the UK to complete his architecture degree. The pair didn't appear worried about their relationship becoming long-distance. 'We had to go our separate ways when we went back to uni last year,' Ben told Matthew. 'Izzie was keen to accept the Canadian placement, and I wasn't prepared to transfer from Cambridge.'

'But we'll be closer geographically now,' Izzie reasoned.

'Yeah, I think,' Matthew said, as she led him to the doorway, 'Craig might have sent out a text about your move to Sweden. Congrat—'

Thwack!

The rattle of glass. A twinge in one shoulder. Matthew went to move sideways. Couldn't.

Izzie yelped and said, 'You're stuck in the door, you poor thing.'

Trapped. Sandwiched between a window and a potted tree. Why couldn't he have got the smaller sized wings? The breadth of these, despite being narrow like those on angel costumes, had proven to be a hazard.

The pressure in his shoulder eased. The window he was jammed against gave way. But was it a window? Someone was taking out a stopper from the floor, someone with hair of red, orange and yellow. 'Ah,' Matthew said. 'Glass double doors. Didn't see that for the foliage.'

'Neither did we,' said Izzie. Mischievously she added, 'We'd better keep both doors open then, in case any other roosters turn up.'

'Who are you calling a rooster,' Matthew growled.

'Sorry. Seagull then.'

'Almost. Seagull without the "s".'

A slender, light-haired woman in a hoop-skirted gown glided up. She stepped between Ben and Izzie, draped her arms around them and said, 'How are we going, kids?'

'Marie Antoinette?' said Matthew. 'No, wait a sec...' He knew that face. 'You're Lena, mother of Ben.'

Looking surprised, Lena nodded. 'Right on all counts. And you are...?' Her eyes widened. She smiled in recognition. 'I know you.'

'Matthew Weissler,' Izzie told her. 'Sara's former stepdad.'

'Of course. Wow! You moved to London, didn't you? But that was years ago! Are you back in Sydney now, Matthew?'

'Only for a couple of weeks. I'm on leave. Wanted to check out some real estate over here.'

'You haven't aged in the slightest!'

'I was about to say the same of you.'

'Ah well. Can't argue with the scientists, can we?'

'About the crystals slowing the ageing process? Yeah, the studies are speaking for themselves.'

'So you decided to join the fun,' Lena said. 'Good for you. You'll get a shock when you see Craig. He's here as a chestnut.'

Craig. Good at shocking people. Matthew tended not to speak to him these days. Emails were more businesslike than phone calls anyway. Less inclined to include details of the boss's personal life.

'So you've only just arrived,' Lena said slowly, 'and you're here by yourself. Or is there a partner tucked away in the dressing room?'

'I don't have a partner tucked away anywhere.' Relationships, since Rosetta, had been light and sweet, but empty, each unfairly subjected to the shadow of comparison.

Lena was watching him carefully. 'I suppose you've heard about Angelica?'

'Who's Angelica?'

'She's Jannali's daughter.' Standing beside him, Lena turned to the dance floor where invitees had joined hands and were stepping forward and back in response to instructions blared through loudspeakers. 'See the woman with the dark-blue butterfly wings? The one with the long black hair? That's Angelica. I think she'll be sitting out the slow dances tonight.' As Lena said this, she turned and gave Matthew a nod as if to emphasise the significance of that statement.

He scanned the rest of the dance floor, dreading seeing Rosetta there with Craig. No-one amongst the technicolour assortment of faeries, elves, mer-people and body kings looked remotely like her. Realising Lena's talk had continued, he turned back to her, displeased with himself for getting so distracted. He wasn't at all sure who Lena was talking about now. All he knew was that the word 'she' had been uttered a couple more times.

'No way. Not with Craig. Not tonight.' Lena indicated the curtained stage. 'He's covered in a whole lot of spikes.'

Ah. Craig unable to be danced with because of his prickly costume. Lena would have been referring to Rosetta.

'Great to see two people so happy though,' Lena said. 'You knew about them, didn't you?'

'About them being engaged?' He hated the chest ache accompanying those words. Was there anyone in the Crystal Consciousness team who didn't know that? They'd been threatening to get married for years.

'Engaged, yes! We were up in the NT on holiday when they made their wedding announcement. March twentieth, 2026.'

'So they've finally settled on a date.'

'Sure have. Craig and Angelica. Two peas in a pod.'

For a moment Matthew was unable to speak. 'But...' he said. 'But Rosetta...'

Lena looked amused. 'Rosetta's fine. The break-up was ages ago. Her decision of course. She's over at the drinks table on the Grudellan side of "Elysium Glades" if you want to talk to her.' Her tone became confidential. 'Footloose and fancy-free.'

Drinks table. He needed to find the drinks table, and he needed to find it fast.

'Just look out for an Orahney.' Lena smiled wryly. 'I'm looking out for a Napoleon.' She laughed, shaking her head. 'My Andrew. If you see him strut by, could you usher him in this direction?'

Matthew winked and nodded, grinning to himself at the idea of Lena's husband strutting. What stuck in his memory was Andrew's super-relaxed amble when they'd strolled the neighbourhood many years earlier, after one of Rosetta's dinner parties.

He drew in a breath. Rosetta single! Could this be as good as it sounded? Only one way to find out.

○

ROSETTA STOOD BY THE DRINKS TABLE, enthused at seeing her associates meet each other and celebrate at this seventeen-year anniversary of the Elysium Heart Crystals.

The past decade had been a hectic whirlwind, and the years had brought rewards she could only have dreamed of. Business trips to oversee both Crystal Consciousness franchise start-ups and CEGS volunteer projects had unlocked a door to the rest of the world, a door she'd thought was forever sealed. And along with the chance to meet many beautiful people from cultures that intrigued her, she'd been free to hear the accents, languages and traditional melodies floating about each new locale. She'd tasted the best of cuisine and fancied she could replicate it once home, with her trusty copper pots, often with less-than-inspiring results.

She waved to Lena, looking as elegant as a Regency-romance heroine in her dove-grey satin crinoline, complete with pearly fan and pale ringlets, then plucked up a cracker from the drinks table and crunched on it, her thoughts flitting back to her travels. How lucky was she to have lounged in the grandeur of Viennese coffee houses; hummed along to Edith Piaf songs with Parisians at a Parc Monceau singalong; strolled through steep, multicolour villages on the Italian Riviera and the grounds of storybook castles in Germany; and breathed the pristine air of dusk-wreathed Norwegian forests that Pieter and Maleika might have once called home.

Despite the sheer joy of globetrotting, retreating to an empty house after acquainting herself with all those new crystals venues and contacts was almost a relief at times. Barring Sidelta the cat, she had to admit she was completely on her own, but her home was a cosy retreat from business-related issues: a cliffside two-storey charmer on Sydney's Northern Beaches. Its stained glass windows, gracious gables and elaborate ceilings evoked the same atmosphere that had made the

Burwood bungalow feel so much like home. Turning out to be a satisfying hobby was working in the lush garden, a generous blend of century-old shade trees and sweeping ocean views.

It was good to be single again. Really good. And that silly little thought flitting around her tonight, about being the only one solo amongst her friends, was just the unwholesome voice of insecurity. She did not need reminding that she was getting older, or that she might have got too set in her ways to share her life with anyone. People did that all the time: lived alone and survived. She was sure she could do that too if the future refused to provide a permanent King of Hearts.

She'd been contented with Craig. His steady predictability and monopolising affection was a soothing balm after Matthew had flung her aside without explanation. Truly happy? Most of the time, hence the wedding they'd planned delegated to the blurred-out zone of 'next year'. She could never hurt someone as kind as Craig, and they'd both joked that their engagement was too good to turn into marriage.

Some nights, though, she would creep downstairs from the vast bedroom she shared with him and stand on the back verandah, watching the starry reflections in the swimming pool. Its deep, dark blue was a strangely sweet reminder of the sea at Balmoral on her first date with Matthew, a night that had brimmed with enchantment.

And then fate intervened at one of the Dalesfords' barbecues when Jannali introduced Craig to her petite dress-shop-owner daughter. A flicker of interest had crossed Angelica's face, and although Rosetta hadn't seen Craig's expression, she'd gathered from his gestures that the interest was mirrored. Not that she'd perceived Angelica as any kind of fiancé-stealer. There'd been a subsequent flicker of embarrassment when Rosetta was introduced as 'Craig's lovely partner'.

Half-a-year later they'd been walking back from boating, a group of friends meandering alongside a Queensland river the day after an interstate CEGS conference. Jim and his wife led the way down the palm-tree lined path, followed by a row of three: Conan Dalesford, Angelica and Craig.

Rosetta trailed behind with Jannali Dalesford, commenting with amusement on the navy ribbon of Angelica's straw hat, how it swished cartoonishly with each turn of her head. And then Rosetta noticed that the ribbon seemed to swish an awful lot to Angelica's right, even when Conan, at her left, was talking. The woman was eager to observe each of Craig's reactions.

Rosetta and Jannali's chatter was interrupted by a small scream. Angelica had tripped over a tree branch on the track and Craig had heroically caught her. A hurried detachment. A guilty backwards step. It was the moment Rosetta realised that Craig was no longer hers.

She'd broached Craig on the subject the next day. Told him Angelica seemed lovely, but he'd misinterpreted her comment. Appeared to view it as an accusation and answered with a moody grunt.

'Craig,' she'd said. 'About our relationship—'

'Rosetta, our relationship's as good as it's ever been.' After a lengthy silence Craig had added, 'And there's no way I'm interested in Angelica.'

'I never said you were. But now that you mention it, I think you *are* interested in Angelica. Let me rephrase this.' She'd drawn in a deep breath. Closed her eyes to shut out the sad sight of Craig's discomfort. 'I think the two of you are meant to be together.'

'Rosetta, that's ridiculous!'

'Let me put it this way. I'll always love you, Craig, but I don't think we make a great match. It was fantastic at the start, but what I'm sensing these days is that you're feeling just as restricted as I am.'

They'd talked. Craig conceded their union had become lukewarm, and they agreed to part on good terms. A few months later, Craig traipsed into their Alice Springs office and told her, self-consciously, that he and Angelica had started dating.

And despite working alongside her newly-in-love ex, Rosetta noticed that the squirmy agitation of feeling second-best, which began with Angus's abandonment and impressed deeper onto her heart when Matthew went back to Dette, had somehow ceased to haunt her. The crystals had healed the bulk of her pain. She was no longer afraid of being alone.

Rosetta watched her vivacious guests floating around the drinks table, many of them battlers like herself before the crystals arrived in their lives, and relished for a moment a feeling of pride. Tonight had finally arrived, the night of all nights, all pressured plans and deadlines surrounding it now sailing into the past. Her relief at everything unfolding as hoped was probably much the same as a bride's. Flowers, *tick!* Gown, *tick!* Celebratory cake, *tick!* Handsome husband...well...everything had a limit. 'Can't be *too* greedy,' she murmured to herself. 'The party's more than enough.'

Izzie had said in the morning, after they'd shown the caterers through to the galley, that she wouldn't be surprised if something really exciting happened.

'Our party's happening, Izzie,' Rosetta had said. 'Isn't that exciting enough?'

Izzie, stepping forward to rescue a fallen vine, had responded with, 'I meant exciting in the universal sense. Heaps of us thought The Silvering would happen in 2012 because of the Mayan calendar. And then nothing became of Conan's prediction. He was *sooo* certain it would happen twelve years after the Mayan prophecy, but The Silvering didn't happen in 2024 either.'

'The future's not set in stone, Iz.'

'The Silvering could still happen I guess. Maybe Conan's got the timeframe part of his prediction wrong. But that could mean it's a lifetime away, and I'd much prefer it to happen now. Today, of course, would be ideal.'

'Sure would!'

'Today or tonight.'

It could be any day. *Any day or night.* The words tarot-reading speedster Maleika / Molly Carr had chosen, to hint at a soulmate encounter. Pushing away images of a vanishing rabbit and cherry-coloured Jag, Rosetta had said, 'I think The Silvering might have already happened. Either that or it's in the process of happening.'

Izzie had agreed that the miraculous effect of the crystals could indeed be the catalyst for mass transformation. 'Although...' Izzie's voice had become pensive. '...I always imagined The Silvering would be in some way unmissable. Flashes of light or something, but what would I know?'

Eyeing the drinks table now, Rosetta plucked up a glass and scooped herself a generous amount of the strawberry-and-mint strewn punch.

'I'll have one too if you don't mind. The pineapple pieces in that are addictive!' Eadie was shuffling across to the table, grey ears bobbing forward as she peered into the punch. 'Get a move on, Rosetta! This rabbit's dying of thirst!'

MATTHEW MOVED INTO THE BALLROOM fully, found a path beside a sign marked *Elysium Glades* and marched through a blur of crimson and emerald, only vaguely aware of the autumn trees and veils of mist that surrounded him.

At the other side of the indoor forest, guests were stationed around a table laden with crystal punch-bowls and varying sizes of bottles. Two ice sculptures, a sombre sun and smiling moon, sparkled under a chandelier.

A pretty brunette in a long orange dress sashayed up to him. *'Oh Em Gee,'* she said. 'Your costume is gorgeous!'

'Gee thanks,' he said. 'You look great yourself.' He scanned the crowd ahead. He could see Eadie, a pregnant Eadie, done out in a rabbit costume, ears flopping forward and back as she nodded in answer to someone obscured by the ceiling's trailing vines.

The woman in orange remained beside him. 'I'm Caroline Trent,' she said. 'I owned the first Crystal Consciousness prior to Rosetta's purchase of it.'

'The one in Martin Place?'

'Yes! The one in Martin Place!'

'I knew that one quite well.'

'And now I manage Rosetta's Burwood franchise. So how are you linked with all this?'

Matthew told her about his role in London, which led to another question, and then another. Their conversation wore on. Matthew kept an eye on the rabbit's bobbing ears.

'So you're Storlem obviously,' Caroline was saying. 'You won't believe this. I'm Orahney.' She smiled rather bashfully. 'Coincidence hey?'

While Matthew tried to determine why this should be such a coincidence, he glimpsed a flutter of red to the side of Eadie's ample belly. The flutter took form. Exotic eyes, smooth olive skin, a shapely figure swathed in layers of fiery silk.

Rosetta.

Eadie caught his eye, threw him a friendly wave, then drifted off to the drinks table. Matthew turned to Caroline, hastily excusing himself, and moved towards Rosetta. He had to speak to her. Now was his chance.

She was turned away slightly. Her hair was piled on top of her head attractively, just how it was the night they'd first met. He could see the curve of her cheek and the curl of her eyelashes as she turned. Her gown fell about her like a Grecian robe. A Greek goddess. Technically speaking, Rosetta wasn't Greek.

Greek-speaking goddess then.

And then they were opposite each other, Matthew breathing unsteadily, Rosetta staring at him in surprise.

'Rosetta,' he said. 'I have to speak to you.'

Rosetta said nothing. Just continued to stare with uncertain eyes.

Was he really here? Was he here, opposite the woman he worshipped, knowing she was no longer with Craig?

She unclipped her evening purse, reached in, drew out a card and handed it to him. 'Call my office on Monday if you like,' she said, her manner-of-speech untypically haughty. 'My assistant will be happy to help.'

Ignoring the aloof dismissal, Matthew studied the card. Lawyer. Melki-Delorey Legal. Printed across the centre in rainbow-flecked silver was the name Odetta Melki.

'Odetta?' He lifted his eyes to gaze at her.

Without wasting words, Rosetta spoke again. 'My business name.'

'Odetta, Rosetta, Lucetta...' Smiling, Matthew shook his head. 'Maleika, Orahney, Marani. I've known them all.'

Rosetta was taken aback. She watched him. Warily now. 'What do you mean?' Her back stiffened. 'Actually, don't worry.'

'Odetta,' Matthew repeated, glancing back at the card. He took a step towards the wary goddess. 'I still like Rosetta,' he said.

An understatement.

'Still...really...*like* Rosetta.'

Another understatement. And then, in an impulse of besotted recklessness, he said, 'Love her in fact.'

He breathed out slowly. Glanced away, then back at the woman standing before him. It was done now. He'd laid all his cards on the table. All he could do was await her response.

Rosetta attempted to say something. She hesitated, eyes downcast. And then, before Matthew had time to think of anything coherent to add, she darted away from him.

Within seconds she had vanished into the indoor forest, subtly and swiftly, like autumn leaves in the breeze. He dashed back into the forest to pursue her, emerging at the other side just in time to see her sweep out of the ballroom. He rocketed towards the exit, dodging chattery partygoers who persisted in marring his way. At last he was at the door.

Thwack!

The wings. How could he have forgotten he was wearing the wings?

A small spiky-haired figure sprang up and took out the stopper on the door beside it. History repeating. Same man who'd opened the first lot of doors Matthew had got stuck in, and he looked familiar. Aha! It was none other than Jippie, the guy who had a habit of cropping up whenever Rosetta was around. 'Thanks, Jippie.' Matthew shuffled impatiently into the open air.

'Zhippe.'

'Huh? Of course. Zhippe as in Zhippe and Carlonn. Great water-sprite costume.'

'Full moon tonight,' the undine-man commented. His joined-together words were butter soft. 'In Aries. A time of new beginnings.'

Matthew surged forward.

He had to find her.

He pressed through the carnival crowd, vaguely aware of the undine-man gabbling something more. Whatever it was had dissolved with distance; had dwindled into little more than hushed murmurings, sounds that seemed to echo the words 'magic' and 'ancient prophecy' although Matthew couldn't be sure.

Chapter Twelve

ROSETTA SURVEYED THE HARBOUR'S muted pinks and blues. She felt safe on the Luna Park wharf, away from the party, away from Matthew and his calculated, empty words.

How could he have done that to her? Again? Had he decided she hadn't been hurt enough the first time?

She'd been talking to Eadie when she'd spotted him in the crowd. The glimpse of a tall man with wings had caught her attention. A tall, highly attractive man.

'Oh God,' she'd said to Eadie. 'I've just spotted Matthew Weissler.'

Eadie had looked at her in concern. 'You okay, Rosetta?'

'Fine.' Trying to ignore the drumming of her heart, she'd stepped out of Matthew's line of vision and whispered, 'What's he doing? What's he doing now?'

Eadie had turned and stared in Matthew's direction, her fluffy belly and glass of juice swivelling slowly in unison. Willing Eadie to appear less obvious, Rosetta had clicked her fingers, whispering, 'Eadie, don't let him see you looking.'

Still staring, Eadie had said, 'He's talking to someone.' Loudly she'd added, 'He's talking to Caroline. Ha! Flirting more likely. Oops! He's spotted us. Ooh, he *is* good looking isn't he?'

'How far away?' She'd grasped Eadie's arm. 'No! Don't look this time!' But Eadie was already looking.

'About six metres. No...no, that's not right. About four. He's looking again!' Eadie had lifted a paw and waved.

'What do you think you're *doing*,' Rosetta had hissed.

Eadie had given a satisfied nod. 'You're in luck. He's coming over. Have fun, darl. I'll leave you to it.'

'Eadie, Don't g—'

'Rosetta...'

She'd looked up. Matthew had been there, still wholly and utterly gorgeous, perhaps even more so, bronzed from a summer spent in the Northern Hemisphere.

Her breath had caught in her throat. She couldn't think, or speak, or act. All she could do was watch him. Stupidly.

Escaping to the solitary wharf where Milsons-Point-bound ferries docked each hour had been all she could think to do, and now she was contemplating the silver turrets of the ballroom's facade, reluctant to rejoin her guests.

His words rang back now, in hollow echoes.

Still really...like Rosetta. Love her in fact.

Uttered straight after he'd been chatting up Caroline from the Burwood store.

She stared into a luminous patch of blue-green where the water was crystal sleek. Why did it have to remind her of those eyes? Dusk-tinted wavelets bumped and kissed; pale, playful glimmers disrupting the harbour's smoothness.

He'd made a good show of pretending he loved her. Back then, and again tonight. Matthew didn't know how to love. He only knew how to impress and discard. Only Matthew would have the audacity to torment her after the damage he'd caused.

'Rosetta!' His voice. From a distance this time. She couldn't face him.

He was here though, and there was nothing she could do about it, advancing towards her from the Luna Park exit. Matthew dressed as Storlem, almost comical with his wings jolting about him in lethargic bounces. Rosetta noticed then that one of the wings was broken. Its feathered edges brushed the ground in large, sad, sweeps.

He was at the wharf's steps now, a cross between angelic messenger and swashbuckler, his clothing obviously designed to emphasise athletic leanness. Criss-crossed lacing held the top of his shirt-front together in eighteenth-century style. An open waistcoat hung loosely over the broadness of his shoulders.

He descended the wharf steps.

Cornered now, Rosetta turned away from him, half wishing a freak wave would emerge from the harbour to wash her away.

'I need to speak to you,' he said.

'I'd prefer that you didn't.'

'I need to clarify what happened to our relationship.'

'You did that years ago. I left before you got to the part about you going back to...' She couldn't continue.

'That's what I need to speak to you about.'

'Don't trouble yourself. It's gone and forgotten now.' Rosetta willed herself to remain calm. 'It would have been nice, though, Matthew, to know you were alive and well back then, before I rang all the hospitals. It would have been nice to have been informed of your change of heart. Sure, I would have been devastated, but the truth would have shown a smidgen of respect on your behalf. Instead I go to visit Grant and find *you* there. Living with Dette and—'

'Bernadette wasn't living with me.'

'I couldn't reach you! It was as though you'd turned to stone.' She tried to still the quiver in her voice. 'You ignored me, Matthew. For four whole weeks.'

'And for four whole years *you* ignored *me*.'

Matthew's inability to recognise how many years had passed stung like an icy slap.

'Four years times four,' Matthew added. 'Plus one. The single four sounded better as a retort. You'd understand, being a lawyer, yourself.'

She tried to suppress a smile.

The top of his wings curled as his shoulders dropped into a slump. 'Short of asking Craig to pass a message on to his fiancée—and don't think I didn't consider it—I'd exhausted every method of getting in contact with you.'

She thought she heard him sigh.

The seventeen-year mantra kicked in. Nothing to her. No-one. After the Punchbowl episode, she'd shrugged off his rejection and banned any thought that hinted of him even remotely; had said to her friends, 'It didn't work out', a statement that efficiently closed the door on any concerned enquiry.

Matthew was frowning down at the wharf boards. Gently he said, 'Did it ever occur to you, Rosetta, that you may have been wrong?'

The long-buried grief surfaced unexpectedly. Facing him squarely, Rosetta flung back, 'She was in your flat! She'd just stepped out from the shower!'

'Correction. She stepped *in* from *a* shower.'

'Do forgive me,' Rosetta droned. 'She stepped *in* to the lounge room from *a* shower.'

'Incorrect. She stepped into *my flat* from a shower. She'd got caught in the rain. It was teeming down that day.'

Rosetta turned away from him. Sighed theatrically. 'Caught in the rain wearing *your* bathrobe. Hm. Funny that.'

He was amused. She'd made him laugh. What right did he think he had, to compound his lies and then chuckle as though it didn't matter?

'Do you remember an email you once sent me?'

Now he was changing the subject! To avoid the subject at hand! Easily seen why he was once drawn to politics.

'You sent Izzie an email attachment to give to Sara. It concerned Craig's management role.'

The letter she'd composed in New Zealand. 'What does that have to do with you and Bernadette?'

'A lot. I never received it until that day at the flat.'

'I *knew* you'd go back to her,' Rosetta said, sadness seeping into her chest. 'What was I thinking?'

Over in Luna Park, the Ferris wheel was slowing to a stop, a dazzling asterisk piercing the darkened sky.

Resigned now to conceding the part that she, herself, had played in their crumbled romance, Rosetta threw up her hands. 'It was arrogant of me to think you were over your marriage.'

'I would never do that.' Matthew's tone was emphatic. 'Never. I could never leave you for someone else.' He told her then that Bernadette had turned up unannounced with rained-on hair and mud-spattered clothing. She'd been living with Grant in a nearby suburb and had only called in to hand over the email attachment from Sara's belongings; was drying her skirt on the heater when Rosetta knocked on the door of Grant's old flat. 'Prior to that, the last time I'd seen Bernadette was the same day you had. At Harrow's.'

He'd sounded as though he really meant it, but seventeen years gave him ample scope to build a credible fib.

'Is that true, Matthew?' she whispered.

'Absolutely.' He was gazing at her intently. 'I was over my marriage long before I met you.'

Rosetta searched his eyes. She wanted so much to believe him. 'Is that really true, Matthew? Those weeks I couldn't reach you though. You were—'

'Alone. Sinking into a shabby couch and full of self-pity. I was convinced that losing my money meant losing you.'

How could he have thought she'd be shallow enough to ditch him over a change in status? A memory flitted back. Grant's flat...2008...Post GFC, sitting on a sinking couch and hearing Matthew's halted explanation, a fumbling blend of confusion and remorse when he told her of his financial losses. At last she said, 'Just what sort of a person did you think I was?'

'A beautiful, accomplished woman who has always had money.' He hadn't known her at all. 'For me, stumbling economically meant I had had very little to give.'

'But I'd never been so happy! And it had absolutely nothing to do with what we were worth.' She'd done it now, carelessly revealed her weakness for him. And now, perversely, she wanted to reveal another flaw. 'Matthew, I have something to confess.'

'We have a fair bit to catch up on, haven't we?' Matthew gestured to a seat on the wharf. 'Let's sit down then.'

Rosetta sank onto the seat, feverishly aware of Matthew's nearness as he sat beside her. How would she put this? Shakily, she began her confession. 'You're not right in assuming I was born into wealth. You were justified in thinking that. I had every opportunity to put you right.' She glanced down at the wharf boards. Bit her lip. 'Truth is, when you and I first met at the bar Adam took me to, I was a struggling single mum.' There. She'd said it. Unable to meet his eyes, she contemplated a small pebble by her foot and mashed her toe down against it.

She told him about the repossessed home and the mortgage Angus had lumped her with and the frenetic flit between jobs throughout Izzie's primary-school years to avoid bankruptcy. 'Our house was gone by the time Izzie started high school, but making ends meet still wasn't easy. There's no security in renting. Being forced to move house again and again took its toll.' And then she owned up to initially letting him believe she was a lawyer rather than a law student, and talked about how she'd kept up the pretence of having owned Craig's BMW by buying an identical one. 'But up until the autumn of 2008, I was a shop-girl: a retail-assistant. And a tarot reader.'

'A professional tarot reader? Unbelievable!'

'And I refuse now to be ashamed of that.'

'How could you have thought hardship would make me think any less of you?' Matthew's voice was warm with concern. 'If anything, I would have thought more of you. Any sort of struggle builds strength. It's what I tend to admire in people.'

'As in oyster plus aggravation equals pearl?'

'That's it. Beauty through adversity or whatever it is.'

So many times! How many times had she gone to talk to Matthew about her biological parents? She'd always stopped herself at the crucial moment, reasoning that mentioning Daniela's fortune might cause her to blab about the stringent life she'd led. 'You told me at the flat that you weren't well-off until you got an inheritance,' she said. 'I didn't say it at the time, but an inheritance changed my life too.' She went on to tell him about the legacy that had spun her stressed-out routine into a philanthropist's heaven. 'The accomplished lady you mentioned describes my mother more than it does me. Someone I'd always looked up to.'

'So you knew your birth mother?'

'Only from her album covers. She was a singer.'

'Yeah?' Matthew was impressed. 'Would I know of her? What's her name?'

Rosetta told him Daniela's stage name.

Matthew turned to stare at her. 'Danna Nolan?' He shook his head. Laughed. 'Danna Nolan. Wow! I heard one of her songs on the radio tonight! The cabbie was singing along to it.' He shook his head again, whispering, 'Danna Nolan!' Turning once more to Rosetta, he said, 'Easily seen now why you sing so well.'

Courage gained, Rosetta confessed to more. 'I was a cleaner too. I cleaned the offices you worked at. I used to get disparaging little notes from the traders.' Would she tell him about the note he'd once written? She'd figured out, soon after she'd started seeing him, who M.P.W. was. 'One of those notes said, *Don't miss the floor.* That was one I replied to.'

He surprised her with a grin. She watched him fold over, winged shoulders shaking with laughter. *'Banker, please don't miss the bin.* I remember it. That was you!'

'That was me.' The same response she'd given when Matthew had mentioned at Amaretti's 'The Piper' poet, the very words she'd used when his description of a bunny-chasing madwoman blocking the road rang of horrifying familiarity. And now she'd said it to him again. *That was me.* She smiled. Half to herself she said, 'Isn't it always?'

Matthew's response was swift. 'Always,' he said. He was watching her now with heart-sparking tenderness. 'Rosetta, it's always been you.'

All those vicious assumptions...the incandescent certainty that Matthew was immune to commitment...everything that had weighed her down with the ache of despair...was falling away softly, like petals from an autumn rose. This was real. Matthew was admitting to caring for her, perhaps even as much as she cared for him. He'd made plenty of attempts to talk in the past, but an excruciating sense of betrayal had deafened her to his pleas.

Behind them a train clattered over the Harbour Bridge. Back in Luna Park the nineteenth-century carousel whirled into another round, its music conjuring hope-filled notes of yesteryear.

'Well then,' Matthew said. 'We've both been victims of Gold's Kin values. Both of us measured our sense of worth against how much or how little we owned.'

'And I just realised something! *Worth* doesn't just mean worthiness. It's also used to describe money.'

Agreeing with this, Matthew cited an instance at a New Years' Eve party he and Dette once hosted at his Milsons Point penthouse. 'One of the guests' new partners was in awe of the place.'

'Doesn't surprise me. It was a magnificent home, Matthew.'

'Sure. But I overheard the guy saying to his date, "Whoa! What would *he* be worth?" He tended to defer to me a bit throughout the evening, which made me uncomfortable, and it struck me that he'd placed me on a hierarchy and perceived himself to be on a level below. Pretty unfair if you ask me.'

'Why is it that people are valued more if they become wealthy?' Rosetta said. 'Everyone works much the same hours. These days I don't seem to get revered for it so much, and I'm pleased about that. It's like most are choosing to value actions over status. Maybe we've all matured! Have you noticed this, Matthew?'

Matthew conceded that he now rarely heard anyone speculate on another person's finances. 'We've got our crystals to thank for that,' he said, 'or at least, the transmissible harmonisers they contain. I wonder if we've all gone through The Silvering without realising.'

'I've wondered that too. Izzie's not so sure.'

Matthew was ponderous. 'Say if The Silvering has already come about. What then, do you think, would we name the body-king influenced age we've only just emerged from?'

'Hard to say. I'd probably describe it the same way you did. I'd call it the Body King Age.'

'Or The Golding perhaps?'

'The Golding! Great term, Matthew! But now that you've given it such a glittery name, I almost feel sorry it's on its way out.'

WHILE THE SKY AND WATER DEEPENED to violet, Rosetta settled back into the wharf seat and talked with Matthew, hungry for news on the years that had passed. She laughed along with him as though he were her most treasured and reliable friend, a long-time companion she'd never had to lose.

Matthew brought up The Silvering again, and Rosetta conveyed her certainty that it hadn't yet happened. Even though hatred and territorialism appeared to have diminished in the past seventeen years, the world still had a long way to go before serenity and safeness could comfortably reign. 'The greed-lack cycle might take another century to fade out,' she said.

Matthew responded with: 'I used to think that, but now I feel positive the Currency of Kindness can return in our lifetime.'

Rosetta's evening purse quivered to signal a text. She reached for her circular pocket-watch-style phone and scanned the screen. Izzie conveying a message from Craig: Did Rosetta want to be the one to draw the raffle? Or was he okay to go ahead without her?

Intent on savouring her moments with Matthew, she answered she was fine with Craig announcing the winner, and added she was catching up with an old friend.

Old friend? Izzie texted back. *Would that be the same friend who turns Worcestershire sauce into hazelnut coffee syrup?*

Rosetta switched off her phone abruptly and shoved it back into her purse.

As subtly as she could, she looked at Matthew. He was lost in contemplation, seemingly transfixed by the harbour's purpled dapples.

'Love your costume,' he said at last. 'That lace-up belt you're wearing. It's a lot like the one you wore when Adam introduced us at the bar.'

'I *loved* that bar! I remember its beautiful lampshades.' Rosetta placed a hand on the belt and thought back to the evening of Matthew's work send-off. 'Would you believe it's the same belt? I found it in an old shoebox the other day. I still can't believe I've hung on to it all these years. I couldn't decide whether to be the Gypsy or the faerie, so decided to combine the two.' Criss-crossed laces, she realised, were very 1770s. She only had to look at the other guests or Matthew in his poet shirt to arrive at that. Picturing the world without conveniences like elastic and zippers said a lot about the resourcefulness of prior generations. 'I guess you could say I'm a mix of the ancient world and the seventeen-hundreds.'

'That makes two of us. I'm regretting these wings though. I got stuck in the door twice. And that sharp-shooting daughter of yours insists I'm a rooster.'

'There's no mistaking you're an eagle.'

'A legal eagle?'

'A regal one. Storlem was a palace guard, after all. You getting stuck in the door reminds me of a dream you once wrote about, in an email.'

'The one where my wings wouldn't fit in the plane? Yeah, tonight was a case of *deja vu.*'

'Nice French!'

'*Merci, ma cherie.*'

'*Mon dieu!* You've progressed quite a bit since your calendar reciting days!'

Grinning, Matthew said, 'You're determined to overlook the fact it was only ever meant as a joke.' He eyed the damage to his wing. 'Bad decision. Shouldn't have listened to her.'

'Shouldn't have...listened to...who?'

'To Harriet. She's someone you know by name, Rosetta. Harriet Neilson. I met her years ago. In Cornwall. Glynis and Dudley's Friday Fortnight group. Harriet's the one who transcribed the Lillibridge letters.'

'Er...Okay..er...'

'She became my...Well, she married m—'

'Is *that* the *time?* I'd better get back to the—'

'...my brother's wife's brother. Became my sister-in-law.'

'Sorry, what did you say?'

'I said that Harriet married a brother-in-law.'

'Oh good! Glad she didn't end up with your brother's friend.'

'Kirk Rummery, you mean? Me too. He did her a favour by scarpering. He's doing well, by the way.' Matthew related a decision not to press charges. Kirk had returned the bulk of Matthew's money, swearing it had always been his intention to pay it back. Matthew reasoned that the man was already being punished enough for his other crimes, and the gift of a crystal was starting to bring about promising change. 'They released him on a good behaviour bond. Model prisoner, apparently. He's in social work now. Helps young offenders to reform and advises them on the phenomenal benefits of Elysium heart-crystals.'

'Matthew, that's brilliant.'

'Yeah! He reckons the prisons would be empty if everyone owned one of our crystals. Fun, isn't it, speculating on their far-reaching effects.'

'So you're here as Storlem,' Rosetta commented when they'd said all they could about the Crystal Consciousness network. 'But you're also someone from the 1700s. Ned Lillibridge?'

'Ned's father.'

About to ask why he hadn't chosen to emulate the actual author of *Our True Ancient History*, Rosetta halted, remembering the dream she'd had on her flight to Christchurch in 2008. A field awash with the brightness of dandelions and buttercups. A scattering of scarlet blooms. Faeries. Hundreds of tiny faeries greeting her with smiles...the awareness of wearing a long skirt overlaid with an apron, and a bodice similar to this shoebox belt she had on now...a man writing with a quill, a man who referred to her as Lucy.

'Of *course*,' she whispered. 'Of *course* you're Edward Lillibridge!'

Rosetta shook her head. How strange it was that Matthew and she had so much in common, as EGS colleagues for a start, yet were virtual strangers for well over a decade. Why had she misjudged Matthew so terribly? He was nothing like Adam or her dishonest ex.

The moon was hovering above the Harbour Bridge like a suspended coin, smiling dreamily down on them, beckoning them into a haze of nostalgia.

Matthew's hand slid tentatively over her wrist. The electric jolt of his touch seemed to spin her to the stars and back.

'I feel as though we're meant to be together,' he said, his fingers enclosing hers. 'You might feel differently of course. I...' His voice trailed off.

'I don't feel differently, Matthew. Not at all. I keep receiving these...images. They're like dreams but more real. Visions I guess you'd call them.'

'I know what you mean about the visions. That's what I experienced when Pieter visited me. And these days I'm getting a lot more of them.'

'Lately I've been getting visions of being underwater,' Rosetta told him. 'They're a lot like the dreams I used to have: I'm diving through coral gardens, and when I look back at my feet, I see only a dolphin tail. But in these visions there's always the faint sound of singing, something like a choir.' Rosetta hesitated. Would Matthew laugh if she admitted to the next thing? Deciding to take the risk, she continued. 'I'm beginning to wonder whether I existed here at some point in time as a mermaid!'

'Probably because you did,' Matthew said mysteriously. 'In some other reality, you having a fishtail is perfectly normal.'

Back in the ballroom he'd referred to her as Lucetta and a handful of story characters. The faerie Orahney. The elf Maleika. Marani had been the last name he'd mentioned, the siren in Edward Lillibridge's retelling of a Cornish legend that Matthew retrieved from a 1761 issue of *The Tintagel Times*. Was it possible she'd had a life connected with the Mermaid of Zennor? Could that be what those dreams and visions were about?

'And in those images, Matthew, you're always there. You're always nearby, making me feel safe.'

Matthew turned and met her gaze. In a low voice, he said, 'The vision I've been getting is of a huge auditorium with a crystal dome roof. It's got a futuristic feel to it.'

'Sounds like the Sonic Unity Gathering that the elves saw.'

'Has to be. And my claim of being part of it is purely competitive since you often claimed that you were in the book.'

'I *am*,' Rosetta joked. 'For sure I am! Along with my silver feline and fire-haired daughter.'

'Anyway, I'm there listening to someone address an audience. I turn to the woman next to me to whisper something...' Rosetta felt the pressure of his hand as he gave her fingers a squeeze. '...And that woman is always you. So, based on that vision of mine, we might as well say that we both appear in *Our True Ancient History*.'

Playing along, Rosetta said, 'Absolutely. And because you've had all those dreams about Pieter of the Brumlynds, you're more than likely the numeral-obsessed "fellow" in the "red chariot" at the start. How unthinking of Lillibridge to forget to mention our names.'

Matthew glanced at his watch. 'I'm keeping you from your party. We'd better get back.'

He rose, and Rosetta accepted the hand he offered. When he helped her to her feet, she luxuriated for a moment in his protective hold, not wanting to fight the gossamer-fine ropes of feeling that linked her to his presence.

'There's something I'd like to give you,' he said, patting the front of his waistcoat. Inside the waistcoat's pocket was a velvet jewellery case. Bigger than an engagement ring box, not that Rosetta would have minded. 'I'd better first give you a background on this. I got it at Sotheby's. I won the bid for Lillibridge's original manuscript, and then I bought something else Anna Callan put up for auction.'

Rosetta blinked and stared at Matthew. 'What did you just say?'

'I was saying Anna Callan owned this as well as the manuscript and—'

'The manuscript,' Rosetta said. 'What did you say about the manuscript?'

'I bought it. Had pretty tough competition though. Another bidder pushed the price up enormously.'

The undisclosed buyer who'd outbid her broker! Someone she knew, someone she adored, someone standing opposite, was in possession of that much-desired document! 'What's in it? Is there more to it than the published version? Are there any extra mentions of Lillibridge? And what's his handwriting like?'

'To be honest, I don't know. It's still in its package.'

Was Matthew serious? Was the manuscript still in its package five months on?

'I bought it for you, Rosetta. I felt its rightful owner was the founder of Friday Fortnight.'

'Matthew, that's so beautiful of you. But way too generous!' Feeling guilty, Rosetta turned away from him. She already had inside knowledge. Knew for certain he'd paid a ridiculous amount for it, and all because she'd told her broker to outbid any competition!

'I wanted to post it from England, but I kept up the hope of delivering it personally. Ulterior motive. I wanted to be beside you once you first looked through it.'

Unable to contain her joy, Rosetta laughed and fake-punched the top of Matthew's arm—awkwardly—because she couldn't fully conceal her need to caress him, and if she started, she wouldn't be able to stop, or hear what he next had to say.

'So when can I get it to you? Tomorrow morning okay?'

'Perfect. Let's meet for breakfast.'

'It's a date.' Matthew reached into his waistcoat again. 'Here's a letter from Anna Callan. She asked me to pass it on.'

The envelope he handed her was adorned in the palest of pink roses. Eager to see what Anna had written, Rosetta tore the envelope open. A floral perfume wafted from old-fashioned writing paper.

She read the letter aloud:

'Dear Rosetta,

I was so very pleased when Matthew told me he'd purchased the manuscript for you at Auction. I believe that someone who has devoted a website to my husband's ancestor is truly deserving of this.

The reason for my letter involves a peculiar discovery. The names Rosetta and Matthew...' Rosetta stopped. 'I can't make this part out. Oh, wait a minnie, I can. It says...*appear in...'*

Rosetta squinted at the elaborate script. 'Matthew, I can't quite understand Anna's handwriting here. Can you...'

Matthew drew closer and placed a hand on her back.

Zingity-Zingity...Zing-Zing-Zing!

'What can't you understand?'

Cool air flitted over her neck. 'Ooh, the wind's sprung up!' A breeze ruffled the letter. The breeze grew into a gust. The letter trembled, then flew from her slackened fingers as though snatched away by unseen hands and paused restlessly on the wharf boards.

Matthew stooped to pick it up, but the letter, springing to life once more, skittered across the wharf. Matthew stepped after it.

Rosetta leapt forward then back and jogged anxiously on the spot while Matthew raced to the wharf's edge. 'Can you see it?' she called to him.

Matthew was examining the water beneath. 'I can't believe it.'

'Believe what?'

'The letter's fallen into the harbour.'

◠

'PITY THESE WINGS OF MINE don't flap,' Matthew said. 'I could have swooped down and rescued it.'

'I'm so sorry, Matthew! I should have—'

'Not a problem. Nothing you could do. That breeze flew up from nowhere.'

'I'll contact Anna tomorrow and ask her what she wrote.'

'So what did you see in the letter before the wind took it from you? What did Anna think our names appeared in?'

'That's as far as I got.'

'Well, we're both mentioned a bit online.'

'An occupational hazard.'

'So probably that's what Anna was referring to.' He nudged her elbow. 'Unless she was talking about the unpublished manuscript.'

Rosetta tried to remain serious. 'Perhaps she was saying we appear in that!'

Matthew's voice melted into laughter. 'Told you we were in the book!'

They laughed together for some time, although Rosetta knew her jovial mood was sparked by Matthew's proximity more than anything else.

Matthew opened the small box in his hand. He withdrew something sparkly from its satin cushioned interior, something displaying a single jewel. 'Anna found this in a locked box along with Edward's last letter, the letter he wrote to Ned.' He held the jewellery piece up so that she could see it in the darkness. Light danced over a lunar-gilt chain. Rosetta shook her head, beaming deliriously. He'd got her an antique necklace! The chain melded delicately with an oval encasement, a filigree of silver-gold flower petals framing a white gem. 'Matthew, it's exquisite,' she said. 'The metal surrounding the gem...it's like lace!'

Matthew moved his hand, and the gem dipped sideways into the moonlight. Shards of coloured light bounced over it, illuminating the central stone. She could see the stone's true colour now. Pale and pink, the colour of Elysium heart-crystals and identical to the gem in a picture Izzie had drawn as a teenager. Its beauty held her mesmerised.

'Lucy Lillibridge's magic pendant,' Matthew said. 'Stolen from an Australian tribesman and given to her in 1760.'

'The crystal fragment from Orahney's wand,' Rosetta whispered. 'The one that silvered Eidred!' She ran a finger over its intricate frame. 'To think we've read about it and now...This silver-gold metal. The Elysium mer-people transmuted it from a remnant of Eidred's lace sleeve!'

Her thoughts slid over the crystal's history. As with Lillibridge's evolving book, the jewel had journeyed far. Its healing power had sprung from a Norwegian autumn sprite's heart when her beauty-creation was drained in a magic-robbing ceremony; stored in a crystal vial and fashioned into a wand, Eidred's fragment of it having chipped from the wand when the sorcerer Rawhor flung it in rage during her crystalling. Then on it travelled to Lemuria, or that 'Great Southern Land' of Australia, in the form of a pendant on Eidred's neck. Passed down from Eid to the indigenous tribespeople. Pilfered by a seafarer who passed it to his captain who sent it to the Gypsy Lucetta in England as a token of his love. And here it was, returned to Australia.

Matthew placed the necklace over her head and levelled it against her collarbone, his fingers brushing warmly against her neck.

Instinctively Rosetta closed her hand around the stone. It seemed to pulsate. A radiating rhythm flickered steadily with each heartbeat. It surged over and around and through her. She had become as tiny as a speck of stardust yet as vast as the ocean. Rosetta's heart was already brimming with love for the man before her. Now it was expanding into another kind of emotion, a feeling of honour for every living thing.

She threw her arms around Matthew. Kissed him with abandon. Champagne happiness...his mouth against hers. The return of a man whose name was once Storlem and the gift of her autumn-sprite heart had transformed her future into something sublime.

Matthew's voice was low and intense. 'How could I have allowed money to deny me of someone I loved?'

'Maybe to bring us to this moment,' Rosetta said. 'This moment right now. It's somehow...silvery.'

Matthew held her close. She sighed into his embrace. 'I think I get it now,' he said, his voice a soft growl. 'Wall Street's bulls and bears brought me to this.'

Rosetta thought she heard an echo. *Bulls and bears.* She had! She'd heard someone say it just a second ago, someone from far away.

A backwards-rushing sensation engulfed her.

In her mind's eye, she was travelling away from Matthew and into another world.

'Bulls and bears.' An echoing voice. She was standing beside a man in robes, whose sapphire eyes weren't altogether dissimilar to Conan Dalesford's. 'Maleika, watch this scene from the future,' he said. She peered through a window edged with cloud. Appearing behind the window was the interior of a building. Its clear, domed ceiling mirrored hints of rainbows.

The words had been spoken by a man addressing an audience. Seated on the stage to one side of the man was Izzie. Her face had taken on a radiant composure, and her hair sparkled with something that looked like a tiara. The man's eyes were darkly bright and otherworldly. 'This is the meaning of the Oracle's final verse,' he said. 'Horned ones were a symbol of success through upward-rising markets within the world's stock exchanges. They were the bulls. The "grizzly" beast part of the verse refers to the downward swipers of years gone by, the "bear markets".

'Within the past decade, those who have upheld these financial centres have made the historic decision to phase out the Gold's-Kin initiated system. On account of Kindness Merits having become the preferred currency, old-style exchange is now almost obsolete.

'As we all know, traders the world over have honourably embraced their returned sprite qualities.

'Only one market has remained open, more through tradition than anything else. Upon closing, it will transform into one of the world's first Halls of Compassionate Learning, a place where science, art and education are both explored and enhanced via Dream Sphere connections and made accessible to all who wish to know more.

'It therefore gives us great joy to inform you that this one remaining stock exchange, to which the Oracle has referred as "the horned ones' Wall", and known more commonly as New York's *Wall* Street, has today, on this ninth day of August 2026, graciously closed its doors for the final time.'

An elated roar rose up from the audience.

'A symbol,' said the speaker, 'of our dedication to the Currency of Kindness.'

He quoted two lines from the Oracle's final verse.

Then crumbled is the horned ones' Wall
Where grizzly beasts are prone to fall

'The final part of the prophecy is now fulfilled,' he said. 'And I might add here that gold was never my favourite headwear.' He was holding aloft a crown, an ornate piece of craftsmanship encrusted with rubies and diamonds, gems devoid of true healing power. 'Crowns are interesting things. Many would agree they fascinate, or promote humble awe, but in a world that no longer defines rulership by ownership, this kind of relic loses its allure. Besides all that, gold is too heavy to wear in this form, and as my wife Izzie would say, crowns are impossibly outdated. And so yesterday, I, Nikolaus Kristofer Glorion Pieter Lars, Wealth for All Committee founder and King of Perelda, made the long overdue decision to revoke the possession of mine.

'And now, I would like,' he said, 'to introduce my mother-in-law, a woman whose website compelled me seventeen years ago to run away from my new overseas home in Adelaide, Australia, in the hope of attending one of her Friday Fortnight groups in Sydney. Along with many others, she has brought both Edward Lillibridge's *Our True Ancient History* and the power of the Elysium heart-crystals to the world's attention. Her innumerable contributions to communities have inspired joy in many, and her exuberant efforts have assisted in elevating whole nations into awakening within themselves enthusiasm for a more harmonious exchange system. On behalf of the Wealth for All Comittee, please join me in welcoming to the podium...Odetta Weissler.'

But now Rosetta was travelling again. Back into that life in Elysium Glades, where her elfin son had woken from the Dream Sphere.

'And what does the leader say to these people at the gathering, Pieter?' she said.

'There is something to celebrate,' Pieter told her. 'A return to the Currency of Kindness. The leader then announces the name of an individual who has been greatly responsible for this.'

'And who should this creature be?'

'The name is...er...it is difficult to recall.'

'Take another sip of Remembrance Essence, Pieter.'

Pieter did so. 'Oh!' he said. 'Det.'

'Det,' she repeated.

'Ah...'

'Take another sip, Pieter.'

Pieter did so. 'Wise...'

She nodded encouragingly. *'Wise.'*

'La!' said Pieter finally.

'Well done, Pieter.' She clasped her hands together. 'You have been shown someone who will one day help in restoring this world to its former beauty. And we now know the sonic signature of this wonderful sprite. Det-ah-Wise-la!'

Surfacing from the memory, Rosetta smiled to herself. Back then, in her life as Maleika, she inadvertently shortened the name that Pieter recalled so accurately, mistaking the second syllable of her current birth name for the first. *Det-ah* was Odetta without the 'O'!

Hopefully the scenario that had just played out, a son-in-law calling her up to speak, was an intuitive vision rather than an airy-fairy daydream. There was nothing she would love more than to take on Matthew's surname.

Whirl of colour...clatter of shade...laughter of snowdrops.

She was clinging to eagle-winged Storlem desperately as courtiers slashed at vines in Elysium Glades, vowing in a trembling voice that she would love him for all lifetimes to come. And then she was speaking to a body-king daughter in the Dream Sphere. 'Not in your lifetime, Eidred,' she said. 'One day though. One day, many millenniums into the future, it will happen.'

The scene changed. The Dream Sphere's clouds were replaced by the rippling sheen of a midnight-blue sea. She was seated on a moonlit rock, splashing her fishtail and weaving coral through her hair while Matthew Trelawney of Zennor serenaded her in tones that made her spirits soar.

The water fell away. She was now watching the man who was her husband, with quiet admiration. He was writing by candlelight, his dear face half in shadow. The edges of the quill he wielded, golden from the flame's luminosity, seemed to impress on her as an angel's wing in sunlight, a hushed glimpse of freedom.

He looked up from the lines he was writing and rested his quill on the table. 'I will work tirelessly, my darling enchantress,' he said, 'to bring about The Silvering. It has every chance of occurring. Within one score year I would say.'

Sorrowful at Edward's words, she shook her head. The sickening feeling of foreboding had unravelled in the depths of her being. Her crystal pendant's powers and Gypsy intuition had caused her to sense a fate drawing near, a shattering fate that would see Edward Lillibridge taken away from her. 'Not in our lifetime, dear-heart,' she said. 'One day though. One day, many years into the future, it will happen.'

The antiquated surroundings vanished.

She was back in Matthew's arms, breathless from that sudden bout of dreamlike journeying.

Strange lightning appeared then, in crystalline flashes. It pulsed above the Harbour Bridge and skimmed the water below.

Matthew drew Rosetta closer. She closed her eyes and savoured his words as he whispered in her ear, 'I feel as though the sky's singing.'

'I feel that way too.'

A barely audible sound seemed to seep from the clouds. The sound wavered in the evening breeze, as though on tiptoe, and wended its way around the harbour.

'Matthew, it is! The sky is *actually* singing!'

Low and haunting. The soft, sweet whistle of a pipe made from reed, a lone quiver that spiralled into a flurry of sylvan bells and sighing laughter.

And then, quite astoundingly, the lightning above them dispersed into sparks, bursts of dancing light that somersaulted into a whirl of lemon and lilac stars.

An otherworldly aura surrounded the moon. The aura had grown brighter and more expansive; was bathing the sky in swirling, stretching, streams of silver.

If she hadn't been so immersed in Matthew's closeness, if she hadn't been so overwhelmed by the power of his kiss after linking him, for years, with a heartache that even the crystals couldn't cure, Rosetta would have been just as stunned at the harbour's unearthly radiance as the crowd emerging from the Crystal Palace Ballroom. But her world right now was a happily-ever-after faerie story, with a certain GEG in the role of devoted winged hero, and all she could feel was a blissful brand of acceptance.

A voice from the ancient past swam back to her, the voice of the Oracle. Its tone evoked the image of a silver-gold ocean...a symbol of the sun and moon united in harmony.

> And once a winged man acts with grace
> By gifting magic framed in lace
> The Silvering will fast descend
> To mark the greed-lack ailment's end

Matthew took her hand and led her to the water, marvelling at the reflections and triumphant display above.

She pressed her fingertips against the pendant's lacy edge. 'I think it's begun.'

'The Silvering!' The moon's dazzle was playing on Matthew's features, caressing with magical light his smile and the green of his eyes. 'It's really happening.'

'In our lifetime!' Rosetta said. 'It's happening in our lifetime.'

Acknowledgements

How does anyone who has published their first three books ever express in a mere page-and-a-half the enormity of their gratitude to all who have given encouragement and support?

My initial thanks must go to my beautiful parents:

My mother's confidence in my ability to complete the project (despite its 'Neverending Story' nickname) was vastly reassuring. Mum, your down-to-earth literary sensibility, honest critiques of all my many and varied drafts and your sense of the dramatic have been invaluable. Thank you for getting to know my characters and for discussing the manuscripts at length. Your insights have helped in enlivening all three books.

I am grateful to my father for his reliable and practical help throughout these past few years and his selfless assistance when professional editing had become an unreachable goal. Thank you, Dad, for envisaging this project as a book series and sharing my hope of making *Epiphany* available to those who wish to discover its outcomes. Your reading and re-reading of the manuscripts and suggestions to sharpen the text led me to the project's completion.

A huge thank you to those who have trial-read the books in manuscript form: Amanda Earley and Vikki Warren, the courageous readers of an early draft, and to readers of later drafts: Kim Jagers, Rose Pollock, Filiz Niyazi and Robyn Kelly. Your enthusiasm for the venture and generosity in providing balanced feedback will never be forgotten.

I can't begin to describe how happy I was to engage the brilliant services of Deonie Fiford who carried out an insightful structural edit and subsequent follow-up review of the manuscripts. Thank you for helping to shape this work.

Thanks also to Abigail Nathan of Bothersome Words for an amazingly helpful early manuscript assessment, generous advice and partial copy edit (any errors are due to my own editing). It's been a pleasure working with you.

My appreciation also goes to Laura Moyer of The Book Cover Machine for the celestial cover; Lorie DeWorken of Mind the Margins for the cover's text and spine; and MiblArt for prompt and courteous alterations to the latest edition's cover for *THE SILVERING*.

Just as the cover is vital to the atmosphere of a book, so too is the look of the pages. My gratitude goes to Rachael Cox of RC Edits for turning my document files into ebooks. I am certainly no typesetter, but thanks to your work on the pages I formatted, I could publish the finals *without* scene-breaks squished out of shape by my less-than-sophisticated software!

A final thanks to you, the reader, for completing the *Epiphany* journey. Hope you enjoyed your travels!

Did you enjoy Sonya Deanna Terry's

Epiphany series?

Unlike books funded by a publishing company,
*the **Epiphany** series was edited, printed and marketed*
at the author's own expense.

Independent authors don't always have the promotional reach
that traditionally published authors have, so online
recommendations are vital — to keep their books in circulation.

Would you consider recommending

E p i p h a n y – THE SILVERING

in a written review on Goodreads and/or the online retailer
you purchased from?

Your opinion matters!

* * * * * * * *

Recommend any (or all) of the **Epiphany** books online for
your chance to win a book addressed to you along with
a personal message from the author

Join the publisher mailing list at:

www.EpiphanyTheGolding.com

then tell us your review's title / first sentence
OR
the alias / reviewer-name used

* * *Giveaways every month up until June 2024* * *

About the Author

Idealism is the driving force behind Sonya Deanna Terry's work.

She is a keen supporter of human rights and animal rights—and unites with you, the reader, in your desire for a happier world.

Sonya can be contacted via:

www.EpiphanyTheGolding.com

Character List

18th-Century England

CORNWALL

Edward Lillibridge...Documenter of *Our True Ancient History*

Ned Lillibridge........Edward Lillibridge's son

Lucetta (Lucy)......................A Gypsy fortune teller

Prehistoric Norway
Portrayed as 'Norwegia' in Lillibridge's
Our True Ancient History

ELYSIUM GLADES
The elfin Brumlynd clan
Nature spirits of devic origin (sprites)

Maleika...............................Clan Watcher

Kloory..................................Maleika's younger son

Croydee................................Maleika's nephew

Zhippe..................................An adopted water sprite orphan

Carlonn.................................Zhippe's twin

Forest creatures

Fripso..A young rabbit

Karee..Fripso's mother

Sluken................................Croydee's dragon

THE GRUDELLAN PALACE
Gold's Kin
Known to the sprites as 'body kings'

Eidred.............................Princess of Grudella

Pieter /Adahmos.................Maleika's son/Eidred's husband

The Solen...........................Gold's Kin Emperor/Eidred's father

Storlem..............................Gold's Kin guard and crystal keeper

Zemelda............................Palace soothsayer/former bewitcher

Rahwor..............................Grudellan sorcerer

Orahney.............................An autumn faerie from another century

The Dream Sphere
A celestial dimension featured in Lillibridge's
Our True Ancient History

Alcor...The Brumlynd clan's Dream Master

Modern Australia

SYDNEY

Rosetta Melki ....Friday Fortnight founder

Rosetta's Friday Fortnight book study group

Craig Delorey ....Lawyer/entrepreneur

Edith Derby (Eadie).........Beauty Therapy student

Royston Leckie..................Youth Counsellor

Lena Morris.......................Health foods shop proprietor

Darren Eddings.................Former Hairdresser

○

Izzie Redding......................Rosetta's daughter

Glorion Osterhoudt.........Izzie's crush

Charlotte Wallace ....Izzie's school friend

Diondra Wallace...............Charlotte's mother/Dette's friend

Dominic Wallace..............Charlotte's father

Matthew P Weissler.........Former Investment Bank Trading Manager

Matthew's former work colleagues

Charlie Sanders.................Trading Director

Adam Harrow...................Trading Manager

Paul 'Davo' Davison ....Trading Manager

Celia Owens ....Executive Assistant

Lila Donevski....................Administrative Assistant

○

Bernadette Weissler (Dette)......Matthew's wife

Sara Belfield................................Dette's elder daughter/Izzie's friend

Laura Belfield...................Dette's younger daughter

Grant Belfield..................Dette's ex-husband/Sara and Laura's father/
Rosetta's former neighbour

ALICE SPRINGS

Conan Dalesford...Author of *Thoughts on Tomorrow's Tycoon War*

Jannali Dalesford...Conan's Wife

Modern England

CORNWALL

Harriet Neilson......................Member of Glynis and Dudley's
Friday Fortnight group

Charles Gloucester................Antique Dealer

Anna Callan.............................Wife of one of Lillibridge's descendants

LONDON

Kirk Rummery.............................Former Associate of Matthew's brother

www.ingramcontent.com/pod-product-compliance
Lightning Source LLC
Chambersburg PA
CBHW010509100726
47902CB00011B/2147